I0618323

INVISIBLE AMONG US

JOY ANN COLL

ISBN 9780989200202

Joy Ann Coll, Vero Beach, FL

Cover Art by Paul Summerfield (www.ageofwonder.org)
Typeset by Michelle Lovi (www.odysseybooks.com.au)

Published in the United States of America

DEDICATION

To my dear husband, Bernard,
who provides me with encouragement,
support, and love while I live in my
fantasy world … I love you more every day.

Author's Note

This story is a work of fiction but
the reality of slavery in the USA
and around the world is very real.

Please support the following organizations
who work to right the wrongs of human trafficking:

FreetheSlaves, Inc.
FBI Human Trafficking Task Force
National Human Trafficking Resource Center
Coalition to Abolish Slavery and Trafficking

and many other government and non-governmental
organizations too numerous to mention.

For every book sold, a donation
will be made to fight human trafficking.

Thank you for your support!

Chapter 1
Miami, Florida

Jason looked at the picture in his hand and knew he had to rescue her. His thumb caressed her stunning auburn hair, cat-like green eyes, and warm smile that called to him, begging him to save her. The wetsuit he wore dried in the hot Florida sun, after a scuba dive with his buddies from the FBI dive team and his best friend, Charles. His body rocked as the sailboat gently tossed on a rolling ocean wave. The halyard clanged on the mast high above him when the sails popped, whipped by a tropical breeze.

FBI Special Agent Matt Chambers pointed at her photo. "Her name's Kathleen McDougal. She's from Miami Shores."

"I remember her." Jason recalled the extensive media coverage of her kidnapping. "She disappeared from Aruba about a year ago."

"That's right," Matt nodded. "The Aruban authorities investigated her disappearance but they never learned what happened to her."

"Just like the others." Jason shook his head. "How many women have to disappear from Aruba before we get some answers?"

"At least four, we know of. But this time, we've cracked the case." Matt beamed with pride. "Or, I should say, Lucy has."

"What?" Jason leaned forward and glanced at the men gathered around him. Charles looked as stunned as he felt. Matt and his dive team leader, Todd Humphries, barely contained their glee.

Todd unzipped his wetsuit. "It's been a long time coming, but we finally have some answers."

"How'd you find her?" Charles' blond hair tossed in the breeze.

"Lucy hacked into the traffickers' computer system," Matt said. "Kathleen's name was listed as the webmaster. She hid her name inside some code that would keep regular computer users from seeing it. Lucy didn't notice it when she first searched their site, but this time she saw some unusual code that wasn't there before. When she unlocked the code, Kathleen's name appeared."

"How weird is that?" Charles looked perplexed.

"Why would slave traffickers take a beautiful woman and keep her to run their computer system?" Jason glanced down at her photo.

"Kathleen's a special person. She's a software engineer ... one of the best." Matt smiled with delight. "She's won lots of awards over the years. Lucy recognized her name right away because they knew each other from computer hacking contests."

Jason barked a laugh. "Contests for computer hackers?" He squinted against the bright sunlight as it bounced off the rippling ocean waves.

"They're legal," Matt smirked. "Kathleen and Lucy were always in the top five finalists."

"Human trafficking is a billion dollar a year business. They needed someone to manage their growing profits." Sarcasm filled Jason's gut. "Someone to keep law enforcement from tracing their financial transactions."

"Well, most law enforcement," Todd chuckled and looked at his boss. "They haven't met Lucy."

Matt nodded. "We hoped you and your foundation could buy her and bring her home."

"Absolutely, where do I need to go?"

"Vancouver."

"Canada? How'd she get there?"

Matt watched a rumbling cigarette boat speed past. "The task force believes women are being taken by ship from Aruba through the Panama Canal to islands in the South Pacific and to Canada, where they're sold into slavery ... primarily to Asian and Middle Eastern buyers. The next slave auction takes place in two weeks. Owners are coming from all over. We'd like to enter your name as a buyer."

"Absolutely..." He looked at Kathleen's picture again, admiring her long auburn hair and wondering if it had been cut.

"We don't know where the auctions are held. We'd like you to wear this GPS tracking device." Matt lifted a small round object from a gauze cover. "It would need to be inserted under your skin."

Jason's eyebrows rose while he processed what Matt said. "You guys have the greatest gadgets."

"The tracking device will lead us to the auction." Matt wiped his sweating brow. "The Canadians will trace the bank transactions then arrest everyone and free the slaves."

"Let's do it." Jason smiled. "I'll put some money in my bank account in the Cayman Islands to buy her freedom."

"We couldn't do these operations without your foundation's private funding." Matt extended his right hand. "Using public money to purchase human beings or pay anything that might be considered a ransom is forbidden. We can't thank you enough."

Jason shook his hand. "Rescuing slaves helps with the guilt."

"Connie's smiling down on you," Todd said.

Jason nodded and thought about the young innocent life snuffed out almost a year ago by angry slave owners. He couldn't save Connie but he and the other members of the foundation he started were determined to save as many victims as they could.

Vancouver, British Columbia, Canada

Two weeks later, Jason landed at Vancouver International Airport on a private jet leased by his foundation to bring Kathleen McDougal home. Matt sat across from him at a small conference table next to large oval windows.

"I'll track your location using the GPS device implanted in your arm." Matt held up an electronic device. "When you stop moving for at least an hour, I'll assume you're at the auction." He looked out the window of the aircraft as it taxied to the front of a metal hangar. "I'll give your location to the Mounties and they'll coordinate the rest of the operation."

"What if I stop at a location that's not the auction? I'm supposed to meet someone in the lobby of the Fairmont Hotel on the waterfront. I don't know how long I'll be there."

"We'll follow you from the hotel. If you arrive at a location that's not the slave auction, you need to move. If you *are* at the auction, then you need to stay there an hour while the Mounties coordinate their teams to surround the location. When your illegal transaction passes through the computer system, we'll get you out."

"Okay." Jason glanced down at Kathleen's photo and wondered if he would recognize her after a year of slavery. He imagined how she might look today to keep from being shocked when he saw her. "I'm not sure if she'll even be there."

"If you don't see her, type this string of code into one of their computers." Matt handed him a slip of paper. "Lucy said this will freeze the computers and they will be forced to bring her out of hiding to fix them."

Jason contemplated his options. "That might be my only chance to save her." As the jet stopped in front of the one-story hangar, a black limousine pulled up.

"There's your ride," Matt said. "I'll get a taxi to meet up with the Mounties while the limo takes you to the hotel."

Jason laid the photo down on the small table between their seats. "She probably doesn't look like this anymore. I hope we're not too late."

"Whatever happens, be strong." Matt shook Jason's hand and watched him leave.

Jason greeted the limo driver and rode toward the Fairmont Hotel on the waterfront. He had never been to Vancouver. The thirty-minute ride from the airport to the downtown hotel gave him a feel for the city. It was vibrant and alive, with tall buildings standing sentinel over the blue harbor off the Inside Passage. He arrived in the late afternoon; a red glow bounced off the shiny buildings as the sun dipped lower in the sky. The limo stopped in front of the hotel lobby where the driver moved smartly to open his door.

The Port of Vancouver stood tall across the harbor as Jason pressed a tip into the driver's palm and stepped up the brick pavers into the lobby. The broad expanse of shiny marble floor was impressive. He walked to the front desk and was greeted by the friendly hotel staff.

"Yes, sir, may I help you?"

"I'm here to meet Mr. Wilson."

The young man nodded and pointed to the men gathered in the seating area in front of the tall windows showcasing the cruise ship terminal across the street. "Mr. Wilson will meet you over there, sir."

"Thanks." Jason moved casually to the area where the other men gathered. He nodded to them and sat down. He looked at the faces of the other buyers who seemed to be from many different countries. Before he could say anything to the others, a short, husky man arrived and stood with his back to the massive windows, glancing around at their faces.

"Good evening, gentlemen. My name is Wilson."

Jason stood with the others and shook Wilson's hand as he moved from man to man, checking off their names on a clipboard. After meeting everyone, Wilson reached into his pocket and removed several zip-top plastic bags and passed them around.

"Take one of these bags. Put your wallet, keys, phone, and any electronic devices in it. Once that's done, we'll be on our way." While the men placed their personal belongings into the small bags, Wilson pulled a larger bag from his pocket and placed the smaller bags inside. "Follow me." Wilson strode toward the lobby exit.

Jason and the other men followed him outside to a large van with dark windows. When Wilson opened the side door and got into the front seat, Jason and the other men got into the van. The driver started the engine and quickly took them from the fancy hotel on the waterfront to the shipping terminal nearby.

A harbor full of container ships waited for their turn to be unloaded by huge gantry cranes. The van passed through the security gate at the port entrance, drove toward a large container ship, and stopped next to it. Wilson got out and spoke to one of the stevedores standing nearby and slipped him a wad of paper money. While he bent over to put a wooden plank across the dock to the ship, Wilson returned to the van and opened the side door. "Gentlemen, follow me."

Jason got out and walked across the gang plank onto the large ship full of containers. After the last man crossed over, the gang plank was pulled onto the ship and off the dock. He felt a sudden thud in his chest and hoped the ship wouldn't be leaving the harbor. If it did, his chances of getting Kathleen off the ship would be greatly diminished. *I don't even know if she's here.*

Wilson led the men down a metal staircase with a chain handrail to a room below decks. The room looked more comfortable than Jason had expected. Carpet, chairs, tables with computer monitors. Red drapes over the portholes hung to the floor, blocking prying eyes.

"Have a seat, gentlemen." Wilson gestured toward the chairs in front of the computer screens. "The show will begin soon." He stepped back through the metal doorway they had just entered and left them alone as they sat in front of the computers.

Soon, the lights dimmed and soft music played in the background. A group of women entered the room, barely dressed, carrying drinks and snacks. Each put a small tray of food and drinks on the tables and stood next to each buyer waiting for instructions.

"Gentlemen," Wilson said in a loud voice, "these beauties are available for purchase." He snapped his fingers and the captives moved around the room in a circle, parading their assets.

Jason watched as women of all shapes, sizes, and nationalities walked slowly around the room as if in a death march. Most were brunettes, some were redheads. Interestingly, none were blondes. Not one had auburn hair like Kathleen's, but he knew she wouldn't be on parade. She had to be working in a back room somewhere. The code Lucy had given him would pull Kathleen from the dark shadows.

Jason checked his watch. *One hour from now, it'll be over.* His concern that the ship might leave the harbor ebbed when he saw the cranes unloading containers. The ship couldn't move while it was being unloaded. When he realized that, he relaxed and focused on his mission. He scanned the room looking at all the women, but there were none who looked like Kathleen.

As the women continued to walk in circles around the room, Wilson strolled behind each buyer, highlighting each woman's assets. "Look at your computer screens, gentlemen, for more detailed information about each slave."

Jason looked at the computer and saw a photo and country of origin for each captive. A list of assets each might possess of a sexual or service nature packed the screen. He looked for a space to enter the code Matt had given him. As he clicked through the group of slave files, he searched for an asset missing from the group that he could exploit.

"Where are the blondes?"

"Blondes are special orders." Wilson stepped toward him. "If you want something special, you need to request that in advance."

"I'm thinking about a feisty redhead."

Wilson glanced over to a dark corner where it looked like a dark-haired woman sat on a wooden chair, her hands grasping the seat.

"Is she a redhead?"

"She's not for sale."

"I want to talk to her."

When Wilson gave him an annoyed glance and strode away, Jason quickly pulled the keyboard toward him, removed the code from his pocket, and started typing. When he pressed the 'enter' key and heard groans from the other buyers, he knew he succeeded. He smothered a smile when Wilson's back turned rigid.

"Get over here!" Wilson yelled at the woman sitting in the corner.

She scrambled to her feet and hurried to one of the computer screens. Leaning over the keyboard she typed something, but nothing changed.

"Hey, come over here and fix mine." Jason pointed toward his computer.

She looked at him with an odd expression. Her wounded, empty green eyes searched his face. Her thin cheeks were a testament to the evil she had endured for the past year.

"Come here, I want to talk to you." He gestured to her with a beckoning finger.

She slowly moved toward him and looked down at his computer screen. Her mind seemed to reel with possibilities for the computer glitch.

Jason slipped the paper with the code into her hand. He looked sideways at Wilson, who was talking with the other buyers about their computer problems. "Kathleen McDougal?" he whispered.

She startled as if he had hit her and looked at him with an intensity that had not been present before. She read the code written on the piece of paper, then looked back at Jason, searching his eyes for answers. "Why are you doing this?" she whispered.

"I'm here to take you home," he whispered. "Do what I say and we'll get out of here alive."

"Save the others," she replied, tossing her head at the younger women.

"I came two thousand miles. I'm not leaving without you."

"My life is over, save someone else."

"You're going home with me." He grabbed her upper arm as he saw Wilson out of the corner of his eye coming toward them. He needed to put on a show.

"Get this computer problem fixed now!" Wilson shouted at her.

Kathleen crumpled the piece of paper in her fist, leaned over the table, and typed a code into the computer. She pressed enter and straightened when the screen changed. She released a slow easy breath when the other buyers cheered.

Wilson raised his hand to hit her, and she cringed.

Jason grabbed Wilson's arm. "I want this woman."

"I told you, she's not for sale." Wilson grew tense. "Get back to your corner." He pointed to the chair and glared at her.

"Stay." Jason pointed at the floor. "Do not leave this spot."

She hesitated, shifting her eyes between him and Wilson.

"Sir, you're wearing out your welcome." Wilson's nostrils flared with anger as he spun and strode toward the other buyers who had resumed selecting women.

Jason watched him leave then turned to Kathleen and clutched her upper arm. "Do exactly what I say. Do you hear me?"

≈

Kathleen glared at the strange man whose dark eyes penetrated her very soul. He must have nerves of steel to antagonize Wilson. His light southern accent seemed genuine but the well-built physique hidden beneath his black suit was not common for a slave buyer. His soft black hair looked tossed as if he had run his fingers through it. Was he nervous or stressed? His deep blue eyes searched hers. Was he trying to tell her something? Why should she trust him? After suffering for a year in this den of misery, she didn't trust anyone ... especially men. *He must be trying to trick me. Even so, going with him would be better than staying here.* If she went with him, she would have a better chance to escape. *Oh, to feel the warm sun of Florida again.* Her bones ached from the damp cold common in this city. *Say yes. Do whatever he wants. I don't care anymore.*

His firm grip on her upper arm irritated her but she couldn't afford to antagonize a buyer. Wilson would make her life more miserable than it already was. She imagined what it might be like to be free again. Evil surrounded her like a dark, wet, cold blanket. She glanced at the stranger and clenched her jaw. "Your southern charm is enchanting." Feeling defiant, she dripped with sarcasm.

"It's equally matched by your southern hospitality."

"Your accent matches your wit." She raised her chin to challenge him.

"Don't make the mistake of comparing my accent to my intellect. Those who have are spending time in prison."

"Cop?" She watched his dark eyes flash.

"Lawyer."

"Fancy suit ... fancy lawyer." She glanced over the luxury material and resisted the urge to run her fingers down the lapel. "What's black and looks good on a lawyer?"

"A Doberman." He released her arm and tried not to smile. "I've heard them all."

She smirked and remembered the bad lawyer jokes she used to tell her brother when he informed her he would be attending law school. This was the first time in a year she felt like smiling. Oh, how she yearned to see her family. They had probably forgotten about her. Briefly, she felt sorry for herself until the strange man said something. "What?" Mesmerized by his black eyelashes, she found it difficult to focus.

"Strip, please." Wrinkles formed on his tanned brow as he glanced toward Wilson and quickly looked back at her with intensity not present before.

Feeling aghast, she sensed his equal discomfort. "A southern gentleman would not ask a lady to disrobe in public."

He glanced at Wilson and she followed his gaze. "You can slap my face later, but right now, you and I are two actors in a horrible play. This needs to look realistic, if we're going to get out of here alive."

"You can at least let me stand behind the computer."

He gestured in that direction. "Be my guest."

"I don't even know your name," she whispered.

"Jason. Now, let's get on with this charade."

"Charmed, I'm sure." She gave him a slight curtsy and a flippant smirk then stepped behind the computer. Grabbing the bottom of her shirt, she looked at his face to make sure he was serious.

"You can turn your back." He spun his index finger in a circle.

She felt an ounce of relief before filling with disgust. Turning her back, she whipped the shirt over her head, placed it on the table, and pushed her sweatpants down to her ankles. She stood motionless in her bra and panties, aware from his silence that he must be looking at her scars.

"Continue," she heard him say behind her.

She flinched. "I hate you right now."

"I know. My mama would be very displeased."

"I'll be sure to mention this to her." She pushed her panties to her ankles and removed her bra. Placing it on the table behind her, she felt mortified. After a year of helping Wilson run slave auctions, this was the first time she had to undress for a buyer. She felt Jason's eyes tread over every inch of her naked body. She heard Wilson's familiar footsteps coming toward her and his annoyed voice. She had heard its piercing tone many times.

"I told you, sir, she's not for sale." By this time, Wilson had grown agitated.

"Why is she so thin?" Jason's fingers caressed her exposed ribs.

"She gives her food away." Wilson tilted his head toward the other slaves.

Jason ran his hand over her skin from her ribs down her round, but thin hips, down her flanks and paused. "What are these marks?"

"She doesn't follow orders." Wilson gestured in the direction of the death-march. "Look at the other women."

"I want this one."

"She's a pain in the ass."

"I like a little fire in my women. It makes things … challenging."

"Oh, she's a challenge all right."

"Looks like you've enjoyed it enough." Jason moved to her front and clenched his jaw.

She crossed her arms in front of her breasts in an effort to hide her scars. *Please spare me some dignity,* she thought. But much to her dismay, he clucked his tongue, encircled her wrists and put them down at her sides. She closed her eyes to avoid his expected look of shock but opened them to something quite different.

Jason's face looked stern and he almost winced as he looked brazenly at her breasts. "What happened here?" He touched her healed wounds.

"I got carried away celebrating New Year's."

"Celebrating? You've got an odd way of celebrating," he glared at Wilson. Jason looked back at Kathleen sympathetically. "Put your clothes on."

She quickly grabbed her bra and shirt off the table and pulled up her pants while Jason moved in front of Wilson.

"Look, sir. As I've said, she's not for sale. You can see she's too much trouble."

"I want her." He looked at the other slaves cowering in front of the other buyers. "Look at them, their fear bores me. I want some fire; some excitement. I can see she's used to pain. I'll enjoy breaking her spirit."

Kathleen's eyebrows rose as she glanced up to see Jason flash a phony smile toward Wilson. This buyer wasn't a very good actor. She hoped Wilson couldn't sense his fake persona.

"Humph," Wilson grumbled. "Who will manage our finances?"

"There are plenty of folks who would turn a blind eye for a share of the fun," Jason crossed his arms. When Wilson hesitated and glanced at

11

her with disdain, she worried this charade would fail. Then Jason cleared his throat to regain Wilson's attention. "I'm willing to pay double."

All of a sudden, Wilson's face softened, his eyes flashed and glazed over as he must have pondered how he might spend the money.

Kathleen prayed that Jason was an honest man. Why would he pay double for her damaged body when the others were pristine?

"Deal?" Jason extended his hand to Wilson.

Wilson's eyes focused before he shook Jason's hand. Kathleen released a breath, not realizing she had been holding it. Wilson stepped in front of the computer screen and typed in the enormous amount of money Jason would pay for her. "Get over here and do this," Wilson glared at her and pointed at the screen.

She moved to the spot he vacated and sat down to type the financial codes that kept their evil dealings protected. She looked up at Jason. "What's the account number?"

"It's in my wallet." Jason looked at Wilson and cocked an eyebrow.

"I'll get it." Wilson stepped over to the armed guard and returned with the bag. Opening it, he dumped the smaller bags onto the table next to her. "Which one?"

"Here…" Jason picked up the bag containing his wallet and removed a business card. Handing it to Kathleen, he flipped it over before she took it.

On the back, she recognized a long string of numbers as the electronic code for international banking transactions. She entered it and pressed a few keys, finishing the illegal transaction. She looked up at the stranger and hoped the intense look on his face didn't mean trouble.

Within minutes, the metal door to the room flew open and several men entered shouting and pointing guns at the armed guard and barking orders. Some of the buyers looked for an escape route but soon learned there was no other way out. Captives hunkered in the far corner, some were stark naked. The slave buyers, Wilson, and the armed guard were handcuffed and gathered together near the door. Commando-like rescuers charged around the room with guns raised, ready to meet any danger. Once secured, they glanced around the room at the scene. When their eyes landed on Kathleen, they walked toward her and Jason, who remained standing at the computer table.

"Montgomery?" the commando said.

"Yes," Jason replied, shaking his hand. "This is Miss McDougal."

The commando nodded. "Follow me." He turned away, still holding his rifle in front of him, and marched toward the door.

Jason put his hand on Kathleen's back and urged her forward as he followed behind. When she got to the door, she heard Wilson's menacing voice.

"You bitch!" Wilson shouted. "I'll get you for this!"

She looked at him before stepping through the door. "I didn't have anything to do with this."

"You're the only one smart enough to pull this off!" Wilson's tight lips seethed with the bitterness festering in his soul. "For as long as you live, watch your back because I'm coming after you!"

"Burn in hell," Jason said and turned to Kathleen. "Let's get out of here." He pressed gently into her lower back, urging her to step through the raised threshold.

Even though Kathleen had been rescued, Wilson's words haunted her. He was evil personified and she knew he meant what he said. She took a deep, steadying breath and walked out of the slave auction toward the main deck and her freedom. She felt exhilarated. Stepping into the night, she shielded her eyes from the bright lights flooding the dock as huge cranes unloaded containers from the ship. When the commando ahead of her stopped, she saw light reflecting off the water and froze. Her breathing increased, her chest tightened.

Jason put his arm around her back and leaned close to her ear. "What's wrong?"

"Water…" she gasped, and began to shake as painful memories flashed through her mind. Her pulse increased while she tried to catch her breath.

Jason removed his suit jacket, put it around her shoulders and raised the collar and lapels to fashion crude blinders. He stepped in front of her to block her view of the gang plank. "Look at me." He took her hands in his. "Only look at me, nowhere else."

"Okay." She grasped his warm palms with her cold ones.

"We're going to take one step at a time over to the dock."

She looked sideways, saw the water and gulped.

"Look at me. Take a deep breath and take one step when I do."

Her tense muscles made it difficult to move. She took a deep breath and stepped forward when he moved backward.

"Again."

She took another step. Her hands shook. The cool night air blew her auburn hair around her back, distracting her from her distress. She watched Jason's blue eyes highlighted by black eyelashes until her foot stepped onto hard solid concrete.

"There, now you're free," he said, smiling. He turned his back to her, blocking the harsh lights and shielded his own eyes as he searched the area for a familiar face.

She peeked around him to see two shadowy figures moving toward them. One dressed in khaki pants and a polo shirt extended his hand.

"Good job, man," he said and shook Jason's hand.

"Thanks."

The two men then acknowledged Kathleen. She felt trapped, surrounded. They were all taller and bigger. She rubbed her arms in nervous reaction.

"Kathleen, this is Matt Chambers." Jason gestured at the stranger. "He's the Special Agent in Charge of the FBI Miami office."

When she shook his hand, relief overcame her and her knees buckled.

Jason's strong hands steadied her at the waist. "It's all right, you're free now."

Focusing on his face until her head cleared, she glanced at Matt. "Why would you come all the way from Miami to rescue me?"

"My office is responsible for Americans missing from Aruba," Matt said. "I'm hoping you can shed some light on what happened to you and the others."

"We'll have time to discuss that later," the other man said. "Right now, we need to know the location of this slave ring."

Matt looked at the other man dressed in a red jacket. "Kathleen," this is Major Featherston of the Royal Canadian Mounted Police. He's in charge of this operation."

She shook hands with the tall man in the stunning red uniform jacket. "Pleased to meet you, Major."

"My pleasure, Miss," the major said. "I don't wish to be impertinent, but we need to know where the slave operation is located. If we don't get there tonight, the trail will go cold." He folded his arms across his chest. "Can you tell us anything about where you've been for the past year?"

"Their warehouse is about five minutes from here, along the railroad tracks."

"Do you know the address or anything else about the location?"

"No, they kept us blindfolded whenever they took us outside. But I did hear train whistles day and night."

"That helps." Featherston handed her a business card with RCMP on it. "Please contact me if you remember anything else that can help us pinpoint their location."

"I will." She took the card from him.

"Let's go home." Jason put his arm around her back.

As Kathleen walked into the dark, cold night toward her first taste of freedom, the other slaves, wrapped in blankets, stepped into a large medical vehicle. Her body was free but her mind remained haunted by the senseless tragedy of the past year. Even though she appreciated being rescued, she felt unsure of her surroundings. Would these men take her home? What would her future be like? Her unsteady gait reflected the unsteadiness of her mind. She would let the stranger, Jason, help her until she could make her own decisions.

Chapter 2

Kathleen lay in her bed in the back of the airplane, staring at the ceiling, unable to sleep. She showered, washed her dirty hair, and put on the pajamas Jason had brought for her. Even though it was after midnight, she tossed and turned. The excitement of her liberation kept her mind too active. She wondered if Jason and Matt were sleeping … such nice-looking guys. Why did they save her? Where were they taking her? Jason said Miami, but were they really going there? She would know soon. It takes five and a half hours to fly there. *Is it possible I'll be home by morning?*

She yearned to feel the heat of the Florida sunshine, to walk on the beach, to paint the color of the ocean. Relief overcame her as she drifted off to sleep, her mind shifting from the beauty of the teal ocean along Miami's beach to the ocean color around Aruba …

Turquoise waters had beckoned her to walk along the beach. The shells around Aruba had been similar to her extensive collection at home, but on this Dutch island, a treasure trove of artifacts could be found. She felt fortunate to find a rare Dutch bead from the 1700s and kept it as a souvenir. But over the past year, it had become her good luck charm. It reminded her of the triumph of slaves over their captors.

Blessed with beauty on the outside, Aruba concealed a sinister evil beneath the smiles and relaxed atmosphere of the southern Caribbean island. Aware that several women had disappeared from there, she and her co-workers agreed to stay together. But even those precautions had not been enough. She heard screams, water splashing, followed by an eerie silence.

She startled herself awake with a chilling scream that echoed off the fuselage of the airplane. Sitting upright like a stiff doll, she struggled to breathe when she heard a light knock on the door.

"Kathleen? Are you all right?"

16

"Yes. Just a bad dream."

The pocket door between her bedroom and the main cabin slid open and Jason poked his head through the crack. "Want something to drink?"

"No." She grabbed the blanket closer to her neck. "I'm okay now. Sorry."

"I'll wake you when we're closer to Miami."

"Thanks." She smiled inside but wasn't sure it reached her face. "I appreciate it."

Jason looked concerned but nodded and closed the door. She recalled tidbits of what had happened to her but didn't want to remember. Soon sleep overtook her. It seemed only a few minutes later, when another knock awakened her. "Yes?"

"Time to get up."

"Okay, thanks." She stretched her arms outward giving her muscles a good pull. Rubbing her eyes, she released a low groan when she heard footsteps followed by a light tap on the pocket door.

"You'll find some clothes in the dresser."

"Did you guys think of everything?"

"We do our best. There's a toothbrush in the bathroom. When you're ready, we'll have breakfast."

"You two are unbelievable." She heard a hearty laugh and footsteps walking away. After washing and dressing, she found a hair brush on the sink top and ran it through her stringy hair. Even though she had washed it a few hours earlier, it still looked thin and dull. She lamented at its poor condition. It looked nothing like what it used to … before Aruba. Gazing at her reflection in the mirror, she attempted to bolster her self-esteem. "Okay girl, get yourself together. This is the first day of your freedom. You should be happy," she heard herself say, but she didn't really feel it deep down. Not sure why, she felt depressed and angry. Blowing out her lips in a fit of frustration, she headed toward the main cabin.

When she slid open the door, the aroma of coffee lightened her mood. Her stomach growled as she walked through the rear galley where the coffee pot steamed a luscious brew of strong-smelling liquid caffeine. Impressed by the china and crystal stored in the glass-front cabinets, the galley looked more like a luxury hotel. Silver flatware waited on the granite countertop alongside real cloth napkins. This airplane had more luxurious amenities than her old apartment. She walked past the two divans where Jason and Matt slept last night, their sheets and pillows removed. The low roar of the engines seemed louder in the main cabin.

Jason and Matt sat at a four-seat conference table next to large oval windows where a sliver of light peeked over the horizon, the dawn of a new day, the first day of her new life. She stopped and marveled at its beauty until the men looked up from their electronic devices.

"Morning."

"Good morning," Jason said. "Did you get any sleep?"

"A few hours, did you?"

"A little ..." Jason set his smartphone on the table.

"Yeah, someone kept screaming." Matt cocked an eyebrow at her.

Feeling sheepish, she muttered, "Sorry," and sat down in the seat next to Jason. "Thanks for the clothes." She tugged at the elastic waistband. "This helps."

"We weren't sure what to expect," Jason said. "It'll work until you get home."

"I really appreciate everything you both have done for me." She glanced at their smiling faces. "When do you think we'll land?"

Matt checked his watch, Jason his phone. "One and a half hours," Jason said. "Want some breakfast?"

"Yes, I'm starved." She glanced toward the galley. "Can I get some coffee?"

"Go ahead," Matt said. "Are you sure you can eat?"

"I'll try." She remembered how she gobbled her dinner the night before. Not used to such good food, it came right back up. She had felt mortified when she reached for the puke bag. Incredibly, Jason had held her hair back. What a surprising man. She picked up the coffee pot and poured herself a mug. Jason followed her with his empty cup, which she filled.

"Matt?" She lifted the pot in the air.

"I'm good."

Jason sipped on his black coffee and watched her face as she stirred some cream into her mug. "I was thinking … maybe if I give you a little food at a time, it might help."

She thought about being restricted by this handsome man and it turned her off. Emancipated, only to be controlled by another man? No, I think not. "Ummm … that's okay; I'll try on my own. But thanks." She turned and walked over to her seat. Jason stayed in the kitchen. She heard him clanging dishes, glasses and utensils. "Can I help?"

"I've got it."

"He's very handy in the kitchen. He'll make someone a good wife." Matt tossed back his head and laughed.

"I heard that." Jason pretended to be stern but Kathleen could tell he was joking.

She smiled at their friendly banter while sipping her coffee. The hot, steamy liquid bit her tongue. Not bitter but very strong. "You guys like really strong coffee."

"Yep," Matt said. "We usually like espresso but they didn't have any on this plane."

"Wow, I don't think my stomach could have handled that."

Jason brought two glasses of orange juice to them. "Good thing they were out." He set the drink in front of them and returned to the galley.

About five minutes later, Jason brought her a plate full of hot, smelly food. "Thanks. I didn't expect to be served." She eagerly took the plate from him and set it down in front of her. Scrambled eggs, link sausage, and a few hash-brown potatoes looked and smelled great. She smiled her thanks at Jason and couldn't wait to dig in.

"Go ahead, eat." Jason soon returned with plates for Matt and himself, sitting next to her by the window.

Faced with the aroma from the steaming food, she could almost taste it. She stabbed the eggs with her fork and gobbled them. She couldn't help it. Nothing she had eaten over the past year had tasted so good. When she sensed four eyes watching her, she looked at Matt and Jason, then swallowed the wad in her mouth.

19

Jason cautioned her, "If you keep eating like that, you'll throw up again."

"I'm okay." She paused briefly before returning to her mission. A minute later she had finished. She glanced over at Jason's plate. He wasn't half done. Matt wasn't too far ahead of him. They had self-control. Of course they did. They weren't starving. "What's the plan when we get to Miami?" She sipped her coffee.

"We'll take you to the FBI safe house," Matt said. "You'll be protected there until we can arrest the traffickers."

She thought about that and looked at Jason. "Would I live there by myself?" When he nodded, she wasn't sure she wanted to be alone so abruptly. "My parents will want me to go home." She looked at Matt. "I want to visit with them and see my friends before going into hiding."

"I understand," Matt said. "You've been gone a year. But for your safety, staying at the safe house would be a better choice. When I called your parents and told them you were coming home today, needless to say, they were more than shocked."

"I guess so." She felt almost frightened at the thought of seeing them. How would they react to seeing her? She didn't exactly look the same. "Did they think I was dead?" A silent pause filled the void.

Jason gave her a sympathetic look. "Let's just say, you've been gone so long, they feared the worst." He spoke in a gentle tone and polished it with a reassuring smile.

"I understand." But she really didn't. How could her family think she was dead? How could they give up on her? Stop believing in her? How could they? She felt almost betrayed. She finished her coffee and went to the galley.

"More coffee?" She held up the carafe to the men.

"Sure," Jason replied, while Matt smiled his agreement.

"Thank you, ma'am." Jason's good southern manners charmed her.

She filled Matt's cup and realized the two pilots in the cockpit probably would like some as well. She knocked on the cockpit door and it soon opened. "Would you guys like some coffee?"

"No thanks," the pilot said. "We've been drinking it for the past couple of hours."

"My name's Kathleen. Thanks for doing all the work up here. If I knew how to fly, I'd give you a break."

The pilots grinned. "We're glad to do it. Would you tell Jason we'll be landing soon?"

"Sure." She returned the carafe to its heater before settling in her seat next to Jason. "The pilot said we'll be landing soon."

"Good." Jason gazed out the window at the sunrise. "I'll be glad to be back in the heat. Vancouver was a nice city but it's cold up there."

"Try living there, with no coat." She shivered just thinking about it.

"Bastards. Oops. Sorry." Matt smiled an apology. "As soon as you're ready, I'd like you to come to the office and meet with our Human Trafficking Task Force. It's a team of professionals who work to liberate folks from slavery. They want to debrief you about how you left Aruba and arrived in Vancouver."

Kathleen remembered her dream from that night and cringed. "I'd like to get settled, spend some time with my family, can we meet after that?"

"Absolutely, how about in two days?"

"How about three?" She buckled her seatbelt when she heard the plane's flaps lower. Her stomach shifted. She felt uneasy as she anticipated seeing her parents and brother. The next few days would prove to be very unsettling.

The pilots guided the Gulfstream jet to a smooth landing and taxied toward the hangar where it stopped. Her stomach lurched. After the engines shut down, the pilots opened the cockpit door. She glanced out the large oval window next to Jason and saw her parents' car pull up. Her nerves forced her to swallow a lump in her throat. Her heart raced. She felt ill and excited at the same time. She felt lightheaded and her breathing increased.

"Are you all right?" Jason asked and squeezed her hand that gripped the plush leather armrest between them.

Kathleen swallowed hard and tried to reduce her breathing but couldn't. Her face must have turned pale because Jason grabbed the puke bag and handed it to her. That was the last thing she needed to see because up came her breakfast. She turned away from him and tried to get out of her seat but her seatbelt resisted. Jason pulled her hair away from her face and twisted it lightly down her back to keep it out of the way. Feeling embarrassed, she mumbled, "Sorry."

Jason went to the galley and returned with a wet cloth. "Here." He pressed her cheeks with it and looked at the pilots who were ready to open the cabin door. "We need a minute."

Her shaky hand took the towel from him and wiped her forehead and neck. She soon felt better but her mouth tasted bitter. "I need to brush my teeth." She rushed into the bathroom in the back of the plane. While the men talked, she brushed her teeth, gargled, washed her face, brushed her hair, and looked at herself in the mirror. "Okay, girl, you look halfway presentable. Now try not to throw up on your family."

She walked into the main cabin and waited for the men to acknowledge her. Matt, Jason and the two pilots looked concerned. "Sorry about that. I'm a little nervous, I guess." She forced a weak smile.

"That's understandable. I can't imagine what it must be like to come home after a year ... it must be overwhelming." Matt gave her a reassuring smile.

Jason rubbed her back. "We can spend as much time here as you want. Don't rush yourself."

"I'm ready. I think the greasy sausage didn't agree with me."

"Okay." Jason looked up at the two pilots standing by the door. "Let's do this."

The pilots opened the cabin door and lowered the staircase to the tarmac. "Want to go first?"

Matt looked at Kathleen and must have sensed she still felt a bit nauseated. "You go. We'll delay as long as possible."

Jason gazed out the window. "There's no rush. Charles is with your family. He'll keep them entertained."

"Charles?" She looked out the large oval window.

"He's my friend and business partner. He has quite a personality."

That news helped her feel better. Her mother, father, and brother waited with a tall blond man dressed in a tan, smart-looking suit. He dressed like a lawyer. She soon felt calmer, eager to see her younger brother, to whom she had grown very close before she was taken. "Can we go now?"

"Sure." Jason stood up with her.

Matt left the cabin while Jason helped her onto the ramp. Bright sunlight burned her eyes. Shielding them with her left hand, she looked for the first step at the top of the stairs. She grabbed the handrail and slowly descended several steps to the tarmac. When her foot touched the ground, she heard a squeal. Kathleen looked up to see her mother running toward her with a hand over her mouth. Her father and brother followed close behind.

Her mother stopped short in front of her. Her wide eyes perusing her body from top to bottom, muffling a groan with a shaking hand.

Kathleen spread her arms. "I'm okay, Mom. I'm alive."

Her mother grabbed her completely around her back. "I can't believe they found you," she yelled. "Oh my God." She burst into tears and hugged her so tight Kathleen thought she might not be able to take another breath.

Tears filled Kathleen's eyes as she looked into the faces of her father and brother, who were more mild-mannered than her mother. "I'm okay." She attempted to loosen her hold. When her mother finally released her, Kathleen stepped over to her father who had tears in his eyes and opened his arms. She quickly went into them and held him for what seemed like several minutes.

"I love you, sweetie," her father said. "We're so glad you're home." He let go of her and gave her time to hug her younger brother, Sam.

"Hey, Sis." Sam encircled her in his arms. "Welcome home. We sure missed you." He patted her on the back and let her step back to take in the scene.

"I need to introduce you to my new friends." Kathleen turned to Jason and Matt who stood nearby with Charles.

"Oh, we know Matt." Her father extended his hand. "Nice to see you again."

"Glad to bring you some good news for a change." Matt shook her father's hand.

Kathleen glanced at Jason. "This is my brother, Sam; my father, Harry; and my mother, Brenda." She touched his arm. "This is Jason. He rescued me last night." She felt a warm glow as her family shook hands with him.

"This is my friend, Charles." Jason gestured toward him.

She shook his hand. "Nice to meet you. Thanks for entertaining my family while I gathered myself."

Charles smiled warmly. "Welcome home. We're very glad the FBI found you."

"It was a team effort." Matt slapped Jason on the back. "We'll talk more about that later. First, we need to get Kathleen settled at the safe house."

"Safe house?" Harry said. "She's not coming home with us?"

"Under the circumstances," Matt said, "the traffickers will be looking for revenge. We think it best she be kept in a secret location for now."

"My baby's been missing for a year," Brenda said. "You're not going to keep her from me any longer."

"Matt's right, Mrs. McDougal," Jason said. "We don't want to jeopardize her safety until the key players are in prison."

"Well, I don't like that at all," her mother insisted. "I want my baby home."

"They're right, Mom," Sam said. "When the head of the organization finds out, all they have to do is look up the name McDougal in the Miami phone book and they'll come here to kill Kathleen."

Brenda looked at her family with fear and desperation. "I don't like this. I want my baby back." She hugged Kathleen close and started to bawl. "I won't take no for an answer. You're coming home!"

"Okay, Mom," Kathleen rubbed her mother's back as she watched Jason's concerned expression. "I'll go home with my family."

"I don't support that decision," Jason said. "Your safety should be the first priority."

Kathleen pulled away from her mother who glared at a determined Jason. Squeezing his arm, Kathleen hoped he would back off a bit.

Matt's cellphone buzzed. "I need to get back to the office. I hate to impose on you Jason, but could you take Kathleen where she wants to

24

go?" He gave her a serious look. "While I can't make you go to the safe house, I highly recommend you do." He reached into his pants pocket and removed a key. "Here's the key, if you change your mind."

"I'll be okay for a few days. I'll move to the safe house when things heat up." Kathleen wondered if she meant with the slavers or with her mother.

Jason took the key from Matt. "I'll get her settled at home for now."

"Thanks. I owe you." Matt shook his hand and turned to Charles. "I appreciate your help with these operations."

Charles shook Matt's hand. "If it weren't for Jason, I wouldn't be so community oriented. He keeps me grounded."

Matt smiled. "Mr. and Mrs. McDougal, if you need anything, give me a call. Sam, good luck with law school."

Sam grinned. "Thanks for everything you've done for my family."

"My pleasure. Kathleen, see you in three days." Matt turned to leave.

"Wait." She ran after him and gave him a big hug. "Thank you for saving me." She kissed him on the cheek and let him go when he looked embarrassed.

"I'd really prefer you stay at the safe house."

"I know. I'll go as soon as everything settles down."

When Matt left, she returned to Sam who put his arm around her shoulders.

"I'm going to get her settled," Jason said to Charles, "then I'll come to the office to catch up on things."

"We've got the office covered. You need some sleep."

"Things will get too backed up."

"I received an email from you early this morning. I know you were working. I admire your dedication, but you won't be any good if you can't stay awake. Take a couple days off. Our staff is perfectly capable of keeping things running. Besides, if anything exciting happens, I'll be there."

"All right." Jason shook his hand. "Thanks for coming out to welcome us home."

"We worry about you, buddy." Charles squeezed his shoulder. "You can put yourself in some sticky situations."

"I wouldn't have it any other way. Otherwise, life would be pretty boring."

"I'm ready for some boring." Everyone laughed at Kathleen's comment, but she was serious. When she heard beeping, she moved aside. A jet porter pulled the Gulfstream airplane into the hangar. A beautiful aircraft she hoped never to ride in again.

Jason touched her arm. "We need to talk. Would you ride with me?"

Brenda frowned but Kathleen knew they needed to chat. "Sure, I'll make sure you don't get lost." She hugged her family before they got in their car and left for home.

Jason opened the passenger door of his silver Cadillac Escalade and helped her into the seat. After shutting her door, he moved around to the driver's seat and got in. "I'll take you home, but I still don't agree with it."

"I know you're concerned, but I don't think the slavers will come after me in the next couple of days."

"I'd be more comfortable with you hidden away." Starting the truck, he followed her parents out of the airport. "We don't know how far-reaching this operation is."

"I'm willing to take a chance for a couple of days." He sighed with frustration at her resistance. "Besides, I'm free after more than a year. I'd like to enjoy it a little." She smiled at his tense lips and gazed out the windshield, reveling in her newfound freedom to make her own decisions. It felt good to be independent again. Although she knew he was right. The slavers were ruthless people who cared little for the value of human life. Moving to the safe house would help protect her and her family from those evil people.

As they traveled in silence, she scanned the city to see what had changed during the past year. "Look at all the new skyscrapers."

"There's been a renaissance of building downtown. You should come see it. People are living and working downtown again. It has revitalized the city."

"I'd like that. Is the FBI office downtown?"

"No, it's in North Miami Beach. When you go there, you'll meet the folks who worked to bring you home."

"I'd like that. I mean to thank them in person."

"Matt said your brother is in law school?"

"Yes, you two should get along well. Living at home with our parents must be difficult for him. And now I'm back."

"Law school's tough, but passing the bar exam is even harder."

"When I get settled, maybe Sam and I can get a place together."

"Don't rush your recovery, it'll take time."

"I want to be back to normal in one year."

"That's ambitious. If you push yourself too hard, you could have a breakdown."

"I've already lost a year of my life. I'm willing to take a year to recover from it but no more." He didn't say anything. He probably thought she was too unrealistic about recovering but what did he know? He was a lawyer not a doctor.

Chapter 3

As Kathleen rode with Jason toward her parents' house in Miami Shores north of the city, she was reflective. It felt strange to be going home to stay with her parents. After she left to attend the University of Miami ten years ago, she would return home for only brief visits. Her neighborhood had always been stuck in time, and as Jason drove her back she could see that nothing had changed in the last year either.

When her family pulled into their driveway, Jason looked in the rearview mirror. "There's a car behind us. I'm going around the block."

She glanced at the side mirror and saw a white sedan behind them. "You don't think they'd be here the first day ..." She shook her head and thought he was being ridiculous.

"I'm not taking any chances." He drove past her parents' house, turned left, and drove around the block until the car behind them slowed and entered a driveway. Jason made left turns until they were back on her parents' street. He looked in the mirror again and this time pulled into the driveway. "Quick, get inside."

She hurried to the front door where awkwardness set in. Should she knock or walk in? She knocked a couple of times then opened the door and entered. "Hello." She looked around the empty living room.

"Back here," she heard her mother say from the rear of the house.

Kathleen walked across the tiled floor toward her mother's voice and saw her family sitting outside on the lanai. Behind their home was a well-kept, landscaped garden. The familiar pebble path led to a wooden walkway over the sand dunes that ended at the beach. She had missed the smell of salt air, tropical sea breezes, and myriad sounds of nature.

"I made your bed and cleaned your old room." Her mother smiled and set snacks on the table. "You can sleep in there."

"Just like old times." Kathleen cringed and glanced at Jason, who gave her a sympathetic look followed by consternation.

"Sit down, Katie." Her father pulled out a chair for her with a loving smile. "Tell me what you want to do first."

"I'd like to put on my own clothes, get some money out of the bank, and maybe call Tara and Chandra."

"Is that all?" Harry chuckled.

"Who are Tara and Chandra?" Jason asked.

"Tara is my best friend from college and Chandra is my friend from work who went to Aruba with me on business." She gulped as the others looked at her wanting to probe for more information, but they resisted asking the question everyone wanted to know.

Harry looked at Brenda, who grimaced. "Sweetie ... we donated your clothes to charity and sold your household goods."

"We sold your shell collection to that big store in the Keys." Her mother looked sheepish. "We kept your paintings and personal things. They're in storage."

"You sold my shells?" Feeling devastated, Kathleen remembered the years she spent collecting hundreds of unique seashells. How could they get rid of her things? She rubbed her forehead trying to relieve the stress she felt. "What about my car?"

"Sam's using it for school."

"You can have it back, sis." Sam offered her a weak smile.

"That's okay. Keep it. I'm not ready to drive." She felt her stomach roll. The stress of coming home caused too much anxiety. She needed to focus on her recovery, not her past.

"We kept the money in your savings account," Harry said. "But we'll need to talk to the bank about what paperwork they need to let you have it."

"I can help with that." Jason looked at his watch. "We can go to the bank first then head to the storage unit to get your things." His leg jerked rapidly under the glass table as if he were nervous or anxious. "Ready?" He looked at her. "It'd be better to get to the bank before they break for lunch."

"Ummm, okay." She didn't understand the rush. She just got home.

Jason looked at his smartphone, thumbing through his messages. He probably wanted to get her settled so he could get back to work.

Her mother got up from the table. "I'll get the bank information and the key to the storage unit." She soon returned with papers and keys. "Here's a spare key to the house."

"Thanks, Mom." She took the keys and stuffed them in her pants pocket next to her Dutch slave bead, rubbing it for good luck.

Jason put his smartphone in its holster and helped Kathleen into his truck. He followed Brenda's car to the bank where they met with the bank manager. While the manager had been thrilled that she had been rescued, she also explained that her parents had declared her missing and presumed dead, which froze her accounts. Kathleen felt relieved when Jason understood what needed to be done to reverse that situation. She couldn't seem to focus on details. She shook the manager's hand, followed her mother outside, hugged her goodbye, and got into Jason's truck.

"I can't believe they declared me missing and presumed dead. I can't touch my own money." She snapped her seatbelt around her hips.

"Don't worry." Jason started the engine. "I'll take care of the paperwork."

"I'm just annoyed they gave up on me."

As they followed Brenda into acres of orange and white storage buildings, Kathleen realized her muscles ached as if she had caught the flu. She rubbed her arms hoping to relieve the tension and anxiety. When Jason pulled up next to her mother's car, Kathleen jumped down from his truck and handed him the storage locker key. He unlocked the orange overhead door and rolled it to the top of the track.

Kathleen glanced around at the stacks of boxes, old bed frames, and miscellaneous furniture left there to be forgotten.

"Here are your things, Katie." Her mother pointed to a stack of boxes along the side wall.

Shocked by the small number of boxes, Kathleen stiffened her spine, and forced herself not to show her distress. There weren't many boxes for a life of twenty-eight years.

Jason gave her a sympathetic glance and loaded the boxes into the back of his Escalade while Kathleen and her mother talked. How did he know what she was feeling at every turn?

Brenda smiled. "Next we can talk to the credit card companies about opening your accounts again."

"Whoa. Not so fast." Kathleen raised her hands. "I don't have any income."

"You have your savings."

"I'm going to be much more frugal than I used to be."

When Jason finished loading her boxes, he pulled down the overhead door, locked it, and gave the key to Brenda. They said goodbye before Jason opened the passenger door and helped Kathleen inside. He waited for her mother's car to start before leaving the storage facility. Impressed by his good manners, Kathleen wondered about his mother. She'd taught him well.

Riding home in silence, she pondered her feelings when a lump formed in her throat. She rubbed it away, refusing to shed a tear for mere things. When she sniffled, Jason glanced over at her but remained quiet. He knew what she was thinking, again. She looked over at him with a sense of amazement. "At first, when my parents told me they had given away my things, I felt angry. But when I thought about my old furniture, I didn't feel anything. I didn't really care about it anymore."

"That's good."

"I've changed." She glanced out the side window. "I used to enjoy decorating my apartment."

"You've gained a different perspective."

"I care more deeply about people than I did before."

"That's a good thing. My father taught me from a young age to give back to the community and to care for others. It's a lesson I've cherished all my life."

"Your father sounds like a good man."

"He is. I'm always trying to make him proud." Then he laughed. "And outdo him."

"I think that's typical for father-son relationships, don't you?"

31

"I suppose. What about mother-daughter relationships?"

She sighed. "They're a challenge. Women compete in subtle and vindictive ways."

"Your mother doesn't seem very subtle," he chuckled.

"That's because she sees you as competition."

"That's a first. She's more like a momma bear protecting her cub."

She snorted a laugh. "She's a good person really, just a bit overbearing."

Minutes later, they arrived at her parents' home where he backed into the driveway. Before he could turn the engine off, a car sped down the street, crashed over her parents' mailbox, and squealed tires as it sped around the corner. Jason sprung open the glove compartment, pulled out a gun, and aimed at the car. There were kids playing nearby. He cursed and raised the pistol in the air without firing.

Shocked by the entire episode, her mouth fell open. Was she more startled by the car crashing over the mailbox or his reaction to it?

"You need to move to the safe house." He looked at her determinedly.

"That was a coincidence. It couldn't be them."

"You don't know that."

"Neither do you." She raised her eyebrows. "Now let's unload my boxes."

Jason sighed with exasperation and returned his pistol to the glove compartment. He helped carry Kathleen's boxes inside and put them in the corner of her childhood bedroom.

"That's it." She stood in the doorway with her arms crossed. "This is all that remains of my former life."

"You need to start fresh, anyway." He began to unbutton his shirt. "I'll fix your mailbox." He removed his dress shirt and undershirt and tossed them over the back of the sofa.

She admired his well-built shoulders and chest when he wasn't looking. She wondered if he lifted weights then glanced away when he looked at her.

"Do you have a shovel?"

She led him to the garage where he selected a shovel. While they picked up the pieces of the crushed mailbox, her mother pulled into the driveway and carried groceries toward them. "What happened?"

"Someone ran over the mailbox." She had a hard time believing a slave trafficker would have done this. They were in jail. "We're going to stand it up in a bucket for now."

"I'll get a post from the hardware store tomorrow and fix it," Jason said.

"That's nice of you, but I'm sure my husband will want to do it himself." She stepped closer to Kathleen. "I'm cooking your favorite dinner tonight."

Jason stomped the tip of the shovel into the ground.

"You're welcome to join us, Jason," her mother said.

"Thank you, ma'am, I'd like that." He glanced at Kathleen for her tacit consent. She smiled and nodded. He looked down at his dirty slacks. "I'll go home and clean up. What time should I come back?"

"We eat around seven. If you want to have a cocktail before that, come about six."

"Thanks, I'll be here." He dug out the broken post and lifted the mailbox as her mother took the groceries inside.

"Mom's right, Dad will probably want to fix this his way."

"We'll see if he has time. I have time, if he doesn't." He stood the mailbox in a five-gallon bucket, stepped back, and looked at his handiwork. "At least you can get your mail today."

"Thanks for digging it up. That's the hardest part." Kathleen smiled and avoided staring at his sculpted chest.

"I'm too dirty to go back inside for my clothes. Could you get them?"

"Sure. Be right back." She went inside, picked up Jason's shirts, and took them outside. "Thanks for your help today." She reluctantly handed him the clothes. An unfamiliar throb between her legs was something she hadn't felt in more than a year. As she walked with him to the truck she pondered this reaction.

"I'm not leaving until you're inside the house."

"Okay, I'm going. See you later." She stood inside the front door and waved as he disappeared around the corner. Exhausted, she made her way to her old bedroom, where she laid her head on the feather pillow and drifted off to sleep. Her escape from slavery had been unexpected and hurried. The sudden realization that she had been freed seemed overwhelming. Intense dreams ruled her sleep, flashes of words, colors, and screams. Were they her screams?

She awoke a couple hours later to the aroma of slow-roasted veal shanks. She freshened herself and helped her mother in the kitchen while she waited for Jason. Time seemed to stand still. Being at home with her parents seemed like an old dream that would soon end, and she would wake to find herself back in Vancouver. She shook her head trying to erase those memories and realized her head ached. At six o'clock the doorbell rang. She hurried toward the door and opened it.

Jason looked refreshed. His polo shirt and dress shorts were an improvement over the black suit he had worn to the auction. His muscular legs led to feet slid into brown leather sandals. Sunglasses balanced on his head sporting neatly trimmed black hair. His dark blue eyes danced when he saw her. He carried a bottle of wine and a box.

"What do you have?" She took the wine and box.

"I wasn't sure if your mother had dessert. They're cupcakes."

"Thank you. You're very thoughtful." She led him into the kitchen where Brenda had prepared drinks and snacks. "Look what Jason brought." She handed the wine and cupcakes to her mother.

"My goodness, you seem to anticipate whatever's needed."

"You noticed that too?" Kathleen smiled at his handsome face.

Jason looked almost embarrassed as he opened the sliding glass door, allowing Brenda to carry the tray of drinks and snacks onto the lanai. Harry and Sam relaxed around the table. Kathleen followed her mother and smiled at Jason as he sat down next to her.

In the backyard, palm trees swayed in the tropical breeze. She could hear waves crashing on the beach, making a roar that served as pleasant background noise. She still wore the casual clothes that Matt and Jason had bought her. "I can't wait to walk on the beach. I missed it so much."

Jason smiled at her. "Want to go after dinner?"

Filled with anticipation, she found it difficult to contain her glee. "I can't wait." Her excitement sent a tingle down her arms.

"Vancouver must have been quite a change from Miami," her father said.

"It was bone chilling." She took one of the margaritas her mother made and sipped it. Worried that alcohol might not agree with her uneasy stomach, she enjoyed the taste and relaxed in her seat. Jason looked worried when she winked at him.

"Where'd you get those clothes?" Brenda asked.

"Jason and Matt bought them for me."

Her mother snapped her tongue. "We'll go shopping. Have a mother-daughter outing."

Kathleen had forgotten how controlling her mother was. It's odd how absence blurs character flaws from your memory.

"We'll get you some nice trendy shorts. The fashions changed since you left."

"I don't think so."

Her mother looked at her with an odd questioning gaze. "You know it's too hot to wear long pants in south Florida."

"I don't wear shorts anymore."

"Katie, it'll only get hotter. I'll get you some trendy Bermuda shorts."

"I'm not wearing shorts." She hoped that wasn't as blunt as it sounded. She rubbed her forehead and thought the top of her head might explode. *Why won't she listen?*

Sam had gone inside to grab a beer from the refrigerator and returned to sit next to his father. He watched his mother with a surprised look while sipping the naked end of the beer bottle.

Brenda's surprised expression subsided. "Are you hungry?"

"Starved, I missed your great cooking."

"I'll get dinner ready." Brenda went into the kitchen. A few minutes later, she handed her daughter a plate with a veal shank sunken into mashed potatoes.

Kathleen eagerly grabbed the plate, set it in front of her, and began to gobble her food. When Jason reached for her plate, she couldn't imagine what he was doing, until she looked up and saw everyone watching her with amazement.

35

"Let me help you with that." Jason cut some veal off the bone, put a few pieces on her plate with a small amount of mashed potatoes, and slid it in front of her. "After each bite, count to twenty."

She appreciated his help but he made her feel like a child. Her parents looked at him with annoyance but didn't say anything. Her head throbbed. She couldn't afford to throw up again. She didn't have much to eat today and there weren't any puke bags here. Besides, she needed to put on a brave face for her family.

"So, Katie, tell us what happened to you in Aruba," her mother said. "How'd you get to Canada?"

Kathleen gulped and put her fork down. "I don't want to talk about that."

"But why were you in Canada? Were you there a year?"

"Not now, Mom." Her nightmares were bad enough without rehashing everything. When she started to shake, she rubbed her aching head.

"This probably isn't the time for questions." Jason rubbed her back and looked concerned. "Let her rest a few days. When she's ready to talk, she will."

Brenda looked at Jason with fierce eyes but Kathleen felt relieved that he spoke up. She felt a knot form in her stomach. Jason squeezed her hand that rested on the table. Her mind drifted off while her family talked with him about law school, work, and their interests. She finished the last bit of veal on her plate. She made sure to take her time. So far, her stomach felt comfortable. Maybe this meal would stay down. She had no doubt the mashed potatoes settled her stomach.

When Jason took Kathleen's plate again and passed it back to her, Brenda's face grew apoplectic. "We appreciate what you've done for Katie but you don't need to bother anymore."

"It's not a bother," Jason said.

"I'm sure you're very busy. Besides, I'm a nurse. I can take care of her now."

"Yes ma'am." Jason smiled graciously, but Kathleen sensed he didn't like being pushed away. "If that's what Kathleen wants, she'll tell me."

Brenda sighed and glared at Jason. "Why are you so interested in my baby?"

"Mother ..." Kathleen rubbed her aching forehead and tensed.

Sam rolled his eyes and looked down at his food, avoiding eye contact.

Jason replied calmly. "I want to make sure she's safe and gets a good start on her recovery."

"She'll recover just fine, we'll see to that. We appreciate what you've done, but we'll take good care of her from now on." Brenda patted her daughter's hand.

Kathleen felt exasperated and exhausted. She couldn't explain all the things that happened to her. They were too painful ... too awful. Her nightmares were frequent. Her sleep was short. This afternoon she dreamt about words that didn't make any sense. She couldn't remember where she saw them or what they meant, but recalling them upset her.

"Katie, dear, when you want to talk about what happened, I'm ready to hear it."

"Stop asking me what happened!" Kathleen snapped. The surprised looks on her parents' faces hurt her briefly. Then she remembered she felt bad and didn't really care what they thought.

"Let's go for that walk." Jason rose from his seat and extended his hand to help her up.

She let him escort her down the backyard path toward the beach and over the dune walkway, where he stopped to remove his sandals. She put the flip flops he bought her next to his and stepped down onto the white sandy beach. A low groan rumbled from inside her. "This feels wonderful. I forgot how great sand feels."

After being in Canada for a year, the warm temperatures felt good to her bones. Her long sleeves and pants warmed her like a gentle toaster oven. She walked up the beach alongside Jason who zigzagged through beach goers and kids who ran back and forth to the crashing waves. She bent down to look at some seashells but tossed them down when she saw they weren't special like those in her collection.

"I had a great seashell collection. I spent years collecting them. I can't believe they sold them." Kathleen almost choked back tears thinking about the years she spent on her favorite hobby.

Jason rubbed her back, trying to soothe the hurt she felt.

She brushed away a tear and tried to collect herself as they walked slowly along the edge of the ocean.

"What about work?" he said. "Would you like to go back?"

"Yes, I need income and health insurance. But, they probably won't want me back. And, to be honest, I don't know if I could concentrate on the details. Plus, I'm very irritable."

"I noticed." He put his hand on her shoulder and flashed a cock-eyed grin. "It's normal for victims to feel overwhelmed at first. I know you've set a goal of one year but that's really ambitious."

She winced at being called a victim. She thought of herself as a survivor, not a victim. His comment annoyed her, but she'd let it pass for now. She owed him a lot. "I know a year is ambitious, but I want a stretch goal."

"You also need to see a doctor. Do you have one?"

"My parents do. I haven't been to him since I was a teenager."

"You need to get a referral from your doctor to see a therapist."

"I'm not talking to a shrink!" She glared at him, amazed at his audacity.

"I think you need to. I have a friend who knows a female therapist. She'd be perfect for you."

"I'm not ready to talk about what happened!" She felt annoyed and couldn't help the strained tone of her voice.

"Okay. Let me know when you are." He walked beside her in silence while she collected herself. Soon, the rhythmic sounds of the ocean relaxed her. A tear rolled down her cheek.

"I have to start over from scratch." She gulped.

Jason reached around her back and pulled her to his chest and held her while she cried. "It's okay. You can replace your things."

She sniffled into his polo shirt. "I feel like I've lost myself all over again." She choked on a wad of tears clogging her throat.

"Shhh ..." Jason held her until she calmed down. He put his finger under her chin and lifted it to look at him. His thumb wiped a last tear from her cheek.

She felt isolated and alone. But this man, he was still here, helping her. He put up with her moods, her throwing up. He cared. She had forgotten how irritating her mother could be. Funny how absence helps people forget the negative traits of those they love. Her dad was still the same good-natured guy who loved her mother and tolerated her faults.

Jason's dark blue eyes seemed to be trying to read her thoughts. She almost wanted to kiss him but she didn't even know him, really. *What a handsome guy. Why isn't he married? Maybe he is. No ring. Maybe he's gay. Maybe Charles is more than a business partner.*

She looked out into the ocean as a dolphin came up to catch a quick breath. When they returned to her parents' backyard, Brenda had already cleared away their dishes and brought out the gourmet cupcakes Jason brought.

Kathleen had not eaten sweets in over a year. She didn't know how her stomach would react. When she put a bite in her mouth, her cheeks puckered from the super sweet sensation. She stopped at one bite, just to be safe, and slid her plate in front of Jason.

"You need to eat more," her mother said. "You're very thin."

"I'm trying." She smiled at her mother. "A little bit at a time. I've already thrown up on Jason twice. He's helping me eat more slowly." Her parents looked at her with their mouths ajar. "With all this good food, I gobble it down like a starving savage. We Americans are so spoiled when it comes to food."

"Amen to that," her father said. "Just tell us what you want to eat and we'll get some."

Kathleen swallowed hard and glanced at Jason. She didn't think she could ever live at home again. She felt sure of that already. Once this investigation came to an end, she would get another apartment.

"Tell me Jason," Harry said, "when is this slavery business going to be over?"

Jason shifted in his seat. "This operation is very complicated. It could take a long time. The Mounties don't know where the traffickers' head-quarters is located. And Aruba has so much corruption the FBI doesn't know who to trust. When the traffickers find out who brought them down …" He glanced at Kathleen. "They might come after you and your family."

She felt shocked when he grabbed her hand. "I'll have to change my name. Is that what you're telling me?"

"You'll be protected at the safe house. Let me take you there."

"She can stay here as long as she wants." Brenda smiled as though it was a challenge.

"You're missing my point, ma'am. They'll come after any McDougals in Miami."

"I'm not changing my name." Harry tugged his wife around the shoulders. "I'm proud of my Irish heritage and I'm not running away from evil that may never come. Right, dear?"

"Right, McDougal." Brenda smiled at her husband. "We're stubborn Irish to the end."

"Maybe we can do something not so drastic," Sam said. "We could set up a revocable living trust and put all our assets in the name of the trust. They couldn't trace us that way."

"Interesting idea, let's talk about it some time." Harry laughed. "You can do all the paperwork."

Jason smiled but Kathleen didn't feel like smiling. She didn't relish the idea of her family's safety being in jeopardy. They didn't understand who they were dealing with. She needed to think about changing her name, but she didn't want to. She was a proud Irish lass, too; but not if it meant her life. She stifled a yawn and gave an apologetic look to her parents.

"I'd better leave you good folks." Jason flashed a charming smile and shook everyone's hand. "Thanks for the delicious dinner."

"Thanks for all you've done for our Katie," Brenda said.

"I'll see you out." Kathleen walked behind him to the front door where he paused and turned to say goodbye. She put her hand on his muscular shoulder and kissed him on the cheek. "Thanks for bringing me home."

"I could never have left you there." He touched her cheek and reached into his pocket. "I brought you my spare cellphone." He handed it to her.

"Keep it and use it all you want. I forgot the charger, I'll bring it tomorrow."

"Are you sure? You've done too much already."

"I'm just getting started. I'll call you tomorrow." He opened the door, cautiously stepping outside as a car sped down the street past the house.

She waved goodbye and closed the front door before heading to the kitchen to help her mother. Picking up a dish towel, she reached for a wet pot her mother just washed.

"I'm not sure I like Jason having so much control over you."

Kathleen laughed at the irony of her comment. "I'll be careful. I don't trust men anymore but he's been very good to me. He'll lose interest in me when he goes back to work. For some reason, I'm his hobby."

"He's a nice young man but he's a bit overpowering."

Kathleen laughed again. "He's a lawyer. That comes with the job."

"Yes, I suppose you're right. Sam has started to be very forceful in his tone with me. I know they teach them that for the courtroom but—"

"Sam's a good man and he'll be a good lawyer." As she dried the dishes her mother washed, she thought about Jason and felt content.

Happy to be free, happy to be reunited with her beloved but dysfunctional family, and happy to be cared for by a good man, she felt disconcerted by the warm feelings she felt toward him. Should she trust him? Why was he so interested in her safety? He could be a bit of a pain at times, but he seemed to genuinely care about her. She would miss him when he went back to work. Would he miss her?

Chapter 4

Jason drove into the parking garage beneath the building where his law firm filled one of the upper floors. He parked in his reserved spot and noted that Charles' car stood in its usual place next to his. The elevator swept him to the twentieth floor where the doors opened onto an elegant lobby. Potted palms reflected in the shiny wood floors. Tall double doors with gold lettering read Schumacher & Montgomery, Attorneys-at-Law. Grabbing the brass door handle, he stepped inside where his shoes sunk into plush carpeting. As he approached the office of his assistant, Mrs. Bailey, he paused in her doorway. "Good morning, Mrs. Bailey."

"Mr. Montgomery. You're back."

"For a few hours. Bring me any papers I need to sign but hold my calls."

"Yes, sir." Mrs. Bailey smiled and spun around in her chair, reaching for a stack of folders.

Jason headed toward his office on the left. Charles' office door stood open on the right. He walked to his large wooden desk in the middle of the room. A backdrop of floor-to-ceiling windows looked out onto the skyscrapers along the Miami River and the Biscayne Bay. A side wall with bookshelves full of legal tomes served as the backdrop for a seating area with small leather sofas and side chairs for intimate counseling sessions.

He wasn't in his office for two minutes before Mrs. Bailey brought in his signature folders. "Thank you, ma'am." He sat behind his desk and scanned the papers, signing them as he flipped them over when he heard a knock on his door.

"I thought I heard you," Charles said, walking toward him.

Jason stood and shook hands with his best friend.

"How'd things go with Kathleen?" Charles leaned on the back of a leather side chair.

"Good. She's settled at home. We spent last night with her family."

"We …?" Charles raised an eyebrow.

"I had dinner with Kathleen and her family."

"She's sweet, buddy, but she's got too many problems. You should gracefully back away from her and all her troubles."

"Probably, but—"

"Uh oh, but …" Charles chuckled. "That's trouble."

Jason smirked. "I have a chance to help someone recover. Not just send her home on an airplane and forget about her, but to help her through the complete process of recovery. I want to experience what that's like."

"That's very noble, but don't you think you'll get too involved with her problems?" He sat down in the chair opposite him. "I mean, she's got physical and mental challenges that'll take years to overcome, if she ever does."

"Bringing her home and dumping her is leaving the job unfinished." Jason stood up and turned to look out the windows toward the river. "The foundation can give her medical help, counseling, job training. Eventually, I'd like to have our own safe house full of folks we've rescued who are transitioning back to freedom."

"I like your foundation's goals and fully support what you're doing. I'm just saying, if you personally take on her recovery, it might get messy."

"Messy?" Jason cocked one eyebrow and turned to his friend.

"Well, you know what I mean, psychological problems. Not to mention what happens if the traffickers come after her?"

"I'll be there to protect her."

"You're just trying to rid yourself of guilt because of what happened to Connie. There wasn't anything you could have done to save her. The slave owner came after her and took her before we even knew what happened."

"Now I know what's happening. This time I'll be there to stop them."

Charles sighed and looked down. "Whatever you decide, I'll be there to help. I just don't want to see you get hurt."

"I'll be ready for them this time." Jason crossed his arms. "Kathleen needs a job. I'm going to call her employer and remind them of their responsibilities toward their employees and see what I can work out for her."

"Okay." Charles rose to leave. "I'll leave you to it. Let me know if I can help."

"Thanks. Remember we're having the Board of Directors' meeting on the sailboat this Sunday."

"I'll be there." Charles left the office, then poked his head back around the doorway. "I'll bring the dancing girls." He laughed and disappeared from view.

Jason shook his head and smiled. He continued to review and sign documents, but his mind wandered. He thought about what he would say to Kathleen's employer. They had probably filled her job and didn't want to pay her medical bills. He might have to ask his foundation to share paying her expenses with her employer. He made a note to add that to the agenda for the Board of Directors' meeting.

Remembering Charles' warning, he considered several ways to keep Kathleen safe. Once she returned to work, the public would know she had been rescued. There would be publicity. How would he protect her? The slave traffickers could follow her to the safe house and to her family. They would kill her for what she did ... just like they killed Connie. His thoughts turned to the young, kind housemaid who helped him clean after special events. Charles was right. There was nothing he could have done. *If I had minded my own business, she would still be alive.* He wiped the sweat from his brow and refocused on his task.

He signed more papers, set up client meetings for the next day with Mrs. Bailey's superb assistance, and talked briefly with Kathleen's employer. The president of the company had been shocked to hear that she had been rescued from traffickers in Canada. His concern for her wellbeing seemed sincere. Jason thought he might be reasonable when it came time to discuss an agreement about her re-employment. He swore the man to secrecy because her return hadn't been announced by the FBI yet.

Feeling good about what he accomplished, he drove back to Kathleen's home later in the afternoon to bring her downtown for a tour and dinner. When he knocked on the front door, Sam yanked it open. Panic twisted his face.

"Kathleen's sick, help me." Sam trotted toward the dining room.

Jason took long strides to where she sat on the floor, shaking, rocking, and moaning. She had opened her boxes. Painting supplies lay scattered around her on the floor. He pushed aside the paints and brushes and sat down on the floor in front of her.

"Kathleen!" He squeezed her shoulders. "Can you hear me?" Her haunted green eyes chilled him as she rocked. "Where are you?"

She moaned and rocked. "Venezuela."

Jason felt like someone hit him with a baseball bat. "Venezuela?" He held her while she shook and stroked her auburn hair down her back. "It's okay, you're safe. You're in Miami."

After a few minutes, her shaking waned, her moaning stopped. She lifted her head from his shoulder and blinked as if she just realized who he was. "What happened?"

"You had a flashback," Jason said. "You're starting to remember what happened. What triggered it?"

When she looked up behind him, he followed her gaze. She had set up her easel and painted a wicked-looking black painting overtop an old ocean scene. The canvas had a large black hulk in the center of it, a screaming mouth with red lips, and the words RUB and TAR painted across the chilling background.

He looked at her drawn face. "I want you to start talking to a therapist."

"No, I'm not ready."

"Kathleen," Jason took her hands in his, "if you want to recover in a year, you need to get started soon."

"Stop pushing me. I can't even sleep at night. If I see a therapist, I'll never sleep."

"You'll recover faster if you get started now."

"Don't lecture me." She let go of his hands, got up from the floor, and stormed toward the living room.

Jason followed her. "Kathleen, listen to me …"

"No!" She held the sides of her head. "Leave me alone!"

Jason sighed, exasperated by her resistance and glared at Sam. "I'm going back to work." He walked past her toward the front door and paused.

She stood in the middle of the room with her arms folded around her waist watching him with vacant eyes.

His frustration with her peaked. "Call me when you want help." He quickly went to his truck and headed back to his downtown office. Maybe Charles was right. Maybe he should back away. This would be a perfect time, but he could not let go of his concern. She needed to talk to a therapist. She needed a medical exam. He was not naïve enough to believe she hadn't been raped. She needed to be tested for diseases and treated for injuries. Her physical scars were most likely matched by psychological ones. But she wasn't ready. Not yet anyway. Someday soon she would need to talk to a therapist and he needed to be prepared. Her recovery would require lots of time and patience … from both of them.

≈

The next morning, Kathleen met her mother at the mall to buy basic things for everyday living. She had made a list last night after Jason stormed out of the house. She felt terrible about their disagreement and had spent the evening thinking about how to make amends. She missed him and wondered if she called his office if he would hang up on her. She was rude to him. After all he had done, she sent him packing without a care in the world. *Bad form. I need to grow a spine and apologize.*

When the time came for her mother to leave for work, they said goodbye at the mall exit and went in opposite directions. She'd bought a few things to make life easier. Before her captivity, she would have splurged on several unnecessary items. Having more than one bra and different shoes for various outfits seemed decadent somehow.

Kathleen picked up her shopping bags and headed for the bus stop. After a ten-minute wait, the bus arrived and soon lumbered toward her home. Jason would not approve, but getting a taxi at the mall proved difficult. As she rode home, a man walked up the aisle from behind her. She leaned away from him and watched every move he made until he waited at the front of the bus to get off. Agitation consumed her. When the bus neared her stop, she wrestled her bags through the door and headed home.

Stepping along at a lively pace, she heard a sound behind her and turned around. No one was there. When she heard someone cough, she realized a man was following her. She ducked into an entryway of a small shop and waited until he passed. When he didn't look back, her anxiety eased and she continued her journey. Maybe Jason was right, maybe she did need help. *I'll call him and apologize.*

Excitement filled her to overflowing when she saw Jason's silver Cadillac Escalade parked in the driveway. She ran to the front door and fumbled for her key when the door abruptly opened. She gasped before seeing Jason's smiling face. "Oh, thank heaven."

"Did you leave anything at the mall?" He chuckled at her armload.

She smiled and felt relieved he wasn't mad anymore. That was a good start, but she still needed to apologize. "What a nice surprise." She put her bags in his outstretched arms.

"Did you pay the taxi?"

"Ummm, I took the bus." She cringed and waited for a tirade.

He tilted his head to one side and gave her a questioning look but stayed silent. He carried her bags to the sofa in the living room.

She closed the door behind her and followed him. "Look, Jason. I'm sorry I was so bitchy yesterday. I'm really having trouble adjusting. I do want your help. I just want to do it at my speed ... not yours."

He put her bags on the sofa and turned to her. "Okay, I'll try not to be so pushy."

"Friends?" She extended her open hand to him and he shook it.

"Friends. My life moves at a pretty fast pace, but I'll try to slow down around you."

47

"That's a deal. Did you go back to work?"

"I got some superficial things done, but tomorrow I have several client meetings. I won't be able to pick you up for the FBI meeting."

"That's okay. Sam said he'd take me."

"I do have this afternoon off. Would you like to tour downtown and have dinner?"

"Sure." Her heart skipped a beat at her heated response. "Do I have time to shower and change?"

Jason smiled. "Go ahead, I'll occupy myself."

Kathleen grabbed her shopping bags from the sofa, and hurried off to the bathroom to quickly shower and wash her hair. When she put on her new sundress and looked in the mirror, she sighed with disappointment at the whip marks on the backs of her legs. "I'll have to take this back. I'm not wearing a dress until I get some laser treatments." Instead, she pulled on a pair of long, white skinny jeans that stopped just above her ankles and perused her reflection. "Perfect ... no marks." She chose a pale green long-sleeved tunic and a white belt that highlighted her slender waist. She liked the way the color set off her auburn hair and green eyes. Satisfied, she left her room to look for Jason. With the living room empty, she explored further and found him standing in front of her painting.

His fingers rubbed his chin. "You're very pensive." He flinched and ran his eyes over her outfit. "Very cute. Much nicer than what we picked out. Aren't you worried about them being too hot?"

"You sound like my mother." She looked down at her long pants and sleeves and back up at him. "No one wants to see my ugly marks."

He looked sympathetic. "I don't think they're ugly. Anyway, your outfit's very flattering." He turned to her painting and squinted.

She joined him and shivered. "I can't believe all that anger and fear came out of me."

"I'm trying to figure out what these words mean, RUB and TAR. Do you remember?"

She shook her head and tossed her hair over her shoulder. "I wish I knew."

"I'm sure you'll think of it." He turned toward her. "Ready?"

"Yes, I'll tell Sam I won't be home till later." After speaking to Sam, she and Jason went to his truck where he helped her inside.

He drove south to Bayfront Park along the shore of Biscayne Bay where Adirondack chairs sat empty on an urban beach. At the point of land where the Miami River merged with the Biscayne Bay, a wide concrete walkway along the river provided space for dog walkers, joggers, and bicyclists.

Kathleen marveled at puffy white clouds scattered across the bright blue sky that echoed off mirrored buildings lining both sides of the river. Some were hotels, some offices, others condos. The tall, striking exteriors reflected their statuesque forms on the water far below. A sightseeing boat full of visitors passed as runners and walkers merged together.

"Living downtown gives you time to have a personal life during the week, not just on weekends," Kathleen said.

As they strolled along the river, Kathleen's stomach became queasy. She didn't understand why until she realized ... the smell. As she passed the Epic hotel, she felt nauseated and covered her nose and mouth. She quickened her pace to get beyond the oriental aromas. In Vancouver, she had eaten enough Chinese food to last a lifetime. Smelling that again caused her discomfort.

"Are you okay?" Jason strode next to her, rubbing her back. She nodded and kept walking. "Are you sure? We can go back."

She shook her head and removed her hand from her mouth. "I'll be okay as soon as I'm away from the soy sauce."

He pointed to the river. "Quick, let's cross the draw bridge before it opens for that freighter."

As she quickened her pace, she watched the traffic below on the Miami River and mindlessly stepped off the curb without looking. A car honked as Jason grabbed her arm to keep her from entering traffic.

"Careful." His strong arm held hers.

Kathleen gasped. "I wasn't paying attention." When the street light changed, she walked across the bridge to the Easter Island-inspired statues in front of the Viceroy Hotel. "I love those." She walked next to

Jason down Brickell Avenue where he stopped at several restaurants to look at dinner menus.

"This is a steakhouse with outdoor dining right on the river. That would be too much for you to eat." He grabbed her hand and led her across the street. "The River Seafood & Oyster Bar is this way."

When they arrived at the corner of South Miami Avenue, she saw huge Live Oak trees draped with Spanish moss and fell in love. "What's that?" She pointed toward an area a couple blocks away.

"That's Mary Brickell Village. You'll like it." When they entered the village, Jason led her through the winding paved walkways beneath huge trees strung with white twinkling lights.

As her eyes scanned the variety of food, shopping, and fun, she felt delighted. From Italian to Irish to Mexican to Seafood, the choices were endless. She felt awed by the experience and couldn't choose one above the other. "I love the bright blue neon lights at Oceanaire. But I'd love to sit outside and people watch."

Jason chuckled. "Let's have a drink at Oceanaire, then dinner at Toscana. They have half portions."

"Can we sit outside?"

"I'll check." He stepped to the outdoor greeting station to speak with the hostess.

Kathleen wondered if this was a goodbye dinner. He would return to work full time tomorrow and become immersed in his fast-paced life. She would see him at the FBI human trafficking task force meeting tomorrow, but after that? She wanted to see her old friends again but they didn't even know she was alive. If she called Tara, she would probably have a heart attack.

Jason made his way through the growing throng of patrons to where she stood on the sidewalk. "I made a reservation at one of the outdoor tables in an hour. That'll give us time to wander more and have a drink at Oceanaire."

As they entered the bright blue neon bar and seafood restaurant, their eyes adjusted to the charming setting where folks of all ages enjoyed an art-deco atmosphere. Jason led her to a stool at the ultra-modern bar, ordered two glasses of wine, and relaxed on the steel stools in air-conditioned comfort.

While they avoided the heat of the sun with a quick drink surrounded by bright blue neon, she forgot about their argument and gained a sense of friendship with this handsome man. An hour later, they returned to Toscana where the hostess led them to a table along the sidewalk. Kathleen smiled at Jason when he pulled out her chair. *I must remember to compliment his mother.*

Jason ordered a bottle of red wine, which the waiter poured into large, round glasses while they scanned the menu.

Surprised by the quality of choices, she felt overwhelmed. "Wow, how could anyone ever decide what to order." When he looked up from his menu, all she could see were his black eyebrows and dark blue eyes dancing with happiness.

"I'd be glad to make some suggestions."

"Please do." She laid her menu on the table.

"The pappardelle is particularly good. Plus you can get a tapas portion."

"Sold." She smiled and sipped the dark red nectar in her wine glass and swirled it over her tongue tasting dry, oaky flavors. When a man skated by, she marveled at his long hair and flashy earring and wondered if he might be an undercover police officer. She waited for Jason to order and watched the waiter hurry away. "So tell me what you do when you're not babysitting me."

He chuckled. "Charles and I own a sailboat that we use a couple weekends a month. One of my passions is scuba diving. Once a quarter, we take the FBI dive team sailing for a special dive challenge."

"The FBI has a dive team?"

He nodded and lifted his wine glass. "Believe it or not, they have dive teams that travel all over the world. I'm one of their dive instructors."

"No kidding." Amazed by his answer and his hobbies, she pressed on. "You volunteer with a foundation that rescues people like me?"

"Yes, we've rescued several victims in the past fifteen months. Most were brought here to pay off debts or were tricked into slavery."

51

Kathleen felt annoyed when he called her a victim but let it pass. "That's really sad, especially in the land of the free." She sipped her wine and savored its strong aroma.

"Human trafficking is big business around the world and unfortunately it's come to America. Folks are brought here for jobs that turn out to be scams. They end up making nothing picking fruits and vegetables or cleaning buildings. Some even serve as sex slaves."

Feeling shocked, she wondered why he looked sad. "You have a very busy life."

He smiled. "I like to keep busy. I also mentor at-risk kids who no one else wants to bother with. That's one reason why I carry a gun."

She shook her head. "Why would you put yourself in that position?"

"If no one helps them escape the gangs and violence in their neighborhoods, nothing will ever change. Someone has to do something, why not me?"

"That scares me."

"Most of the kids use bravado to hide their fear; they act tough to fit in and to keep from being bullied. Once you get to know them, they're good people."

"Amazing, you're very brave."

"Not really, you're the brave one."

When the waiter brought their meals, she ate slowly, savoring the unusual flavors of the food, and enjoying every bite. No nausea. That pleased her. She admired Jason's shoulder muscles and quickly looked away.

"Excuse me for saying so, but you obviously work out." His broad shoulders and powerful-looking biceps caused a heated twinge between her legs.

"I lift weights and run several times a week to keep in shape."

"How do you find time for all your interests ... now you've added me?"

"If I didn't think I could handle it, I wouldn't have offered."

As the sun set, daylight dimmed to a soft amber. Seated under Live Oak trees, adorned with Spanish moss and small twinkling lights, she felt like she had landed in heaven. The charming setting enhanced by good food, a handsome man, and a glass of wine brought feelings of peace and lust. She didn't want this to end.

"Speaking of the foundation, thanks for buying me and helping me get settled."

He reached over and squeezed her hand. "I didn't buy *you*. I paid for your freedom. That's a subtle difference but a big one."

"I don't know how much longer I could have lived under those circumstances. I do appreciate everything you've done for me."

"Sounds like you're saying goodbye. Are you?"

"Ummm … well, I assumed so. You're going back to work, aren't you?"

"Yes, but I do have a personal life." He smiled. "Do you want my help or not?"

"That depends."

"On what …" He cocked one eyebrow.

"On whether you keep calling me a victim. I'm a survivor." She flashed a confident smile. "I appreciate what you've done, but I don't want to be dependent on you. That only keeps me weak."

"I don't want to keep you weak. It would be a privilege for me to see you grow stronger and become independent again."

She lifted her glass of wine. "I'll toast to that."

Before he lifted his glass, his cellphone rang. He looked down at the screen to see who called. "Excuse me, I need to take this." He pressed a button to accept the call and covered his mouth with his hand so other diners could not hear his conversation. "What's up man? I'm downtown. I can pick it up. No problem. See ya." He ended the call and put the phone back in its holster. "Charles asked me to pick up some papers from one of our clients for tomorrow's meeting. We can stop there on the way home."

"Okay." She rubbed her long sleeves. "I'm glad I wore this shirt. It gets chilly along the water in the evenings."

"Yes, this time of year …" He stopped speaking when the waiter asked if they wanted anything else. "Dessert?"

"No thanks. I'm stuffed." She smiled at the waiter. When the check

53

came, Jason took it and reached for his wallet. She dug into her pocket for cash.

"Put your money away, please." He opened his wallet and put a card on the check.

She smirked. "There you go making me dependent already."

"I invited you to dinner. Besides, my momma taught me how to treat a lady."

She scoffed at his remark. "I'm far from being a lady, at least, not anymore."

He cringed as he reached over to squeeze her hand. "I think you're a very brave lady. You can pay next time, if you insist."

"In that case, next time we'll have pizza at home." She laughed but appreciated his warm smile and flattering remark. She had to ask the FBI tomorrow about calling her employer. She needed income and her own place to live.

A group of young ladies wearing tall spiked heels beneath short sparkling dresses headed upstairs where low rhythmic music emanated from the Blue Martini. Kathleen envied them; thinking back, she used to enjoy dancing. Perhaps she would again someday.

After Jason paid the bill, she walked with him toward the people mover train station where they waited for the single automated train car to stop on the platform. Once onboard, the people mover whisked them along an elevated track above the city and stopped briefly at four stations before arriving at Bayfront Park.

She marveled at the colorful lights on the skyscrapers and noticed that Jason had become quiet and wondered what was on his mind. If she asked, would he tell her? They were friendly but not close.

Jason helped her into his truck and drove north and east toward the Port of Miami. Huge cranes stood sentinel over the port. Some worked to unload containers from ships while others stood dark and idle.

"Charles and I have a lot of clients at the Port. We assist them with import-export matters." He pointed to one of the idle cranes. "These new cranes are being built to handle the super-sized ships coming through the widened Panama Canal."

"Unbelievable how big they are. Imagine the view from the top."

He pulled up to a guard house at the entrance to the fenced-in port area. "Reach into the glove compartment and get out my ID card, it's on a chain." She opened the glove compartment and gasped at the pistol resting inside a holster. "Under the gun." He reached to take it from her as his window lowered. He showed his identification as the guard came to his window.

"Name?" The guard glanced at his clipboard.

"Montgomery, Seaside Shipping."

The guard raised the gate arm. "Have a good evening, sir."

Jason returned his identification to her while he drove toward the container ships.

She grew tense and silently counseled herself. *These are just ships,* she told herself, *just containers full of junk, not people.*

He pulled up to an office door with an outdoor security lamp. "I'll be right back." Hopping out of the driver's seat, he disappeared inside. The sign over the door read Seaside Shipping Corporation. Her mind flashed through memories of blindfolds, bright lights, dark containers, and the smell of bananas.

Jason returned with a legal-size folder of papers and tossed them on the flat-top console between them before driving by the ships along the dock.

Her heart raced; she opened her mouth to get more air. *Don't look at the ships. Keep looking straight ahead.* She heard Jason say something but didn't know what he said. She looked at him when he squeezed her hand.

"Are you okay?" His brow wrinkled with concern.

She tried to breathe but her lungs squeezed tight with tension. "Can we leave?"

"Sure." He turned the steering wheel toward the exit and headed north toward her home in Miami Shores. When they reached her parents' house, he walked her to the front door.

"Thanks for the tour and dinner. I enjoyed getting to know you."

He grasped her extended hand and squeezed it. "I did too."

"Do you want to come in for coffee or something?"

"Not tonight, I have an early day tomorrow."

Awkwardness consumed her. "Good night then." She stood on her tiptoes and kissed him on the cheek.

He released her hand and smiled warmly. "Get inside and lock the door."

As she pushed the door closed, a motorcycle sped down the street. Stopping in front of her parents' home, the rider threw something at the living room window, breaking it. Wearing black leather, the rider blended into the darkness as he sped off around the corner.

Jason ran to his truck then chased after him as she slammed the door and threw the deadbolt when her father ran into the living room.

"What the heck is going on?" He looked her over, then glanced at the floor where a rock rested on the tiles amidst broken shards of glass.

"There's a note on it." Kathleen picked it up and removed the paper. She gasped when she read it. "Forget Aruba or else!" Her father's shocked face made her breathing quicken, her mind raced. She heard Jason's truck pull into the driveway and opened the front door.

When Jason came inside, he saw glass on the floor and the note in her hands. He read the note and his back stiffened. His eyes flashed a fierceness she hadn't seen before. Grabbing her elbows, he pulled her close. "You're going to the safe house, right now."

She held his pulsing biceps, still startled by the note and its meaning. His blue eyes pleaded with her.

"I'm not moving tonight."

"Then come home with me." He still held her elbows.

She was shocked. "I'm not going home with you."

"I have two spare bedrooms." Jason looked at Harry's stern face. "Your parents can stay in one; you can stay in the other. Sam can sleep on the sofa."

Harry grunted. "I'm not moving out of my home because some punk threw a rock and broke my front window."

Jason's lips tightened. "Mr. McDougal, I can't tell you how important her safety is. Do you want to lose her again?"

She gasped at his audacity. "How dare you say that to my dad?"

"He needs to understand what's at stake." Jason's eyes were intense. "You of all people know what they're capable of."

Feeling stunned by his bluntness, her mind raced. Yes, she knew, but how did he know? What did he know that he wasn't telling?

Jason gently shook her from her thoughts. "If you didn't know, you wouldn't be having nightmares and flashbacks. Am I right?"

She nodded and glanced at her father. "He's right, Dad. Come with me to the safe house."

"I'm not moving out of my home and that's final!" Harry stepped closer and clutched her arm. "You go. We'll be fine."

"Okay! Okay!" She threw her hands in the air. "I surrender! I'll move to the safe house."

Kathleen walked to her bedroom with Jason following close behind. Her head spun with myriad possibilities of who could be terrorizing her family. She couldn't imagine that anyone from Aruba or Vancouver would be involved. Wilson was in jail for heaven's sake. And the folks in Aruba, the casino workers, fishermen, dock workers ... they didn't even know her name. Who could be doing this? She stuffed her meager belongings into the boxes from the storage unit and handed them to Jason and her father, who helped load them into the back of the truck. She wished she had moved to the safe house in the first place and avoided this assault on her family. Now, they were involved in her misery. She hoped they wouldn't become targets.

Chapter 5

The next day, Kathleen rode in the elevator with Sam to the second floor where the FBI human trafficking task force gathered for their regular meeting. "It's really nice to spend some time with you. I hope I'm not taking you away from your studies."

Sam smiled. "I'm so happy you're home, I can't concentrate." When the elevator stopped, he gestured for her to go first when the doors opened. "I'll hit the books this weekend."

She stepped into a hallway of drab tile with limited decoration and no color. The headquarters for the FBI Miami Division resided about five minutes from the safe house. It reminded her of the military facility she drove past on her way to work. She looked down at the note from the receptionist and checked the room numbers.

"This way …" Sam pointed down the hall.

As they neared the meeting room, she heard loud, deep voices talking and laughing. She tensed. Her footsteps hitched. *Deep male voices gathered in a small room.* Anxiety filled her very core. Her heart raced. Her lips parted. She stopped at the doorway and attempted to compose herself. When she saw her reflection in the glass door, her appearance startled her.

Sam reached for the doorknob and opened the door. "This is it."

Male voices became louder, too close, frightening. She couldn't move her feet. She froze. Her lungs tightened, she couldn't breathe. She clutched her throat and gasped for air.

"Kathleen?" Sam's piercing blue eyes focused on her like lasers. "What's wrong?" He grabbed her arm and held it. His side-swept brown hair reflected the harsh fluorescent light from the ceiling.

Unable to handle the pressure, she pried Sam's fingers from her upper arm and ran down the hall to the end where a door stood open. She ducked into the large white-walled room. A small table and a few chairs were placed in the center. A tall file cabinet in the corner seemed welcoming as she sat on the floor between it and the wall. She gasped for air, tucked her knees to her chest, and clutched them. Too many male voices. Her eyes glazed over. She couldn't focus. She heard footsteps before a shadow blocked the light in front of her. Someone grabbed her hands and said something. All she could hear was her heart drumming. Those hands seemed familiar. She closed her eyes and focused on breathing. Breathe ... breathe ... her heartbeat slowed. Soon she breathed easier and could hear a man speaking.

"Take a deep breath; blow it out your mouth."

Kathleen opened her eyes and felt calmer as soon as she saw Jason's dark blue eyes surrounded by long black eyelashes.

His Carolina drawl warmed her while his thumbs rubbed her fingers. "There you are."

Concerned by her reaction, Sam and Matt remained near the door. She shivered as all eyes were upon her.

Jason glanced at Matt. "Do you have a blanket in your hurricane supplies?"

"I'll get one." Matt disappeared from behind Sam, who edged closer and knelt nearby.

"What's wrong, Sis?"

"Men. Too many men. Small space."

Jason squeezed her palms and gave her a sympathetic look. "Get some water, Sam. It's in the conference room."

Sam left when Matt returned with a blanket and handed it to Jason. He broke open the plastic bag, shook it, holding it by the corners. "I have a nice warm blanket. Would you like this wrapped around you?"

When Kathleen shivered and nodded, Jason put the blanket behind her and pulled it forward over her shoulders. "There, nice and warm." He dragged his hands down her arms.

Soon, she stopped shivering and realized she was sitting on the floor next to a filing cabinet. Embarrassed, she shifted her weight to stand. "Can I get up now?"

Jason extended his large hands and helped her stand. "Sit here." He pulled one of the small chairs near her.

She sat down, wrapped in the blanket and looked from Jason to Matt. "Sorry."

"You sure say sorry a lot," Jason said.

"Oh, sorry." Then she chuckled, realizing she had done it again.

Jason smiled then turned serious. "You don't need to be sorry about anything. What happened to you wasn't your fault and you have nothing to apologize for."

"This isn't like me. I mean … the old me."

"You've been through a lot," Jason said. "That's okay."

Matt stepped closer. "No one could go through what you did and not change."

Sam returned carrying a pitcher of water and a glass. He poured some and set the pitcher on the table. "Here, Sis."

"Thanks." She sipped on the water a little at a time.

Jason turned to Matt. "My suggestion is we ask the task force members to go into the witness room." He tilted his head toward the glass wall on the other side of the room. "They can see her and ask questions without her seeing them."

"Good idea. We'll start as soon as she feels up to it." He touched her shoulder and smiled. "Better now?"

"I'm good. I can do this now."

When Matt left, Jason pulled up a chair next to her. "Want to take the blanket off?" He folded a flap down around her neck.

"No, I like the feel of it. Mind if I hang onto it?"

"Of course not." Jason smiled and patted her arm.

Kathleen heard footsteps as a large group of people moved past the door and entered another area down the hall. They were silent when they entered another room and shut the door behind them.

Matt returned carrying an easel and put it in the far corner facing her and the glass wall. "Are you staying Sam?"

"I'd like to, if it's allowed," Sam said. "I can leave when you discuss secret stuff."

Matt chuckled. "You might be asked to keep some things to yourself, but nothing's classified here."

She smiled at Sam and set the glass on the table. "That'll give him practice at being a real lawyer." Pulling the blanket down, she wrapped it around her hips.

"I think I can handle it." Sam flashed a sarcastic smile.

Matt sat at the table across from her. "We appreciate your coming into the office today. I know it's probably too soon after your return, but we wanted to take advantage of any fresh memories you might have." He gave her a sympathetic look. "They're probably too fresh for you, but we'd like to ask you some questions. When you start to feel uncomfortable, say *red* and we'll take a break. Okay?"

"Yes, sounds good." She stared at the map on the easel that showed North America, Central America and the southern Caribbean ABC islands of Aruba, Bonaire, and Curacao.

"Can you tell us what you remember, starting at the casino in Aruba?" Matt said. "You were last seen playing poker. What happened after that?"

"I was winning and wanted to play longer. My friend, Chandra, got tired around nine o'clock and wanted to go back to the hotel. The casino staff brought us drinks to keep us there, I guess. But she left anyway."

Matt flipped through his folder. "Chandra Nix attempted to leave and was stopped by a casino worker. Do you remember what he looked like?"

"No sorry." Kathleen realized what she said and sighed at Jason. "He was a typical casino worker, nothing special about him." Remembering the scene, she tensed. "He tried to stop her from leaving and one of our male co-workers saw the guy grab her arm. He intervened and they left together. I remember that specifically because she staggered out the door. She would never drink enough to stagger."

Matt glanced at his report. "Chandra was drugged, the same way you were, in your drink."

That revelation stunned her. Her confused expression relaxed when the intercom beeped and a male explained, "Benzodiazepine was found in her bloodstream."

61

Matt smiled at the glass wall. "Thanks, Chad. He's our Drug Enforcement guy."

"Hi, Chad." She waved at the glass wall.

"Hi, Kathleen, nice to see you back."

"They tried to take both of us?" She glanced at her companions in the room.

Matt nodded. "The only reason Chandra wasn't taken was because your co-worker took her back to the hotel. By the time he got her to her room, she couldn't walk. He called the front desk for medical help."

She sighed. "Missed her by that much." She put her thumb and forefinger close together.

"Yes, she was lucky," Matt said. "Now, how did they get you from the poker table to Vancouver?"

"One minute I was playing cards, the next thing I knew, I was riding in the back of a truck inside a dog cage. It was pitch black. Every now and then we passed a street light that I could see through my blindfold. I don't know how long I was knocked out but it was still dark. When the truck stopped, a couple men carried my cage to a wharf. I could hear the putt-putt of an engine in the distance. Eventually a smelly fishing boat arrived and they put me on it." She reached for her glass of water and sipped.

"Take your time." Jason patted her back.

"I was on the boat maybe two hours. When we docked, they loaded me into the back of another truck. We rode about twenty minutes and stopped at a well-lit seaport. There were lots of lights and sounds. I heard lines and rubber tires rubbing against boats and piers. Waves rocked the boat."

"It was still dark?" Matt said.

"Yes. The men put me on an oil tanker and steamed south."

"How'd you know the direction?" Matt said.

"The men spoke Spanish. That ruled out Bonaire and Curacao. When we arrived at a much larger port, I was carried off the tanker and taken inside a warehouse. I heard other women moaning. Someone opened my cage and tossed in some bread." She started to shake, closed her eyes and took a deep breath. *Skip the next part ... jump ahead. No, tell them.* "After we ate, they took us out of our cages and lined us up. I could feel the heat from another person on my arm." She paused to gather courage. "Then, two rough hands squeezed my breasts before moving on to the next in line. Some of the women gasped, some yelled, some were taken away. I heard splashing and screaming, then silence."

Jason winced while Sam looked at his shoes. Matt, Mr. Tough Guy, listened to every word she said, but didn't react. He took notes while she spoke and waited for her to continue. He must have heard everything in his job.

"They loaded the rest of us into a container. I didn't see sunlight for days." She held her elbows and shook. Jason looked concerned. "Pink." She stopped short of the safe word, red.

"We'll take a break." Jason touched her forearm.

She shook her head. "Let's get this over with."

Matt pressed a button on an intercom box. "Joe, let's start with you."

The door opened and an older man entered. His receding hairline showed a prominent forehead and the old-fashioned mustache above his lips reminded her of the 1980s. He grabbed a small chair and moved it to the table and sat down. "I'm Joe Hargraves. I work for Immigration and Customs. "

She shook his hand. "Hi, Joe."

"Was the container refrigerated or fresh air?"

"Refrigerated, but not too much, if you know what I mean. It wasn't cold like a refrigerator. The temperature was comfortable the entire trip."

"Did you see any numbers or writing on the container?"

She paused and gazed into the distance. "No, we were inside a container home. There were bunk beds, a kitchenette, and a toilet that didn't flush. I didn't see any numbers."

Jason grunted. "A container home, I've never heard of that."

"We use them for natural disasters," Matt said. "Construction companies use them for temporary housing. Folks are even living in them for eco-housing."

"It was self-contained," she said. "Food and water were in the kitchen.

63

Labels on the packages read Venezuela." Joe's eyes widened. "One odd thing, we smelled bananas the entire trip."

Matt turned to Joe. "What ports handle banana shipments?"

"Several in Venezuela, Columbia, Costa Rica …" Joe said.

As she remembered her painting, Jason's expression changed from curious to serious as he grabbed his iPad and looked up something. He moved to the easel where he drew a point of land below Aruba and placed marks on the map. "Cabo San Roman is the northernmost point in Venezuela. It's only seventeen miles from Aruba." He pointed to a peninsula. "Right here is a fishing fleet and a refinery."

"Sounds like the fishermen are catching more than fish," Matt said. "They're using their boats at night for a much more lucrative market."

Jason moved his finger south of the fishing village. "Right here is Maracaibo, a large seaport."

Joe had an odd expression on his face. "I'll research the companies that moved containers from Maracaibo to Vancouver a year ago."

"Good deal," Matt said.

"Let me know if I can help," Jason said. "I represent a few shipping companies at the Port of Miami."

Joe laughed in a mocking way. "I'm not a fancy lawyer, but I think I can handle this."

Jason looked puzzled. "What happened once you were loaded on the ship?"

Kathleen smirked inside as Mr. Smooth let Joe's snide remark bounce right off him. "We took off our blindfolds and checked out the container home. A few of us had watches so we marked the time and days on the wall. We figured we were in there about ten days. When the rumble of the engines stopped, they moved our box. We rode a short distance, stopped a few minutes then rode another ten minutes. We sat inside the container for hours before some men opened it, blindfolded us, and walked us to a warehouse. It was freezing cold and dark. We didn't see anything."

"Tell them about the words you painted," Jason said.

"Oh, RUB and TAR?" She shook her head. "I don't know what they mean."

Matt walked to the easel and wrote the words at the top. "Any ideas?" He looked at the glass wall.

The intercom beeped. "Words on barrels?" said one man.

"Rub tar on pilings?" said another. "Tar is a byproduct from refining fuel."

"Tar is slang for a sailor," another man said.

Matt checked her face for clues but she shook her head and shrugged. "Let's take a break and we'll talk about Canada next."

Eager to rest, Kathleen went to the ladies' room where she splashed water on her face. Amazed that Chandra had been drugged too, she felt a longing to see her and Tara. When she walked back to the meeting room, she saw an old acquaintance. "Lucy?"

The Asian-looking woman turned and smiled. Her glasses reflected the glare from the overhead lights. Her straight, black hair pulled back into a ponytail reminded her of the last time they met. "Welcome back, Kathleen."

Kathleen shook her hand. "I haven't seen you in ages."

Matt returned and joined their conversation. "Lucy's the one who discovered your name in the webmaster code."

Kathleen pumped her fist in the air. "Yes!" Putting her arms around Lucy, she hugged her. "I should have known it was you when Jason handed me the code he had entered. That was from the last contest."

"Yes, I seem to remember you won that contest." Lucy smiled warmly.

"I believe I did. Thanks for discovering me."

"It's a thrill to see you home. Matt suggested I stop by to see if you remember any passwords and usernames from the traffickers' computer system."

"I think so. I'll write them down for you." Kathleen sat at the small table, slid a tablet and pen toward her, and wrote down all she could remember. Handing it to Lucy, she felt doubtful. "These are all of them, but they're probably changed by now." Before Lucy could respond, a tall man entered the room. She startled and looked toward the door when she saw a big reflection. "Hi, I'm Kathleen McDougal." She extended her hand.

"Major Whittington. I'm the Liaison Officer for the RCMP in Miami."

"Nice to meet you." She felt relieved when Jason and Sam returned.

Matt shook the major's hand. "Major Whittington, this is Jason Montgomery, he's our private funding source and this is Kathleen's brother, Sam." After greeting each other, they all sat down.

"Miss McDougal," the major said. "I'd like you to come back to Canada to testify against the men we arrested in this trafficking business."

She gasped at his frankness. "Aren't they going to be in jail for a while?"

"Perhaps," the major said.

"What do you mean, perhaps?" Jason said. "You're not saying they could get out on bail are you?"

"They claim to know some very important people," the major said. "Very rich people."

Her heart raced. "This can't be. Wilson can't possibly be eligible for bail. He's a flight risk."

"That'll be decided by a judge," Major Whittington said.

"I'll do whatever I have to." She wrung her hands and looked down.

"If that happens," Jason said. "It's a payoff."

"Slave trafficking is a complex web that stretches around the world," the major said. "We've stopped one small piece by working with the FBI on this task force. But cutting off a piece of spider web only makes the rest of the web strengthen and relocate."

"You're right," Matt said. "We need to identify the folks in the casino, on the fishing boat, and the shipping folks who are involved."

The intercom beeped. "There's possible corruption in Aruba. We'll need to work with Interpol and the Netherlands to root out the bad guys."

"That's right," Matt said. "That's Nathan with ATF."

"ATFE," Nathan said.

"They've changed your agency's name again?" Jason asked.

"Yeah, we've added explosives to Alcohol, Tobacco and Firearms," Nathan said.

"Good," Matt said. "We need an explosives expert." Looking at Kathleen, his appearance grew serious. "Speaking of explosives, this brings us to your security. I'm holding a press conference at five o'clock to announce that you've been rescued. That will allow you to begin living a normal life."

"Normal, hell," Jason said. "They'll kill her."

Kathleen startled at Jason's firm response and flashed him a concerned look. He seemed to realize that he scared her because he grabbed her hand and gave her a sympathetic look.

"You'll be able to return to work," Matt said, "visit your family and friends. The only thing I ask is that the location of our safe house be kept secret. You can't even tell your family or friends." He looked at Sam. "That includes you Sam."

"Sam brought me here, sorry."

"I can keep a secret." Sam acted annoyed. "I'm a grownup now, Big Sis."

"I know." She squeezed his arm. "I don't want you dragged into this mess because you know where I live."

"Don't worry about me. I can defend myself."

Kathleen felt exasperated. Talking to men can be frustrating. They're so macho, they take everything personally. "I need to get my own place to live anyway. How long will I be able to use the safe house?"

"We don't need it right now," Matt said, "but that can change overnight. You need to begin discussions with your employer about going back to work." Matt looked at Jason. "Do you want to discuss that now?"

"I'm taking care of that," Jason said.

Her mouth fell open. "What?"

"We don't need to waste the task force's time discussing personal stuff," Jason said. "We'll talk later."

"Summarize it for me, counselor." She twisted her lips into a smirk.

"I've spoken with the president of the company. He's willing to discuss your return to work but not in your former position." He grabbed her hand and squeezed it. "Let's talk after the meeting."

Stunned and surprised, she couldn't believe Jason had already spoken to her employer. He did lead a fast-paced life. "But my friends and co-workers think I'm dead."

"After the press conference, everyone will know you're back," Matt said.

"Including the traffickers." Jason gave him a helpless look.

"The other option is the witness protection program," Matt said. "You and your family could—"

"No," Sam said. "We're not changing our names and we're not running for the rest of our lives."

"Then the other option," Matt said, "is high security. You'll need to wear a disguise and be picked up from work. Never go directly home or to your parents' house."

"You're scaring me," Kathleen said.

"These people will do anything," Jason said. "You need to be scared."

Her eyes widened as she looked at his serious face. She bit her lip and took a deep breath. "I don't have that kind of money."

Jason squeezed her hand. "Later."

"Okay," Matt said, "Back to Canada. The shipping company and the Port of Vancouver are stalling our efforts for information about their involvement. What's the latest on that, major?"

Major Whittington cleared his throat. "Because of the international nature of shipping, the legal hurdles are numerous. We're working through that. Several folks were arrested in Vancouver." He flipped through his notebook. "A man named Wilson refuses any cooperation. The rest are keeping their mouths shut. They seem afraid of something or someone. We've done forensics on the computers, traced the banking transactions to the Middle East, Asia, South America, and the Caribbean." He looked at Matt. "The next step is a bail hearing for the defendants. The judge will set a trial date and the hard work of proving the case begins." He turned to Kathleen. "That's where you come in. In order to prove this case, we'll need you to return to Vancouver. Are you willing to do that?"

"Of course," she said.

"One last question," Matt said. "Did you ever see the names Natalee Holloway or Robyn Gardner in the computer database?"

"No, but they were blondes weren't they?"

"Yes … what difference does that make?" Matt said.

"Blondes and young boys were special orders," she said. "They weren't entered into the computer. They were ordered directly through Wilson and were paid for in cash."

"Did you ever see a list of special orders?" Matt asked.

She shook her head. "Wilson kept it locked in a safe in his office. No one was allowed to see the list but him."

Matt pounded his fist on the table. She raised her eyebrows. Mr. Tough Guy had a chink in his armor. "That would be too easy." He looked at the major with frustration.

"Where is this safe?" the major said.

"It's behind Wilson's desk in the far corner where the boards are loose in the floor."

The major sat back in his chair as if she slapped him. "Do you know the combination?"

"No, I wasn't allowed near it. If Natalee and Robyn went to Vancouver, their names would be on that list."

Matt rubbed his temples with his hands. "I was hoping you would have an answer for their families." He craned and rubbed the back of his neck. He quickly recovered and sat up straight. "Let's move on to the press conference. Jason said he's not interested in participating. Are you?"

She glanced at Jason, whose dark eyes watched her. "I don't think I'm ready for that. Maybe someday, is that a problem?"

"Not at all," Matt said. "I'm simply going to announce you've returned and answer any questions the media might have. Would you like me to read a statement to the media?"

She thought for a minute. "I guess I should. I'd like to thank the FBI human trafficking task force and Impact Ten—"

"No," Jason said. "Impact Ten is an anonymous donor. We don't want any publicity."

"Okay." She turned to Matt. "I'd like to thank the FBI team who worked to bring me home. I'd like to ask the media for privacy while I

69

recover from my captivity and ask that they give my family and friends' privacy while we work to readjust to our new lives."

"I'll have my assistant write something along those lines," Matt said. "I'll show it to you before I read it to them."

"Are we done?" Jason said.

"She's all yours." Matt grinned and closed his files.

Jason stood up and nodded to Sam. They walked out of the room together and headed for the elevator. "I thought we'd go downstairs to talk about your job and your security needs. The press conference will start in half an hour." He glanced at his watch. "If you want to watch it, we can sit in the back of the room."

"No thanks."

Jason held her hand as they left the elevator and headed down the carpeted hallway. He opened the door to a large meeting room and stepped back, smiling at her. "Go ahead." He gestured inside.

Uncertain, Kathleen stepped into the lighted room and heard a cacophony of voices yell, "Surprise!" She covered her mouth to keep from screaming. When she scanned the faces, she saw her parents, relatives, and friends. "Oh my God." Squeals erupted as Chandra and Tara ran toward her with tears in their eyes. She bit her lip as a chill ran down her arms.

Chandra and Tara grabbed her in a group hug and jumped up and down while the others laughed and clapped. "I can't believe you're here." Chandra still had a short pixie haircut with side-swept bangs that framed her charming smile. She looked exactly like Kathleen remembered her.

Tara, her best friend and college roommate, had shoulder-length, curled blond hair with dark lined brown eyes. Her long legs and model-shaped body covered in fashionable clothing betrayed her twenty-eight years of age. "I'm so glad you're home." Tara hugged her, crying.

Tears ran down Kathleen's face as she looked at her friends and family gathered around her in the brightly lit room. She hugged all of them one by one and talked with her friends and extended family as Matt and the human trafficking task force announced her return to the world. She glanced at Jason and Sam who smiled broadly and watched her happy reactions as they talked with Charles.

With tears streaming down her face, she turned to Chandra and Tara. "I want you to meet my new friends." She gestured toward Jason and Charles.

"Are those the guys who rescued you?" Tara said.

"The one with black hair rescued me. The tall blonde man is his best friend and business partner, Charles."

Tara looked at Charles and smiled broadly. "I like how Charles looks. We blondes have to stick together." She laughed as her eyes flashed.

"Let's meet them," Chandra said. "Your brother is looking better than ever."

Kathleen smiled. "You two are hopeless." She walked toward Jason and he smiled at her, his eyes twinkling. He obviously felt pleased about her reaction to this gathering. She wiped away a tear from her cheek and stood in front of him. "Did you put this together?" she rested her hand on his arm.

"I like to stay busy." Jason smiled warmly.

She wrapped her arms around him and he put his arms around her and held her a minute. She smelled his manly scent, not sweat, not cologne, just natural musk. "You're so sweet." She kissed him on the cheek. "Thank you," she whispered to him and turned to her friends. "I want to introduce my friends." She touched Chandra's arm. "This is my friend, Chandra Nix, and this is my college roommate, Tara Kelly."

Charles assessed Tara with an admiring gaze and smirked at her short skirt. "Do those legs ever stop?" His sparkling eyes reflected his thoughts.

Tara barked a laugh and tossed her blond hair. "Stick around and you might find out." Tara grinned and batted her heavy eyelashes at Charles.

Kathleen raised her eyebrows at their playfulness and thought she heard Charles growl but dismissed it.

"I call them the three musketeers," Sam said. "They do everything together."

"Thanks for inviting us," Chandra said. "We're very happy to have

Kathleen back home." Chandra reached around her back and hugged her, touching their heads together.

"So are we," Jason said. "You might want to get something to eat before the FBI task force arrives. They eat everything in sight."

"Yeah," Charles said, "they're like locusts." He reached out for Tara's hand. "Let's tour the food tables." He walked away with her, smiling as though he had won a special prize.

"Feel like a snack?" Jason rested his hand on her shoulder.

"I think so." She rubbed her stomach. "But I could really use a soft drink."

"I'm going to check out the press conference," Sam said. "I'll be back."

"Oh, well," Chandra said. "I guess he's not interested."

"In you or the food?" Kathleen felt a twinge of sympathy.

"Neither." Chandra's disappointment showed on her face.

"He's going through a rough time," Kathleen said. "Why don't you check out the press conference? You and I can hang out tomorrow and catch up on all the news from work."

Chandra grabbed her hand and kissed her on the cheek. "You're so perceptive."

"Get going before he slips out a side door and goes home." Kathleen patted Chandra's back.

Chandra looked at Jason. "It was great meeting you. I won't be long."

"Take your time with the young squire," Jason said. "You'll have years to get reacquainted with Kathleen."

Chandra flashed her warm, charming smile and headed for the press conference.

Kathleen looked at Jason and grabbed his hand. "Come with me, I want you to meet my family." She walked toward her aunts, uncles, and cousins and introduced him to everyone. She enjoyed watching him smile and shake hands with her extended family members. He finally received the accolades he deserved but shied away from.

She had a warm tender spot in her heart for this fine, young man who showered her with attention and care. He had invited her friends and family to help rebuild her life. His awareness of her needs seemed uncanny. How did he know what she needed and when? Whatever drove him must be very powerful. She felt happier than ever and wondered how she would repay him for everything he had done.

Chapter 6

The cork popped and flew across the salon of Jason's sailboat, nearly hitting the men gathered around him. Dressed in a short-sleeved shirt and casual shorts, Jason offered a drink to the cheering men who stood with champagne flutes in hand. When he finished pouring glasses for everyone, he set the bottle down and raised his glass to his foundation's Board of Directors. "A toast ... to Kathleen McDougal, our first American woman rescued from slavery."

"To Kathleen." The men raised their glasses and sipped.

Jason stood at the front of the salon, glass in hand, and reached for a folder of papers he had brought from home. "Before we leave on our sailing adventure, I thought we'd get our Board meeting out of the way. First, I'm sure you saw the FBI press conference on Friday night." The gathering applauded and cheered. "Kathleen would have been here today to thank you in person, but she has a fear of small rooms full of men and rocking boats. Considering the makeup of this Board and the location of our meeting, there was no way."

"What an odd phobia," Marcus the architect said. "We're the most innocent, harmless men I know." He glanced around at the others who nodded and laughed.

"I've asked Dr. G to address her needs." Jason nodded to his friend, Dr. Gregory Chase, and sat on a stool.

Doctor Chase set down his glass. "After talking with Jason about Kathleen's symptoms, it's my opinion she has classic symptoms of PTSD."

"Post traumatic stress disorder?" Charles said. "Like war vets?"

"Yes, anyone who has suffered severe trauma can get PTSD," Dr. Chase said. "My recommendation to the Board is to contract services

74

from Dr. Jennifer Powell. She's trained in psychological trauma such as PTSD and counsels rape victims. She's board certified in her field and is highly recommended by her peers."

"I've spoken with Kathleen's employer," Jason said. "They're willing to re-hire her in a lower-level position until she regains her ability to work full-time. Their medical coverage only provides for eight weeks of therapy before the employee begins to pay. Since her income has been reduced and her medical needs will be extensive, I'm proposing we pay for Kathleen's weekly therapy sessions once the employer coverage expires."

"What is Dr. Powell's prognosis?" Marcus said. "How many sessions would she need?"

"Without talking to Kathleen, she can only surmise based on her symptoms, but her plan would be to treat Kathleen with Cognitive Behavioral Therapy," Dr. Chase said. "Her initial recommendation is for a six-month plan but she anticipates needing a year."

"How much money do we have available?" Doug the engineer asked. He looked at the banker, Edward, who served as the foundation's treasurer.

Edward peeked at the bank statement he brought with him. "Our current balance available for services is just over $500,000."

"In that case," Charles said, "I make a motion for the Board to approve funding for six months of once-a-week therapy sessions, to be re-evaluated at that time."

"Seconded," David, the CEO said.

"All in favor?" Jason said. Everyone in the salon said yea. "Opposed?" No one spoke. "Seeing no opposition, the motion carries unanimously." He reached for his iPad and turned it on. "On Friday, while the press conference was going on, we hosted a reception for Kathleen's family and two close friends. That was her first chance to see her extended family, friends and to meet the FBI task force. We took some photos to share with you," he said, handing the tablet to Charles. "Would you pass the iPad around?"

Jason heard footsteps topside and assumed they were from Sam, whom he had invited. "Down here."

Sam walked down the steps into the salon where the men greeted him.

"Gentlemen, we invited Kathleen's brother, Sam, to meet you. He's a young squire attending the University of Miami Law School. He hopes to graduate next year, in case any of you are looking for a new attorney."

Sam smiled and shook hands as the men welcomed him with enthusiasm.

"Is there any other business?" Jason said to the Board members. He heard nothing from the floor. "I declare this meeting adjourned." He turned to Charles. "Captain, we're ready to cast off."

Charles saluted him. "Aye, aye, sir." He laughed a hearty bellow, welcomed Sam, and went topside to set sail.

Jason felt pleased about the Board members' support for Kathleen's recovery. His foundation would ensure she had a successful experience. Unlike the others he had rescued and sent home without support, Kathleen would benefit from Connie's death.

＿

Meanwhile in Miami Shores, Kathleen attended church with her parents, who proudly introduced her to all their friends. Her parents' church members were very kind. They held a social after the Sunday services where the congregants gathered in fellowship and offered her their strength. She appreciated their kindness and wallowed in the warmth of caring they extended to her. She felt herself healing inside with all the affection she had enjoyed this weekend. The previous day, she had met Tara and Chandra at the Bayside Marketplace where they enjoyed the day laughing, sharing stories and catching up on what had happened over the past year. The night before she went to a Miami Marlins baseball game with her parents and Sam and explored their art-deco-style stadium.

As the church social drew to an end and people filtered toward the parking lot, Kathleen tried to peek at her mother's watch. She had told Tara and Chandra she would meet them at Jungle Island around one o'clock.

Brenda noticed her daughter's fidgeting. "It's a little after noon. We'll drive you down there, but how are you getting home?"

"I'm not sure," she said. "I'll decide when the time comes."

"Where's Jason today?" Brenda failed at hiding her sarcasm. "Did he finally cut you loose?"

Kathleen blinked and swallowed. She hoped not. "He's very busy and so am I. He has a Board of Directors' meeting today with the foundation that paid for my freedom."

"What foundation?" her father said.

"It's called Impact Ten. It's a group of men who donate money to rescue people from slavery."

"Never heard of it," Harry said.

"They shy away from publicity. They paid for the plane that brought me home and for the reception on Friday."

"They're very generous but these security concerns are malarkey," Brenda said. "Taking taxis to meet your family and friends, is overkill."

"Maybe, but I'm going to do whatever the FBI says. They're the experts."

"I think Jason just wants to control you for some reason." Brenda lifted her overstuffed purse and slung it over her shoulder. "He sees you as a victim that he can use to his own advantage."

"He's treated me very well."

"Now he's working on Sam," Brenda said. "Sailing ... that boy needs to be studying, not gallivanting around with spoiled rich boys."

Kathleen tensed with exasperation. "Mother ... Jason and Charles like Sam. They have taken an interest in him and I'm hoping they'll mentor him." She looked around the room and saw that most folks had left. She couldn't wait to leave too. "It would benefit Sam to know someone in the legal field when he starts looking for a permanent position."

"I don't want them using Sam to get to you," Brenda said. "Now that we have you back, I'm keeping an eye on you."

Kathleen stared at her father for help. "Jason's a good man; he's not using me or Sam."

"Yes, but ..." Brenda said.

"I don't want to be late. Dad, can we go?" Kathleen gave her father a pleading glance.

"Sure sweetie," he said. "I'll thank the pastor. Then we'll leave."

Harry walked over to the pastor, shook his hand and said some things. Then she felt guilty about not doing the same. She walked behind her father and shook the pastor's hand and thanked him.

Her father led the way out of the church hall toward their car. She felt odd getting into the back of her parents' car. It made her feel like a child. She really needed to talk to Jason about her job. They didn't get to talk much at the reception on Friday and they both had been busy all weekend. Maybe he would call her tonight after he got home.

Harry drove about fifteen minutes south to Jungle Island near the Port of Miami where Tara and Chandra were chatting near the entrance gate. When he pulled up to the curb, Kathleen kissed her parents.

"Thank you for a wonderful weekend. I'm starting to feel whole again."

"Have fun, Katie," Brenda said. "I'll call you."

"Have a good week. Call me if you need anything," Harry added.

Kathleen hopped out, closed the car door, and scurried toward her friends. She encircled them in her arms as if she hadn't seen them in years. *Oh, the love of good friends*, she thought, *there's nothing like it.* "You guys are the greatest friends. Thanks for supporting me."

"We wouldn't do anything else," Tara said. "Let's go in. There's a Liger show in an hour. But first, I want to see a friend who's in a fashion show in the ballroom."

"Is this someone from your modeling class?" Kathleen asked.

"Yes, I met her there," Tara said. "She's struggling to get a break too."

As they got in line at the ticket window, she realized what Tara had said. "What's a Liger?"

"It's a cross between a lion and a tiger," Chandra said. "They're really beautiful."

She dug into her pocket for some cash and bought her ticket at the entrance window. They walked through the turnstiles and into the amazing exhibits of wild animals. She followed behind as Tara stepped quickly toward the ballroom where the fashion show would be held. Tara had always hoped to be a professional model. She certainly had the beauty and the pizzazz. Kathleen and Chandra had always supported her dream but it was a tough business to break into.

Before the fashion show, everyone was asked to turn off their cell-phones. Kathleen reached into her pocket and took out the one Jason loaned her. She turned it off and shoved it back in her pants pocket.

Tara's eyes sparkled with glee at the anticipation of seeing one of her friends in the show. Looking nervous, she put her hands between her knees to keep her legs from jumping. Settling into chairs around the cat-walk, Tara screeched when her friend strutted down the raised floor in the latest fashions.

Kathleen wasn't sure whether Tara was more excited about seeing her friend or the fashions. Always trendy, Tara wore large hoop earrings almost as big as her head. Kathleen chuckled to herself. She didn't even own a purse.

After the show, Tara went to speak to the man who organized it and gave him her business card. Tara's marketing strategy involved passing out as many business cards as possible, hoping one day someone would call her. She returned with a broad smile on her face while the man watched her walk away, checking out her long legs.

"What did he say?" Kathleen felt annoyed by the man's behavior.

"He said to send him my portfolio and he'd consider me for a show," Tara said. "Can you believe that? I might finally get a break." She laughed boisterously and grabbed Kathleen's and Chandra's arms and walked away with them. "Who wants to see the kangaroos?"

Kathleen enjoyed the day at Jungle Island so much that it seemed almost like a dream. It felt too good. It couldn't be real. But she never woke up. Her thoughts drifted to her new friend, Jason. He had invited Sam to go sailing with him and the Board of Directors today. Was her mother right? Was he using Sam? Why? For what purpose would he do that? What would Sam have that Jason couldn't get on his own? Abso-lutely nothing; he was obviously successful, he wore nice clothes, drove a nice car, and owned a nice boat. He simply wanted to help her. It was a charitable need of his … a gift from his father. Why did her mother always try to stir up controversy where none existed?

After the Liger show, they visited the albino alligator then took pictures with the macaws and monkeys. By late afternoon, Kathleen started to feel tired when the sun dipped behind some live oak trees. "I'd love to have an ice cream cone."

"Great idea." Tara led them toward the café.

Kathleen sat outside licking her ice cream when a man approached. He looked familiar. Was he a former teacher? The closer he got, the more nervous she became. He stared at her then reached into his pocket, pulled out a camera and took her picture. "You're Kathleen McDougal, aren't you?"

Startled by the camera and the strange man, she looked at her friends with wide eyes then glanced back at him. "No, you're mistaken. I don't know who you're talking about."

"I'd know you anywhere," he said, "your picture's been all over the TV for a year."

"Nope. Sorry." Kathleen got up and threw away her cone. "Come on, let's go." She gestured for her friends to follow. As they threw their cones in the trash can and followed her toward the exit, Kathleen looked over her shoulder to make sure the man wasn't following her. The mass of people coming and going blurred her view of the café tables. *Where did he go? Was he following her? Who was he?* She walked faster toward the exit, pushed through the turnstiles, and stopped at the curb where Chandra caught up with her.

"What's wrong? Did you know that guy?"

"No," Kathleen said, "and that's what scares me. I need to get out of here." She looked around for a taxi stand and didn't see one.

"We'll take you wherever you want to go," Tara said. "I drove, we can go together."

"We can't go home, in case he follows," Kathleen said. "I'm not allowed to let anyone know where I live." Her panic rose. "Where can we go?"

"Let's go somewhere isolated, where we can see when a car is following," Chandra said.

"On a Sunday, every place is going to be busy," Kathleen said. She heard footsteps and spun around to see who followed. A small family walked up behind her and gave her a strange look when they saw her staring at them. They walked around her, glaring as they passed. "Let's just get in the car and go. We'll figure out where to go once we get out of here."

"We'll turn opposite of where everyone else is going," Chandra said.

Tara pulled away quickly and turned in the opposite direction of the traffic. She drove for about ten minutes and stopped the car when the land ended at the old lighthouse at South Pointe Park. They got out of the car and walked toward the lone tall structure at the point where the Atlantic Ocean met the Biscayne Bay. When a car drove into the parking lot, they panicked and ran toward the lighthouse.

"Hide in the bushes." Kathleen pointed at the base of the lighthouse. She was out of shape and soon lost her breath. She walked briskly toward the dim light at the base of the structure where she hid in the bushes. Kneeling on the ground, she pulled her cellphone out of her pocket. "Darn, I forgot I turned this off."

"Me too," Tara said. "Should we call 911?"

"We can't," Chandra said. "This isn't an emergency."

Annoyed, Kathleen glared at Chandra who didn't understand what kind of situation this might be. Better not tell her, she might overreact. When a lone man came toward them, her heart raced. Her breathing increased. She opened the phone and called Jason. It didn't ring. It went directly to voice mail. No doubt he was still on the sailboat. She dialed Sam and the same thing happened. She closed the phone and shoved it back in her pants pocket.

When the man approached, her heart pounded so hard, she couldn't hear. He walked past them, removed a key from his pocket, and unlocked the door to the lighthouse.

She let out a long, slow breath and collapsed on the ground.

Tara and Chandra both started laughing and walked out of the bushes and waited for her to follow. As the sun inched lower in the western sky, daylight dimmed around them. The huge light at the top of the lighthouse came on and began to sweep around in circles.

"This place is creepy," Kathleen said, "let's get out of here." She walked toward Tara's car when two bright lights entered the parking lot and sped toward her. She panicked. "Run to the car." She ran as fast as she could, opened the back door, hopped in, and slammed it shut.

Tara got in the driver's seat and Chandra got in the passenger seat. Kathleen laid on the backseat and covered her head.

"What are you doing?" Chandra said.

"Lock the doors!" Kathleen yelled. "They're coming for me!" She heard the vehicle stop and the doors open.

Tara and Chandra screamed when their doors jerked open.

Kathleen screamed, at what she didn't know.

When Tara laughed and Chandra said, "Good grief," she grew suspicious as the back door opened and Jason pointed his gun at her.

"What on earth?" He put his gun in a shoulder holster and lifted her easily out of the car.

She began to shake and tried to catch her breath. When her knees buckled, she clutched his shirt.

"What in heaven's name are you doing here?" Jason held her up until her knees locked.

"We were being followed," she said.

"Are you sure?" Jason said.

"We thought so, but then he turned out to be the lighthouse keeper. When we realized our mistake, we walked toward the car." She glanced over at Sam, Tara and Chandra. "Then you came roaring across the parking lot right for us." She took a deep breath. "We thought you were him."

"Who?" Jason said.

"The man at Jungle Island," Tara said. "He took her picture and knew her name."

Jason wrapped his arms around her and held her close until her breathing calmed and her shaking subsided. "You're okay, sweetheart." He tilted her chin upward and planted a quick, tender kiss on her lips.

Her heart skipped a beat, not from fear but from passion. When he drew away, she looked into his dark eyes and witnessed his concern. "I guess my mind got carried away."

"Maybe not," Sam said, walking toward her with Tara and Chandra.

"What do you mean?" she said.

"It's Mom and Dad," Sam said. "Their house was ransacked while they were at church."

"What?" Shocked, Kathleen looked at Jason. "Who is doing this?"

"No one knows," Jason said. "Just to be safe, you're coming home with me."

"I can't," she said.

"Why?" Jason said.

"My mama taught me better."

Jason paused and tilted his head. "I'm not inviting you into my bed. I have a spare bedroom you can sleep in." He looked at Sam. "Actually, I have two spare bedrooms, if you'd rather not go home tonight."

"I'm not leaving my parents alone," Sam said, "but thanks for the offer."

"You can stay at my place." Chandra's hopes rose in her eyes.

"Thanks, but I'm not running scared," Sam said. "Besides, I need to help my parents put everything back together. The place was tossed."

Chandra looked disappointed but she should be getting used to Sam pushing her away. He's been doing it since before they went to Aruba. Kathleen wished she could mediate somehow but she thought Chandra might be ready to give up. "I should go home with Sam and help them."

"No way," Jason said. "I can go over and help but you're not going anywhere near their house."

"We can help them." Tara winked at Chandra.

"My car's at the marina," Sam said. "If you'd drop me there, I can drive myself home."

Chandra picked up on Tara's wink. "Tara and I'd be glad to help clean up the mess. We'll follow you home."

"Good," Jason said, looking at Kathleen. "You'll be safe and your family will have help, problem solved."

Kathleen hugged her friends. "Tell my mother I'll call her when I get settled at Jason's." She sniffled at the affection showered on her by her friends and squeezed their hands. "Thanks for helping us."

Tara and Chandra watched her with a mixture of concern and amusement. They didn't grasp the seriousness of the situation. She stepped into Jason's truck and waited for him to close her door before putting on her seatbelt. Tara's car pulled away with Chandra and Sam headed for the Miami Marina.

Jason got into the truck and followed Tara out of the lighthouse parking lot until she turned into the marina. Kathleen saw the tall buildings in the downtown area and leaned forward.

"Are you okay?" Jason said.

"I'm okay. I just can't believe all these incidents are coincidences."

"You know they aren't. You can stay with me for a couple of days until things cool down."

"I don't have anything to do at your place. You'll be at work all day."

"There's plenty to do. If you want to go back to work, you need to have a complete physical exam including blood work." He looked at her when the traffic light turned red. "Plus, your employer is concerned about possible psychological problems."

"They think I'm deranged?" She felt insulted.

"No. They have a responsibility to their employees to keep them safe. If they bring you back to work and you cause someone to be injured, they're responsible."

"Oh," she sighed. "What do I have to do?"

"First, you have to pass a physical. After that, you can return to work under one condition."

"What's that?"

"You have weekly sessions with a therapist." He pulled away from the traffic light.

Kathleen groaned and looked out the side window. *Am I ready to face my fears? Should I move home with my parents?* That possibility made her gut clench. Jason was right, but he wasn't saying it. If she wanted to recover in a year, she had to return to work, she needed her own place to live, and she had to start talking to a professional. She released an exasperated sigh. "I guess I'll have to."

Jason smiled, obviously pleased at her conclusion. "I think that'll help with your nightmares and flashbacks."

"Maybe, but going back to work would be great."

As they entered the downtown area, she grew curious about his home. When he entered a gated underground parking garage, she looked up at the tall building standing over it. Her mouth fell open. *Oh my goodness ... he lives in one of these.* She felt like an idiot. No wonder he knew so much about the downtown area, he lived there.

They rode in the elevator to the fifteenth floor where her stomach wiggled from the fast ascent and stop. The elevator doors opened onto shiny marble floors where potted palms enhanced marble walls that reflected her image. She followed Jason to a wooden door where he stopped to unlock it. He went in first and turned on the lights. She waited just outside the door.

"Come in."

She slowly stepped inside where the marble floors changed color to a light tan. Jason walked ahead of her, turned right into the kitchen, and threw his keys into a bowl on the granite countertop. Spacious cabinets glowed warm brown colors surrounding stainless-steel appliances.

"Very nice."

"This way." He left the kitchen through the other side.

Kathleen followed him to a bedroom where he flipped on the lights. "This is your safe place. You'll sleep in here." He went in and pointed down a hallway. "Your bathroom's in there. I'll get you something to wear." He left her standing in the center of the bedroom.

She sat on the bed and found it very comfortable. Glancing around the room, the white painted furniture looked bright and cheerful. The red patterned rug under the bed gave the room some much-needed color.

He returned holding a T-shirt and long pajama bottoms. "I haven't worn these." He handed them to her. "You can have them."

She held them in front of her and wrinkled her nose at the orange and blue design. "Gators? You expect me to wear University of Florida clothes?"

"It's that or nothing." He raised an eyebrow.

His smirk amused her. "Very funny, they'll do for a couple nights."

When his home phone rang, he went to the kitchen to answer it. Laying the pajamas on the bed, she went into the bathroom, washed her face and brushed her long red-brown hair. She noticed a blush of sunburn in the mirror. One more thing she needed to buy, sun block. Her skin looked pale from living indoors for a year. When she saw herself in the mirror, she assessed her look as unhealthy, thin and pale. At least she hadn't thrown up in a few days. That small bit of progress pleased her.

When Jason didn't return, she went into the kitchen looking for him. He wasn't there. She moved through the kitchen into a hallway that led to the living room, which was decorated with oriental rugs and leather furniture. Glass table tops reflected lights shining from other buildings through the wall of windows on the other side of the room. His home proved to be as masculine as he was, yet softened by a breathtaking view. As she walked closer to the windows, reflections bounced off the water far below.

He emerged from another room. "Finding your way around?"

"Yes, your home is beautiful."

"Thanks." Stopping at the entertainment center, he flipped on some soft jazz and moved next to her. "You can't see it now, but over there is the Miami River where we walked the other day."

"Yes, I see where we are now. Since it's my turn to buy dinner, can we order pizza?" She laughed at his amused face.

"Pizza's fine. We've both had a long day."

"I need to call my parents first."

"It's better to order the pizza and go downstairs to get it. Why don't you call your parents and I'll get the pizza." He ordered the pizza but refused the money she tried to give him.

She called her parents and spoke to her mother, who was rattled but sounded resolute and philosophical about the break-in. When she learned Tara and Chandra had helped them put things back together, she felt relieved. After changing into the Gator pajamas, she felt instantly at home.

When the doorbell rang, she assumed it was Jason with the pizza.

She opened the door and gasped. "Charles." She patted her chest from the shock.

"Well, hello, hello ..." Charles considered her obviously male Gator pajama set, grinned and crossed his arms. "Jason left me to clean the boat so he could get you into bed?"

"No!" Her voice sounded strained. "Why would you say such a thing? Don't you know my parents' house was invaded?"

"I know, kitten," Charles said gently. "Is everything okay?" A look of concern crossed his face as he caressed her cheek.

"Sam and my friends helped them clean up, but I'm scared."

"You'll be okay. Tell Jason—"

"Tell Jason what?" Jason said as he appeared with the pizza.

"Hey, man. I stopped to see what happened with Kathleen but I can see my timing is bad. You obviously have everything in hand." He leered with meaning.

"It's not what it seems," Jason said. "Come inside, my neighbors don't need to hear my business." He led them inside and put the pizza on the kitchen counter. "Want some pizza?"

"No thanks," Charles said. "I'm beat. I'll just watch the news and go to bed."

Jason opened a drawer and glanced at Kathleen. "Our friend, Dr. Greg called. He said you can stop by his office tomorrow and one of his partners will give you a physical."

"How'd you arrange that on a weekend?" she asked.

"Greg's on the Board of Directors," Jason said. "These male-bonding trips pay off." He removed paper plates and napkins from the cabinet and put a piece of pizza on each one. He handed her a plate and pointed toward a bar stool at the counter.

Kathleen moved to the raised counter and sat down. Charles watched her every move. He seemed intrigued by her. She bit into her slice and chewed slowly while he watched her. "Is something wrong?" Feeling a bit miffed at his intimate perusal, she glared.

"Your hair is shinier, your cheeks aren't as hollow," Charles said.

Jason sat down next to her, bit into his pizza and looked at her while he chewed. "You *are* filling out a little." He touched her cheek and looked down at her ribs.

"Stop inspecting me," she said. He gave her an amused look and continued eating. She glanced at Charles and gave him an annoyed look.

"Put your claws away, kitten," Charles said. "I don't bite unless invited." He laughed, reached for her hand and kissed it. "I'll see you in the morning buddy."

"Thanks for taking care of the boat," Jason said with his mouth full.

"Everyone helped. Have a good night," Charles said as he left the kitchen.

"Why did he call me kitten?"

"Maybe because of your beautiful green eyes." Jason smiled. "Charles has lots of women friends. I call them his harem, he calls them his pets."

Her eyebrows rose. "Really?"

"Maybe he plans to add you to his collection."

She scoffed at that. "I used to dream of having a husband and a kid or two but …" she swallowed hard, "all that's been ruined."

His concerned face flashed with anger then disappeared. "You feel that way now because your memories are fresh. When you start talking to a therapist, you'll see things differently."

"Maybe *I'll* see things differently, but what man wants to marry damaged goods?"

Jason winced and squeezed her hand. "Any good man would be happy to have you for his wife."

"I could always join Charles' harem." She laughed with caustic bitterness.

"You are a strong, brave, and intelligent woman. Don't sell yourself short." He raised her chin to look at him. "I want you to give Charles a wide berth."

"Why?" She looked into his dark blue eyes.

"He enjoys dominating women. If you let him, he will." He looked at her with concern. "You've had enough male domination for one lifetime."

She swallowed hard when his meaning hit her. "You mean he likes to tie up women and … um, have sex with them?"

"He would never hurt anyone, but he enjoys bondage. Don't let him intimidate you."

"Okay, but he's such a charmer."

Jason chuckled. "A charmer he definitely is. I love him like a brother." He turned more serious. "Now about work ... with this break-in, I think you need to start wearing a disguise."

"Like a hat and scarf?"

"That's fine, plus sunglasses. I'll pick you up at work.

"No, you've done too much." She raised her hand to stop him. "I can't ask you to pick me up from work every day."

"You didn't ask. I offered."

"But you have work to do."

"When I have to work late, I'll ask someone to pick you up so you always know who to go home with."

"I won't be getting into any strange cars. I can take the bus."

He gave her an incredulous look. "We've had this conversation." He returned to eating his slice of pizza and glanced at her. "Are you nervous being alone with me?"

She flinched and hesitated. "Maybe ... a little."

"Thanks for being honest. I want you to lock your bedroom door tonight."

Startled, she looked tentatively at him while chewing her pizza.

He grasped her hand. "I want you to feel comfortable in my home and being comfortable starts with feeling safe."

"I feel safe with you." Her auburn hair partially blocked one eye. "But I'm still nervous."

He brushed the hair out of her eye and wrapped it behind her ear. His gentle hand lingered there caressing her soft lobe when he leaned close and kissed her with a tenderness she hadn't experienced in a long time. His whiskers brushed her chin as his warm lips pressed against hers. Her breathing increased causing a throb of warmth to course down between her legs. What an odd sensation. Until recently, she hadn't felt aroused in a very long time.

He pulled away and smiled. "There, we both got that out of the way.

Now there's nothing else you need to be nervous about." He caressed her cheek. "You are a beautiful woman Kathleen ..."

Uh oh, here it comes. You're pretty but ... your body turns me off.

"I would never do anything to scare you. I want you to lock your bedroom door and put a chair under the knob if that helps you feel better. I'm very attracted to you but I don't assault women who sleep in my guest room."

Her stomach fluttered with his admission. Who would be attracted to her? She had stringy hair, her ribs were exposed, her cheeks were sunken, not to mention her disgusting slave tattoo, whip marks, and cigarette burns. She grabbed her arm where her tattoo was hidden under her shirt and shook her head.

He gave her a sympathetic look as if he heard her self-deprecating thoughts. "Also, never open the front door like you did for Charles unless you look out the peep hole first. There's a security guard in the lobby but make sure you know who's at the door before you open it."

She nodded. "Okay. What time do you get up?"

"Six. You can sleep in if you want. I'll leave the address to the doctor's office on the kitchen counter. You can take a taxi when you're ready."

"If you don't mind, can I go to bed early?"

"Do whatever you like. Your bedroom is your sanctuary. You can stay in there all you want." He looked over at her. "If you want to watch television, I stay up to ten. You're welcome to join me." He raised one eyebrow in a questioning gaze.

"Um, maybe some other time, I'm exhausted."

"How are your parents?"

"Good. They're tough Irish folk."

"Like their daughter?" He smiled at her.

Kathleen appreciated his compliment but she didn't feel too strong right now. Maybe when she went back to work and started her therapy sessions, she would begin to heal. She finished her pizza, wiped her mouth with a napkin, and hoped for a good night's sleep. Excitement about going back to work might keep that from happening. Her mother was partly right. These security precautions were tiresome. She'd put up with them while she lived at the safe house, but when things settled down, she would get back to living a normal life. Would that include Jason? For the first time in a long time, she felt intrigued by the possibility.

Chapter 7

Later in the week, Kathleen returned to work for the first time. She sat in front of a computer screen reminiscing about what happened that morning when Jason brought her to work. When she walked into the lobby, her co-workers cheered, waved signs, and held balloons. The president of the company shook her hand and welcomed her back. Before she greeted her co-workers, Jason kissed her on the cheek and left her surrounded by smiling friends.

Everyone had surrounded her to say hello including her old friends, Anita and Chelsea. But now they didn't seem to want to be associated with her sordid affair. They welcomed her back but their friendship seemed distant. That saddened her. As she pondered the warm welcome she received, footsteps came up behind her. She jumped and turned quickly to see Chandra, then released a long breath.

Chandra leaned on her door frame. "Want to take a break?"

"Might as well. This project is so boring. I hope they give me something more challenging tomorrow."

"Tomorrow? You mean you'll have it done today?"

"Sure, it's pretty simple." She left her office and walked down the hall toward the break room with Chandra at her side.

"What's it like living with Jason?" Chandra flashed a wicked grin.

"I moved back to the safe house. I stayed with him a couple nights but I wanted my own things around me." She sighed. "It was kind of nice though. He has a beautiful condo downtown in one of those high rises. His friend, Charles, lives upstairs."

"Wow, they're pretty successful for young guys."

"Yeah, they started their partnership right out of law school and worked hard growing their business for about five years until Charles's

92

father died. Apparently his father was a big-time lawyer for the shipping industry so they took over his clients. They're partly successful from their own hard work and partly from luck, I guess."

"Cool, I like to see folks who work hard become successful. They must be about thirty-five then."

"They're thirty-three and unattached." She elbowed Chandra in the side. "Watch out for Charles though. He stopped by after the break-in and practically undressed me. Jason told me to steer clear of him because he likes BDSM."

"Really, who knew? He does seem very much in control now that you mention it."

"I thought that was a lawyer thing, but Charles likes restraining his ladies in bed." She giggled when Chandra did. As they entered the break room, she grabbed her water from the refrigerator and sat down at one of the tables.

Chandra poured a mug of coffee from the pot. "Speaking of BDSM, they did a movie about that popular book."

She shook her head. "I don't know if I could watch that. I lived the evil side of it for the past year."

Chandra looked sad then grabbed a nearby newspaper. "Let's see what else is playing." Shock covered her face. "Oh my god ..." Chandra stared at the paper, her mouth ajar.

"What?"

Chandra pointed to a photo. "You're in the paper."

She grabbed the news and read the headline. "McDougal home ransacked." She put her palm on her forehand. "Why did they publish my picture?"

"Money ... it's all about money. That guy at Jungle Island probably got a lot for a close-up photo of someone famous."

"I'm not famous."

"You are now."

Kathleen sighed. "The FBI isn't going to be happy. I'd better call Jason." She dialed the cellphone he loaned her and listened to it ring.

"I saw it," Jason said when he answered.

93

"What am I going to do? Now they know where I work and where my parents live."

"Sam and I are going to take turns picking you up after work. He already knows where the safe house is and that gives us more flexibility. Don't worry." He paused and spoke to someone in the background. "I've got a meeting, sweetheart. We can talk tonight."

"Okay, see you around five fifteen." She ended the call and looked at the time on the phone. "We'd better get back." Walking back to her office, her eye caught something odd outside the window.

Chandra stopped short. "Look at them, they're like vultures."

She looked at the mob scene in front of the building. Photographers waited for her to appear. She hadn't expected to become a celebrity when she came home. She tensed and glanced at Chandra. "How am I going to get to Jason's truck?"

"I'll go out the front entrance wearing your scarf and my sunglasses. You go out the back entrance."

"I can't ask you to get in the middle of this mess."

"I'll run through the gauntlet and be at my car in no time. We youngsters are more in shape than you oldsters." She laughed at Kathleen's dubious gaze.

"Go ahead, rub youth in my face. What are you, 24 or 25 now? I've lost track, sorry."

"I'll be 25 in August. Same age as Sam, but he'd never notice."

She sympathized. Chandra cared for a man who didn't notice her and she had a man that cared for her who she could never hope to have. She wasn't good enough for him.

Chandra patted her on the shoulder. "You finish that boring project and I'll go round up the troops to walk out with us after work."

She returned to her office, tackled the simple project, and sent it to her supervisor before preparing to leave for the day.

Chandra stopped by and borrowed her scarf to cover her short haircut.

Kathleen put on her floppy hat and sunglasses and joined their co-workers in the lobby. Splitting into two groups, half walked out the rear entrance with her while the others ventured out the front toward the horde of photographers.

Surrounded by her co-workers, she walked toward Jason's truck waiting at the end of the sidewalk. She thanked her friends and got into the truck as they scattered to their cars in the parking lot. She smiled at Jason and Sam, who sat in the backseat. "Well, my two favorite men. How lucky can I get?" She buckled her seatbelt.

"Hi, Sis. How was your first day?"

"Interesting ... Not as bad as I thought."

"Good," Jason said. "You'll be promoted before you know it." He smiled and squeezed her hand then drove around the side of the building to the front and paused to watch Chandra come out with her guardians. The photographers ran toward her, cameras flashing, and video cameras taping. They barked questions at her and tried to stop her when she ran toward her car.

"They're pushing her," Sam said, opening the door. "You go ahead, I'm taking Chandra home." Sam left the truck and ran toward Chandra and the hoard of paparazzi.

Kathleen and Jason waited to see what happened. Sam started shoving the photographers away from Chandra. One fell down. Sam put his arm around her protectively. Kathleen rolled down her window and heard him yell at the pushy journalists.

"Leave her alone. Leave my family alone." Sam pushed through the photographers toward Chandra's car and helped her into the passenger seat. He got in the driver's side as the photographers snapped pictures through the windshield and side window. Sam pulled away slowly and sped away as he cleared the group of vultures. Her co-workers stood around their cars watching the escape.

"They're okay now," Kathleen said.

"Dumb jerks." Jason followed Sam out of the parking lot. Sam drove toward Chandra's home on the west side of town while Jason turned toward the safe house. "Are you worried about your first session with the therapist tomorrow?"

"Yes. I don't really want to talk about my ordeal."

"Give her a chance to tell you what she thinks. Maybe that's not the kind of therapy she's planning for you."

"There are different kinds of therapy? I thought you lay down and told the doctor your life story."

Jason chuckled. "That's what happens on television. I think the real world is more complicated." He glanced at her and smiled.

The FBI safe house was hidden in plain sight, just minutes from her parents' home. When Jason pulled to the curb in front of the house, she felt at home. Its Florida Cracker-style construction, all one story with sweeping wraparound porches, gave her a warm feeling. The silver metal roof reflected bright sunlight pouring from the intense blue sky.

Jason pressed a code into the front gate of the three-foot metal white picket fence. "Remember, when the security system is on, don't touch the fence, it's electrified." He grabbed the rubber handle on the front gate and pushed it open.

"Yes, I remember." As Kathleen walked up the sidewalk toward the front porch, she smelled fresh-cut grass. Its bright green color was quite a change from Canada. She followed Jason up the front steps to the door and waited while he unlocked it. He disappeared into the dark interior as she followed him inside.

Jason opened the plantation shutters covering the windows to allow some light to brighten the cool, dark interior.

She recognized the casual, comfortable furnishings that had welcomed her into the living room a few days earlier. The kitchen was a good size, with white appliances and sand-colored countertops.

Jason stood next to her. "On Saturday, I'm mentoring a teenage boy. Would you like to join us?" He put both arms around her waist.

She hesitated and admired his warm smile. "Oh, he probably wouldn't want me to interfere in your session. You know what they say, three's a crowd."

"I'm not inviting you for his benefit. I'm inviting you for mine." He smiled at her and pulled her close to his chest.

His warm genuine smile caused a heated throb between her legs. "In that case, I'd be happy to join you."

Pleased by her answer, he leaned down to press his hot lips on hers. Her breathing increased as he teased her lips. His breath brushed her cheek as he pulled away from her. "Now that's something to look forward to."

She closed the door, turned the deadbolt, and heard him walk through the gate. When his truck pulled away, she leaned back against the door. He was such a nice man. Why is he so interested in my recovery? He has a very busy life but insists on helping me. Why? Whatever it was that drove him, she felt thankful. He would be a good friend to have, a protector, and a friend to confide in. He was a little pushy sometimes, not in a mean-spirited way, but in a caring way.

She enjoyed being back in the safe house with her painting supplies and personal things, even though it was too much space. Besides, the noises at night time drove her crazy. Popping and cracking made it sound like someone was trying to get inside. It unnerved her so much, some nights she laid awake for hours watching for beams of light against the walls. She had developed a plan to hide in the closet in an emergency. Plus, she kept Jason's cellphone next to her bed. Tired from her first day of work, she decided to relax in front of the television with a big bowl of popcorn.

As she stared mindlessly at the television with the popcorn bowl in her lap, she chuckled at the Gator pajamas she wore. They were so big she tied them into knots to keep them from falling off. Before she could eat another handful of popcorn, her cellphone rang. She glanced over to see it was her best friend, Tara Kelly.

"Hello, Tara."

"You won't believe this!"

She held the phone away from her ear. "What happened?"

"I got a job in a fashion show!" Tara shrieked. "It's next week! Everyone has to come!"

"Tell me where and when and we'll be there." Her broad smile reflected how thrilled she felt for Tara. This might be the break she had been waiting for. She chatted with her for at least a half hour about the fashion show, her first day at work, and their plans for the weekend. She felt so happy at the end of her phone call that she finished her popcorn and went to bed. Even though her first therapy session was tomorrow, at that moment, she didn't feel like she needed any. Wouldn't it be great if happiness, family, and friends helped make her strong again?

≈

The next day, Kathleen took a taxi from her workplace to her therapist's office. She had to recheck the address because the home she stood in front of didn't look like a doctor's office. Nervous tingles ran up her arms in anticipation of what might happen. She stepped up to the front porch where flower boxes hung over the railings and wicker chairs with soft cushions encouraged folks to sit and rest. A wreath of magnolia blossoms hung on the front door above a gold nameplate that read Dr. Jennifer Powell. Her hand shook when she reached for the doorknob and entered a carpeted reception area. Glancing around, the room seemed like someone's living room. She approached the desk where a young lady sat.

"Can I help you?" the young lady acknowledged.

"Yes, I have an appointment at noon."

The receptionist glanced at her computer. "Miss McDougal?"

"Yes."

"Please have a seat. The doctor will be with you shortly." The receptionist gestured to the wicker chairs sitting around the walls of the casual room.

Kathleen sat in a chair and reached for a magazine. Before she could get interested in an article, a door opened and a middle-aged brunette with a gentle smile came out to meet her.

"Miss McDougal, I'm Jennifer Powell. I've heard a lot about you." She extended her hand to Kathleen. "Come in, we'll get started." She led the way into her office.

Kathleen's anxiety ebbed as she glanced around the doctor's private office. She had imagined heavy leather chairs and sofas, but the room was decorated in a casual wicker style. When she settled into a soft cushioned chair, the doctor sat across from her and smiled.

"I understand you're friends with Jason Montgomery."

"Yes, he's a new friend but a good one."

"I've spoken to a friend of his, Dr. Gregory Chase. Jason told him that you're suffering from vomiting, headaches, irritability, nightmares, flashbacks, low self-esteem, and eating disorders. Is that correct?" The doctor glanced up from her notepad.

"That about sums it up." She felt somewhat embarrassed. "Plus, I'm jumpy when I hear sounds behind me and I'm having difficulty concentrating."

"I believe your symptoms are associated with PTSD," Dr. Powell said. "My plan is to treat you with cognitive behavioral therapy."

"How does that work?"

"CBT is the leading form of therapy for anxiety. It's found to be more effective than medications."

Kathleen sat back and exhaled. "I don't have to take medicines?"

"Not unless you feel you need them."

"I'd rather not. How exactly does this work?"

"Instead of focusing on your childhood, your family, or your dreams, CBT helps change negative thoughts and your reactions to anxiety triggers. The first step is to recognize when you're stressed."

"I usually start shaking."

"When you start to shake, I want you to write down what triggered your response. Then write down how anxious you were on a scale of one to five. Once we identify your triggers, we'll work together to substitute positive thoughts."

"That sounds easy enough. Then what happens?"

"Next I'll have you work on facing your fears. Tell me something that makes you shake."

"Boats and water. I was taken from Aruba on a boat and some bad things happened." Kathleen rubbed her arms just thinking about what happened in Venezuela.

"Okay. We can start with that. Do you enjoy any hobbies where you can work on facing this fear?"

"I like to paint and I run for exercise."

"Good, I'd like you to start running at least every other day. If you can run every day that would be super, but I know that's probably impractical." She scribbled something down on her notepad. "When you run, I want you to think about a boat on the water. I want you to let yourself shake. Tell yourself it's okay to be afraid. Then we'll replace your fear with some positive thoughts. Would you like to take a ride on a boat?"

"Someday. Jason has a sailboat but I'm too afraid to get on it."

"That's perfect. After you've faced your fear, then I want you to imagine yourself on the sailboat having fun."

Kathleen liked what she heard. "I can do that."

"Perfect, now let's talk about some other things that are bothering you."

Kathleen told Dr. Powell about all the anxieties and panic attacks she had since returning home. She and the doctor prioritized what they would work on for their next session. "Thanks for seeing me at lunch time. I'm worried about taking too much time off."

"I'm happy to do it." Dr. Powell smiled warmly.

Kathleen shook hands with her new therapist and left her office, holding the hardback journal she had given her. She felt stronger already. Armed with a plan to attack her fears, she returned to work on her new computer project.

At the end of the work day, Kathleen and Chandra put on their floppy hats, scarves, and sunglasses. "I really appreciate your doing this for me."

"This is kind of exciting. It adds some excitement to my boring life."

Kathleen felt sad for her sweet friend. "What happened when Sam took you home last night?"

Chandra looked disappointed. "No excitement there. I seem to be invisible to him. I guess I need to start looking for a man who's interested in me."

"I'm sorry." Kathleen grabbed her hand. "I don't know what's wrong with him. Believe me, it's not you."

"I've tried to get his attention for more than a year. I guess it's time I got the message." Chandra sighed and donned a floppy hat over the scarf tied around her chin. "Ready to run the gauntlet?"

Kathleen laughed. "Ready." She walked down the stairs to the lobby followed by Chandra. A few co-workers mingled around waiting for them. "Thanks guys, hopefully they'll get bored with me soon."

But the paparazzi hadn't given up. They returned to take more pictures of Chandra disguised as Kathleen. Her co-workers split into two groups and gathered around them as Kathleen walked out the back entrance toward Jason's truck. Chandra waited for her to leave before she went out the front.

Kathleen walked with her crowd of supporters to the back parking lot where she got into Jason's truck.

"Hi, how are you?" Jason's smiling face greeted her as she buckled her seatbelt.

Reaching across the center console, he squeezed her hand. "I'm good."

He drove around the building to the front. "Did you like your therapist?"

"I did. She asked me to call her Jen. Her office is warm and friendly and I felt comfortable with her." When he stopped at the front of the building to watch Chandra come out, she lowered her window. In addition to the usual photographers, tonight there were television trucks with satellite dishes on top. "Oh brother, this is getting ridiculous."

"Speaking of your brother, he asked me to let him out so he could help Chandra get to her car."

"Really ..." She looked for Sam in the crowd of people.

When Chandra came out of the building, the media throng ran up the sidewalk toward her. She pulled her hat down and ran forward, laughing when everyone gathered around her snapping photos and sticking microphones in her face. One photographer grabbed her hat and tried to pull it off.

Sam rushed forward to help Chandra when another photographer tried to pull off her hat as the cameras clicked. Sam shoved the photographer. "Leave her alone." The man got mad and shoved him back. Sam pushed toward Chandra who was being jostled. When he got to the photographer who first tried to pull off her hat, Sam punched the man

101

in the face. Sprawled on the ground, his expensive camera floundered under feet.

"I'll have you arrested!" the photographer yelled.

"Go ahead!" Sam went to Chandra's side.

Kathleen reached for the door handle. "He's getting into a fight!"

"You stay here. I'll go." Jason left the truck and ran toward the crowd. Dressed in a fancy black suit and shiny shoes, he looked the role of a lawyer. He pulled men in the crowd apart as he pushed toward Sam and Chandra.

Her co-workers pushed through the crowd in the opposite direction. Some of the crowd helped the man lying on the ground. Another photographer grabbed Chandra. She screeched.

"Keep your hands off her." Sam hit a man's arm away.

A brawl ensued when someone grabbed Chandra's hat and pulled it off. It fell to the ground and everyone pushed forward to get the best angle of the famous ex-slave. A videographer pushed forward, grabbed her scarf and tugged. She clutched it with her fist and held tight.

Sam punched the man in the side of his head, knocking him sideways.

"Hey man," he said to Sam, "that's battery!"

Someone snatched the scarf off Chandra's head, exposing her short haircut. Silence fell over the crowd. "She's a fraud! This isn't Kathleen McDougal!"

Jason pushed through the yelling, shoving men and pulled Sam, whose fists held onto the shirt of one of the photographers. "Stop now!" Jason shoved Sam and the photographer apart.

"I'll sue for assault!" the photographer yelled, pointing a finger in Sam's face.

"Sue away, jackass!" Sam lunged at the man.

Jason grabbed Sam and held the leaner, younger man away from the photographer before things got more difficult. "Sam, stop."

"Who's this, your nursemaid?" the photographer said.

"I'm his lawyer." Jason stuffed his business card in the man's shirt pocket. "If you want to talk about suing, call me. We'll see who gets sued." He put his arm around Chandra and pushed through the photographers, who weren't taking pictures any more.

Chandra's pixie haircut gave away the scheme. She picked up her hat and took her scarf off her neck and walked slowly to her car. She seemed to be almost disappointed that the excitement had ended.

As Sam helped Chandra into her car and left with her, Jason walked back to the truck. The television crews and mob of grumbling photographers dispersed as she raised her dark window.

"This is getting too crazy," she said as Jason got into the truck.

"We can't use Chandra anymore. They'll be looking for you now."

She sighed and sat back in her seat. "Maybe I can work from home."

"Is that what you want to do?"

"Not really. I want to be around other people."

Jason pulled away and drove toward downtown. "Did you bring your running clothes?"

"Yes, it's funny. Dr. Jen wants me to run to face my fears. When I told her we were running after work, she smiled and told me how to work through one thing that terrifies me."

"What's that?"

"Boats on the water. When I'm running I have to think about a boat and the water and face what happened."

"Interesting."

They changed clothes in his condo and went down to the lobby to the street. Jason introduced Kathleen to the security guard before they left the building and ran along the Miami Riverwalk past outdoor dining, skaters, dog walkers, and strollers.

Kathleen thought about Aruba, the fishing boat, the truck, the ship. She shook but kept running. *Stop thinking about that … no think about it. You have to. Force yourself to think about that.* She ran for twenty minutes and felt she needed to rest. She stopped and leaned against the railing along the river when Jason came back to her.

"You go ahead." She gasped for air. "I need to rest."

"I'm not leaving you alone." He rested his hands on his hips.

"I don't want to keep you from exercising. I'll wait here for you."

"No way, sweetheart." He went to a nearby vendor and bought a couple bottles of water and brought them back, handing one to her.

"Thanks." Eager to taste the cool, wet liquid she tossed her head back and drank almost half the bottle. She wiped her brow and enjoyed the cool feeling inside. She shook and realized Jason watched her.

"Are you okay?"

"I guess. This is harder than I thought."

"Let's walk the rest of the way. You can run a little farther each day until you get into shape."

She strolled along the water watching gentle ripples on the river and shook a bit more. She gasped when tears welled up in her eyes. "I don't want to think about this anymore."

He stopped, put his arms around her and held her close.

Kathleen shook in his arms but enjoyed the warmth of his embrace. A few tears fell as she shuddered from the memories of Aruba and Venezuela. She couldn't help but push them away. The memories were too painful. She wiped a tear from her cheek and looked up at him. "Sorry."

He kissed her lips, his breath on her cheek, she felt safe and loved. He pulled away from her but stayed close to her face. "Stop saying sorry," he whispered and pecked her on the cheek. He pulled her under his arm and walked along the river, holding her against his side.

"Oh, before I forget. Tara will be in a fashion show next week. Can you and Charles come support her?"

Jason smiled. "Sure, sounds like fun." He rolled his eyes.

She punched him playfully. "I know it's not a guy thing, but it's really important to her."

"That would be the only reason I'd go. Charles on the other hand, might go if he's not busy. But for Tara, he might change his plans."

She raised her eyebrows and looked at his amused face. "Are you telling me he likes her?"

"He's intrigued by her. I'll say that." He smiled and kissed her on the head as they walked along the water. He looked down and pulled her close. "I miss having you in my condo."

Surprised, she scanned his face to see if he was kidding. His eyes looked sincere. "I liked staying with you but I like having my own space. I only wish my friends could come visit me and I could visit them. Having to meet in safe locations is getting very tiring."

"Hopefully the FBI will discover who is involved in Aruba. Once they're arrested, you'll be free."

"I miss relaxing at home with my friends, watching movies together, playing games ... You can't do stuff like that when you meet at a public place."

"I know it's frustrating."

"Speaking of friends, I used to be friends with Anita and Chelsea at work. Now they're distant like they don't want to be associated with me or my sordid affair."

He pulled her closer. "They aren't true friends. You know who your real friends are. Cherish them."

"I am and that's why you're coming to the fashion show next week." She laughed when he laughed at her. Feeling playful, she ran ahead of him until he caught up to her and pulled on her ponytail.

"The only reason I would attend a fashion show is because you wanted me to."

She liked his honesty and his flattering attention. They ran side-by-side for another ten minutes until she got winded. "I'm done this time." She leaned against the bougainvillea planter to catch her breath.

"I have an idea. After the fashion show, we can all go over to Lincoln Road near the beach. The Van Dyke has late-night jazz."

"That'd be great. We could relax, listen to good music, talk and have some laughs."

"Perfect end to a fashion show." He laughed and checked the time. "We'd better head back."

She followed him across the street and walked alongside him, headed toward his home when they passed an open-air restaurant. Bar stools filled with men watched pedestrians stroll past. When she heard her name, she startled and looked toward the television behind the bar that broadcast local news. She couldn't believe what she saw, a video of the paparazzi pushing and shoving Chandra and Sam. "Look, it's on TV."

105

She felt a sudden dread come over her. Why wouldn't they leave her alone? How would she get to work on Monday? She had to think of something to stop this madness.

Chapter 8

At the entrance to the Children's Museum, Kathleen walked next to Jason while Carlos, the at-risk teen he mentored, walked on his other side. Carlos had not been pleased to see her, but she had been polite and cordial to him. How could she win him over?

Carlos was thin and seemed awkward. He stood about her height, five feet seven inches, but he was still a teenager. Uncomfortable in body and spirit, he had probably seen everything at the tender age of fifteen.

They spent a couple of hours walking through the exhibits where they learned how to use a bank, how to shop in a grocery store, and even how to navigate a cruise ship. When they arrived at the Port of Miami exhibit, Jason explained to Carlos how countries imported and exported products on ships. Carlos learned to operate a gantry crane that unloaded containers. At the 900-gallon aquarium, he watched undersea creatures with amazement.

"Would you like to go underwater sometime?" Jason asked.

"I might be scared," Carlos said, "but I'd like to try it."

"I'll take you one weekend," Jason said. "We'll set a date before you go home."

In the Meet Miami exhibit, they walked from neighborhood to neighborhood learning about various cultures that comprised the city.

Kathleen noticed Carlos seemed very interested in one particular neighborhood when he stared at the wall-size buildings. "Do you know this neighborhood?"

"I grew up here." Carlos pointed to a run-down looking apartment building. "This is where I lived when my mom died."

"I'm so sorry. Where's your father?"

"He works in the fields. I don't see him much." Carlos walked away toward Jason. "Jason, I've decided to work in the fields next year."

Jason's face reflected his shock. He put a hand on Carlos' shoulder. "Your mother and father wouldn't want that for you."

"Some men came to see me. They said I could work next to my dad." Carlos looked at Jason with sad eyes. "I want to be with my dad. I know it'll be hard work but I need to be with him."

Jason took a deep breath, put his arm around Carlos' shoulders, and walked away from the cultural exhibit. "You really need to think hard about this."

"I want to escape the violence in my neighborhood," Carlos said.

"The fields are an endless trap. Once you're in them, you'll never get out."

"If I don't escape the gangs, I'll end up being one of them."

Kathleen followed behind through the last neighborhood exhibit and joined them as they entered the water play area. Jason took Carlos to the water pistols and paid for two. They chased each other through the maze firing their weapons at each other. They laughed, got soaked and enjoyed their game of pretend violence.

"Now that's the kind of violence I like," she chuckled. "You two are soaked." She handed them towels to wipe their faces and hair. "I think you got the worst end of the bargain." She laughed at Jason and sat on a nearby bench while they dried themselves. She admired how Jason interacted with Carlos. He seemed to care for the boy more than a typical mentoring relationship might suggest.

Jason laughed and ruffled Carlos' hair. "Next time I'll soak you."

Carlos laughed and seemed to enjoy his time with Jason. He turned in his towel to the attendant and walked outside toward Pet Central.

"Do you have any pets?" Kathleen asked Carlos.

"No. But there are lots of dogs in the neighborhood. Some don't belong to anyone. They fight for food in the streets. Gangs use them as status symbols."

"Better to use dogs as status symbols than guns," she said.

"They use those too. Dogs, guns, drugs, violence ..." Carlos brushed the toy dog in the veterinary clinic and lost his train of thought.

"I found that when someone uses violence against you," she said, "you have to keep your mind strong to get your body through it."

"What do you know about violence?" Carlos gave her a mocking glance.

"I know plenty." She pulled up her sleeve and showed him the tattoo on her forearm. "See this? It's my slave number. I was a slave in Canada for a year before Jason rescued me. I survived and so can you."

The shock on Carlos's face mirrored the stunned surprise on Jason's. She had hidden her tattoo during his inspection of her at the auction but now, she chose to share it with someone who might understand and benefit from her pain. Pulling down her sleeve, she straightened her back and proudly walked toward the next exhibit.

Kathleen enjoyed her outing with Jason and Carlos. Even though he had been testy at first, Carlos seemed to come around to her presence after a few hours. Sharing her pain with him seemed to help. When she said goodbye, he actually smiled. *One small triumph,* she thought, *now back to my own challenges.*

≈

On Sunday morning, Jason swam above the coral reef in his scuba gear searching for a place to hide. The twelve-member FBI dive team hunted for him using side-scan sonar, metal detectors, and full-face masks that enabled them to talk to each other while working under-water. He enjoyed these quarterly exercises with Matt's dive team, not only because he loved scuba diving, but because it allowed him to work with state-of-the-art equipment used by the team to find underwater bodies, evidence, and explosives worldwide. He felt privileged to have the opportunity to work with the FBI and their team of professionals.

As he scanned the clear water behind him for signs of frogmen, a man-atee lumbered across his path headed for the shallow sea grass beds. He kicked his fins toward deeper water where sea turtles and dolphins darted away. He stayed alert for sharks. They made this country boy nervous.

When he spied an outcropping of jagged rocks, he removed his pistol and buried it in the sand. He kicked away when he heard Todd giving directions to his team of divers who followed a short distance behind. The sonar allowed them to map his path as he swam through obstacles like sunken ships. When a metal detector beeped, everyone stopped.

"Found something here," Todd said.

Jason watched as a diver removed a small shovel from his waterproof rucksack and dug into the ocean floor. When the metal detector screeched, the diver raised Jason's handgun for the rest of the team to see and put it into an evidence bag.

Jason smiled and swam over the coral reefs where spiny lobsters and stone crabs ducked under rocks. Brightly colored tropical fish swam in schools around him, unfazed by his presence. He felt free underwater. The overwhelming beauty of sea life inspired him to keep improving his skills. His camouflage wetsuit made it difficult for the dive team and anyone above water to see him. It came in handy when he trained rookie divers. He swam over outcroppings of chimney coral and ducked behind them, lying on the ocean floor. "Plan B executed."

Matt monitored the exercises from the sailboat above and directed Todd, his team leader. "Diver down … search and rescue."

"Commencing search," Todd said and gave instructions to his men.

Jason knew they would be coming for him soon. He pulled off his full-face mask and inserted a rebreather in his mouth, which gave him oxygen without expelling bubbles. He took off his heavy air tank and laid against the ocean floor, blending into the sand. They went in the wrong direction, probably to map the ocean floor in a schematic pattern that would eventually bring them over his hiding place. While he waited to be found, his thoughts turned to Kathleen.

She had grown stronger both physically and emotionally. It helped that she liked her therapist. The bail hearing for Wilson would happen soon. He decided not to mention that to her. He didn't want to give her any additional stress. With her parents' house under assault, she had enough to process. Each day she told him more. Her revelations were difficult to hear. He couldn't imagine how painful it must have been to endure them.

When he looked up, the dive team surrounded him. They put down their underwater assault rifles, removed netting and buoyant floats from their equipment bags, and put the net under him as if he were a corpse being lifted out of the water for evidence. He smiled when he confounded their efforts with clumsy, floating limbs. The instructor in him couldn't resist taking advantage of the fact they all put down their weapons in order to work together on the netting. Before they could float him to the surface, he pushed away from them and escaped. Without his full-face mask he couldn't hear them, but smiled when he imagined their curses.

As Jason swam toward the targets set up earlier, the team chased him with their assault rifles ready. He approached the first target and darted behind it. The divers raised their weapons and fired. He looked over his shoulder and saw another man swimming toward him. Kicking his flippers, they propelled him through the clear blue water toward another target. Dipping around it, the team raised their weapons and fired. The bullets whizzed through the water, slowed by its powerful force until they hit the target. Several divers raced toward him. His heart rate increased as he sucked air from his rebreather and kicked toward his sailboat. If he did not move fast, they would capture him. He plowed like a dart toward the keel of the boat in the distance. He climbed the ladder on the stern and stepped up onto the deck where Matt and Charles waited. "How'd we do?" He glanced at his dive watch.

Matt smiled. "You really know how to put them through their paces."

"I try to make it interesting."

"I thought they'd capture you this time," Charles said.

"They were having too much fun with the guns." Jason laughed as the divers from the FBI dive team followed him onto the boat.

Todd extended his hand. "That was an excellent test of our anti-terrorism skills."

Jason shook Todd's hand and smiled. "The targets got a good workout."

After the team loaded their equipment onboard, Jason sailed toward the slip at the marina, where someone waited on the dock. A small, slender person … was it Carlos? His visit with Carlos yesterday disturbed his sleep. After Connie died, he tried to mentor the boy as best he could. He had promised her husband, Hernando, he would watch out for their son. He needed to stop going to tourist attractions and instead help him with homework, interpersonal skills, relationships with friends … something more in depth and more dangerous. Carlos had grown since they first met. His needs were changing from companionship to something deeper and he couldn't put his finger on it. Next week he would sit down with Carlos and have a man-to-man talk.

Charles came back to the helm, grabbed the lines, and prepared to toss them over the pilings. "Who's that on the dock?"

"Carlos?"

"You're starting to need glasses, buddy," Charles smirked. "He has a long red ponytail."

"Kathleen?" Jason blinked at the slender figure standing with its arms crossed. "She wouldn't come near a boat or the water."

"Looks like that therapy is working." Charles spun the sails around the masts, securing them, and then tossed lines over the pilings while Jason maneuvered the sailboat into the slip.

While Charles drew the sailboat closer to the dock, Matt and his dive team gathered their equipment. "Hello kitten."

"Hello Charles." She uncrossed her arms and clasped her hands together as she stepped back from the boat.

Jason put the leather strap over the wheel to keep it from turning and stepped to the side railing. "Is everything okay?"

She rubbed her arms, recoiling from the boat and the reflections off the water. "I remembered something."

Jason looked at Matt who stood nearby. "I'll get the gangplank." He retrieved the board from its storage spot, put it across to the dock, and unsnapped the line blocking the exit. "Want to come aboard?"

She shook her head and rubbed her arms. "Not yet, maybe next time."

"Okay, give us a few minutes to unload." Jason faced Matt and lowered his voice. "She wouldn't come here unless it was important."

Matt nodded while he picked up his tanks and wetsuit. "I'm in the mood for some new leads." He stepped across the gangplank, put down his equipment and said hello to Kathleen.

Jason helped the team move their equipment from the sailboat to the dock then secured everything below, bringing up the coolers to the dock trolley.

Kathleen stepped back when all the men gathered around her. She nervously grasped her arms and looked around for an escape route.

Noticing her anxious reaction, Jason put his arm around her waist and gave her a reassuring smile. "This is a first. What brings you this close to the boat?"

"Um, I had a flashback last night." She looked up at him. "I remembered something I thought might help Matt."

Matt drew closer. "What did you remember?"

"The words RUB and TAR. When I left the casino, they tied a T-shirt over my eyes to blindfold me. My eyes were open, I guess from being drugged, and when they put the shirt on and off, I saw the words, *ARUBA STAR*. That was the name of the boat that took me from Aruba to Venezuela."

"Excellent," Matt said. "I'll talk to the Aruban authorities tomorrow and see what we can do to set a trap for the bastards. Oops. Sorry." He smiled at her and turned to leave.

"There's more."

Matt stopped dead in his tracks and turned around as his team continued to their vehicles at the end of the dock.

She shielded her eyes from the sun's glare and repeated the horrible scene she had witnessed many times.

Jason's gut wrenched as he listened to her agonizing story. His admiration for her courage grew more each day.

≈

A week later, Tara strutted down the catwalk in a full length emerald-green satin dress. Slit to her upper thigh, the dress almost hinted at her sexuality while a slit from her chest to her navel covered very little.

Kathleen glanced at Charles whose eyes glittered. No doubt, he imagined slipping her out of that dress later. Tara looked seductive as she strutted to the end of the runway and turned, swinging her slender hips to swirl the flowing dress behind her. The audience cheered in response to her pizzazz. With her blond hair swept up into a formal look, her flashy earrings reflected her love for the runway and it showed on stage.

Kathleen smiled at Jason who seemed more interested than she thought he would be. He was a good man. He didn't like fashion shows but he did like her friends and that touched her heart more than he knew. She glanced at the manager of the fashion show who had leered at Tara at Jungle Island.

With his arms crossed in front of his chest, he seemed very pleased with her performance. He definitely liked the audience reaction to her work. As Tara stepped off the catwalk, he nodded and said something to her. Once all the models had finished displaying the clothes on the runway, they came out for a final showing while the audience stood and cheered.

"That was fun. She looked good." Kathleen smiled at Jason and glanced at the others who agreed.

After Tara changed, she came out from behind the stage where they waited for her. "The manager liked how I looked on stage and he said he would call me when he had another job." She laughed and bowed as they applauded.

To celebrate, they drove to Lincoln Road near South Miami Beach where pedestrian traffic rules the road. She strolled along looking at the stores and restaurants. When she saw the distinctive red awnings of the Van Dyke Café, she knew they had reached their destination. The night air was humid but folks enjoyed the evening at the outdoor tables under the stars.

"Let's go upstairs," Jason said. "Jazz starts at nine."

"Can we eat up there?" Tara said. "I didn't eat anything before the show."

"They have great food," Charles said. "My favorite is the salmon pizza."

"Yum." Tara looked at Kathleen and Chandra. "I'm sold." She took Charles' arm and walked ahead of them to the second floor.

Once upstairs, Kathleen sat on the small banquette with Jason. Sam and Chandra sat in barrel chairs to one side while Charles and Tara sat together in chairs on the other. Literally surrounded by her friends, old and new, she felt exhilarated and content.

Sam actually talked to Chandra as if he was interested in what she had to say. That was a first. He finally came around but was it too late? Had Chandra moved on? She seemed happy on the outside but what was she really thinking?

"A toast ... to the prettiest model in the show." Charles touched glasses with Tara, whose smile was broad enough to reach across the room.

Tara looked flattered by Charles' attention and Kathleen wondered if she should warn her about his sexual interests or keep her mouth shut. *Would I want to know?*

While they waited for the jazz musicians to set up, they ordered a salmon pizza and other small plates. Kathleen sat back on the banquette and relaxed, listening to her friends' conversation, wallowing in the glory of their love. Musicians carrying a saxophone and a guitar tuned-up on stage. A round blues singer in a tight dress leaned on a stool and hit similar notes along with them. When they started to play, she zoned out to a comfortable place where heaven met earth.

When Jason squeezed her hand, it brought her out of her solitude. "Let's dance." He stood up, taking her hand with him.

Stunned, she watched his face to make sure he was serious. He looked sincere. She walked with him to the dance floor. "Let's see if I remember how to do this." Reaching for his shoulders, she hesitated.

He put her arm on his left shoulder, his around her waist, and pulled her toward him. He clutched her right hand on his chest and nuzzled his lips near her ear. "How's this?"

"Good ... very good." His scent aroused her senses. The music had a sensual rhythm matched by his dance movements. She felt mesmerized and closed her eyes to wallow in her feelings of arousal. Her heated response made her vagina swell and throb from the sensuous assault on her body and mind. When the music ended, she opened her eyes and looked into dark blue ones surrounded by black lashes.

"Happy?" he said, holding her waist in the middle of the dance floor.

She nodded and smiled. When the next song started, he resumed his rhythmic dancing and nibbled on her earlobe. She moaned and felt a heated throb drive straight down to her vagina with an explosion. She stifled a gasp and continued dancing, closing her eyes to dream.

"Come home with me." He nuzzled her cheek.

"I can't." She kept her eyes closed.

"I know your mama taught you better but I still want you." He bit her neck below her earlobe.

Chills ran down her arms. "You're moving too fast for me, counselor."

"If I go any slower, sweetheart, I'll have to buy a monk's robe and learn Gregorian chants."

She laughed and surveyed his amused face. He meant what he said, but his eyes still wrinkled at the corners betraying his hilarity. "I'm not ready." *Why did I say that? My body is ready, my mind is resisting.*

He leaned down and kissed her mouth with hot, searing lips. "When you are, we'll set the bed on fire."

She hid her face from his intense gaze. The possibility of a sexual encounter with him both thrilled and frightened her. Her mind waged war with her body at the thought of him thrusting into her. Her heart skipped a beat just thinking about what it would be like. Her breathing increased at the possibility of holding his strong shoulders while he made love to her. A shudder went through her from fear and arousal. *I need help from Dr. Jennifer.*

Chapter 9

By the end of the week, the FBI had worked with Aruban authorities to devise and set a trap for the casino staff and fishing boat captain in Aruba. Eager to find out what had happened, Jason kept his smartphone with him at all times. After picking up Kathleen from work, they ran around Brickell Key near his home on the Miami River. A concrete path around the outside edge of the man-made island in the Biscayne Bay permitted her to run without stopping for traffic or other distractions. He and Kathleen had run together almost every day. He felt pleased that she had increased her running time to thirty-five minutes without resting.

Kathleen ran beside him, her reddish-brown ponytail jumped up and down as she ran. With her eyes half closed, she seemed almost in a trance.

Jason wondered what anxiety trigger she worked on this week. Did it involve him? He had called her therapist to ask how Kathleen was doing. She wouldn't share any details but inferred that Kathleen had a strong will to return to normal. The doctor had been impressed with her rapid improvement. Jason asked her to call him if he could help but she didn't seem likely to do that. She had been polite but resisted his request. He understood why her doctor protected her patient's privacy because he did the same thing for his clients.

When he rounded the corner of the key running alongside Kathleen, he saw two men watching them. He wracked his brain, questioning if any cars had followed him when he picked her up from work. As he drew closer, he realized the figures were Charles and Matt. He grabbed her arm. "Slow down, sweetheart, we're stopping." Coming to a halt, Jason shook Matt's hand. "What brings you downtown?"

"Bad news, I'm afraid. Our trap in Aruba was sprung."

Stunned by the turn of events, he felt disappointed and looked at Kathleen, whose eyes were wide with disbelief. "That's too bad."

"What happened?" Kathleen said.

"The female decoy we set up in the casino was taken but released the next morning. The fishing boat, Aruba Star, exploded and burned completely, right down to the hull."

Kathleen returned his gaze with sad eyes and leaned into his side as he put his arm around her and held her against him.

"Easy kitten," Charles brushed his finger down her cheek. "They'll get them next time."

"There won't be a next time," Jason bristled at his intimate gesture.

Perplexed, Matt looked quizzical. "What do you mean? We'll try again."

Jason felt incredulous but suppressed an urge to show it. "Who tipped off the casino staff and who blew up the boat?"

"We'll find out," Matt said.

The interrogator in Jason kicked in. "Who knew about the operation?"

"Just the human trafficking task force," Matt wiped his perspiring brow.

"Exactly," Jason placed his hand on his hip. "You've got a mole on your team."

Matt looked stunned and fell silent. "Someone in Aruba could have tipped them off."

"Maybe," Jason said. "Until you find out, I'm not working with your team anymore."

"Now wait a minute." Matt raised his hand. "Don't be hasty."

"Nothing against you, man ..." Jason tugged Kathleen closer. "Kathleen and her family are too important to me to risk their lives."

"You either have a mole on your team or there's one in Aruba," Charles said.

"You'll need to set another trap," Jason said, "a very sophisticated one that will fool the bad guys and the mole."

Matt sighed and nodded. "Man, I'd be really disappointed to find out it was someone on my team. I always assumed the corruption was in Aruba."

Jason felt Kathleen grab the back of his shirt with a clenched fist. Her eyes looked intent and distant. No doubt she recalled everyone she met, looking for clues to a possible traitor. Could it be Chad, Lucy, Joe, Nathan, the Canadian, an official in Aruba? The possibilities were endless. But to continue his foundation's mission, he had to eliminate the task force as the source of the leak.

"I trust you," Jason said, "but I don't know the others well enough to work with them anymore."

"I'll talk with headquarters and develop a plan to expose the traitor," Matt said. "Will you work with me on this?"

"Definitely. You can count on me any day." He shook Matt's hand and smiled. "Want to join us for dinner?"

"No thanks. I just stopped by to let you know what happened. My son has a baseball game tonight." Matt turned to leave. "I'll be in touch next week."

Jason waved goodbye and looked at Charles. "Interested in dinner?"

"No thanks, I'm headed to the club. You should come along." Charles winked and grinned.

Jason smiled at Kathleen. He knew she wouldn't enjoy a club where men wore black leather and were served by almost naked women. And that was in the public room. In the private rooms, the women knelt at the men's feet and did exactly what they were told or were playfully and happily punished. That would be too much like the past year for her. Besides, she wouldn't understand a consensual master/slave relationship that gave both men and women pleasure. If he suggested it, she would look at him like he had two heads. "Maybe some other time, have fun."

Charles grinned. "I will." Before leaving, he reached for Kathleen's hand and kissed it with great fanfare then stared into her green eyes. "One of these days, I'll have you kneeling at my feet."

"Ha!" She almost barked. "In your dreams."

Charles laughed and released her hand. "I can always dream, kitten." He spun on his heels and headed toward home.

She looked up at Jason. "He's nuts. That'll never happen in my life-time."

Jason chuckled and held her close to his side as they enjoyed an eve-ning stroll along the river. After sharing a light dinner together, as he anticipated, she declined to go home with him. Reluctantly, he drove her back to the safe house. He knew what her answer would be, but it didn't hurt to ask. He would keep asking until she said yes. He was determined to have her. He somewhat envied Charles. Some female companionship would be welcome, but he told Charles earlier that he was committed to Kathleen and he meant it. He would wait as long as she wanted him to, no matter how painful his morning showers had become.

~

Jason got into his bed, looking forward to a good night's sleep before an early morning deposition. He dozed off and was soon awakened by his ringing smartphone. He lifted it from the nightstand and saw that Sam was calling. "Hello?"

"Jason," Sam said, "sorry to call so late but it's Kathleen ..."

He heard a scream in the background and sat up erect in bed. "What's going on?"

"We watched a movie. She dozed off but when she woke, she screamed and shook and tore at her clothes." He paused to catch his breath. "She's rolling on the floor. We don't know what to do. She won't stop."

"We?"

"Mom and Dad are here." Sam sounded sheepish.

That made Jason mad. They were told not to share the safe house location. Now her parents knew and if anyone had followed them, so did the bad guys. He repressed his anger and tried to speak calmly when he heard Kathleen scream. "I'll be right there."

He jumped out of bed, threw on his clothes, and rushed downstairs to the garage. He sped north on the interstate toward North Miami

Beach and arrived at the safe house about twenty minutes later. By the time he arrived, Kathleen's pajamas were soaked from sweat. She rolled on the floor in front of the television, surrounded by her distressed family. He knelt on the floor, touched her hair, and put his face close to hers. "Can you hear me, sweetheart?"

She moaned. "I'm burning." She almost popped the buttons on her shirt when she grabbed it and pulled it away from her skin.

"Okay, baby." He touched her head. "Sam, bring all the ice cubes and anything frozen from the freezer."

Sam ran to the kitchen while Jason tried to comfort her.

"We tried to hold her down," Brenda said, "but she just screamed."

"Please don't touch her," Jason said to Kathleen's parents while caressing her hair. "You'll be okay, sweetheart."

Sam returned with ice cube trays and frozen food, piling them on the floor. He and his parents knelt behind Kathleen. When Brenda touched Kathleen's rear end, she screamed in agony.

"Mrs. McDougal," Jason said in an exasperated tone only to be met with a defiant glare. He took the ice cube trays and broke them open on the floor. "Take two handfuls of cubes or frozen food and rub Kathleen's skin under her pajamas. Mr. McDougal can do her shoulders and upper back, Mrs. McDougal you do her lower back to her upper thighs and Sam you do her legs and feet." He handed out the frozen items to each of them. "I'll do her front." He pulled her pajama top toward him forming a gap and reached beneath, rubbing ice over her chest, down her waist, over her thighs to her feet.

She moaned as the four of them doused the heat from her burning skin. Jason lay down in front of her and touched her cheek. "Okay, baby? Any more burns?"

"Left side."

He rolled her face down while the others rubbed her with cubes. Lying in front of her, he noticed her eyes focusing on his face. "Better?"

The pain which had emanated from her eyes eased when she stopped moaning and concentrated her gaze on his eyes. She reached up to him. "I love you."

121

"I love you too, sweetheart." Jason tickled her soft lips and looked at her parents, who seemed shocked. "Ma'am, would you get a towel, fresh pajamas, and a robe? There should be a pair of Gator pajamas in there."

Brenda looked askance at him; none too pleased, and went into Kathleen's closet. Meanwhile he helped Sam and Harry pick up the melted ice cubes.

Jason encircled Kathleen's upper arms and helped her sit up. "There you go." He rubbed her back. Her face looked haunted. His thoughts turned to the agony she had suffered that caused these flashbacks.

"Can I go home with you?" Her green eyes pleaded for his affirmative answer.

"You're always welcome in my home."

She rubbed her arms, cold from the frozen treatment. "I don't want to live alone anymore. I don't feel safe here." When her mother returned with a towel and helped dry her she still shook from whatever evil had possessed her mind. She looked at Jason with fearful eyes. "Can I move in with you?"

Jason felt stunned but pleased by her hasty decision yet hesitated. "We'll talk about it."

Her mother touched her hand. "Honey, you can move home with us."

"No thanks, Mom. I've outgrown living with my parents."

"If my little girl is going to move in with you," Harry said, "you and I need to visit." For the first time, Kathleen's father looked piqued and protective of his daughter.

Jason smiled inside but outwardly showed his poker face. He reached into his wallet for a business card and handed it to Harry. "Here's my work address. We can meet for lunch tomorrow, if you're available."

"I'll make myself available," Harry said firmly. "I'll be there at eleven-thirty."

"I have a deposition that will probably last until after eleven," Jason said.

"I'll wait," Harry said.

Jason helped Kathleen to her feet. "Change into some dry clothes and pack for the next couple of days. Then we'll talk. I want you to be sure."

"I'm sure," Kathleen said.

"If you move in, you're not moving out. You're not going to toy with me like that." He grasped her chin and looked into her green eyes to make sure she understood. She sighed and went into her closet.

Brenda looked at Harry, infuriated with her daughter and with Jason. She couldn't stop what was happening and she clearly was not pleased.

After securing the safe house, Jason helped Kathleen into his truck, said goodnight to her family, and drove to his condo. Once inside the safety of his home, she went into the guest bedroom and settled in as if she belonged there. Jason felt pleased to have her back. She brought warmth and happiness to his otherwise cold abode. He returned to his bed, eager to get a few hours sleep before his deposition.

Later the next morning, Jason finished his deposition. The questioning had been intense but he got the witness to say some things he could use in the upcoming trial. That went well—now he had to face an angry and disappointed father. He left the conference room, walked past Mrs. Bailey's office, and saw Kathleen's father standing in his office looking at his wall of books. Dressed in a navy blue blazer and tan slacks, he looked like the accountant he was.

"Mr. McDougal." Jason's black suit and tie coordinated with his black hair while his light blue shirt highlighted his eye color. He shook hands with Kathleen's father, who seemed older today.

"Impressive office. If my daughter moves in with you, I guess you should call me Harry."

"We'll see, sir. I don't want her to move in if she's running away from something."

Kathleen's father smiled and winced at the same time. "What kind of legal business are you doing here?"

"We represent shipping companies at the Port of Miami, as well as other businesses around the city. We provide legal counsel and manage the paperwork."

"You are the managing partner?"

"Charles and I manage the company together."

He nodded and looked out the wall of windows at the view. "Oh yes, we met him at the airport, I forgot."

"We've known each other since college and went into business together eight years ago." Jason joined him at the window. "Mr. McDougal, I want you to know I care very much for Kathleen. I would never hurt her."

He looked at Jason with wounded eyes. "Letting her move in with you is hurting her. We're church-going people. It's a sin for her to live with you."

"She'll have her own bedroom, sir."

Harry's face softened somewhat. "That helps. I can see you're capable of supporting her financially. But I'd like to know more about you and how you'd treat her."

"That's fair. If I were you, I'd want to know the same things." Jason turned away from the windows. "Let's head upstairs to the restaurant where we won't be interrupted." He walked toward the elevator lobby and heard footsteps behind. Harry stood next to him as they rode to the top floor where the restaurant provided a 360-degree view.

Jason led him to a large leather booth away from the other diners. "We call this booth 'the cone of silence.'" He chuckled. "No one can hear what's being said when you sit here."

As Jason slid into the booth, his smartphone buzzed. Kathleen had sent him a text message. "Kathleen says she survived hell on earth. Now, she wants to make her own decisions."

Harry smiled. "She's getting her independent streak back." He took the Arnold Palmer offered by the waiter and took a sip. "What happened to her? Last night she seemed almost insane."

"She's suffering from severe trauma." Jason took a glass of sweet tea from the waiter. "She survived unspeakable cruelty. The details might keep you awake for a few nights."

"I have a right to know what happened to her."

"I'll tell you what I know. You can decide what to tell her mother."

Harry nodded. "I want to know everything. Don't hold anything back."

"If you insist ..." Jason began the story in Aruba, told of Kathleen's trip to Venezuela and Vancouver. When he described how he made her strip at the auction and what he saw on her body, Harry clenched his fists so hard his knuckles turned white. Jason paused, giving him time to gather himself. "Do you want me to continue?"

Harry nodded but looked ill. "Tell me."

"Since coming home, Kathleen has remembered some of the more painful things her mind had blocked. Last weekend, she told me when they arrived in Venezuela the women were lined up and groped. Some were taken away. She heard screaming and then silence. She never knew what happened, until she got to Vancouver."

"What happened?" Harry clenched his teeth.

"Apparently, slave buyers don't want women with breast implants. Rather than waste money feeding and transporting them, the kidnappers check to see if they have them. Those who do are disposed of."

"Good God." Harry rubbed his forehead and closed his eyes.

Jason cleared his throat. "While she was in Vancouver, they would take her and those who weren't bought at the auction out on a boat. They'd tie ropes around their waists with cement blocks on the ends. They never knew who would be thrown overboard and who would return to shore. If the men liked a slave, they would shoot her in the forehead before throwing her in the water. If they didn't, they'd throw her in the water and let her scream until she drowned. Every month, Kathleen agonized about the ones who went overboard, but she soon realized they were the lucky ones."

"Lord, have mercy." Harry looked down at the table with his fists clenched. Taking a deep breath, he looked up with tears in his eyes. "It's obvious you and Katie want to be together. I won't stand in your way, if that's what you both decide."

"I appreciate that, sir. I'm sure this is difficult for you." Jason was glad to have Kathleen's father's blessing, although he didn't need it or want it. On the other hand, his approval would help Kathleen feel better and her feelings *were* important to him.

That night, after Jason picked Kathleen up from work, they ran along the Riverwalk. After taking showers, they put on comfortable clothes and stood in the kitchen cutting up vegetables for a salad.

"After dinner," Jason said, "want to watch that movie that won the Academy Award?" He glanced up from the cutting board into her pretty green eyes.

"Good idea, I've wanted to see that." She finished the salad and put a crabmeat quiche in the oven for dinner.

Jason took a bottle of wine out of the refrigerator. "Let's have a glass while the quiche cooks."

"I might need one." She pushed her hair over her shoulder. "How was your talk with my dad?"

Jason twisted the corkscrew. "Your text message set the tone for our conversation." The cork squeaked when he slid it out of the bottle. "When I told him what your text said, he smiled and said you were getting your independent streak back."

"I'm glad I sent it." Kathleen smiled and extended her empty wine glass. "Was he really mad about me moving in with you?"

"I wouldn't say mad, I'd say uncomfortable. Once I explained how you felt about surviving and some of the things you went through, he relented. He actually had tears in his eyes at the end."

"Boy, you must have given a powerful speech," she chuckled.

Jason filled her glass and shrugged his shoulders. "I gave him a good mental picture. I warned him he might not sleep for a couple nights, but he insisted that I tell him everything."

"Everything?"

"He insisted." Jason poured himself a glass. "But he's not telling your mother, it'd be too much for her." He gestured toward the living room sofa and led the way as she followed.

Kathleen sat down next to him. "Thanks for talking to him. I know that's the last thing you needed after a short night and a busy morning."

"If his blessing puts your mind at ease, I'm glad to help." He grabbed her hand and squeezed it. "Now, tell me about work. How are you doing?"

"They trust me enough to give me some more challenging projects, so I'm happier than I was."

"You've done really well with your recovery. I think they're recognizing that." He sat back on the sofa. "I don't think it's as much about trust as it is about not wanting to overwhelm you."

"I guess you're right. It just seems kind of degrading to be given such childish work."

"You think it's childish because you haven't lost your abilities." He sipped his wine.

When the buzzer on the oven sounded, they enjoyed dinner and discussed the news of the day. Later, Jason started the movie on the television, put his arm around her shoulders, and sat back. By the end of the movie, Kathleen's head laid on his chest.

"I can see why that won the Oscar," he said into the top of her head.

She nodded. "I'll be thinking about it for days."

When she looked up at him for confirmation, he kissed her. Sensing her warmth and her need, he kissed harder and longer. He gently rubbed her breast through her top and felt her nipple harden. Her breathing increased. *If I unbutton her shirt, will she bolt for her bedroom?* When he unfastened the first button, she didn't shake or resist. He continued slowly and reached for her stiff nipple and caressed it around and over the top. She moaned. He cupped her breast in his palm and squeezed her nipple with two fingers. His breathing increased and his erection twitched. He lowered his lips to suck on her nipple and felt her quiver. Unsure of her reaction, he continued. When she began to shake, he stopped and kissed her neck and held her, biting her at the base of her neck and shoulder until she stopped. He covered her breast and snuggled her into his side until his erection softened. Reaching for the remote control, they watched the late evening news until she fell asleep. He kissed the top of her head. "Let's go to bed, sleepy head."

She woke up but her eyes were half closed. She smiled at him and lifted her chin to kiss him.

He returned her kisses in an unhurried manner, ending with kisses down her throat. He stood up, pulled her up with him, and held her hand all the way to her bedroom door. "Good night, sweetheart." He closed her bedroom door behind him.

Over the next couple of days, Jason enjoyed having Kathleen in his condo. He made sure not to press her on anything. She needed to come to him or their relationship would not be what he wanted. Their friendship had grown over the past few weeks and he didn't want to ruin what they had achieved. He was content with her living in his home and wanted her to feel comfortable and safe.

When he picked her up from work on the third night, she seemed anxious and jumpy. Those nervous symptoms she had when she first came home had subsided. He knew something bothered her. Running was the best thing for her to do when she felt anxious. An afternoon thunderstorm kept them from running outside. He took her down to the second floor health club in their condo building. Treadmills, stationery bikes, and weightlifting benches filled the fitness center. A small staffed kitchenette allowed residents to get water, juices, and snacks.

Kathleen chose a treadmill in front of the windows. Her skin-tight exercise suit showed off her figure, which had begun to fill out. Her slender torso had developed a soft gentle shape. With her auburn hair pulled back in a ponytail, it flopped behind her head as she ran with her eyes closed and faced her demons.

Jason ran on the treadmill next to her before he moved to a stationary bike where he rode until he got bored. He moved to the weightlifting area where he lifted one hundred pounds. Between lifts, he glanced over to check on Kathleen. Sure she was safe, he added more weights and lifted until another man began running next to her. He noticed the man kept looking over at her. He tried to engage her in conversation but she ignored him or couldn't hear him in her trance-like state.

Jason tired of him bothering her. Wiping his face with a towel, he strode toward Kathleen and stepped near the strange man. "Please stop talking to her."

"Who are you, her keeper?" the stranger said.

Jason threw the towel around his neck. "I don't recognize you, do you live here?"

"I just moved in last week," the man said. "I'm trying to meet some of my neighbors."

"My name's Montgomery. I live in 1503."

"Stephens," the man said as he ran. "1012."

"She's busy working." Jason nodded toward Kathleen. "She doesn't talk while she's running."

"I see," Stephens said. "What are you, her husband?"

"Close enough." Jason walked around to Kathleen's side. When he saw her floundering, he turned off the treadmill and caught her as she finished running and almost fell down, exhausted. With little effort, he picked her up and carried her to the snack counter. He sat down on a stool with her across his lap. "Water, please," he said when the clerk stopped wiping down the counter.

Jason held the water while she drank half the bottle without taking a breath. "Easy sweetheart." He tipped the bottle away from her lips.

Charles had arrived while they exercised and sat on a stationary bike. He peddled away and smiled at them. When Charles finished he came over and sat on the stool next to them. "Welcome to Riverside, kitten."

Kathleen smiled at him and laid her head on Jason's shoulder. "Thanks."

"Are you planning to stick around this time?" Charles smirked.

She looked up at Jason. "I'm hoping to, but we need to talk."

Jason kissed her lips tenderly, not concerned about who saw him. When he pulled away, he noticed her eyes were misty. He pulled her into the kink of his neck and nuzzled her ear.

"You two need to get a room," Charles said.

Kathleen blushed while Jason smiled and rubbed the light pink shade on her cheeks. Rising from his lap, she brushed away a stray hair. "I think I'm okay now."

"Sit here, kitten." Charles moved down one stool.

She sat on his vacated stool and laughed. "It's nice and warm."

"It's hot for you, baby." Charles grinned and got up. "I'm done here." He glanced at Kathleen. "See you tomorrow?"

"I'll be here." She seemed more confident and smiled.

"Are you done?" Jason asked her.

She nodded. "Yep."

"Hold the elevator," Jason said to Charles, "we'll go up with you."

Jason took her hand and walked out behind Charles to the elevator.

They got off at the fifteenth floor while Charles headed higher. Jason opened the door to his condo and let her enter first. He wasn't normally a jealous person but he didn't like that stranger talking to her. He needed to ask around about that man, just to make sure.

After taking a quick shower, he opened a bottle of wine. Kathleen seemed nervous about their scheduled talk. He shouldn't have put a time limit on her staying with him. That was a rookie mistake. Grabbing the wine, two glasses and some cheese and crackers, he put it on the coffee table in front of the sofa. He had enjoyed their evening chats after work. He heard a noise and glanced over the back of the sofa to see Kathleen coming toward him. She hesitated.

"Come sit down, sweetheart." He patted the sofa next to him. She sat down looking nervous.

He pushed her hair behind her ear. "You're uncomfortable and I never intended to do that. Let's talk another time."

"No, I want to talk now."

"Okay." He brushed her cheek with his fingers. "I'll start. I've enjoyed having you share my home and I don't want you to leave."

She stared with her mouth ajar. "You don't mince words do you?"

"Hey, babe, I'm a lawyer. That's what we do." He laughed and handed her a glass of wine.

Kathleen smiled, took the glass and sipped. "I still have a lot of things to work through."

He pulled her toward him and kissed her passionately for several minutes. Putting down his wine glass, he rubbed her breast through her shirt and felt her nipple harden. Her breathing increased while he continued to kiss her. He knew her body wanted him but her mind ... that would take time.

She pulled away and put her forehead against his face while her breathing slowed. "I want to stay."

"You can stay until you're back to normal. Then you can decide what you want to do."

She put her arms around his chest and snuggled into his neck. "That might take a year."

"I'm willing to try living with you for a year. I just don't want you moving in and out and jerking me around."

"I won't." She smiled against his shirt.

"We can move your things on Saturday morning and have a low-key welcome party in the afternoon."

"You don't have to do that."

"I want you to meet your new neighbors." He kissed her, tasted her mouth and felt his erection thicken. A year of living like this would be painful. He needed to talk to someone who understood rape victims.

On Saturday morning, Kathleen felt excited about moving into Jason's condo. She was surprised at how relaxed she felt. Moving in with him felt so right for her. She didn't feel nervous at all, only excitement at moving their relationship to the next level.

Jason drove her to the safe house and loaded her clothes and boxes into his truck. It didn't take them long to load everything so they spent some time cleaning the house for the next tenant.

When she got back to Jason's condo, she put her clothes in her bedroom closet while he stacked her boxes in the spare bedroom. When she finished hanging her clothes in the closet, she went to look for him and found him in the spare bedroom.

"You can set up your paintings in here." He looked around the room with his hands on his hips. "This will make a good artist's den."

She smiled and felt welcome. "Don't your parents come to visit?"

"Once a year to escape the snow. You can use it the rest of the year." He put his arm around her shoulders and walked out of the spare bedroom with her when the doorbell rang. "That'll be the caterer." He left her and went to open the front door.

A man and woman carried in trays of sandwiches and small bites of various things. Jason took care of everything in the kitchen and paid them before they left.

"Do I have time to take a shower?"

Jason stored the food in the kitchen. "Go ahead. Folks should arrive in an hour or so."

Kathleen went to her bedroom and selected the sexy dress she bought at the mall and pulled out the tights that Tara convinced her to wear underneath it. She admired Tara's excellent fashion sense. She would never have thought of wearing tights under a dress to hide her whip marks. The revelation gave her a feeling of being totally free and self-assured again. Once she had dressed and styled her long hair, she put on some light eye makeup to highlight her green eyes and primped in front of the full-length mirror in the corner. She slipped her slender feet into some sexy high-heeled shoes to show off her legs and giggled. *Wait until Jason sees this.* She spun around admiring her new look then tiptoed into the kitchen.

Jason was busy removing food and drinks from the refrigerator and putting ice on the counter. He didn't hear her. When he glanced up, he froze. Standing upright with wide eyes, he scanned her from head to toe. The animal print dress clung to her slender figure and ended high above her black tights.

"Holy cow." He smiled broadly. "Where have you been hiding that?"

"The dress or the legs?" She chuckled.

"Both. You need to get more dresses." He put his arms around her waist and pulled her close. Kissing her with hot lips, he devoured her when the doorbell rang. He caressed her cheek and hesitated. "Should I get that?"

"The party was your idea."

He reluctantly released her and answered the door.

She heard Charles' voice before he flew into the kitchen carrying two bottles of wine. "Hello kitten." He bent down to kiss her cheek. When he saw her dress, he stepped back to admire her and growled at the animal print. "You keep wearing things like that, and I might have to move in on Jason's territory."

"You keep your distance, buddy." Jason laughed but sounded serious at the same time.

Kathleen went to Jason's side and hugged him around the waist. "I'm not trying to get *your* attention," she said to Charles.

"You've got mine, babe," Jason said, pulling her to him.

Charles smiled. "You'll be on your knees begging me one of these days."

"Not a chance, Sir Charles." She called him a title commensurate with his interest in bondage and domination.

Charles and Jason laughed. "You're an obstinate one," Charles said.

"I'm a survivor."

When the doorbell rang, Jason answered it. She heard her parents and Sam and went to greet them. "Let me take those." She reached for the trays they carried and led them inside. "Come in. The kitchen's this way."

Jason served as host, answering the front door and greeting guests. He introduced his neighbors to Kathleen and helped them with drinks while she entertained everyone in the living room. The guests were mostly young males; some were couples, some were single. Interesting there were no women invited. Just then the doorbell rang and she heard giggles and female laughter. Tara and Chandra had arrived. She was thrilled to have some female companionship.

She hugged her friends and took them into the living room where her parents and some of Jason's friends and neighbors gathered in front of the floor-to-ceiling windows, admiring the view and eating finger foods.

"What a great place," Harry said.

"The view's great, isn't it?" Jason looked at Kathleen's legs and winked.

She blushed, knowing what he meant. After some pleasantries, she gracefully moved away with Tara and Chandra. "Now tell me what happened at the club with Charles."

"Yeah, I want to hear too," Chandra said, whispering.

"Well the men all wore black leather or latex and the women wore skimpy clothes that didn't hide much. The women wore cuffs on their wrists and leashes clipped to a dog collar around their necks." Tara giggled.

"Watch out," Kathleen said, "Charles might try to get you into that."

"He said he had mink handcuffs for his ladies," Tara said, laughing aloud.

Kathleen laughed and looked at Chandra's surprised face. "You're not thinking about trying it are you?"

"We'll see," Tara said, "I might try it just to see what it's like to be restrained and made love to by someone I trust. I'd never try it with someone I didn't know."

"Make sure he wears a condom," Kathleen said, "he gets around."

"He's watching us." Tara glanced at Charles.

"He's probably trying to figure out how to get all three of us in bed," Chandra said. They all laughed and giggled.

Happy to have her friends meet Jason's friends, Kathleen felt surrounded by loving people. "We'd better get back to mingling. We're drawing attention." She saw several folks watching her, including Jason, who was focused on her shoes.

"After you get settled," Tara said, curling her blond hair around a finger, "we'll get together and I'll tell you everything that happened. It was really interesting."

Kathleen, Tara, and Chandra rejoined the party in the living room. "What were you three musketeers giggling about?" Sam said to Chandra.

"Just girl stuff," Chandra said. "What are you doing this weekend?"

"Studying," Sam said. Chandra looked disappointed. "But, hey, everybody needs a break. How about we go see that new movie?"

Chandra's eyes sparkled above her bright smile. "Absolutely," she said, fingering the ends of her pixie haircut.

Brenda had finished her drink, and scanned the room for her daughter. "Do you have more sweet tea, Katie?"

"Sure, Mom," Kathleen said. As she followed her mother to the kitchen, she glanced over to see Charles with his arm around Tara. When he whispered something in her ear, she giggled and nodded. Kathleen swallowed hard. He moved fast, just like Jason. But Jason was waiting for her. She knew he was getting frustrated. When he kissed her, sometimes she felt his erection against her leg but he would back off and wait. An ounce of frustration wiggled its way into her mind. She wasn't a sexual aggressor. She enjoyed men who took the lead in the bedroom. Not quite like Charles, but she did want a man who would push her a little. *How exactly do you communicate that to a man who is trying not to rush you?* She appreciated his consideration and sensitivity to her past but on the other hand ... She poured her mother some tea and handed it to her.

"Katie," Brenda said, "this is a great place, but how are you going to make the rent payments?"

"Jason won't take any rent," she said. "I'm saving that money for some surgeries I need." She led her back to Jason where she picked up her glass of soda.

Brenda clucked her tongue. "You don't need any surgeries."

Kathleen looked at the floor and tensed. She could never have moved home with her parents. She felt happy to be living with Jason and reached for his hand, squeezing it.

Jason squeezed back, giving her an understanding smile, blending sympathy with a wince.

Harry narrowed his eyes at his wife. "Brenda, you need to be quiet."

Brenda looked at her husband with daggers in her eyes. She wasn't used to him putting his foot down—no doubt a new experience. Kathleen felt proud of her father. Ever since he visited with Jason, he seemed different somehow. What had Jason told him?

The tense atmosphere was shattered when Charles returned with Tara under his arm. "Hey, young squire," Charles said to Sam, "we're hosting a charity event next Saturday. Want to join us?"

"If I can, what is it?" Sam said.

"It's a baseball game between lawyers and doctors—we call it Jawbones versus Sawbones," Charles chuckled.

"It benefits at-risk kids," Jason said. "I have tickets here somewhere." He looked around the sideboard behind him. "Bring all your friends, it's a great cause."

"We could use a good hitter," Charles said.

Sam scoffed. "I'm not a home-run hitter, but I can get a base hit here and there."

"Remind me before you leave, I'll give you some tickets," Jason said.

"Typical males, always talking about sports," Brenda said. "Let's meet some of the neighbors." She led her husband away.

"That woman's a ball buster, man," Charles said without thinking.

When Jason kissed Kathleen's hair and snuggled her to his side, she accepted his apology for his friend. Charles didn't mince words either. These two were a pair.

"Oh, sorry you two," Charles said. "Sometimes my mouth is faster than my wits."

"Hey, I grew up with her," Sam said, "you aren't telling me anything."

"You need to move out," Charles said. "Get your own space."

"When I get a permanent job," Sam said, "that'll be the first thing I do." He looked at Jason. "Kathleen and I were going to move in together, but I guess that's not happening."

"Not if I have anything to say about it." Jason smiled and looked down at Kathleen. "I'm not going to say I'm sorry."

Sam smiled at them. "No, I guess not, you owe me one."

"That I do." Jason squeezed Kathleen's waist and enjoyed her twinkling green eyes.

Kathleen laughed at the men's banter and felt very happy about all the fuss. The neighbors gradually said goodbye and left. Tara and Chandra made plans with her to get together this weekend before they went home.

Harry shook Jason's hand. "Thanks for inviting us. Kathleen looks very happy here."

"We're both happy," Jason said. "Come visit anytime. We'll go downstairs with you and introduce you to the security guard in the lobby." They rode down in the elevator, silence filled the air. Jason let everyone get out first and then followed them toward the security desk.

"Julio, this is Kathleen McDougal and her parents. She'll be living here from now on and her parents will be visiting, unit 1503."

Julio wrote on his clipboard. "Yes, Mr. Montgomery, I'll make sure they're added to the resident's list."

Kathleen said goodbye to her family and watched them get into their car parked across the street. She was about to turn toward the elevators when the back door opened and Sam ran across the street toward the lobby. She stepped through the door onto the brick walkway outside.

"I forgot the tickets to the baseball game," Sam said.

Before Kathleen could say anything, her parents' car exploded. Eardrum splitting sounds buffered her ears. Flames flashed high. Black smoke billowed upward. She screamed. Jason grabbed her upper arms and pulled her back inside the lobby.

"Stay inside," he said.

"No!" She pushed his grip away.

"Do you want to go back to Vancouver?" He grabbed her and pulled her back. She froze. He pushed her inside the lobby. "Keep her in here!" he said to Julio. He ran past Sam who stood in shock on the sidewalk. Jason pulled open the nearest car door and pulled Harry out. His clothes were burning. When he glanced at Brenda, her clothes were burning too.

Screaming, Brenda grabbed her hair to put out the flames and burned her hands. Sam opened her door and smothered the flames with his shirt. When Jason pressed the seatbelt button to unlock it, Sam grabbed her arm, pulling her from the burning car. Brenda gasped at the pain.

"Get away from the car!" Jason yelled as he put his arm around Harry and helped him to lean against a rock wall nearby.

While Sam helped his mother sit on the pavement near them, Julio ran to the car with the building fire extinguisher and doused the flames. Soon a fire truck, ambulance and the Miami Police Department responded to Julio's call.

As Kathleen watched from the safety of the lobby, she covered her mouth with her hand. Her father's right side looked burned but he was talking and alert. Her mother looked worse plus her hair was singed. Kathleen heard heavy footsteps behind her and turned to see several residents gathered to watch the excitement.

Among them was Charles, who rushed to her side. "What the hell is going on?"

"I don't know what's going on." She watched helplessly as Jason and Sam worked quickly to help her parents.

"I'll find out." Charles left her with Julio, who had returned with the empty extinguisher.

She watched as Charles spoke to Jason then Sam. A few minutes later, he returned. "They have burns but seem to be okay."

Relieved something worse hadn't happened, Kathleen slumped against Charles. "Sam got out of the car at the last second. He might have been killed."

Charles put his arm around her and held her against him. They watched as paramedics loaded her mother and father into the ambulance and it left with the siren blaring. Another medic attended to Jason and Sam. He bandaged their lower arms. When he asked them something, they shook their heads and signed a paper. Finally, Jason walked toward the lobby. When he came inside, she ran into his open arms and hugged his smoke-filled shirt. "Are you okay?"

"I'm fine, baby." He held her tight with both arms. "Your parents are okay, too. They have some burns."

While they held each other in relief, Charles came near and looked him over. "You certainly manage to get into some real fixes. Are they going to Jackson Memorial?"

"Yes." Jason rubbed her back. "If you take care of Kathleen, I'll go with Sam."

She lifted her head. "I'm going with you."

"No you're not."

"They're my parents. You're not keeping me from seeing them."

"Wait until they're in a room. Drawing you out is exactly what they're trying to do."

She gasped. "You think they did this?"

"Who else?"

"Maybe it was a malfunction." Deep in her heart she knew that was ridiculous.

Jason gave her an incredulous look. "We're getting too close and they don't like it." He touched her chin.

"But I need to be with them." She pleaded to his blue eyes.

"Sweetheart, you need to wait until I can arrange for security." Jason held her arms.

"You can't endanger other people at the hospital," Charles said to her.

"If they're coming for you, they'll hurt anyone who gets in the way."

Kathleen sighed and clutched Jason's shirt, her eyes widened with fear, then narrowed with anger. One of these days, there would be a reckoning.

Chapter 10

Kathleen awoke with her head lying on Jason's chest. She heard soft steady breathing and looked at his sleeping face. His chin and cheeks were covered with course stubble as morning approached. With his arms around her, she felt safe and loved, but she needed to stretch her legs. She lay next to him on a vinyl-covered lounge chair in her parents' hospital room. Someone had covered them with a light cotton blanket. She traced a finger along his square-cut chin, causing him to open those dark blue eyes that reminded her of her Dutch slave bead, her freedom bead.

He smiled. "Hey, pretty lady," he said in his light southern accent.

"Hey," she said softly, not wanting to awaken her sleeping parents. He kissed her tenderly. She enjoyed his warm lips on hers and relaxed into his embrace.

After a couple minutes, he pulled away and looked into her eyes. "That's a first."

"What?"

"No shaking." His eyes twinkled with desire.

She felt proud of her small but significant achievement. After seven weeks, she finally felt happy and content in his arms.

He pushed her auburn hair back and whispered in her ear. "When your parents go home, we should go away together."

Her heart skipped a beat. She knew what he meant … he meant share the same bed. With her mouth slightly ajar, she concentrated on breathing. "I don't want to take time off from work."

"We can go to the Keys for the weekend." He tilted his head and raised an eyebrow. "If you get cold feet, we can come home." He ran his finger down her ear and squeezed her earlobe.

140

"I'd like that." She felt her heart rate increase. The heated throb between her legs confirmed her body liked his idea too.

When her mother moaned, Kathleen left her cozy spot and pushed the blanket onto Jason's outstretched legs. Moving to her mother's bed-side, she lightly touched the bandages on her hands. "Do you want a pain killer?"

Brenda shook her head. "Where's your father?"

"He's in the next bed."

Brenda looked over to see her husband of thirty years sleeping peace-fully. Scanning his bandages, she turned to Kathleen. "How bad is it?"

"Not bad. You both were lucky. You've got burns where your clothes caught fire."

"I can deal with that."

Jason put his arm around Kathleen's shoulders when he stepped next to her. "How are you feeling, Mrs. McDougal?"

"The pain is searing, like being in a frying pan."

"We can call—" He reached for the nurse's call button.

"It's not that bad." Mrs. McDougal took the call button away from him. "Don't bother the nurses. They've got other patients who are worse off."

He smiled at her. "I'm sure you know what to do when you need help."

"I plan to get out of here before they even know my name." She squeezed Kathleen's hand. "I've seen too much to stay in here."

Kathleen chuckled at her mother's spunk. "The doctor said you could go home as long as someone changed your bandages and watched for infections."

"I know what to do," Brenda said, "I do that every day for others, I can certainly do it for myself and my husband."

"I'm glad, Mama." Kathleen patted her shoulder.

The door to their room opened and Sam entered, carrying a large coffee cup, followed closely by Matt. "Look who I found downstairs."

Matt shook hands with Jason and Kathleen and stood at Brenda's bed-side. "Mrs. McDougal, I'm sorry you've gotten involved in this."

"In what?" Harry said, awakened by the noise.

141

"Hello, sir," Matt said, walking over to his bed and shaking hands. "We're pretty sure this was a warning bomb."

"A warning bomb …" Kathleen felt aghast and clutched Jason's shirt.

"If someone wanted to kill your parents," Matt said to her, "they would have. This bomb was a warning for us to stop what we're doing or next time they will kill them."

"You're right." She leaned into Jason's side as he held her tight.

Hearing a knock on the door, Sam opened it to see the security guard Jason had hired to guard the McDougal family and another man.

"Come in, Nathan." Jason gestured him inward.

"Mr. and Mrs. McDougal," Matt said, "this is Nathan Isenberg. He's with Alcohol, Tobacco, Firearms, and Explosives. He can answer any questions you have."

Nathan greeted everyone and stood with Matt between Kathleen's parents' beds. "Our technicians analyzed the remnants of the bomb and found it contained hydrogen peroxide and acetone, which are easily obtained from hair salons. That confirms our original theory that the traffickers blew up your car as a warning."

"What exactly has stirred them up?" Harry said.

"We set a trap in Aruba with information that Kathleen had given us," Matt said. "Unfortunately, someone tipped off the traffickers and our trap was sprung before we could arrest them. They must know by now that Vancouver is shut down and we're focusing on them. To resume business, they need to draw Kathleen out of hiding where they can kill her or take her again."

"They'll never take me alive," Kathleen said, clenching her jaw. Jason squeezed her shoulder as she looked at his concerned face.

"You aren't planning to stop the investigation are you?" Harry said.

"No," Matt said, "but you won't be safe until it's over. I'd like you and your family to move into the safe house until we can make arrests in Aruba and Venezuela."

Kathleen's parents looked at each other for a minute in silence. Then Harry looked at Matt. "I suppose we'll have to. We appreciate your offer."

Sam clenched his hand into a fist. "I want a gun."

Kathleen gasped at almost the same time as her mother. "What are you planning to do with a gun?"

"The same thing Jason does." He nodded toward Jason's shoulder holster. "Protect myself and my family."

Sam's determined look convinced her not to challenge him. She felt vulnerable too. "I don't want a gun, but I would like something to protect myself." She looked at Matt and Nathan. "Do they still make cyanide tablets?"

"Katie!" Brenda said loudly. "Don't even think about that!"

Her mother's reaction made Kathleen feel incredulous. "Mama, if you knew what I've been through, you would have never said that." She looked at Matt and Nathan. "I'm very serious about this. I will not survive slavery twice. What are my options?"

Matt cleared his throat. "I'm not condoning suicide, but I understand your position."

Nathan pulled a flat round object out of his pocket and handed it to her. "You can have this. We call it a P.E.D."

"What's that?" she said.

"Personal explosive device," Nathan said. "It looks like a mirrored coin, but if you turn the red plastic tab on the edge, it'll explode." He put his hand on his chest. "If you put it over your heart and turn the red tab ..."

"I get the picture." She took the shiny disc from him.

"Most federal agents carry one," Nathan said, "at least those who work on cases where they might be captured and tortured."

"Thanks, hopefully I won't need to use it." She glanced up at Jason's worried face, clenched her jaw, and put it in her pocket. She had no intention of being taken twice.

"Kathleen," Matt said, "You can give your safe house key to your family." Looking at Jason, Matt lowered his voice. "I'd like to speak with you when you have time."

"We can talk now." Jason kissed Kathleen at the temple. "I'll be back in a few minutes."

Kathleen stayed with her parents while Nathan spoke about explosives used in other countries and explained how this case was different. She learned more about bombs than she ever wanted to know, but it was interesting. She wondered how Matt knew Nathan wasn't the mole …

≈

A few minutes later, Jason and Matt pushed through the outside exit door down the hall from the McDougals' hospital room. Jason waited while Matt checked the area with an electronic device and glanced around to see if anyone could hear their conversation.

"I appreciate your willingness to help me with this." Matt ran his fingers through his short-cropped hair. "This mole business is a dirty affair but we can't let it or the bombing stop our plans to send a decoy through the trafficking system."

"It's a risk for the decoy, but I don't know any other way."

"If we're lucky, we'll get the traffickers and a traitor." Matt clenched his jaw. "I'm just relieved the McDougals weren't killed."

"They could have been. It shows the person who did it is an amateur."

"Definitely. I've devised a plan with the Aruba police, Interpol and the Mounties to put a female decoy in the Aruba casino. When she's taken, we'll follow her by GPS to the shipping point. When the container ship leaves the harbor, our dive team will go into the water looking for the bodies Kathleen told us about."

"Won't that tip off the folks in the harbor and on the ship?"

"We'll search at night with sonar and rebreathers," Matt said. "No one will see them or hear them. The evidence will stay underwater until the operation is over." He glanced around and lowered his voice. "The Mounties left the slavers' computer system running and Lucy has worked with them to add spyware. That's where you come in."

Jason crossed his arms. "I'll send a refrigerated shipment of bananas from Maracaibo to Vancouver. When it's delivered and opened, the Mounties will arrest them." He squeezed his hand into a fist. "Then I'll make a payment through my foundation and see where it goes and who gets it."

"If we're lucky, we'll catch the traitor." Matt turned to leave. "By the way, I'm assigning an FBI agent to stay with the McDougals in case the traffickers make another attempt."

"Thanks, man." Jason shook his hand. "That means a lot to me."

"I appreciate your help with an internal matter," Matt said. "I'll let you know when the operation starts so you can prepare."

Matt left him alone on the outdoor stairwell where he pondered the risks involved in this operation and wondered how it would affect Kathleen's safety. He couldn't bear to lose her.

≈

On Wednesday, Kathleen wanted to exercise but Jason was too excited to be distracted by their nightly routine. He wouldn't stop grinning. "What's wrong with you?" She almost felt annoyed as they drove home. He just laughed. He was almost too happy. His jubilant behavior almost got on her nerves but who could be annoyed with someone so cheerful? She thought he must be really excited about their trip to the Keys that weekend. If they were going to consummate their relationship, she needed to stop at the pharmacy. How was she going to make a discreet purchase with him tagging along? Good heavens. Maybe Chandra could take her at lunch time.

"We need to pack for the weekend," Jason said. "We're leaving after work on Friday."

"Oh, I thought we were going down on Saturday."

"The full moon is Friday night. We'll miss the party if we leave on Saturday."

"Oh, okay. I don't want to miss that." *Two nights in the same bed.*

"Pack light, we're taking my car."

"You have a car? I've never seen one in the garage."

He nodded. "It's a convertible, so bring your hat and scarf." He disappeared into his bedroom.

Friday after work, he picked her up in his convertible and drove south toward the Florida Keys. The hustle bustle of the city gradually turned into smaller towns and neighborhoods until they reached Homestead, where a large air force base stood along the highway. Fighter jets flew low over the narrow road on their way westward. The loud rushing wind over her scarf and hat buffered her hearing, making it difficult to talk. Soon, the car slowed down, the wind decreased, and she could hear again. She enjoyed the calmer journey until they pulled off the road.

As they drove past farm laborers working in the fields, Jason pulled over on the side of the road. Kathleen watched as he scanned the workers. "Who are you looking for?"

"Carlos' father," he said, squinting.

Stunned, she jerked her head to look at the men picking crops. Most were Hispanic-looking men, some taller, some shorter, all thin. "Do you see him?"

"No." His voice laced with sadness, he pulled onto the highway and drove south at a slower pace, deep in thought.

She decided not to engage him in conversation. She felt bad for Carlos. It obviously bothered Jason that the boy he mentored might end up in the fields with his father. After several minutes, she wondered aloud. "Do you think Carlos will go into the fields next year?"

"Not if I have anything to say about it. Those folks are slaves, just like you were."

She gulped. "Once they get you, they'll never let you go."

"Exactly." He reached for her hand and squeezed it. "You'd be surprised how many slaves work in this country. They're landscapers, cooks, office workers, housekeepers ..." His voice broke when he couldn't continue.

She nodded. "They're invisible among us." Her gut clenched when she thought about Carlos becoming a slave. He was a good kid that needed his father. She would talk to Jason later about what she could do to help. She wondered if they used a computer system to keep track of their indebted slaves.

Soon the agricultural fields turned into the Everglades and the highway became a one-lane road in each direction. The beauty of the water, mangroves, and wading bird life rolled over Kathleen like a sponge bath.

She relaxed and pulled off her hat to let the sun beat down on her face. Her scarf flapped in the breeze as it held her long auburn hair against her head.

The Everglades, a sea of grass, faded away to become the Overseas Highway where small islands were leapfrogged by long bridges that crossed bright turquoise water speckled with fishing boats. Small islets dotted the horizon. Flat bottom boats stopped on sandbars to fish. Jason flipped down the visor to block the bright sunshine as he drove toward it. While Kathleen's sunglasses lessened the glare, she couldn't stop thinking about Carlos and his father.

About an hour later, quenched by the beauty of several Keys and sea-side towns, Jason pulled into the entrance to Cheeca Lodge in Islamorada where he stopped at the guard shack and gave his name. When the guard handed him the room keys and a map of the resort, Jason handed the map to Kathleen and she directed as he drove to their room at the east end of the property.

When Jason parked in front of their bungalow, Kathleen walked around to the beachside, where their deck welcomed her to the Atlantic Ocean. Climbing the spiral staircase to their room, the couple's chaise lounge on the deck called to her. She followed Jason inside and smiled at the whirlpool tub in the corner. A king-size bed in a bamboo frame surrounded by gossamer netting loomed large in her mind. She rubbed her arms, pressing down the goose bumps. As she scanned the beach, a long pier extended into the ocean where kayaks, boats, and paddle boats waited to be rented.

While the ride down to the Keys was one of her favorites, she couldn't wait to explore the property and stretch her legs. After unpacking, they walked through dense landscaping around the spa and came into an opening where several piers crisscrossed over a shallow pool of turquoise water beneath a tall waterfall. She marveled at the unbelievable beauty of this hidden sanctuary. "I wish I had a camera."

"Here." Jason handed her his smartphone. "Use this."

She stood in front of the waterfall, raising the smartphone in the air. "You need to be in the picture too." She grabbed his hand and nudged him into camera shot. He smiled and put his arm around her until she took the picture. She laughed at their picture. "That's perfect." She strolled down a dirt path until it came out onto a golf course. Exploring further, they meandered through the lobby, passed a waterfront restaurant, and walked toward the beach where a wading pool held tropical fish. As they walked down the beach toward their private world, she snuggled her fingers through his.

Exhilarated by her walk along the beach, Kathleen decided to start a new shell collection. After taking a shower in the granite bathroom and dressing for dinner, Jason drove her across the street to Islamorada bayside where they enjoyed a romantic dinner at Pierre's on the second floor outdoor deck. "I'm glad we came down early for the Full Moon Party." Several bonfires built in the sand below glowed bright yellow. A beautiful sunset along the waterfront ended a perfect meal.

"Let's go down to the Green Flash Lounge," Jason said, "we can listen to the Reggae band before the party starts on the beach."

Once downstairs, Kathleen settled back into an Adirondack chair and took the margarita Jason handed her. Before he could sit down next to her, his phone rang.

He checked the screen and stood up. "Be back." He walked to the edge of the Florida Bay as he spoke into the phone. Standing at the water's edge for several minutes, he mostly listened.

She turned her attention to the Brazilian dancers, stilt-walkers, fire-blowers, and balloon artists that wove in and out of the revelers. The balloon man came over to her and made a balloon hat that fit her head perfectly. She gave him a tip and laughed when Jason returned with a smirk on his face.

"We need to talk," he said, standing in front of her.

Not sure what he meant, she hesitated. "Do we need to go home?"

"No, we need to dance." He extended both hands to her.

She stood up, left her sweater in the chair, and took his hands. His odd look turned into a smile. "You have a devilish look, counselor. Care to explain?"

Jason grinned. "That was Matt. The fake shipment we sent from Venezuela passed through the system. The container's on its way to Vancouver."

"Woo-hoo!" She grabbed him around the neck and kissed him.

He laughed at her enthusiastic response. "Let's celebrate. Come on." He led her by the hand to the sand dance area in front of the band.

Remembering what it used to be like to slow dance Kathleen put her arms around his neck and tucked her head next to his jaw. She swayed to the music under the stars held in his strong arms. The brightness of the full moon lit up the sand where small groups gathered to celebrate the once-a-month event. Feeling happy and safe in his arms, they danced several more times until they decided to head back to their bungalow. With the roof down in the car, her hair flew backwards. Without her scarf or hat, she felt free.

When Jason pulled up to their bungalow, he put the top up and held her hand as they climbed steps to their private room. Kathleen felt a bit nervous because everything seemed orchestrated. She felt like she had to perform. Not that she didn't want to. But this was too planned. Nonetheless, her anxiety didn't deter her underpants from soaking up the wetness from her heated arousal.

Once in their room, she brushed her teeth and changed into her pajamas. When she emerged from the bathroom, she looked around for Jason but didn't see him. She assumed he went outside on the deck to watch the stars. When she walked onto the deck, he looked at her clothes and laughed.

"You aren't wearing those to bed are you?"

"Ummm ..." She looked down at them. "Yes."

He struggled to contain his laughter. "You're not serious."

"No one wants to see my ugly skin." Thinking about her scars, she crossed her arms to protect herself.

"You see lash marks and burns. I see beautiful creamy white skin that's soft as a baby's bottom with beautiful pink nipples on plump breasts."

Kathleen blushed and nervously ran her hands down one of the seat cushions.

"Come sit with me." Jason opened his arms, beckoning her.

149

She joined him on the couple's chaise lounge and rested her head against his shoulder. "The stars are so close down here. You can see so many constellations." As she watched the stars, cuddled by the man she was coming to love, she fell asleep in his warm embrace.

The next morning, she awoke in the king-size bed inside Jason's arms. He had laughed at her pajamas with palm trees but he didn't insist she take them off. They'd never slept in the same bed before. He never tried to make love to her, which she was thankful for. It was difficult enough just sleeping in the same bed let alone having sexual relations for the first time. He must have realized she was nervous. Of course she was nervous, but she also had an urgent need for some lovemaking. She hadn't made love to a man in so long. Rape didn't count. There was no climax during rape. Besides, Wilson just took her when he wanted her. While she loosened a few of his teeth, he got his revenge by whipping her afterwards.

When Jason showered and came into the bedroom with a towel wrapped around his waist, her eyes scanned his sculpted muscles. Feeling a heated response to his masculinity, Kathleen considered pursuing him but tossed the thought away. She showered and dressed before they drove to Bob's Bunz for breakfast. When they entered the little shop, she couldn't believe the variety of pastries for sale. Both the sticky buns and cinnamon buns intrigued her. Unable to decide between them, she bought some of each to take home and freeze.

After breakfast, they rented bicycles at the lodge and rode side-by-side down the bike path. When Jason saw a marina, he looked over at her. "One day I'm going to get you on my sailboat." He nodded at the marina. "We could sail it south of Miami and stop at all the hidden places I know."

"That sounds fun." She gripped her handlebars and smiled.

"They have a boat at the resort that takes folks out at sunset, if you feel up to it."

She shook her head. "I'm working on that, but I'm not ready. Maybe next time ..."

"Okay, there's always fishing, golf, tennis, a massage at the spa ..."

"How about laying on the deck and reading a good book?" She chuckled.

"Oh, right. There's a whirlpool tub in our room ..."

She laughed. "Do you ever relax?"

"This is relaxing." He laughed and pulled ahead of her.

She followed him to the end of the Key where they turned around and headed back to Cheeca Lodge. Back at the main lobby, she rode behind him onto the cobblestone foyer where they returned their bicycles. "Let's walk down the beach." She took his hand and meandered toward their room where they climbed the spiral staircase to their deck and went inside.

"Did you bring a swimsuit?" Jason asked.

Kathleen gave him a disbelieving look. "I don't own a swimsuit."

"Okay, that eliminates the pool, the spa and the beach." He walked over to her, took her hands in his and squeezed them before kissing her. While his mouth consumed her lips, his hand moved between them, underneath her top and rubbed her nipple back and forth. When he pulled her cotton top over her head, she stood in front of him in her bra with a look of uncertainly. He pushed the straps down her shoulders, deftly reached behind her, unsnapped her bra and let it slip to the floor. While he nibbled her shoulders and breasts, his hands moved down her butt and pressed her into his erection. He kissed her open lips and pushed her slacks down her thighs until they brushed the floor.

She wobbled and uttered a delighted moan. The heat and agony between her legs drove her mad. Pulling his shirt out of his shorts, she pressed her hands on his chest. Her fingers walked up the steps of his firm muscles.

He pulled off his shirt and tossed it aside giving her room to run her slender fingers over his firm muscles and down his arms.

She squeezed his biceps causing a heated throb to erupt inside her. A shudder went down her spine as he sucked her nipples, one after the other.

He lifted his head and looked at her with half-closed eyes. "Let's get in the tub." He tilted his head at the whirlpool in the corner.

She followed his gaze, saw the candles, soaps, towels, and nodded.

He led her to the tub, unfastened his belt and removed his shorts, tossing them over the back of the desk chair. His erection bounced in the air as he stepped inside the tub and sat down. "Come on sweetheart, stop stalling."

Kathleen stepped out of her slacks and followed him, self-conscious about her body, trying to cover her skin with her hands without success. She poured some bubble bath into the tub, turned it on, and sat down next to him. As the water squirted with powerful force into the tub, the bubbles grew and grew, rising higher and higher. She looked at Jason with concern when the bubbles kept building. "They aren't stopping!" She giggled.

When the bubbles rose above his shoulders, he tossed his head back and laughed. "They're going to overflow." He grabbed some bubbles and put them on her nose.

Laughing, she brushed them away. "All I see is your head." When a blob of bubbles wilted over the side of the tub, her heart rate increased. "Turn it off!" Jason laughed so hard, he couldn't move. She stood up with bubbles clinging to her body, got out of the tub, and reached for the wastebasket by the desk. Scooping suds, she carried them toward the bathroom.

"Where are you going?"

"The shower." She dumped them in the shower stall and returned with suds sliding down her body. Hurrying back with the empty wastebasket, she gathered more suds, and deposited them on top of the others. On her third trip, he still sat in the now-still tub of suds. "You could get out and help, you know."

Still amused, Jason stood up with blobs of suds clinging to his chiseled body. He grabbed an armload of suds and walked gingerly into the bathroom and threw them on top of the pile she already put in there. Working together they lowered the level of suds in the tub to an acceptable point before they stopped to look at each other and burst out laughing.

"We might as well wash ourselves off." He turned on the shower and got in. Standing thigh-deep in suds, she hesitated outside the shower stall waiting for the water to diminish the bubbles. "Come on." He pulled her inside. "I've already seen you, remember?"

"Who could forget?" She remembered her humiliation at the auction.

"I enjoy looking at your body." He reached around her waist. "Now let me see it." He pushed her under the shower, soaking her hair and washing the suds away. She screeched and tried to cover her eyes.

He kissed her lips and pulled her toward him pressing her round soft breasts against his hard chest muscles. She relaxed into him and enjoyed his kisses. He kissed down her neck to her breasts and paused to suck her nipples until they were both hard. Her breathing increased as he teased her with his teeth. When he gently bit down on one nipple she inhaled sharply and moaned, biting her lower lip.

He kissed her belly, stuck his tongue into her belly button, and knelt on the shower floor. When she tilted her head back into the shower to rinse bubbles from her hair, he ran his fingers through her hot, wet folds, searing her tender skin like molten steel. Flashes of pain, fear, anger. Her knees buckled. She gasped in response to her conflicted feelings. He held her up then stood up and pulled her close.

"Okay, babe?" He held her against him, his erection throbbing on her belly.

"Please don't stop." She held his shoulders with desperation. *He isn't Wilson, this isn't rape.*

He tilted her chin up and searched her uncertain eyes. "Are you sure?"

"I want you." She reached down to hold his erection in her hand, squeezing his penis.

He flinched and groaned, clenching his jaw. "Baby, you're killing me." With agony in his voice, he closed his eyes then opened them part way as he tilted his head back into the shower.

She rubbed his stiff penis then caressed his tight balls while squeezing his pulsing bicep.

He hissed and closed his eyes, seeming to count to himself. When he opened his eyes, he grabbed her around the waist and pushed her back against the shower wall until the water ran down his back. He kissed her lips, bit her neck, and pressed his erection closer to her throbbing vagina. He hesitated and looked into her eyes.

"Please, honey." Kathleen closed her eyes with a gasp when he pushed himself into her. Touching the cold marble wall behind her, sensations of cold marble against hot, aching need made her head spin.

Jason thrust into her, slowly at first then more insistent as his breathing increased.

She moaned and adored the feeling of him pushing into her, the ache grew to a hot desire that only he could fill.

He thrust harder, rapidly, until he came inside her for what seemed like several minutes. Satisfied, he slumped against the wall, one arm supporting him, and the other squeezing her butt.

She didn't reach orgasm but she was relieved to have overcome a major hurdle on her way to normalcy. From now on, she wouldn't fear intercourse and hoped to someday enjoy it.

His tender kisses searched her mouth while he pressed her into his softening erection.

She wanted more of him and felt empty when he pulled out of her. Anticipating more lovemaking later, she looked forward to another session with her new man.

After they dried off and dressed, Jason convinced Kathleen to buy a pair of shorts and a skimpy top at the resort boutique. He didn't seem to mind her scars, even though they still bothered her. When they returned from the shop, she put on her shorts and halter top and laid back on the couples lounge on the deck to soak up the warm rays of the sun. She felt free and brazen in a way but reveled in the radiant heat against her naked skin. Oh how she missed the warmth of Florida sunshine. Relaxed to the point of almost snoozing, Jason startled her when he came out on the deck carrying a bottle of suntan lotion.

He sat down next to her. "Sit up, babe. Let me put this on you."

She hesitated while he squirted it into his palm. Biting her bottom lip, she sat up. When he rubbed the cream all over her body with his strong hands, she felt pampered and cared for.

He finished applying the lotion and snapped the top shut. "I'm hungry. Let's order room service."

"Good idea. I'd rather not shower again, although it was delightful." She flashed him a devilish look.

He took off his shirt before ordering sandwiches then handed her a drink from the mini refrigerator before joining her on the lounge.

She relaxed on the deck for hours reading a good book, and watching fishing boats return from their morning excursions. Large brown pelicans dove into the water catching fish. Jason took a walk when he got bored with sunning. She knew he was doing this for her. *He's not used to idle pursuits.*

That night, they were served dinner on the beach in front of the resort's main building. Kathleen couldn't believe the resort staff put the table right in the sand under a large canopy. Potted palms blocked the corner poles and added freshness to the tropical setting. While they enjoyed their last bites of dinner, the sun drew lower in the sky.

"Let's watch the sunset from the pier." Jason nodded in that direction.

She looked at the long pier jutting into the Atlantic Ocean. Several folks had the same idea and were mingling around the lights all the way to the end. A chill ran down her spine.

He squeezed her hand and gave her a concerned look. "What about it?"

She bit her lip. "I'll try."

"We'll take our time." After signing the bill for dinner, he squeezed her hand and led her toward the pier.

As she got closer, her heart thumped against her chest and her feet dragged. By the time she stepped up on the boards, she was almost hyperventilating.

Jason turned and hugged her. "It's okay, baby. Nothing's going to happen to you." He stepped backwards onto the wood decking of the pier and pulled her along with him.

She held his hands firmly. He waited for her to calm before he put his arm around her waist. He held her close to him and walked one step at a time down the pier. Many visitors took photos of the sunset and toasted it with their drinks. Lovers kissed and hugged. She envied them, then looked up at Jason and realized how lucky she was to have a man who seemed to care for her despite all her problems. She smiled when he looked down at her.

He held her close as the sun flashed bright green before it disappeared from sight. He posed with her in front of the sunset and took their picture as the sky behind them streaked shades of pink, red, and orange across a bright blue background. He showed her the photo. "Congratulations, baby." He kissed her lips. "You amaze me. Every week you accomplish something new."

She felt proud of herself and smiled. With her arm around his back she snuggled close to him as they watched the sky darken and the pier lights brighten before heading back to their bungalow.

Jason leaned down to kiss her, caressing her face with his thumb. "You're not wearing pajamas to bed tonight."

She flinched but nodded. Her anticipation grew as they neared their bungalow. Her throbbing clit eagerly awaited their encounter. Once upstairs, he slowly undressed her and wrapped her in one of the luxurious resort robes from the bathroom. She shook briefly but felt determined to continue.

He put his arms around her and held her for several minutes. Pushing aside her auburn hair, he buzzed across her warm lips and moved her robe aside but left it on her. He squeezed her breast and rubbed her nipple until it hardened against his probing fingers. Kissing her skin from her breast downward, he soon knelt between her legs.

When his tongue gently touched her engorged clit, rubbed it on each side, and flicked over the top, she tossed her head back and inhaled. Her breasts swelled with anticipation. He must know she was hot and wet, why was he teasing her? The agony of his caresses drove her crazy. He ran his fingers through her wetness until she thought her head might explode. As her hips bucked against him, an orgasm seemed close, but it went away as fast as it appeared. She breathed rapidly, squeezed his shoulders with both hands and felt dizzy. Her eyes went black. Her mind lost all thought.

When she regained consciousness, Jason held a wet washcloth and dabbed her face, tenderly touching her forehead, cheeks, neck and chest. Sensations of cold against hot brought her back to reality. She batted her eyelashes. "What's wrong with me?" she whimpered as a tear ran down her cheek.

Brushing it away, he murmured. "Nothing, sweetheart, it takes time." He pressed his lips to hers and she eagerly moved hers in a sensuous dance. When he moved her off his lap and laid her on the bed, disappointment consumed her. After undressing, he got in bed next to her and put his arms around her.

She laid her head on his chest and rubbed his hair mindlessly with her fingers. She felt incompetent and useless. Next week, Dr. Jennifer would need to help her with this.

The next morning, Kathleen and Jason shared coffee on the deck and watched the sun rise over the ocean when her cell phone rang. "Hello?"

"He called!" Tara yelled into the phone.

"Who ..." Kathleen thought she meant Charles.

"The manager of the fashion show ..." Tara said. "He wants me to audition for a commercial, can you believe that?"

Kathleen laughed then remembered the sleazy guy that watched Tara like a cat stalking its prey. "Congratulations!" She glanced at a curious Jason. "When is it?"

"A couple weeks," Tara said. "He has to make all the arrangements."

"That's great. I can't wait to hear all about it. How about we get together this week?"

"Okay," Tara said. "I'll call you after you get home."

"Take care." Kathleen hung up the phone.

She and Jason decided to play a quick nine holes of golf before going home. When he hit another shot into the trees, the look on his face made her laugh.

"Do you want to search for another ball?" He looked askance at her.

She smiled and looked down at the score card. "My suggestion is we cut our losses and agree never to play this game again."

He laughed and hugged her. "Ready to head home?"

157

"I'm not a defeatist but I'll admit to being defeated by this game." She snickered and dropped her club in the golf bag.

"We could try tennis."

"I'd rather go home. We have a lot to do this week."

She enjoyed the slow ride home. A balmy breeze pushed her scarf back from her face. She wondered what the week would bring. Tara's audition, her parents living at the safe house, the container shipment to Vancouver, a Board of Directors meeting in Jason's condo, not to mention her sleeping arrangements at home. She glanced over at him as he drove over the long bridges that crossed clear turquoise waters.

"Did you have fun?" Jason reached for her hand.

"It was wonderful." Kathleen smiled and grasped his offered hand. He probably wouldn't like it, but she planned to sleep in her own bedroom. She enjoyed the privacy and the comfort her own space provided. *I hope he understands ….*

Chapter 11

Kathleen enjoyed her weekend getaway to the Keys and felt relaxed and rejuvenated for a couple days until her nightly routine took a shocking turn. After work on Tuesday, she decided to run on a treadmill in the fitness center. As usual, Jason ran next to her for twenty minutes before heading to the weightlifting area.

With her eyes closed, she visualized standing on his sailboat, riding the waves, when someone got on the treadmill next to her. While she concentrated on the sailboat lurching up and down, the bow cresting over wave after wave, a strange male voice interrupted her concentration.

"McDougal?"

Startled, she opened her eyes and spun her head to face the man on the treadmill next to her. "Who are you?"

Stephens grabbed her elbow. "Wilson says hello." His lips curled into a menacing snarl while he squeezed her elbow until it ached.

She shrieked. "Get away from me!" Wrenching her elbow from his grip, she got off the treadmill and scanned the weightlifting area for Jason. Her exercise suit stretched across her chest with every labored breath as she glared at the stranger. "Wilson's in jail."

"Not for long. He'll get out on bail ... and when he does ... you'd better watch out!" His cheek twitched when he clenched his teeth.

"Get out of my life!" She clenched her fists and everyone in the fitness center stopped what they were doing. An eerie silence filled the room, as Jason realized what was happening and raced towards them.

"Tell your boyfriend to back off." He pointed a finger in her face. "Or you'll both be dead!" He ran out the door just as Jason approached.

"What'd he say?"

159

"Wilson knows where I am." Panic filled her gut. "He's coming for both of us."

He put his arm around her back. "Go upstairs and lock yourself in your room. I'll go after this guy."

Charles watched the scene unfold and got off a stationary bike to come to her aid when Jason ran out the door. "Who was that guy?"

"He said the man from Vancouver is coming to kill us." She held her breath and wrung her hands, watching the door as if Jason would come back through it any minute.

Charles put his arm around her. "I'll go upstairs with you."

"I have to get out of here." She glanced around the fitness center. "How'd they find me?" The other residents slowly returned to their exercises. Was there another traitor?

Inside the condo, Kathleen paced the living room with her arms crossed in front of her while Charles stood nearby providing comfort by his presence. Finally, she recognized Jason's footsteps as he entered the condo.

"Stephens isn't a resident," Jason said, walking into the living room. "I went to his condo and it's been empty for weeks. Julio says he had a guest pass to get into the fitness center."

"How'd he get that?" Charles said.

"He's checking. We need to be extra careful from now on," Jason said.

Kathleen went into his arms and squeezed him hard. She reconsidered sleeping alone. His bed suddenly seemed much safer than hers. When he nuzzled her ear, Charles cleared his throat.

"I'll see you two tomorrow," Charles said and walked toward the front door.

"Thanks, man," Jason said.

Kathleen felt insecure. "Can I sleep with you tonight?"

"Of course." He kissed her temple and rubbed her back.

Immediately, she felt safer. Held in his arms all night, she would be able to sleep. Maybe her nightmares would stay away for a change. How did they discover where she lived? Now Wilson would know too. When would Wilson get bail? How did Stephens know he would get bail before there was even a hearing? Was there another mole? Who could she trust? She had so many questions but no easy answers. Suddenly, she grew suspicious of everyone around her.

≈

The next day, Jason waited in his office for a return call from Matt. How did Stephens know Wilson would get bail? The only way he could know that would be if the judge had been bribed. When his assistant, Mrs. Bailey, entered his office he noted her handful of papers.

"Mr. Montgomery," she set the papers in his mailbox, "these are the papers we discussed." The gray-haired lady wearing a tailored suit turned away and walked toward the door.

"Thank you, ma'am," Jason said in his light southern accent. He removed the stack from his inbox and proceeded to review them when his phone rang.

Mrs. Bailey returned to his desk and picked up his phone. "Schumacher Montgomery, May I help you?" She handed the phone to him. "It's Matt calling you back."

"Hey, Matt, what's happening?"

"I spoke with the Mounties in the Vancouver office," Matt said. "There is a bail hearing scheduled for Wilson this week."

"How'd that happen?" Jason gritted his teeth.

"Must have been a bribe," Matt said. "When he was first arrested, they set bail at two million dollars. There's no way he came up with that kind of money."

"He only has to pay ten percent. The traffickers could easily pay that to get him out."

"I've asked the Mounties to fax me the evidentiary paperwork from the hearing so we can see what facts have been discovered. I'll fax it to you as soon as I get it," Matt said. "Let me know if Kathleen remembers anything that will help us tighten the noose on these jokers."

"Will do. Talk later." Jason hung up the phone and resumed reading the documents Mrs. Bailey had brought him when his smartphone buzzed. A text message from Matt read: "Fax from Mounties being sent now." He finished reading the documents and signed the bottom as the legal representative and took them back to Mrs. Bailey when he met her coming into his office.

"Here's a fax from Matt." She handed him the stapled papers.

"And here are the papers for our client, they look fine."

"Do you want me to set up a meeting to discuss them or should I send the documents to their office?"

"Send them by messenger today with a note to call me after they've read them." Jason turned toward his desk, glancing at the fax, as Mrs. Bailey left. Reading the summary on the front, he stopped dead in his tracks. He read and re-read and couldn't believe what he saw. His biggest client, Seaside Shipping, had been named as an accomplice in slave trafficking in Vancouver. Their shipping container was the one sent from Venezuela to Vancouver with the captives. He clenched his fists, squishing the fax. Tension rose up his arms into his chest and he bellowed an anguished yell that echoed off his office walls.

Mrs. Bailey and Charles ran into his office and stared at him in disbelief. "What on earth?" Charles said.

"Are you alright, Mr. Montgomery?" Mrs. Bailey blanched as she stood in his doorway.

Jason threw the fax on his desk and turned to look at Charles. "You'd better come in and close the door." He moved to the windows, his mind reeling with possible scenarios as he gazed over the city.

"Mrs. Bailey," Charles said, "would you please close the door on your way out?"

"Yes, Mr. Schumacher."

Jason's mind spun, analyzing what this evidence might mean. There was a long silence while Charles waited for an explanation. Crossing his arms, Jason turned toward his friend. "It's been fun man. But you might want to get a new business partner."

"What the …" Charles said. "I'm the one who talked you into starting our business. I have a say in this, don't you think?" He put his hands on his hips.

"I have a conflict of interest with one of our clients."

"If you have a conflict, I have a conflict."

"I can't represent our biggest client anymore. They've been implicated in slave trafficking."

"What?" Charles moved closer, shocked by what he heard. "How could they be involved without us knowing about it?"

"How long has this been going on?" Jason glared at his best friend.

Charles looked stunned. "Are you saying my father knew about this?"

"I don't know. Did he?"

"We didn't know." Charles became defensive, crossing his arms and widening his stance.

"I need to know the truth. I couldn't sleep at night if I found out we benefited from slavery. That's dirty money, man," Jason said, watching Charles' reaction.

"My father would never do anything like that. He was an honorable man." Charles stepped near and lowered his voice. "I laugh at and tolerate the bad lawyer jokes but I have no intention of ever becoming a sleazy lawyer. We've worked too hard to build our reputation to have it ruined. If we lose our biggest client and have to start over, then so be it. Our honor and integrity are more important than a fancy office and condos downtown."

Jason liked what he heard and put his hand on Charles's shoulder. "Where are the records from your father's law firm?"

"In a storage warehouse. Why?"

"I need to see them. There must be a clue about what's been happening."

Charles stepped to Jason's desk phone and pressed the buzzer. Mrs. Bailey answered. "Mrs. Bailey, order the records from my father's archives to be delivered here right away."

"All of them?"

"All of them," Jason said.

Efficient Mrs. Bailey had the records delivered to his office that afternoon. Jason began combing through the records and asked one of his young legal aides to assist him. Digging into the papers, he lost track of time and later realized he needed to pick up Kathleen from work. It was too late to ask Sam.

He spent the day reviewing correspondence between the elder Charles Schumacher II, Esq., and the Seaside Shipping Company. Naturally, everything he read pertained to legal issues Charles' father handled for the container shipper. Would he have to subpoena his own clients' records? How would this change his relationship with Charles? *If I discover his father knew, what will I do?* Jason agonized over some possible answers to his questions while he drove to Kathleen's workplace, unaware of his mounting foul mood.

≈

Meanwhile Kathleen grew worried when Jason didn't show up on time to pick her up from work. Her mind raced with reasons for the delay, increasing her anxiety. Did he have a flat tire? Was he tied up at work? Did his truck blow up too? When she saw his Cadillac Escalade enter the parking lot, she felt relieved. Considering her parents' car had exploded and now she was being stalked by the man in the fitness club, she didn't know what to expect next. She trotted to the passenger door and hopped inside.

"Sorry I'm late." Jason leaned over to kiss her when she got in. He didn't flash his customary warm smile.

She kissed his unresponsive lips and put on her seatbelt. "That's okay, but I was worried."

"I called your cell phone. Where is it?"

"I left it home. No one calls me."

"I call you." He sounded annoyed. "You need to carry it with you every day from now on."

"Yes, sir." She saluted him, but he missed the sarcasm in her voice. He seemed preoccupied. "I was thinking about making stuffed meatballs for the Board of Directors meeting, or would you rather have crabcakes."

He drove intently, his eyes focused in the distance.

"Did you hear me, hun?"

"Uh huh, whatever ..." His eyes remained focused on the road.

Realizing a conversation would be fruitless, she looked out the window until they got home a few minutes later. She didn't have time to exercise. She wanted to make food for the foundation meeting tomorrow. Jason was hosting it and she wanted to do something special for them. This would be the first time they met her and her first opportunity to thank them.

An hour later, she finished rolling the last stuffed meatball in her palms and placed it on a cookie sheet to freeze and bake the next day. Jason stood across from her at the center island, mindlessly tearing lettuce apart for a salad. He still looked preoccupied when she washed her hands in the sink and dried them on a kitchen towel. Hanging the towel on its hook, she wondered why he was so distracted. She felt ignored and became annoyed. "Your attention span is about as long as a gnat's brain."

He glared at her then threw down the towel that had been draped over his shoulder. "I had a perfectly good sex life before you came along."

"Wow." Stunned, she raised her hands and backed out of the kitchen toward her bedroom. While she sat on the side of the bed, trying to process what he said, how he felt, how she felt, she saw him standing in her doorway.

"Sorry, babe. That didn't come out right."

"It's okay." A tear streaked down her cheek while her hands covered the place in her belly where she felt wounded.

"I'm going for a run." He sounded solemn and left her alone.

Kathleen closed her eyes and let the tears flow over her cheeks. A few minutes later, she heard the front door open and close and knew he left. She tried to breathe, tried to understand his position. Her mind wasn't clear when the doorbell rang. Thinking he forgot his keys, she opened the front door to see Charles. "Oh, I thought you were Jason. He went for a run along the Riverwalk, you might still catch him."

Charles squinted and assessed her as she brushed a tear away. "What's wrong kitten? And don't say 'nothing.'"

She hesitated, not knowing what to say without getting too personal.

"Have you given up?" Charles said.

Surprised, she looked at him and sniffed. "No, but Jason has."

"Never ... he's just frustrated."

"Why don't you bring him one of your lady friends?"

"He knows where to get a woman if he wants one. Besides, he's committed to you. He doesn't want anyone else." He stepped inside and closed the door.

She stepped backward, giving his large frame room to stand in the foyer.

Charles raised her chin. "I'd be glad to bring you a few toys to try."

She almost smiled at the mental picture that flashed through her mind. "Stimulation isn't the problem. It's mental."

"Oh. Can Dr. Powell help?"

"I won't see her until Friday. This is getting unbearable." Kathleen's throat tightened in an attempt to quash her anguished desire.

"Recovery takes a lot of time, but mostly patience. It's only been two months and look how far you've come."

"I haven't come, that's the problem." She smirked at his raised eyebrows.

Charles considered her with caring pale blue eyes, then cleared his throat. "I see. Well ..." He clutched her shoulders. "If Jason wasn't like a brother to me ... I'd enjoy helping you overcome that problem." He smiled like the charmer she thought him to be.

She tensed and hoped he wouldn't try to kiss her. When he let her go and backed away, she felt relieved.

"Tell Jason to call me," he said and left.

Once she gathered her senses, Kathleen prepared more food for the Impact Ten meeting. Jason wanted to have it catered but she offered to make homemade food for those who paid to buy her freedom. She needed to thank them but wasn't sure she could handle all the men together in the living room. Determined to try, she had been working on entering rooms full of men in her mind. Her thoughts turned to only one man who she desperately wanted to have in her life. Was he growing impatient with her slow progress?

166

≈

The next morning, as Jason drove Kathleen to work, he glanced over to see her glum expression. She wasn't happy and neither was he. She was jerking him around. He told her he didn't like that and now it was happening. Rather than moving in and out of his condo, she was moving in and out of his bed. The previous night she had slept in her own bed again. His frustration with their sleeping arrangements festered. Initially, he was happy just to have her living in his home. But things had changed. Their relationship had grown. It had progressed to the next stage, but it stood on shaky ground.

Jason reached for her hand and squeezed it. "I'm sorry about blowing up at you last night."

She glanced at him with a subdued aura and seemed a bit nervous.

Hell, I can't dump my frustrations on this sweet, precious lady.

"It's okay," she said. "I know you must be very frustrated with my slow recovery." Her hopeful look encouraged him.

"I knew your recovery would take time, I just wasn't prepared for the uncertainty and its unpredictable nature."

"That makes two of us."

"We'll have lots of ups and downs, babe."

"As long as you're with me, everything will be okay."

"You can count on me. We're in this together." He relished the loving smile she gave him and leaned over to kiss her goodbye when he pulled up to the curb.

As Kathleen scurried up the sidewalk into work, he drove away. Anxiety about his love life combined with agitation about his client's involvement in slave trafficking felt almost unbearable. He went to work faced with the prospect of finding something that would bring down the traffickers without losing his best friend and business partner in the process.

During the day, Jason toiled for long hours until his leg fell asleep. All he could do was pace before resuming his search. He cross-referenced shipping manifest data with the dates of all the kidnappings from Aruba, supplied by his legal aide. His eyes dried and grew weary from hours of reading. Shipping codes, freight rates, billing information blurred when he rubbed his eyes in an effort to stay awake. Where was the list of billing names and addresses? Who got paid for the shipments that matched the Aruba kidnappings?

After hours of scanning documents, Charles walked past his office on his way back from his assistant's office. He stopped at Jason's door. "Any luck?"

"This reminds me of law school," Jason chuckled. "Not much so far, but it looks like all the shipments around the time of the Aruba kidnappings included bananas, which matches what Kathleen said. Bananas require a reefer container."

Charles stepped into his office. "That means they could legitimately ship produce requiring a higher temperature with humidity and ventilation controls and at the same time, slip in some human beings."

"I think so. Naturally, the manifest doesn't say human beings, but it does say bananas. What we need to find is something that shows a link between shipping bananas and the kidnappings in Aruba when the delivery point is Vancouver."

Charles sat down next to him among the boxes. "Where do you want me to start?"

Jason smiled. Charles had a lot to lose in this process and he admired him for wanting to learn the truth about his father. "I'm going backwards in time; you can start looking in here." He opened another box. "Only look at records for banana shipments around these dates." He handed him the dates of former Aruban kidnappings.

Charles worked alongside his partner searching through manifests for shipments. When he finished one box, he sat back and rubbed his lower back. "You're right, this is like law school." He laughed and pointed to the stack of papers he pulled from the box. "Somebody in Canada sure eats a lot of bananas."

Jason stopped pulling records from his box. "When we're done with these, let's look through each pile and see if we can come up with something similar about all the banana shipments to Vancouver."

"Okay." Charles sat back against a leather couch.

Jason stood up, put his hands on his hips and groaned as he stretched backwards. He poured a glass of water from the pitcher on his sideboard, drank half of it, and returned to the leather chair in front of his desk. He extended his legs in front of him and flipped through the pages for each shipment. He made a few notes about each one and when he finished, he traded Charles for his. Working together they finished within a couple hours.

When Jason sat back and reviewed his notes, he looked for similarities and oddities. "Huh." He flipped to the next page and recognized an odd pattern. "Do any of your shipments have the shipping code 666?"

Charles checked his paperwork. "There are two codes for all banana shipments: 215 and 666." His hand dropped to his lap when he looked at Jason.

"Someone has an evil sense of humor." Jason thought the shipping code wasn't funny but it certainly said a lot about the shipper and the receiver. "Separate all the shipments that have code 666." He split the shipments into two piles and went to his office door. "Mrs. Bailey, would you come in here please?"

His short, gray-haired assistant entered the office and looked at the stacks of paper scattered around the office. "Yes, sir?"

"When our firm combined with the late Mr. Schumacher's company, did we computerize the Bills of Lading from our new clients?"

"Yes, sir," Mrs. Bailey said. "Remember, we hired a summer intern to enter all the data into a computer database because we had to manage reports for all the shippers."

"Excellent." Jason bent down and picked up the pile of banana shipments. "Take these shipments and print out a detailed report about each one." He extended the documents toward her.

"Let me get a box." When she returned, she held the box while he loaded it. "This might take a while."

"Take as long as you need to do it right," Jason said, "but do this before anything else. We have a board meeting tonight, so take your time."

"Yes, sir." She hurried toward her office.

Pleased about his day's work, Jason sensed he was getting closer to an answer. But the more he learned, the less he knew about the role of Charles' father. He didn't want to think the worst of him. Did he know or didn't he? Had he discovered something? Did he confront those responsible? Had he been killed? Jason didn't even want to mention that possibility to Charles.

I need to investigate deeper to learn the answers, but I might never know.

That evening when his condo doorbell rang, Jason opened it to see Dr. Gregory Chase. "Doctor G, thanks for coming early."

"Not a problem." Dr. Chase stepped inside. "You had questions about Kathleen?"

"I know you can't talk about a patient, but if you could talk to me about rape victims in general, that would be helpful."

"Ah, having some issues?"

"This is very delicate, but basically, she's having sexual dysfunction."

"That's normal," Dr. Chase said. "Most rape victims experience problems in that area."

"She doesn't seem to respond to stimulation," Jason said.

"The issue isn't stimulation. Rape victims experience hyper-arousal and exaggerated responses to stimuli. They're over-stimulated physically."

"Do you have any suggestions?"

"The mind is the greatest sex organ in the body. When you've won the mind, the body will follow." Dr. Chase sat on the living room sofa, where Jason led him. "Women are very complex creatures when it comes to sex. While men want to quickly get to the physical sex act, women want to be romanced, pursued, and aroused mentally. A woman's feelings toward a particular male who wants her is what brings her to climax."

"I see. I never realized that." If romance is what she needed, he would

170

make his best effort. Perhaps sailing to his favorite secluded cove, eating a picnic on the beach would fill the doctor's prescription. But first, he had to get her on the sailboat.

A few minutes later, the rest of the board members arrived for their monthly meeting. Jason had told Kathleen a few days ago that he wanted her to meet them. Her green eyes widened but she agreed. He knew she was nervous, but she needed to thank them.

The men gathered on the leather sofas in his living room as Jason glanced down at the agenda. "The first order of business is the rescue of Connie's husband, Hernando Rivera. Their son, Carlos, is being recruited by slave traffickers to work in the fields when he turns sixteen next year. We've got to rescue Hernando before that happens."

"What if we pay off his debt to the traffickers?" Edward said.

"They'll keep our money and Hernando," Jason said. "His debt to them will never be paid. If we pay for their costs for bringing Carlos here for medical treatment, they'd add up all the other costs for food, housing, clothes, and Hernando would never be free."

"These people are insidious," David said.

"That's not the half of it," Marcus said. "You weren't here when Connie reported them to the FBI. When they found out, they killed her, cut off her hand and foot and mailed them to Jason."

Jason's gut clenched at the memory. He never knew what happened to her body but he recognized her hand by the rings on her fingers. He knew she was dead. His guilt at convincing her to call the FBI still raged inside him. This time it wouldn't happen. They weren't going to get Kathleen. He shook his head to clear away some of his guilt and continued the meeting.

"Traffickers move the workers every day," Jason said. "I drove past them on the way to the Keys last weekend and Hernando wasn't among them. When the FBI finds him near the roadway, we have to move quickly."

Kevin leaned forward. "I'll put together a plan that can be implemented on a minute's notice. I'll email it to the Board for approval."

"The McDougals are in the FBI safe house after their car exploded,"

Jason said. "When we pick up Hernando, we won't have access to the house."

"We need our own safe house," Doug said. "If we're going to rescue all these folks, we need to have a place that's safe, protected, and provides services they need."

"We need to look for a good piece of real estate," William said. "We should be able to get a good deal for a large house with lots of rooms and baths and a big kitchen for folks to share. Like a group home concept."

"I make a motion," Steven said, "that we search the real estate listings for suitable homes to be used as a safe house. We could call it SafePlace."

"Seconded," Charles said.

"All in favor?" As Chairman of the Board, Jason directed the voting. The men all responded, "Aye."

"All opposed?" No one spoke. "Seeing no opposition, the motion passes unanimously." Jason glanced down at the agenda and decided this would be a good time for Kathleen to meet the Impact Ten board members. He knew she would stay in her bedroom until she got up enough nerve to come out.

While the men discussed the concept of SafePlace and what services they could offer, he heard Kathleen in the kitchen. She removed some things from the refrigerator and the cabinets. When she rattled some glasses, Charles looked at Jason and smiled.

"There's your church mouse," Charles said and chuckled.

Jason smiled and glanced toward the kitchen. She wasn't going to show her face unless he forced her. "Kathleen, would you come here please?" Silence filled the room. Finally, small footsteps made a tapping sound down the hallway toward them.

Halfway, she stopped dead in her tracks, rubbed her arms, and gave Jason a pleading look. Her long slender legs concealed by white tights disappeared under a flowery sundress. She looked so cute it distracted him for a minute.

He couldn't resist helping her. Putting down his papers, he went to her and gently squeezed her arms. "It's okay, sweetheart, no one here wants to hurt you."

Kathleen nodded and moved slowly forward when he stepped aside and walked with her toward the sofas. When the men stood up to meet her, she flinched but stood her ground.

"Gentlemen, this lovely lady is Kathleen McDougal." The board members said hello but stayed where they were. Jason put his arm around her and led her forward. "I'm going to introduce you to each person. We'll walk to the left in a circle until we get back to Charles."

She nodded and shook briefly, then stepped to her left.

"This is Dr. Gregory Chase," Jason said. "We call him Dr. G because we're too lazy to say his whole name."

She shook his hand. "Thank you for introducing me to Dr. Jennifer, she's wonderful."

"You're very welcome." Dr. Chase smiled and released her hand.

"Next is Doug. He's an engineer, but we don't hold that against him," Jason said and stepped around the circle. "This is Marcus. He's an architect. And Edward is a banker who's kind enough to serve as our Treasurer. This is William, the Vice President of West Miami Industries. Next is Steven, a professor at Miami."

"Go 'canes," Kathleen said, making her hands into the sign of a U.

Steven smiled and returned the gesture. "Welcome home."

"This is David, he's CEO of South Florida Chemicals," Jason said, taking another step. "And last but not least, Kevin, our Executive Director."

"Welcome home, Kathleen," Kevin said, shaking her hand.

When she stepped in front of Charles at the end of the circle, she felt relieved and grinned.

"You know Master Charles," Jason said, smiling.

"Hello kitten." Charles bent down to hug her. "See ... that wasn't so bad."

Feeling relieved, she faced the gathering and smiled. "Thank you for buying my freedom. I'll always be grateful for what you've done for me." She put her arm around Jason and smiled at him. "Next time we meet, I hope to be able to do it all by myself."

"It takes time," Dr. Chase said.

"... and lots of patience," Jason and Charles said at the same time.

"If you'd like to take a break now," Jason said to the Board members, "Kathleen's made some food."

Everyone sounded happy about that prospect and moved into the kitchen. While the men served themselves, Jason noticed Kathleen had gracefully slipped away to her bedroom. The board members stood in the kitchen eating when the doorbell rang. Jason opened it to see Matt.

"I knew your meeting was tonight," Matt said. "I thought I'd stop by to give you some news."

"Come in." Jason led him to the kitchen. "Grab some food." He gestured with his arm.

"Thanks, but I can't stay," Matt said. "I thought you'd want to know, Wilson got bail."

Jason felt like someone punched him in the stomach. "That's not possible. Who would let him out on bail? He's a flight risk."

"Trafficking is big business," Matt said. "Bribe the judge and you're free. They want to get back to business and they can't do that as long as someone is working hard to stop them." He paused while everyone in the room uttered comments of dismay. "Kathleen is a target. She's a risk they can't afford."

Jason took a deep breath. "I know."

"I don't want to see her end up like Connie," Matt said. "Try to convince her to change her name, will you?"

"Right ..." Jason knew that was a non-starter. It wasn't even worth mentioning. He couldn't bear the thought of her ending up like Connie. He'd never be able to live with himself. Getting over Connie was hard enough. He could never get over the death of someone he was coming to love.

Jason followed Matt to the front door and wished him well. When the board members finished eating, they returned to the living room to continue their meeting. "Next up for discussion is the status of the FBI investigation. I sent you an email summarizing what had been done so far. The shipping container with the Aruban police decoy inside is on its way to Vancouver. After the container ship left Maracaibo, the FBI dive team went into the water around midnight and discovered many skeletons weighed down by cinderblocks."

"God rest their souls," Edward said. "Did they arrest the bastards?"

"Not until the entire investigation is finished," Jason said. "We want to get the traffickers in Vancouver this time."

"Damn right," Marcus said. "But it's sure hard to be patient for justice."

"Won't the decoy suffocate?" Doug said.

"She's in a refrigerated container, called a reefer," Jason said. "The temperature was set for a banana shipment which requires higher temperatures. The container was sealed in Venezuela with a high-security seal that can only be unlocked by Customs officials and the shipment importer."

"She'll smell like a banana by the time she gets to Vancouver," William said.

Jason smiled. "Kathleen still can't stand the smell of bananas." He waited for the chuckling to subside before continuing. "We worked with the FBI to send a shipment with the decoy. Today, Charles and I discovered the two shipping codes used for shipping bananas from Maracaibo to Vancouver. Tomorrow or Monday, I hope to know the name of the person or company that received all the banana shipments."

"If the judge in Vancouver takes bribes," Kevin said, "maybe we should bribe him to arrest the bad guys." He gave Jason a farcical grin. The men laughed and grumbled about corrupt officials.

"When the container arrives in Vancouver next week," Jason said, "the leaders will be exposed and arrested on the spot."

"Someone should arrest the judge," Steven said.

"The Mounties tell us they'll request a new judge if the same one is assigned to this case," Jason said.

"Speaking of traitors," Edward said, "what's the latest on the mole at the FBI?"

"We hoped the fake shipment would flush him out," Jason said, "but no luck so far. The fact that the shipment went through with the decoy proves that the human trafficking task force is the source of the mole."

"Let the entire scenario play itself out," Charles said. "The game isn't over yet, we've got more to uncover."

Jason wondered if Charles was talking about his father or being philosophical, like he got sometimes when he broke up with a particularly intriguing lady. "That's all I've got for tonight, any other business?" He scanned the faces of the Impact Ten team. No one said anything, some shook their heads. "In that case, this meeting is adjourned."

After the meeting, the board members moved toward the front door. Jason followed Charles out of the living room. "Are you using the sailboat this weekend?"

"No, I'm spending time with Mom and Pete." Charles rolled his eyes.

Jason sensed the negative tone in Charles' voice about his mother's new man, but put that aside for later. "Good, then I'll be using it."

"Planning something fun?"

"I'm going to take Kathleen out, if I can get her onboard."

"Good luck with that. Let me know if I can help."

After seeing all the men out, Jason cleaned up the kitchen and went to say goodnight to Kathleen. He knocked on her closed door and heard movement inside.

She opened the door wearing her Gator pajamas and smiled. "Meeting over?"

"For this month. Everyone enjoyed the meatballs."

"I'm glad. Are we getting up at the same time?"

"6 a.m." He reached for her and she quickly came into his arms. Kissing her tenderly, he wanted to continue but decided he needed to think about how to seduce her. He pulled away and stroked her shiny auburn hair. "You did really well meeting the board members."

"Thanks for helping me. They were very nice."

"Considering how well you did, I'd like to take you out on the sailboat on Saturday." She twitched. "Are you up for two challenges in one week?"

"I've been working on it. I'm willing to try."

"Good." He kissed her for several minutes until he felt the beginnings of an erection. Letting her go, he sensed she was feeling subdued. Maybe she was tired. "Good night, sweetheart."

That night, he thought about what Dr. Chase told him and how he might overcome her hyper-arousal problem. He concluded there were very subtle differences between having sex and making love. He had never been the flowers and candy type, but for Kathleen's sake and for his, he would make an effort. His seduction of her would begin tomorrow.

~

The next day, Kathleen sat at her desk working on her latest project. This time it was more complex. She enjoyed the challenge to her considerable skills when someone entered her office. She looked up to see a stranger holding a vase of red roses.

"Miss McDougal?"

"Yes."

"These are for you."

She smiled broadly as she accepted them from the delivery man. Smelling their intoxicating scent, she rubbed their exquisite petals and noticed a card. It read: *Sorry Sweetheart*, followed by a big capital J. *A man of few words*, she thought. She couldn't believe he sent her flowers. He had always been generous but he had never given her flowers. It almost made their spat worthwhile.

Realizing the delivery man was still standing there, she handed him a tip, and held the roses in her arms, admiring them. Her co-workers gathered in her doorway and fussed over the flowers. She experienced a warm feeling for her new beau and felt a tingle rise up her body. Happy that she and Jason weren't just roommates anymore, she smiled the rest of the morning.

At lunch time, Tara collected her and Chandra at work and drove to the pharmacy where she made a couple intimate purchases. When she returned to Tara's car, they headed to lunch.

"You've got to tell us what happened with Charles," Chandra said to Tara.

"Well, I'm not one to talk about private things," Tara said, "but in this case, it's a bit different."

"I'll say," Chandra said.

"Charles is quite a rooster," Tara said.

"Yeah," Kathleen said, "watch out for his cock-a-doodle-do." Uproarious laughter filled the car.

"I told him he was bossy," Tara said. "He calls it being masterful." She glanced at Kathleen. "He wants me to come to his place on Saturday night. I told him I would but I'm really nervous. Are you going to be home?"

"I don't think so." She felt thankful that Jason had plans for them.

"Did Charles say what he'd do to you?" Chandra said.

"He said he'd use the mink handcuffs on my wrists and ankles," Tara giggled. "He said his toys would make me come over and over again."

Kathleen felt envious. But Charles would be too intense for her. She couldn't handle his masterful nature. Her feelings were more inclined toward Jason's temperament. He was strong and confident but backed off when she needed. Charles acted more like a bulldozer.

She enjoyed a quick lunch with her friends and returned to work where she resumed her new assignment. While she was gone, her office filled with the scent of roses. She worked happily the rest of the day thinking about how Jason had transitioned from being her protector and roommate to her new-found love interest.

After work she waited for him in the lobby. The paparazzi had long since moved on to another victim. Thankful she was no longer a big news story, she sniffed the rose buds in her arms. Their heavenly scent caused a heated throb between her legs. When Jason arrived, she couldn't wait to see him. They both had suffered through a difficult week and she was determined to make it up to him. When she got closer to his truck, his door opened and he got out to meet her.

"Thank you for the beautiful roses," she said, smiling at him.

"I'm sorry I've been such an ass this week." He leaned down to kiss her. "Things have been difficult at work."

"I've been so self-absorbed, I haven't thought about what you're going through."

He hugged her, almost squishing the roses. "Let me take those." He opened her door and handed back the flowers once she was seated and had buckled her seatbelt.

When he got in the truck, she admired his strong profile. "We have all weekend to make it up to each other." She hoped her session with Dr. Jennifer would help.

He smiled and squeezed her hand. "Now that's something to look forward to."

The heady, sweet scent of the roses reminded her of their new relationship status. For the next couple of days, she would take a break from her recovery and focus on Jason and his needs. He deserved her full attention. She gazed out the window and smiled to herself as she thought about various ways to make him happy.

Chapter 12

On Saturday, Kathleen tensed as Jason pulled away from the gourmet catering shop and drove toward the marina. She had practiced visualizing herself on the sailboat and the unsteady nature of its journey across the water, but she still felt uneasy about their outing. Trusting in Jason to keep her safe, she knew she would be and cast away her thoughts of anxiety. Instead, she turned to her relationship with him.

"I've been so focused on my recovery, I'm afraid I've been absent in our relationship."

"Not completely absent." His eyes twinkled.

"The past year was so traumatic, my entire life has been altered."

"I understand ..." Reaching for her hand, he held it on the console between them. "You'll gradually leave it behind. One day you'll look forward instead of back."

"I want to look forward now, but I keep getting dragged down."

"You haven't had a flashback since you moved in. Now you're going out on a rocking boat."

"It sounds childish, I know. Sometimes I'm ashamed of my phobias."

"One step at a time." He squeezed her hand then grasped the steering wheel to turn into the marina parking lot.

Kathleen helped him unload the supplies onto the dock cart and walked alongside him as he pushed it toward the gate where he pressed his code on the keypad. When she came to speak to the FBI about what she remembered, the dock master had been kind enough to let her through the gate. But now ... as she neared the boat, her steps faltered. *I can do this, one step after another.*

While she stood next to the boat giving herself a pep talk, Jason loaded everything onboard. She ran her eyes over the sailboat and had to admit it was a stunning vessel. As she walked around, she noticed a main sail and jib, a large open deck seating area near the helm at the rear, a raised cabin with windows, and the maker's nameplate on the side, Gianetti 64, an Italian vessel. That surprised her. Its navy blue hull had a thin red stripe at the water line running to the stern where the boat's name, *Legal Ease*, flashed golden in the bright sunlight. She chuckled at the reference to his occupation.

When he finished loading the supplies, Jason offered his hands to her with palms upward. She shook briefly before taking them and stepping onboard. "Clever name."

He put his arms around her and kissed her tenderly, then lifted his lips away from hers. "Welcome aboard, sweetheart. I'm very proud of you."

She smiled before he lowered his head to kiss her again. With his lips on hers, her thoughts turned to lovemaking and her therapy session. She felt awkward discussing her sexual dysfunction with Dr. Jen but she was glad she did. She had learned something new. Next, she needed to talk to Jason about it. She hated talking about sex. It was awkward, especially with a new lover. How could she broach such a delicate subject?

Jason went below deck to stow their supplies for the voyage.

"You need to teach me how to do the sails," Kathleen said when he came up top.

"You don't do the sails. You hoist them and lower them." He chuckled, but not in a condescending way.

"Regardless of what you call it, you still need to teach me."

"I'll explain things as we go along. The water is calm today because there's not much wind. We'll motor out first. When the sea breeze increases, we'll sail around so you can get your sea legs." He started the engines to let them warm up while he cast off the lines.

She bit her lower lip and grabbed the wheel mount as the boat slowly moved away from the dock.

"Maybe you should wear a life jacket." He steered out of the slip and into the morning sun. "Sit down sweetheart. You can stand when I get a vest on you."

Kathleen sat on the end of a cushioned seating area in front of the wheel and gazed ahead as the sailboat glided over the mirror-like surface of Biscayne Bay. The morning air had a hint of chill. She rubbed her arms to chase it away. Jason insisted that she wear shorts and a halter top under some loose cotton clothes so she could remove the outerwear when they arrived in a place where no one would see her scars. But she thought the weather would be warmer. "Where are we going?"

Jason came up from below with a life vest. "To my favorite hidden cove."

"Where's that?" She put her arms through the vest when he opened it to encircle her neck and tightened the belt around her slender waist.

"It's on a small island between Biscayne Bay and the Atlantic Ocean. We'll stop there for lunch." He noticed the cobalt blue glass bead hanging around her neck and lifted it. "What's this?"

"It's my good luck charm. I found it in Aruba. It's a Dutch trade bead that slaves used for currency in the 1700s."

"Wow, that's old. You've had it all this time?"

Kathleen nodded. "When the Dutch slaves were freed, they threw them on the ground. I kept it as a symbol of freedom. Now it's my good luck charm."

He smiled, kissed her and moved to the helm. When they arrived at the island, he steered the boat as close as he could without damaging the fixed keel. Dropping anchor, he helped her into the dinghy before loading their supplies. He rowed a short distance to shore, jumped into the water, and pulled her and the boat onto the beach where he helped her out.

She lugged a bag holding a blanket and pillow into the interior of the island while he carried the picnic basket. When she came upon an inlet of water swirling into a tidal pool, she paused to admire the mangroves, sea grapes, and palm trees forming a secluded cove.

"I love this place. It's incredible. No one's here."

"We're on the southeast side of the island where people don't usually explore." He set the basket down and took the blanket from her. Shaking it flat on the sand, he placed the bag on one corner in case the breeze picked up.

She sat next to him while he removed items from the basket. "What goodies do you have in there?"

"It's a surprise. First, we'll start with cheese, crackers, grapes and champagne."

Kathleen's stomach growled. "My appetite is getting better." She smiled at another small triumph. Nausea and vomiting had been left behind long ago, plus she boarded the sailboat and survived it. The other night, she met each of the men on the board of directors. Now she had to tackle her nightmares and focus on her love life.

"Care to share those thoughts?"

"I was thinking about the challenges I've overcome and those I still need to face."

"Want to talk about them?" Jason's soft black hair tossed in the breeze.

She blushed then felt her face and chest were warm. "I don't know how to start."

"Allow me. I'm the jawbone." He chuckled and touched her chin. "First, about last weekend." His eyes danced. "I enjoyed our time in the Keys immensely. There were challenges. But there will be for a long time. Second, we had a very crappy week."

"What happened at work that upset you so much?"

"I don't want to talk about it. This weekend, I want to focus on each other."

"But if something upset you, shouldn't we talk about it?"

"If it upset me, it'll upset you." He pushed her auburn hair behind her ear.

"You're not going to tell me?" She felt a sense of disbelief.

He chuckled. "You're getting upset already and we haven't even talked about it. I'll tell you tomorrow." He squeezed her hand. "Today I only want to talk about us." Reaching into the basket, he removed a bottle of champagne and two flutes. "Tell me how your therapy went yesterday." He deftly popped the cork on the champagne, poured a glass and handed it to her.

She looked down at the dancing bubbles. "It was good." Her mind raced struggling to think of a graceful entree.

He poured another glass and returned the bottle to a chiller bag. "But you don't want to talk about it?"

"I want to talk about it, but I don't know how." She sipped some champagne to give herself time. "Would you be interested in going to a session with me?"

He reflected on the possibility as he gazed over the horizon before he looked back at her. "Of course, but don't you want them to be private?"

"Sometimes." She fidgeted.

"What does Dr. Jennifer say about that?"

"She said I can bring you whenever I feel ready."

"Tell me when and I'll be there."

"How about Friday?" She crossed her fingers in her mind, hoping he was free.

He paused a few seconds then looked suspicious. "Why so soon?"

"It's easier if she explains it."

"Easier for you?" He gave her a quizzical look.

She wiggled her toes in the sand while she mulled over how to tell him she wanted to have sex with him on a regular basis.

He put down his glass, pulled his knit shirt over his head and tossed it next to the basket. "Why don't you explain it to me?" He leaned back on one elbow, holding his glass of champagne in one hand and looking like he had all day to listen.

She wished he hadn't taken off his shirt. His chiseled chest muscles distracted her. She swallowed her desire. Her throat seemed dry even though she'd just taken a sip from her glass. Shifting her weight, she tried to think of how to begin. How would he respond?

"Is this about your sexual dysfunction?"

She sighed and felt like a failure. Looking into the dark pupils of his blue eyes, she said a quick prayer. "Dr. Jen suggested I try Karezza ..."

His eyebrows rose. "What's that?"

She glanced at his relaxed body resting on the pillow, ready to listen to her next words intently. If she could only get them out. She shrugged her shoulders. "Karezza is from an Italian word meaning caress. It's an intimate form of lovemaking that bonds a couple together. Some people

184

say it cures sexual dysfunction."

"Interesting ... how does it work?" He raised his glass and sipped.

"It focuses on affectionate touching, stroking, spooning, and gentle intercourse without orgasms." She closed her eyes. *There, I said it.* She opened her eyes and watched his expression change from curious to introspective.

"What is the medical theory behind it?"

"The doctor who named it believes gentle, loving touch without orgasm increases two neurochemicals in the brain, dopamine and oxytocin, which increase pleasure and feelings of closeness, romance, and peace."

"How does not having orgasms help?"

"Orgasms deplete those chemicals. Without orgasms, pleasurable chemicals increase and stay elevated. That increases feelings of happiness and well-being."

"What does Dr. Jen want you to do?"

"She wants me to try a three-week program using what's called ecstatic exchanges." She crossed her fingers. "For the first two weeks, there's no intercourse and no orgasms." She tensed, waiting for his rant.

He looked incredulous and seemed to struggle for the proper words. After a few moments, he regrouped and shook his head. "No orgasms for two weeks? I don't know babe. I'll think about it."

"If you don't want to, that's okay. I know I've asked a lot of you the last two months." She felt her throat close. *Be strong, accept whatever decision he makes.*

"I didn't say no. I'm a lawyer. I don't agree to anything until I hear all the details. And even then, I'll still think about it." He met her eyes and raised his brow with a questioning gaze. "Tell me how this works."

She took a sip of champagne for encouragement. "Ecstatic exchanges emphasize affectionate touching, giving to your partner, and nurturing each other. We'd have to sleep together every night. Before bed, we'd snuggle, kiss, and connect. Maybe spoon for twenty minutes then stroke our bodies for comfort not arousal. For the first two weeks, we wear underpants to bed to remind us that it doesn't involve intercourse."

"That's silly."

"It's just a tool. You don't have to do it. During the third week, you take your clothes off, keep doing the same things and you add intercourse. But during intercourse there's no thrusting."

"No thrusting?" He chuckled. "You want me to undo everything I've ever learned?"

"Not you, just me." She pointed to her chest. "If you don't want to do it, that's okay." She turned away from him and clenched her jaw, forcing herself not to be disappointed. She thought he was committed to her. Even Charles had said so. But she had asked a lot of him.

"Wait." Jason grabbed her arm. "Don't turn away. Lay down with me." He took her flute of champagne and set it in the basket. Tugging her down next to him, she lay on the pillow next to his and looked into his dark blue eyes. "Do these ecstatic exchanges include this?" He reached inside her halter top and cupped her breast.

"Yes." She watched his face as he explored her body.

"Can I do this?" He rubbed his fingers over her nipple, making it hard. Kathleen groaned. "Yes."

He pushed her top aside and replaced his fingers with his lips and licked and sucked on her erect nipple. "Can I do that?"

"Yes."

"And you'll sleep with me every night?"

"Yes." She touched his bare chest and moved her fingers over his hardened muscles.

"There are definitely benefits. I'll think about it." He lowered his head to her breasts and continued to caress and suckle them.

She moaned and lay back on the pillow, enjoying his attentions. Her mind filled with bliss and calm. She explained it to him, everything. Regardless of what he decided, she would have to pay more attention to his needs from now on. She wanted them to be a couple not just roommates.

"Old habits are hard to break." Jason pushed his erection against her thigh. "Besides, I'm not sure Karezza is good for a man's prostate. Babies with birth defects have been linked to old, stale sperm."

"I'm not planning on making any babies." She stroked his chest hairs.

"Neither am I. I'm just saying, new medical discoveries have probably been made since Karezza first came about."

"It's been adapted over time. Besides, we decide how to do it. There isn't a list of things to do."

"At least it's flexible. I'd like to learn more about it before agreeing to do it for three weeks."

"Come with me on Friday." Kathleen gave him a hopeful look.

"I will." He rose on one elbow and looked intently into her eyes. "The next thing I want to talk about is you discussing our sex life with Charles."

She gulped and saw his face change from warm to almost jealous. "I didn't discuss sex with him."

"He gave me some toys to try on you." He cocked an eyebrow.

"He noticed I was upset and guessed the rest."

"Charles is very intuitive. He can read folks like a book. I asked you to give him a wide berth."

"I know. But he's always around. I can't give him a wide berth when he's always in my home. He's a big part of your life and I refuse to be rude to him."

Jason pondered her comments. "I don't want you to be rude to him." He reached into the bag she carried off the boat and pulled out a pouch. "I don't really think you need toys. That would frustrate you even more." He removed a small vial from the bag. "But he did give me something that might be fun to try."

"What's that?" She gazed at the small purple bottle.

"It's oil. I plan to rub it all over you." His eyes creased at the corners when he smiled then leaned forward to kiss her. Kathleen moaned and lay back. Pouring a small amount in one palm, he rubbed his hands together, sniffed them and winked. "You'll like this." Pressing his oily hands on her chest, he massaged her skin, moving his hands in circles around her breasts without touching the peaks.

She closed her eyes and smelled strawberries. "I do like that. Thank heaven it's not banana oil."

187

"Here ..." He handed her a glass of champagne. "Let's finish these before they get warm." He tossed his head back and drank the bubbly down.

She sipped her drink, fearing the bubbles would make her dizzy. Handing the flute back to him, she laid back and listened to the water lapping on the shore. Seagulls squawked as a gentle tropical breeze rustled through the palm fronds. If this is what ecstatic exchanges were like, she could really get used to this every night. What a grand way of connecting with each other before falling asleep. They could try something different each night like a foot massage. She moaned and her crotch throbbed at the thought of the sensuality of it all.

Jason rubbed the strawberry oil all the way to her toes. "What are you thinking?"

"I thought a foot massage would be great."

With that in mind, he rubbed her feet and gently squeezed upward on the arches and took each foot in his strong hands and caressed them. He paused to get more oil and continued rubbing and squeezing her feet until she almost fell asleep.

She moaned and squirmed with delight then raised her head to look at him. "Want me to do that to you?"

"Sure, when I'm done."

When his erection showed, Kathleen felt sorry for him. The poor man had had a miserable week. He ached for her caresses. He hadn't agreed to start Karezza. She forced herself to rouse from her sleepy state. "It's your turn."

She pushed him playfully backward and poured some oil into her palms. Caressing every muscle from his shoulders down his chest to his rigid abdominals, she rubbed his thighs down to his feet, careful not to touch his hardened penis. She soothed the soles of his feet eliciting a groan from him before she reached for his erection.

He flinched and raised his head from the pillow. "Sweetheart—"

"Shhh." With gentleness, she very slowly massaged his penis, balls and perineum with strawberry oil. When he groaned and laid his head back on the pillow, she smiled. Satisfied with his reaction, she squeezed and released his shaft then pressed her fingernails into his groin around his penis to relieve the building tension.

"If you keep this up ..." his breath hitched, "... I'll get blue balls."

"No silly, this isn't blueberry oil, it's strawberry."

He moaned and looked at her with a wrinkled forehead. "I'll explain later."

She giggled. "If you help me do Karezza, I'll do this to you every night for twenty minutes."

Jason groaned. "I don't think I could last twenty minutes." His fists clenched in the blanket as she continued caressing him for comfort, not arousal. He sat up quickly, grabbed her, and pulled her down next to him, laying her on her back. He stretched out next to her, leaned on one elbow, and pressed his erection into her hip.

Kathleen ran her soft hand over his shoulders, loving the strong muscles he used to lift weights. He blocked out the sun and she had difficulty seeing him in the glare.

He leaned down and kissed her tenderly, tasting her lips and biting them gently.

"I think you missed the point of my massage."

"I got your point." He hovered near her lips. "I'm just not sure I can follow the rules ... strictly speaking."

"We make the rules. If you help me, I'll help you." She traced his lower lip with her index finger then ran it along his chin. "Please."

He leaned down and kissed her passionately, inserting his tongue in her mouth, then drew back to look at her. "I'll help you, but next time we'll use manly oil for me."

Kathleen laughed and messed up his hair. "You're the sweetest man ever." She put her arms around his neck and pulled him down on her oily body.

Jason held her and rocked her, kissing her from her face to her breasts. Pressing his erection into her belly, he reached down to her shorts, unbuttoned them and pulled down the zipper. His breathing increased as he kissed her and pressed her down into the pillow. He pushed her shorts down over her hips and pressed closer to her hot, wet vagina.

She shook briefly more from habit than anything else. She wanted him to keep going but he stopped and remained still, looking at her with uncertainty. "I'm okay." She touched his ear and ran her finger down his strong jaw. "Don't stop."

Looking relieved, he kissed her for a long time before sliding his hand into her shorts, sneaking under her panties, and stroking her wet folds.

Turning on her side, she kicked off her shorts and lifted her leg over his hip, opening herself to him. She pressed against his erection to encourage him.

He moved closer and pressed against her outer lips. She was ready for him to enter her but she didn't want aggression and she didn't want his weight on her, not yet. Feeling nervous about her injuries and how he would react to them, she wondered if her body would function properly.

Jason slowly pressed his penis into her hot, wet vagina and stopped when she shook. "Are you okay, sweetheart?"

"I'm okay. I'm just nervous."

"I would never hurt you." He touched her face and waited for her breathing to calm before pressing further inside her. When she gasped and closed her eyes, he stopped and rested until she opened them. "You're a beautiful woman. I like being inside you. Are you afraid?"

Kathleen shook her head and watched his face as he calmly stroked her breasts and nipples, teasing her. "A little."

"You're safe and you're loved." He kissed her forehead, the end of her nose and her lips. His tongue dashed in and out of her mouth. Gazing at her, his large dark irises swallowed her heart. "I'm very proud of you, for all the things you've accomplished."

Tears filled her eyes as they lay together, joined by their genitals. Energy seemed to surge from his penis into her vagina, to her breasts, into his chest and around in a circle, giving her strength and power she hadn't known before. Amazed by the new energy she felt between them, her confidence grew.

Happy with their intimate encounter, she felt calmer than ever and anticipated the day she could completely surrender to his lovemaking. Content to lay in the cove all day joined with him, she became wary when high wispy clouds invaded the clear blue sky. As the sea breeze increased, wind rustled through the Australian pines, making a humming sound that soothed her.

When Jason heard the wind, he lifted his head and looked at the top of the mast on his sailboat. "The wind shifted." He kissed and hugged her, putting his mouth at her ear. "We need to head back."

Thoughts of going home dampened her mood. "Can't we stay a little longer?"

"If you want." He pulled her against him and teased her with small movements of his penis inside her while they rested. She squeezed her muscles around him in return.

Sometime later Kathleen awoke, not knowing how long she snoozed. Jason was still inside her, although his erection had subsided, his breathing came slow and steady. She looked up at the sky that had filled with dark clouds. Gusty winds rustled the palm fronds above their heads. Her quick gasp caused him to open his eyes.

Startled, he looked at the sky. "Storms …" He pulled out of her, fastened his shorts and ran toward the dinghy. Rowing out to the boat, he climbed the swim ladder and went below. He retrieved his computer and set it on the console, looking at the screen.

Kathleen figured he must be checking the radar. She reached for her shorts and donned them. Glancing around, she didn't see any shelter where they could take cover and wondered what he'd want to do. Maybe they could motor to a marina nearby.

Jason rowed the dinghy to shore and waded toward her. Walking into the cove where she sat on the blanket, he joined her.

"Bad news?" She searched his worried face.

"Storms are coming off the ocean toward us. We won't make it back to the marina." He sat opposite her and held her hands. "Listen, sweetheart, we'll have to stay on the boat tonight."

Waves, rocking, seasick, fear rushed through her mind. "Can't we go somewhere nearby?"

"We don't have time to pack and sail somewhere. We'd be trapped in the middle of the storms and I won't do that to you." He squeezed her hands. "You were very brave to get on the boat. I refuse to frighten you unnecessarily." He glanced up at the dark clouds. "We'll sleep here tonight and sail home tomorrow."

The prospect of staying on a boat, rocking all night, sent a chill down her spine. She didn't mind spending time with him, but the fear factor bothered her. When he got up and started packing the picnic basket, she helped. "At least we have something to eat for dinner." She chuckled.

He flashed a reassuring smile. "I have plenty of canned food onboard, plus there are games and cards. We'll have a good time."

A crack of lightning and very loud thunder startled Kathleen, and she huddled low on the blanket. Jason reached for her hand and helped her up. She gathered the sandy blanket and pillows and shook them before tossing them into the large tote bag. She glanced around the area before leaving and didn't see anything else before following him toward the dinghy.

Jason helped her inside and loaded the supplies before hopping in beside her and rowing out to the sailboat offshore.

The skies were ominous to the east toward the Bahamas. When she climbed onto the boat, she looked at the radar. Dark green, yellow and red colors meant heavy rain and wind were on the way. "Are we going to be okay?" She wrung her hands.

"We're very safe. This is an ocean-going vessel. It's built to withstand a lot more than severe thunderstorms." He put his arm around her shoulders. "It's you I'm worried about."

"Me too." She gulped and grabbed him around the waist. Resting her head on his chest, she listened to his steady heartbeat. The soothing rhythm of his thumping chest reassured her.

When the wind blew their hair around and light sprinkles fell on their faces, he opened the door to the salon. "Get below."

She stepped down and entered a world of fine Italian design and furnishings. Light woods with waterproof upholstery welcomed her into the salon. She flipped the light switch and warm, soft wall sconces showered soft light onto the table, counters, and glass doors on the galley cabinets.

Jason followed her down the steps, carrying the picnic basket, blanket and pillows. She walked around the salon running her hand along the granite counters. She peeked down a hallway and saw the entrance to a bedroom. As she headed that way, a room with one large bed came into view. Cushions and pillows were strewn at the head of the mattress. No sheets or pillowcases covered the pillow-top bed.

Jason cleared his throat behind her. "We need to make the bed." The boat began to rock gently. "Let's do it now, while we can stand up."

"Okay." She looked around for a linen closet and opened a narrow door and discovered a bathroom. Poking her head inside, she was surprised to see a shower as well as a tub.

"The sheets are over here." He opened a drawer in the dresser and tossed the sheets on the bed with a couple of pillow cases. Shaking the sheets out of their folds, he quickly stretched the bottom sheet over the box spring and tucked the top sheet in along the side.

She grabbed the pillow cases and put the pillows inside, fluffing them before tossing them on the bed. "There, all done. You've obviously done this before." She smirked.

"No comment." He gave her a warning glance.

She felt a twinge of jealousy run through her, which surprised her. Don't think about his other girlfriends. What's past is past. When she heard wind pelting the small windows with rain, she reached out to steady herself as the boat swayed on the anchor.

"Come into the salon." He reached for her hands. When she took them, he walked backwards like he did earlier and stepped into the larger room. "Sit here." He backed into a small table in the corner.

"Should I put my life vest on?"

"No, you won't need it but if it helps you feel safe, you can." Then he looked up the steps to the deck outside. "It's probably soaking wet now. Want another one?"

"That's okay." She clutched the edge of the table as the boat rocked and swayed.

Jason opened a cabinet and removed some boxes of board games and brought them to the table. He reached into a small drawer, removed a deck of cards and added them to the stack of boxes. "We have lots of games." He said, joining her in the booth. When loud popping sounds came from the windows, he looked up at them. "Hail." He grabbed her hand. "What would you like to play?"

Kathleen tensed and clutched his hand. What if someone didn't see them and ran into them? What if a tornado hit them? Bright flashes of lightning and loud crashes of thunder startled her. Suddenly she worried more about the weather than her memories of sailing in a rocking boat inside a wire cage to Venezuela. He gazed at her with sympathetic blue eyes.

"Let's play this one." He released her hand and grabbed a box from the pile.

He chose a game that would take hours to play. *Smart man,* she thought. This would take her mind off the weather. She eagerly rolled the dice and moved her player around the board. They laughed and played as the boat turned on its anchor, the winds pushing them around. She lost track of time and later realized the powerful winds had died down, leaving only gentle taps of rain on the windows.

"Let's take a break. I want to check the radar." He went to the galley where he left his computer and pressed the screen a few times.

She stood next to him in the galley and watched the radar loop. More rain would be coming but it would be lighter than what they had just been through. That fact encouraged her but it was too dark and too late to head back to the marina. She would be forced to endure a night on the boat. She prayed her nightmares would spare her this night.

"I know you didn't sign up for an all-nighter. At this point, we don't have any choice but to stay here."

"It'll be an adventure." Kathleen smiled and put her arms around him.

He smiled and kissed her. "I'm getting hungry. Let's eat our lunch." Jason moved into the galley and took the food and champagne from the refrigerator.

She opened the drawers in the galley looking for silverware and dishes. Finding some, she set the table and took out some glasses for drinks. The ice maker in the refrigerator had made enough ice for a few drinks.

"Are you upset about spending the night on the boat?" He bit into a chicken leg.

"I was at first. I thought I'd have a flashback, but actually I'm glad not to be home tonight."

"Why's that?"

"Tara and Charles are having a session tonight." She glanced up at him. "I really didn't want to be anywhere nearby. It feels awkward knowing what they're doing."

The corners of his eyes creased as he smiled and looked down at his plate. "Do you think Tara likes BDSM?"

"She's never tried it. She's just having fun. Charles is too intense for her." She lifted her chicken leg and bit it. "Besides, she's got her heart set on a modeling career."

"What's that have to do with BDSM?"

"Well, wearing dog collars and piercings aren't exactly fashionable. She's all about the show."

"She's using him?"

"They're having fun together. No ties, except those on her wrists and ankles." She giggled at her own joke. "When Tara's parents died, she moved in with her grandma. Tara learned how to use her looks to get what she wanted." She reached for more grapes. "She uses what she has to get what no one can give her."

Jason seemed annoyed. "Believe it or not, Charles does have feelings. He might be domineering on the outside but inside he's a marshmallow."

Surprised that he defended him so strongly, she wished she kept her mouth shut. "Do you want me to tell her to stop seeing him?"

"No, we should mind our own business. They're old enough to know what they're doing. Charles tells everyone he has lots of ladies but truthfully, he'd be happy with one good one."

Kathleen felt bad and wished she hadn't said anything. Now Jason knew Tara wasn't serious about her relationship with Charles. "Tara might like being tied to the bed and made love to. No one really knows what happens between people." Jason's annoyed face relaxed and she felt a bit better.

The rain fell throughout the night, hitting the deck above them with a soft drumming beat. When the time came for bed, she laid her head on Jason's chest and listened to his slow beating heart and his calm steady breaths. He had left the nightlight on in the bathroom in case she needed to get up during the night. The low, warm light cast a glow over the cabin's furnishings as her eyes scanned the room. Surprised at how comforting it felt to sleep with him, she decided to sleep with him every night, if he let her. But her quest to build up her dopamine and oxytocin levels conflicted with his need for regular orgasmic release. She needed to find a way to do both for his sake and hers.

Chapter 13

The next morning, Kathleen awoke wrapped in Jason's comforting embrace. She glanced around the cabin. The boat didn't rock. The wind didn't howl. The rain had ceased. Sunlight beamed through gaps in the small curtains covering the windows. She finally fell asleep early in the morning. Poor Jason put up with a lot from her: nightmares, flashbacks, phobias. He was a saint.

She smiled at his sleeping form. Not wishing to wake him, she waited for him to rouse to the sun shining into the cabin. She survived a night aboard a rocking boat in unfamiliar waters with a man who protected and cared for her. Another accomplishment she could be proud of. Next she would focus on resolving her sexual problem, helping her parents recover from their burns, and convincing them to use a false name.

Jason opened his eyes and smiled at her. "You survived again." He pressed her into his embrace as he kissed her, cradling the side of her head. "Ready to go home?"

She nodded her approval before they took a shower, dressed, and ventured on deck to check for damage. Seeing none, Jason unfurled the jib and sailed around the island to show her where they spent last night. A steady wind from the southeast allowed him to sail back to the marina in a peaceful way. Waves lapped the hull and sails flapped occasionally in the wind. He sailed almost into the slip but lowered the jib when he got close and drifted to the dock. He tossed the bumpers over the side to keep from damaging the boat. Throwing lines over the pilings, he tugged the *Legal Ease* dockside.

Kathleen stripped the bed, emptied the refrigerator, and helped him load supplies on a dock trolley and into his truck. Once they got home, she threw the dirty laundry in the washer before they headed to a breakfast joint Jason liked. During the afternoon, she finished a couple loads of laundry, folding a separate stack to return to the sailboat, and then decided to call her parents.

"Hello, Mom. How are you and Dad doing?"

"We're worried sick about you," her mother said. "You were supposed to call last night. We thought something happened to you."

"We were caught in the storms and had to stay on the boat. Sorry I couldn't call you. There wasn't a cell tower out there." She tried not to sound sarcastic but couldn't help but feel that way.

"I'm surprised at you, Katie." Brenda sighed with frustration.

Kathleen felt like a child. Too young to make her own decisions and still under the thumb of her mother. Good heavens. If her mother knew what Tara was doing, she would not judge her daughter so harshly. She smiled to herself and wondered if Tara would spill the story or keep it private. In one respect, she wanted to know what happened and in another, she'd rather not. She had her own problems to sort out with Jason. She needed to concentrate on him and getting herself well again. She felt exasperated. "Is Dad there?"

"Hello princess," her father said. "How was sailing?"

"Peaceful and invigorating, I'd like to go again." She smiled when she remembered their time in the hidden cove and kept that to herself. "How are you feeling?"

"Our burns are healing, but we'd rather be in our own home, in our own bed."

"I know what you mean. The safe house is nice but it's not home."

"No. When can we see you?"

"I'd like to stop by after work this week. What's Mom's work schedule?"

"She's working days. Anytime this week would be good."

"I'll call when I check my calendar and we'll make a plan. I miss you."

"We miss you too. Two weekends in a row has been torture."

"Okay, Dad. I get the message. How's Sam?"

"He's studying at the library. I think these quarters are too close for him."

She chuckled and understood completely. "I love you guys. Talk later, okay?"

"Goodbye sweetie."

Kathleen ended the call, shoved the cell phone in her pocket, and went to the spare room to look at her paintings. Still on the easel, she lifted the Aruba Star, gazed at it and felt nothing. Was she numb or was she moving on? She hoped it was the latter. Setting it on the floor against the wall, she selected a fresh canvas and pondered what to paint. She touched a paintbrush to her lower lip and reflected on her feelings.

Hours later, she emerged from the spare room carrying her masterpiece. She looked around for Jason but didn't see him. Thinking he must have gone for a run, she stood her painting on a living room chair and went outside on the balcony to bathe in the afternoon sun.

Later, Jason stepped onto the balcony. "There you are. Have fun painting?"

"How'd you know I was painting?" She shielded her eyes from the bright light.

"I poked my head in but you were so focused ... I left a note on the kitchen counter."

"I didn't go in the kitchen, but I figured you went for a run." She looked at his running shorts and tank top and knew she had guessed correctly.

"I still need to talk to you about what happened last week. I'll take a shower and we can chat."

"I'll be here." Kathleen lay back on the lounge chair. A half hour later, Jason emerged fresh, clean and wearing shorts and a polo shirt. She wondered if he ever wore a T-shirt or got dirty. He always seemed so well-dressed.

"Come inside, sweetheart." He reached for her hand. "I don't want the neighbors to hear about our saga."

She moved to the sofa, sat down and waited for him to join her. "Am I going to need a drink for this chat?"

"No." He squeezed her thigh and looked serious. "Don't get excited about this, but Wilson was given bail."

"What?" She sat upright with a spring in her spine. "That's crazy!"

"It is, but there's nothing we can do about it."

"He'll come after us. That man, Stephens, said so."

"Wilson has to wear an ankle monitor. The Mounties will track him at all times. Plus, he needs a passport to cross the border. His was confiscated."

She breathed a sigh of relief and sat back on the sofa. Her belly tensed from the prospect of Wilson being free. How absurd was that? He would start right where he left off. Nothing stopped him or those he worked for. "What about the shipping container?"

"It'll be delivered this week." Jason still held her thigh. "I researched the Bills of Lading for banana shipments to Vancouver and discovered a shipping code that seemed to correlate with the kidnappings in Aruba."

"That's great!" She leaned over to kiss him. "You're not happy about that?"

His face turned grim. "The company I represent, Seaside Shipping, was the one that sent the banana shipments with the captives to Vancouver."

Kathleen grunted and felt as if someone had punched her in the stomach. Folding her arms in front of her, she jumped up and paced in front of the balcony windows. Silence filled the room while she tried to sort out the meaning of what he shared. She didn't know how to feel or what to say. He seemed wary of her reaction and anguished by his clients' possible involvement in slave trafficking. She returned to the sofa and they held each other. "What are you going to do?"

"I told Charles I couldn't represent them anymore, and he needed to look for a new business partner."

She gasped. "What'd he say?"

"He said no. I had practically accused his father of making profits off illegal activity. He defended his father, of course, but honestly, neither of us really knows the truth."

She felt sorry for them both and laid her head on his shoulder. "No wonder you were so upset. What if you find out his father knew and profited from it?"

"Charles and I discussed dropping our client and starting over. I'd probably have to sell the boat and the condo. We'd have to move somewhere more affordable."

"We could buy a small house together ... with a garden and maybe get a dog."

"That's sweet." Jason smiled and kissed her. "I'll keep that in mind."

Kathleen rubbed her hand on his chest. "Poor Charles, he must be beside himself."

"Actually, he helped me do the research. I'm very proud of him."

"He's a strong person." She sensed Jason's depressed mood and felt determined to lift his spirits. "I'm in the mood for a movie and a pizza."

"At home or out?" He sounded more cheerful already.

"Home. I'm too tired to go out." She pointed to her artwork standing in the chair. "Did you see my painting?"

"No, what'd you do?"

She retrieved the painting and showed him. "What do you think?"

He smirked. "It's much better than your last one."

"Stop it. It's your hidden cove."

"It's our hidden cove now, sweetheart. I like it. We should hang it where we'll always see it." Jason glanced around for a good spot, took the painting from her, and held it against a narrow wall between the fireplace and his bedroom. "How about here?"

"It looks good there but it's not done."

"Oh, it looks good enough to be finished to me."

Kathleen chuckled and took it from him. "No silly, it needs more detail." She returned it to the spare room and put it back on the easel. She planned to finish it this week, if she had time. Walking back to the living room, Jason checked which movies were available for download.

"Have you seen this?" He highlighted a title on the television screen.

"It didn't get good reviews but they're not always right." She sat next to him while he downloaded the movie. They watched it for an hour and she thought it must have been the worst movie ever made. Kathleen laid her head on Jason's chest and let her mind wander as the movie grew worse. Unhappy with her predicament, she devised a plan of escape.

Slow and sensuous, her fingers moved in small circles over his muscular thigh, inching forward until her palm spread across his crotch.

He reached down for her chin and tilted it upward. Lowering his lips to hers, he kissed her passionately, caressing her mouth with his tongue. His erection thickened as she continued to massage his genitals.

Unzipping his shorts, she pulled out his stiff penis and lowered her head to lick it. She wrapped her lips around the head, teased the tip with her tongue, and swirled it in her mouth like an ice cream cone.

Jason groaned. His fist clutched the shirt on her back as she gently sucked up and down on his swollen staff. He hissed through his teeth. Not sure whether he was in pain or pleasure, she glanced at him. His eyes were closed as the muscles in his jaw twitched.

Kathleen gently massaged his erection until it became dark red. He squirmed, thrust his hips upward, and clenched his fists. Grunting, he squirted semen into her mouth and on her lips. She wiggled her lips to give him as much pleasure as she could until he finished lifting his hips and relaxed onto the sofa.

He gently tugged on her hair. "Come here, sweetheart." She moved to his waiting lips where he kissed her tenderly and passionately, exploring her mouth with his tongue. He rubbed her erect nipples through her shirt until she felt uncomfortable.

"Let's go to bed," she said.

"Yours or mine ..." He raised one eyebrow.

Taking his hand, she stood and tugged as a chill ran down her spine. "Yours." She'd only been in his bed once, after her parents' car blew up. That episode resulted more from fear than strength. Tonight, she asked to share his bed from a position of strength. She would take care of his needs and hers at the same time. She understood his position and he understood hers, now they needed to meet in the middle.

As he led her to his bedroom, she held his hand and followed. He stepped toward the bed as she stood at the end of it, unbuttoning her blouse. When he reached for his belt buckle and yanked his belt from the loops toward her, she gasped, recoiled, and stepped back into the dresser.

Her mind raced with images of Wilson, his belt, anger, pain, humiliation. With her heart thumping against her chest, her first reaction was to flee to her safe place. She turned to run when two powerful arms encircled her, stopping her retreat. Taking rapid breaths, goosebumps rose on her arms as Jason nuzzled her ear.

"Easy sweetheart," he whispered.

She shook in his embrace, trying to control her feelings of anxiety. Looking at the ceiling, she struggled to slow her breathing and shaking. *Damn it, I'd been doing so well.*

He pulled her back against his strong, muscular chest and whispered in her ear. "I would never hurt you, baby."

"I know." Soon her shaking stopped and her breathing calmed.

"I cherish you and your body. I'll undress you and caress every inch of your beautiful skin until you sizzle with desire."

Kathleen felt a throb in her belly and her vagina became heated and moist. Her lips swelled in anticipation of his tender touch. Her nipples hardened as she imagined him nibbling them.

"I promise ... no thrusting," he whispered. "Let me heal you."

His sincere plea made her heart swell with affection. Or was it love? She had never known real, true love. Was this what it felt like? Cared for, loved, protected? Sharing secrets? Trusting each other? She wanted to feel the strength she felt in the hidden cove when they joined together and caressed each other until they fell asleep. Her confidence grew. Turning her head to look at his quizzical face, she smiled and kissed him.

While they kissed, he unbuttoned her blouse, pulled it off her shoulders and down her arms. He dropped it on the floor between them and reached for her light, cotton slacks, untied the string and opened the waist until they followed the shirt. He reached behind her and unsnapped her bra as his other hand rubbed her taut nipple through the fabric. He kissed her neck below her ear then sucked and nibbled on her earlobe.

She moaned and leaned back against his strong body as he slowly and carefully undressed her. Her breathing increased but in a good way, a passionate way. Her breasts swelled as he cupped them in his hands beneath her loosened bra.

203

His fingers circled her hard nipples eliciting a moan from her. Pushing her bra straps down, her underpants soon followed her bra to the floor. He pressed his erection into her butt cheeks, briefly thrusting for a moment before he immediately stopped. He must have remembered what the doctor suggested. "Old habits, baby," he whispered.

She smiled and kissed him while he carefully and completely caressed her breasts until she squirmed with passion. She wanted him inside her, but not on top of her, at least not yet.

He wrapped his strong arms around her and pulled her backwards toward the bed. Stepping slowly, he unzipped his shorts while he kissed the side of her throat, then pressed his erection between her cheeks. He sat on the end of the bed and tugged her down with him until she sat on his thighs.

She laid her head back against his shoulder and enjoyed his gentle caresses. She felt him touch every inch of her while he kissed and nibbled her ear, and bit her shoulder. She could smell the musky aroma of her arousal and thought he did too because his breathing increased.

Jason ran his fingers between her legs and gently caressed her swollen folds. Gently opening her, he pressed his erection inside her a short distance.

She flinched at his intrusion but wanted him there. Opening her legs wider, she made his entry easier as he pressed further until he was deep inside her.

Rock hard, his stiff penis pulsed inside her wet vagina while his hands rubbed her belly and her thighs with gentle caresses. His breathing became labored.

Kathleen wondered who said men had to wait twenty minutes. This one didn't. She felt sorry for him in a way, but reveled in his gentle joining with her. Her clit and vagina throbbed while he stayed quiet inside her. She wanted him to thrust into her, but she resisted the temptation to tantalize him. She remained still, joined with him.

When he wrapped his arms around her and pulled her toward the head of the bed, she wasn't sure what he planned. He laid her on her side facing away from him. Spooning together, he held her from behind. His hard penis throbbed inside her. He kissed her left ear and neck, nibbling at the base while she relaxed and reveled in the pleasurable feelings of her arousal.

She felt safe, loved, and content held in his arms, her heated response to his sexual interplay cooled to a warm heat that soothed her psyche.

Jason cupped her bare breasts and held them. His breathing became steady as he laid his head on his pillow and pulled her left leg over his leg, making it easier for him to press further inside her.

She moaned and cuddled against him, calm, relaxed, taken by her man but not forced. Bliss overcame her as she closed her eyes and entered a calm state of slumber, one with her man.

≈

Jason considered how much he hated Monday mornings as he sipped his coffee behind his desk. Eager to learn what happened over the weekend regarding the shipping container in Vancouver, he had already contacted Matt's office for an update. While he waited for Matt's call, Jason reviewed the report of Bills of Lading for all of the banana shipments to Vancouver and noticed that every container had been inspected by Customs before the contents were delivered to the importer. He looked into the distance and pondered the significance of an inspection. Focusing on a picture in the hallway outside his office door, he worked his logic through a process when Charles came into view.

"You're early." Charles smiled, carrying his briefcase. "Good weekend?"

"Very nice, how was yours?"

Charles grinned. "Quite enjoyable." He entered Jason's office and sat down in the chair opposite his desk. Setting his briefcase down, he leaned his feet on the edge of the desk and glanced at the boxes of files and stacks of shipping papers on the floor. "Do you need help with anything regarding the shipments?"

"Not right now, but there is something you can help with."

"What's that?" Charles put his fingers together in a steeple.

"Kathleen is going through a fragile time right now. I'd like you to back off a bit."

"Are you putting boundaries on me?" Charles raised his eyebrows.

"No, but I will if I have to."

Charles paused in silent thought then looked amused. "Let me know if you need help with the shipments." He clutched his briefcase and rose to leave.

Jason cleared his throat. "By the way, we enjoyed the oil." He paused and waited for Charles to stop and turn toward him. "But it's kind of disconcerting to smell strawberries every time I pee."

Charles bellowed a hearty laugh. "You were supposed to put it on *her*."

"I did. Then she rubbed it on me." He laughed out loud. "If you have some manly smelling oils, I'd be interested."

"What about almond oil," Charles said.

"That's good, or walnut, something like that."

"Any of the nut oils then." Charles laughed and turned to leave.

Jason grinned and shook his head. Charles and Tara must have enjoyed each other. Before Charles reached the door, Matt stepped in the doorway.

"Do you two have a minute?" Matt said.

"Whenever you're on my doorstep," Jason said, "it's not good news."

Matt scoffed. "I had a meeting at the Federal Maritime Commission and thought I'd stop by." He came in and glanced at the stacks of boxes and papers. "Moving?"

Charles cleared his throat. "We read the report from the Mounties. That wasn't exactly welcome news. We're trying to find out if my father's law firm knew about the slave trafficking."

"I'd be interested to know that," Matt said.

Jason huffed. "That makes three of us." He reached for the report Mrs. Bailey had prepared on Friday regarding the banana shipments. "Besides the shipping code I told you about, here's another interesting similarity. All of the shipments were inspected by Customs before being delivered to the importer."

Matt looked intrigued. "That means Customs knows."

"Seems that way," Jason said.

"Damn," Matt said. "I'll call the Mounties and tell them. The decoy is scheduled to be unloaded at the container terminal on Wednesday." Matt stepped closer and grasped the back of a chair in front of his desk. "But that's not why I stopped by."

Jason looked up at him, sat back, and glanced at Charles. "What did I tell you? He's always bringing bad news."

Matt chuckled and looked guilty. "I thought you'd want to know … Wilson skipped bail."

"What?" Jason stood up as panic consumed him. "What the hell happened?"

"He cut off his ankle bracelet and put it around a dog collar. By the time the Mounties realized they were following a dog, Wilson was long gone."

"Holy cow." Jason ran his fingers through his soft, short cropped black hair. "Kathleen will freak."

"Don't tell her," Charles said.

Jason crossed his arms and felt cornered. "What the hell am I supposed to do?" He glared at Matt as he stood frozen near his desk.

"Keep her safe until we catch the bastard. She can always move back to the safe house." Matt smirked at him.

Jason tilted his head and gave Matt an incredulous look. "Not a chance."

"I thought not." Matt grinned and turned to leave.

As Matt and Charles left his office, Jason sat down with the weight of the world on his shoulders. He had to step up his efforts to keep Kathleen safe. He couldn't bear to lose her too.

≈

Kathleen rode in a taxi to the safe house, which brought back lots of memories of her time there. When she paid the driver and got out, a man sitting on the porch in a rocking chair met her at the front gate. She began to press the code into the keypad on the gate.

"Can I see some identification, Miss?"

"Sure, I'm Kathleen McDougal."

"I can see that. Can I see some ID?"

She sighed and reached into her pocket for her old driver's license and showed it to him.

"Thanks." He opened the gate and stepped back, allowing her to enter.

It was strange to have someone guard her family but she was pleased that Matt had taken the car explosion seriously. At the front door, she knocked and waited until her father opened it.

"Hey, princess." He opened his arms wide for a big hug.

She embraced him and spent a minute cherishing the feeling of his love. Even though her life had changed for the better, she missed seeing her father over the last two weekends. "Let me see those bandages." She pulled away and inspected his arms until she heard her mother limp out of her bedroom.

"Hey, Mama." Kathleen hugged her gently. "Have your bandages been changed today?"

"They don't need changing. I should know."

"How do you like living here?" She walked with her to the kitchen.

"It's not home, but I feel safe with an armed guard outside."

"Good. Tell me about your plans."

"I want to talk with the FBI to see how long they think this investigation is going to take." Harry joined them in the kitchen. "Are we talking a month or a year?"

"I want you to consider using fake names," Kathleen said.

"Whoa, stop right there," Harry said. "We said before—"

"That was before your car blew up. You should really use another name until the FBI finishes the investigation. I'm sure Matt could introduce you to someone who prints fake IDs."

"Isn't that illegal?" Brenda said.

"It's not illegal to use another name, unless your purpose is to commit fraud," Kathleen replied.

"Did your fancy lawyer boyfriend tell you that?" Brenda sounded sarcastic.

"Yes, Jason knows about these things." She felt perturbed by her mother's disrespect.

"I don't like the idea of you sleeping with a man without being married," Brenda said with a disapproving tone.

Kathleen reached out for her mother's arm and gently laid her hand on her bandage. "I'm sorry to burst your bubble, Mama, but I've been raped so many times—" she bit down on the painful memories, "your fantasy of a virginal white-dress wedding disappeared a long time ago."

Her mother stifled a scream, turned away and leaned over the edge of the sink as if she was going to vomit.

Harry looked down at the table and cleared his throat. "What's Jason doing tonight?"

"He's working." Kathleen felt a bit guilty but not too much. "The FBI investigation is heating up and some things have come to light that he needs to work through." She heard footsteps and rustling at the front door and looked up when Sam entered.

Seeing his sister, Sam smiled and eagerly hugged her. "Hey, sis, long time, no see."

Her forehead wrinkled. "Not you too ..."

He flashed a knowing smile and checked the daily mail his parents picked up at the post office box they rented.

Kathleen followed him into the kitchen. "Should we talk about putting their house up for sale, setting up a trust, and using fake names?"

Stunned, Sam glanced at his mother at the sink and his father sitting at the table. "We need to have a family meeting."

"Not to mention buying a new car," Brenda said, turning away from the sink to face them. "Where is all this money going to come from?"

"If you sell your house and rent an apartment, you'll have that money to use until things settle down."

Brenda sighed and looked at her husband with sad eyes. "We raised our children in that house."

Harry gave Brenda a sympathetic look but kept silent. He put his hands together on the table and laced his fingers, looking down at them.

When Kathleen heard a knock on the screen door, she glanced around to where Jason stood, and went to let him in. She tilted her head up to kiss him and enjoyed their brief caress. "Hi, honey."

"Hello, sweetheart." He saw her family in the kitchen and walked to the table. "How is everyone?" He pecked Kathleen's mother on the cheek. "How are your burns?"

"They're healing," Brenda said, "but the burning sensation is almost unbearable."

"Next time you have burn patients," Harry said, "you'll be more sympathetic."

"That's for sure," Brenda agreed.

Jason glanced at their faces. "Everyone looks so serious."

"We have some serious things to discuss," Harry said. "Our lives have been turned upside down."

Jason leaned back on the kitchen counter and glanced at Kathleen. "Should I leave you to talk?"

"No way." She squeezed his hand. "This is family business and you're part of my family now." He smiled at her but remained quiet. "We need to find out from Matt how long this investigation will take. They can't buy a car until they live somewhere else. They can't live somewhere else until they're either safe or use a fake name. Getting back to normal depends on how long the investigation takes."

"Investigations can take months or years," Jason said, "depending on their complexity."

Brenda mother groaned out loud and looked at her husband for help. "I can't do this." She came to the table and sat down in a chair, facing her husband.

Harry reached for her hand. "We'll do what we have to." He looked at Jason. "I don't think the FBI will allow us to stay here that long. We need to devise a Plan B."

"I suggest you put your assets into a revocable living trust," Jason said, "and set yourselves up with fake identities." He glanced at Kathleen for help when they moaned. Raising his hand to silence them he continued. "Just until this case is settled."

"He's right," Kathleen said. "I love you guys and I don't want to see you killed."

Harry looked at her, slowly blinked his eyes and let out a long breath. "We'll think about it."

She felt frustrated by her parents' lack of urgency. "You don't seem to understand. These people are ruthless."

"They can't even blow up a car," Harry said, dismissing her.

"Dad, believe me, I know. They'll kill you without hesitation."

"Maybe."

Her parents' stubbornness exasperated her. She glanced at Jason who seemed to notice the tension and diverted the subject to something lighter.

"Are we going to see you at the baseball game Saturday?"

"Definitely," Sam said. "Chandra's coming, plus a bunch of law school students."

"Terrific," Jason said. "How about you folks?" He looked at Kathleen's anguished parents. "Care to get some fresh air on Saturday for a good cause?"

"If we want to see our daughter," Brenda said, "I guess we'll have to."

Kathleen had taken as much as she could from her parents. She knew they were frustrated with their situation. She was too. Hugging her father goodbye, she went to her mother who looked at her with a haunted look. She hugged her but she seemed distant. Brenda sniffed and wiped a tear away.

Jason opened the front door and followed Kathleen onto the porch. "What was that all about?"

"I finally had to give her a dose of my reality." She grabbed his hand and walked down the sidewalk. "Her fantasy about me wearing a white wedding dress had to end."

Jason pressed his lips together and gave her a sympathetic look. Putting his arm around her, he placed a tender kiss on her forehead. "Let's go home, sweetheart."

Kathleen looked out the window as Jason pulled away from the curb. Her mother's fantasy was sweet but died long ago for her. No self-respecting man would want to marry a woman who had been violated, bore scars that reminded him he wasn't her first, and who couldn't enjoy sexual relations. *Who would want me for a wife?*

Chapter 14

Jason's footsteps echoed off the walls as he walked down the hallway of FBI headquarters in North Miami Beach. As he neared Matt's office, he glanced around to make sure no one from the human trafficking task force saw him. He turned the doorknob and slipped quietly inside the reception area. Matt's assistant looked up and smiled.

"Morning, Mr. Montgomery. Matt's expecting you." She rose from behind her desk, headed into Matt's office, and stood in his open office door. "Come in please."

Jason moved through Matt's office door as the assistant stepped back and returned to her desk. Matt stared at his dual flat panel computer screens intent on reading something. "What's happening?" Jason leaned over the desk to look at the screens.

"Nothing, yet," Matt said. "It's still early out there."

Jason glanced at his watch. Vancouver was three hours earlier than Miami. He removed his suit jacket and hung it over the back of one of the side chairs. Loosening his tie, he pulled a second chair around the desk to sit next to Matt and settled into it. One computer screen displayed a video feed from a small seaplane, the other screen displayed the Port of Vancouver's computer system which analyzed the weight distribution of each container and directed the huge gantry crane operator to unload boxes from the container ship without sacrificing the ship's balance.

"How often is the seaplane going to fly over the terminal?"

"Every half hour. The Mounties mingled their unmarked seaplane with the regular flights that take folks to Victoria and Vancouver Island. When the container is moved, their helicopter will follow it."

Jason glanced down at the manifest and Bill of Lading for the decoy shipment and checked the computer screen. "Our container's at the bottom of the ship. It's going to take hours for it to be unloaded."

"Yep, better get comfortable. This is going to take awhile."

As the hours passed, the agony of waiting wore on Jason. He paced around Matt's office, trying to push some blood back into his legs. "Nothing's happening. Something's wrong."

"Nothing's wrong, man. It takes hours to unload a ship. Besides they don't know there are people inside."

Another hour passed while Jason checked his email on his smartphone and responded to text messages from Mrs. Bailey.

"Our box is next," Matt said, pointing to the computer screen.

"Finally." Jason leaned forward then looked up when the office door opened.

The liaison officer from the Royal Canadian Mounted Police, who he met months ago, entered Matt's office. "What did I miss?"

"Not much," Matt said. "Our box is being removed now." He shook his hand. "Pull up a chair." He gestured toward Jason, "You remember Jason Montgomery?"

"Yes," Major Whittington said, shaking his hand, "nice to see you."

"Good to see you, sir." Jason shook his hand in return and sat down.

As the major grabbed a seat, the container was removed from the ship by a gantry crane and placed on a flatbed truck.

"Did your folks change the shipping code to 666?" Jason asked.

"I told them," the major said. "As soon as they entered the new shipping code, special instructions were printed on the Bill of Lading. It said a Customs inspection was required and a new delivery address would be provided."

"Amazing." Matt shook his head at Jason.

Dock workers lashed the box to the truck bed before it pulled toward the Customs warehouse and stopped outside the office door. An inspector came out holding papers and spoke to the driver.

"New papers," Jason said.

"The new delivery address," Matt said.

"He's heading to the Import Distribution Center," the major said.

"All containers have to go through there before being delivered."

As the truck left the container terminal, the Mounties' helicopter followed the truck to a traffic light in front of the Import Distribution Center. When the light turned green, the truck did not turn into the warehouse complex but continued straight through the light.

"He's not turning," Jason said.

"What the heck is going on?" Major Whittington said. "They're bypassing regulations."

"Apparently, this is a special shipment," Matt said, smirking at Jason.

He watched the video feed from the helicopter for about five minutes until, not far from the port, the truck turned down Main Street in Chinatown. Pulling into an empty lot between what looked like two Chinese restaurants, the driver got out of the cab and disappeared down the street.

"An empty lot in Chinatown?" the major said.

"That's it?" Jason said.

"Chinatown," Matt said. He sat back in his desk chair, contemplating the significance of that news.

"We'll stake out the empty lot," the major said and stood, removing his cell phone from its holster. "I'll call our lead man in Vancouver." He turned and walked out of Matt's office as he pressed on his phone.

Jason looked at Matt and felt his gut twist. "Chinatown means the slaves are probably sold and put on the express container ship to China."

"From China, they could send captives to the Middle East or anywhere," Matt said.

Major Whittington completed his call to Vancouver and returned to sit by Matt's desk. "This case just escalated into an international incident."

"What do you mean?" Matt said.

"The Chinese Mafia runs that part of town," the major said. "We'd better make sure we have all our facts correct and concrete evidence before we bring that operation down."

Jason felt concerned. "I didn't realize the Chinese Mafia was active in Canada."

215

Matt nodded. "Canada is a haven for slave traffickers who deal with China and the Middle East."

The major crossed his arms. "There are so many Chinese people in Vancouver; the locals are calling it Hongcouver."

"I had no idea." Jason shook his head. "Good thing we're friendly with Canada." He sat back in his chair and watched the video from the helicopter. Hours passed as the truck and container remained untouched. He glanced at his watch. "How long are you going to watch this?"

"As long as it takes," Matt said. "I'll stay all night if I have to."

"Me too," the major said, "but I'm moving to the sofa." He moved to a small couch, messed up the pillows and reclined. "Let me know when something happens."

Jason sat back, stretched out his legs and wondered how long he should stay. Nothing had happened since the container was delivered around four o'clock. Why would they leave people sitting there for so long? He looked at his wristwatch. Kathleen would be done working soon.

"I need to pick up Kathleen from work."

"Bring her here," Matt said. "She might like to see the end."

"I don't know." Jason wasn't sure she could handle the situation. "Watching other captives might bring back too many memories."

"I think she'll like the end," Matt said. "I mean ... to see justice done."

"Maybe, I'll leave that up to her."

≈

When Jason pulled up to the curb at Kathleen's workplace, she scurried to the truck and hopped in the passenger seat.

"Hi, sweetheart." He leaned over to kiss her.

"Hi, hun." She kissed him and put on her seatbelt. "What happened in Vancouver?"

"They delivered the container to Chinatown." He watched her green eyes brighten then fade into contemplation. She sat back in her seat.

"Is that near the railroad tracks?"

"Right next to the tracks, just like you said. Matt said you might like to watch the end." He tried to read her deeper feelings but saw conflict in her face.

She hesitated as her co-workers left work and got into their cars. "I don't know if I could watch slaves being taken into the depths of hell."

"The FBI and the Mounties won't let that happen. They want to end this racket tonight."

She bit her bottom lip. "I'd like to see them be arrested. I'd like to see their faces when they're taken down." She glanced at him, feeling more confident.

"It's the Chinese Mafia." He grabbed her hand. "Did you see Chinese people when you were in Vancouver?"

"Sure, lots. But I was told there were a lot of them in Vancouver so I didn't think anything about it." She looked out the window. "The mafia ... no wonder they're so ruthless."

Jason put the truck into gear and headed back to the FBI headquarters in North Miami Beach. "Let's stop and pick up some food and drinks for everyone. This might be a long night."

He stopped at Rosanelli's Italian restaurant to pick up some thin-crust pizzas before returning to Matt's office. By the time they returned, most of the workers had left for the day. The only light in the hallway came from Matt's window.

Kathleen opened Matt's office door for Jason and stepped back as he carried the pizzas inside.

"Hey, look who's here," Matt said and stood up to shake Kathleen's hand. "I'm glad you came." He turned to the major. "You remember Major Whittington?"

"Yes." She waved to him on the couch. "Nice to see you."

"Here sweetheart, take my chair. I'm tired of sitting."

"Thanks for the food," Matt said. "I'm starved." He reached for a piece of pizza and gobbled it down.

Jason chuckled. "It's something to do while we wait."

When the sky darkened shortly after sunset at ten o'clock, several Chinese people wearing dark blue shirts and pants unlocked the doors on the end of the container. An eyesore in the middle of upscale Chinese restaurants and shops, the large metal box soon became the center of attention.

"Major," Matt said, "they're opening the box."

Major Whittington rose from the couch and joined them in front of the computer screen. The video feed from the helicopter and seaplanes had ended long ago. A new feed from special cameras set up by the Mounties across the street allowed them to watch as a forklift removed pallets of bananas and took them away. Stepping toward the open container were several Chinese men wearing suits and ties. As the workers entered the container to remove the slaves, they soon backed out of the container with their hands raised in the air.

Kathleen gasped. "What's going on?" She leaned forward and looked amazed when several men walked out of the container with automatic weapons aimed at the Chinese. "Who's that?"

"Todd!" Jason felt shocked and surprised.

"Who?" the major said.

"Todd is the head of the FBI dive team." Jason smiled at Matt. "You seem to have left out a few details."

"Sorry, man," Matt said. "I had to be sure you weren't the mole."

Jason felt incredulous. "Why would someone who rescues slaves be a mole for the traffickers?"

"Stranger things have happened," Matt said. "You'd be amazed."

"Look at their faces," Kathleen said with some satisfaction. "Yes!" She pumped her fist, celebrating their defeat.

"How'd you pull this off?" Jason asked, smiling.

"After the dive team searched underwater for the women who were killed," Matt said, "they boarded the ship, opened the container, and removed the women. Half of the dive team stayed inside the container while the rest locked the door and took the victims to safety."

Jason felt used. "You let me think all along there were women in the container." He watched the video streaming through night vision cameras as at least a hundred people dressed in uniforms surrounded the container and began to arrest the workers and their bosses.

218

"What about the people in Aruba and Venezuela?" Kathleen said.

"They're being arrested at the same time as this operation ends," Matt said. "We'll never know how the slaves were transferred to the express ship to China or the train eastbound."

"At some point in every investigation," Major Whittington said, "you have to stop and arrest the bad guys. You couldn't keep this operation going forever."

"I wish we could have gotten the people involved in the rest of the system," Matt said. "Maybe the workers will talk."

"Don't count on it," the major said. "When the Chinese mafia is involved, folks are too afraid to say anything for fear of reprisal. We're lucky we got this far." The major stood up and shook hands with Matt, Jason, and Kathleen. "It was a pleasure sharing this with you good people, but I'm off to bed."

"Thanks for all your help, major," Matt said. "We appreciate seeing this come to an end."

Jason sat back in his chair, feeling amazed at the sudden and dramatic conclusion to the slave trafficking ring. He glanced at Kathleen, who seemed to have mixed emotions. He reached over to rub her back. "What are you thinking?"

"I wish I could see the faces of the people in Aruba and Venezuela, the goons in the casino, those on the fishing boat, the truck driver, and the dock workers. They should spend the rest of their lives in prison."

"There's a lot of corruption in Aruba," Matt said. "This will probably be a minor setback for them."

She shook her head. "My parents are growing tired of living at the safe house. Can they move back home?"

Jason shook his head. He didn't want her to know that Wilson skipped bail. She had finally stopped shaking and her nightmares were subsiding. He didn't want her to suffer a setback.

"Uh ..." Matt glanced from Jason to Kathleen. "Maybe it'd be best if they waited a bit longer."

She sighed, disappointed.

Jason nodded to Matt. Would these arrests keep Wilson from crossing the border and making his way to Miami? The Vancouver operation was history but the reach of the Chinese Mafia was long. And Wilson knew where he and Kathleen lived ....

≈

On Saturday morning, Kathleen and Jason walked toward the baseball diamond, carrying bats, balls, and gloves for the Jawbones versus Sawbones charity event. She smiled at her parents, Sam, and Chandra as they came toward her with Charles.

"Where's Tara?" Charles asked.

"She got a call to audition for a television commercial," Kathleen said. "She'll be here as soon as she's done."

"That's a shame we couldn't go support her," Chandra said.

"She said we'd make her nervous, anyway. It's just as well we had a conflict." She looked around at Jason. "Where are the kids?"

"They're coming on a special bus." Jason turned to look for them. "Here they come."

The school bus pulled to the edge of the grass behind the baseball diamond. When the door opened, the kids hopped off the bus wearing long, baggy shorts past their knees. The group was a mixture of Hispanic, African-American, and Caucasian kids who looked like ten to fifteen-year-old boys. Most sported tattoos on their arms and legs.

Kathleen recognized Carlos as he walked toward Jason. Shaking his hand, Jason put his arm around Carlos's shoulder and pulled him to his side in a man hug.

"Kathleen, you remember Carlos."

"Yes, I do." She extended her hand to him. "It's nice to see you again."

"You too, miss." Carlos smiled wanly. He turned to his friends and introduced them to everyone.

"It's great to see you guys," Jason said. "Thanks for coming out today. You know your assignments, if you have any problems, let me know. Let's have some fun." He raised his arm into the air and the boys gathered around him in a circle and they shouted "1-2-3 Let's Go!"

Cars streamed into the parking area and filled up the spots on the grass near the baseball field. The bleachers on both sides of home plate soon became crowded with parents, friends, and folks wanting to support at-risk teens. The boys helped to park cars, sell snacks, accept donations, and sell fans and visors.

A local radio personality agreed to donate his time to welcome the spectators, introduce the players, and call the game, making wise remarks mostly about the doctors because he was afraid the lawyers might sue. "Money raised today will support after-school activities, tutoring, school supplies, and clothes for at-risk teens."

When the game commenced, Kathleen observed the men weren't bad players considering they all sat behind desks most days. At age twenty-five, Sam showed up the older men. Chandra smiled broadly. She seemed to be happier than ever. Kathleen felt happy for her. She deserved to finally earn Sam's attention. Her parents seemed to have a good time. A chance for relaxation was good for everyone.

At the end of the game, the boys turned in the money to Jason who locked it in a padlocked bag. The boys sat in the bleachers and ate hot dogs and drinks while Jason counted the money. He joined them in the bleachers.

"We raised $10,000 today." The kids cheered. "You did such a great job I'm treating you to ice cream." The boys cheered again and eagerly talked among themselves while Jason put the money in his truck and joined the adults to invite them along.

"I'm worried about Tara." Kathleen glanced at her watch. "This audition is taking way too long."

Before Jason could reply, Matt's car pulled into the baseball field. "Here comes bad news." He glanced toward Charles.

The passenger door to Matt's car opened and Tara stepped out. She looked haunted and drugged. Matt hurried around to help her as she staggered away from his car toward them.

Kathleen gasped and rushed to her friend. "What happened?" She grabbed Tara's hands and looked into her sad eyes.

"It was all a fraud." Tears welled up in Tara's eyes before spilling down her cheeks. "They drugged me and filmed me for a sex video to be sold on the internet."

Kathleen hugged her friend and rocked her as the others joined them. She heard Matt clear his throat.

"Tara was tricked into doing a sex video, which two men posted on the internet to make money. The Miami Police took her to the hospital for tests and called me since this falls into the human trafficking arena."

Kathleen let go of Tara so everyone else could hug her. She wasn't sure how Charles would feel about this, but he hugged Tara the longest, stroking her long slender back. She decided she would go home with Tara and help her deal with her situation with her grandmother.

"I'm sorry, Tara," Jason said. "I know the audition meant a lot to you."

Tears streamed down Tara's cheeks as Kathleen held her hand and the others struggled for the appropriate words to comfort her.

"What are the chances of catching these guys?" Sam asked Matt.

"Good. Tara isn't their first victim. This has happened to several other women, even a female soldier serving overseas, believe it or not."

"Wow." Chandra moved to Tara's other side and rubbed her arm. "That's unbelievable."

"I'm going home with you," Kathleen said to Tara.

"You don't need to do that," Tara said softly. "Go have fun."

Charles stepped forward. "I'll take her home."

Kathleen glanced at Tara, searching her eyes for her agreement.

Tara gave her a thankful look and glanced at Charles. "I'd like that, thanks." She reached her hand out to him and he took it readily and moved to her side.

"I'll see you later." Charles put his arm around Tara and walked toward his black sedan, speaking softly to her the entire time.

Tara leaned her head against Charles as she walked away with him. Kathleen felt relieved that Tara seemed comfortable with him. She could count on him to care for her best friend.

On Monday morning, Charles walked into Jason's office carrying a metal lock box. "Have a minute?" Not waiting for a response, he sat down in the chair across from him.

"What's up?" Jason rested the papers he was reading on the desk.

"I spent some time with my mother and her itch scratcher this weekend," Charles said, setting the lock box on top of his desk. "I found something I thought you'd want to see."

A knock on the door caused Jason to look up and Charles to turn around in his chair. Matt stuck his head inside his office. "You called?" Matt said, looking at Charles.

"I did, thanks for coming on short notice." He waited for Matt to take a seat next to him. "I was just telling Jason, I spent time at my mother's house this weekend and we got to talking about my dad's papers." He opened the lid of the lock box and pulled out an envelope. "She told me she never opened my dad's papers after he died. She never had the nerve." He flipped the envelope over to show Jason the front. It read: To be Opened After my Death.

Jason's eyebrows rose with surprise. "Intriguing ..."

Charles showed the envelope to Matt before opening the envelope and removing a sheet of paper. "This letter is in my father's handwriting. It reads: 'To Whom It May Concern, I have been approached by a Mr. Stephen Longfellow, a man involved with computerizing shipment records for my client, Seaside Shipping LLC. During the conversion from paper records to electronic, the manager discovered that software can be manipulated in such a way as to hide facts that were not possible using paper records. I have threatened the computer manager with reporting him to the Federal Maritime Commission for violation of the Shipping Act of 1984. He has threatened me in return. If I die unexpectedly, I respectfully request that my body undergo testing for unnatural causes of death.' It was signed, Charles Schumacher II, Esquire.

"Unbelievable." Matt removed his cellphone from his pocket.

"I'm shocked," Jason said. "We need to exhume his body."

Charles nodded grimly.

Matt pressed his cellphone screen. "I'll ask the Federal Maritime

Commission to search their paper files for a formal complaint. While they do that, I'll get a search warrant and arrest warrant for the computer manager."

Jason sat back in his high-back leather chair and sighed. *This situation gets deeper by the day. Was Charles' father murdered?*

Chapter 15

Kathleen sat at her desk researching her software project when Chandra came into her office carrying a long box and flashing a broad smile.

"Look what I found at the reception desk."

Confused, Kathleen accepted the box and set it on her desk. "Jason just sent me flowers. It's not my birthday." As she lifted the lid, Chandra stood next to her eager to share her pleasure. When she saw long-stemmed dead roses, she dropped the box top and covered her nose from the putrid smell of rotten leaves. Chandra looked as shocked as she felt. A note card resting on top of the brown, wilted roses read: *McDougal, I'm here to get you, Wilson.* When Kathleen's knees buckled, she clutched the edge of her desk to steady herself until her knees could hold her weight again.

Chandra grabbed Kathleen's arm to steady her. "What's it say?"

"It's from the man in Vancouver. He's here to kill me."

Chandra blanched as her mouth fell open. "Call Jason, you need to get out of here."

"Wilson will follow us home. I can't let him kill Jason." She snatched her small purse, said goodbye to Chandra, and hurried out the door covering her head with a hat and scarf. She looked around the parking lot for anyone who may be watching and ran to the curb. Hailing a taxi cab, she rushed home, running through the lobby past Julio to the elevators. Once inside the condo, she felt safer. Wilson would have to get through a few layers of security before he could get her.

Kathleen picked up the house phone and dialed Jason's office. His assistant, Mrs. Bailey, answered and told her he was in a meeting with clients and wouldn't be available for an hour or two. "Please ask him to call Kathleen when he can." She hung up the phone and paced around the kitchen contemplating what she should do. She couldn't stay in the condo. Wilson knew where she lived, Stephens would have told him. If Wilson could get into the country, he could easily find a way to get into a condo building. She needed to leave before Jason came home and was killed along with her. When the phone rang, she assumed it was Jason and answered it. "Hello?"

"Is Jason there?" a woman asked.

"Not yet. Can I take a message?"

"Tell him to call his mother," the woman said. "I haven't heard from him in a while. Is he dead?" She chuckled in a snide manner.

"No ma'am, he's alive and well."

"Who are you?" Jason's mother said in a light southern accent. "Are you Connie's replacement?"

Kathleen startled. "Ummm, no. Who's Connie?"

"Oh never mind," Jason's mother said. "Just tell Froggy to call his mother. Goodbye."

She gasped as the phone clicked on the other end. *Froggy?* She stumbled against the refrigerator in a panic. His mother called him Froggy. *He can't be. He's not Froggy Watson. No, tell me no!*

She grabbed her hair in a tight fist and tossed the phone onto the counter and almost ran into the bedroom, pulling open the closet door and looking around his dresser and chest of drawers. She yanked open the drawers, tossing through his clothes and miscellaneous junk. The plastic bag he used in Vancouver was hidden under a shirt. Opening the zipper top, she reached for his passport and read it. His name was Froggy Watson. A Florida driver's license said Froggy Watson. Her hands shook as she read everything inside the bag. Everything said Froggy Watson.

She stifled a shriek when she lifted a photo of Jason with a woman who looked Hispanic. He had his arm around her. They both smiled while holding drinks in their hands. She carried the photo through the living room into the kitchen and stood it on the center island, staring at it for several minutes. They looked happy, although Connie was too short for him. A large cross on a necklace hung around her neck. Christmas decorations surrounded their heads and hung from the ceiling and walls. It was Christmas time, but what year? Her mind raced. What was she to him? What feelings did he have toward her?

She took frustrated breaths while she clutched the photo in her hand and reached for a pen and paper. The note she left Jason read: *Froggy, call your mother!* Scurrying into her bedroom, she grabbed a large bag and tossed in some clothes and personal items. Flinging open the front door, she slammed it before hurrying to the elevator. Once in the lobby, she rushed toward the front doors when she saw Charles coming inside. Before she could escape through another exit door, he saw her.

"Kitten, wait!"

She ran down the street past the Easter Island-type sculptures at the Viceroy Hotel, crossed the bridge over the Miami River, ran past the convention center, and headed toward the people mover station.

Encumbered by his dress shoes, briefcase, and suit jacket, Charles chased her and eventually caught up to her. "Stop!"

She took the steps two at a time to the train platform. Her workouts had been good for her. The bell rang on the platform as the small train car approached. Glancing behind her, Charles stormed across the platform toward her, none too pleased. What would she say?

Charles grabbed her elbow and looked very annoyed. "What's going on?"

"You both lied to me!" She jerked her arm away unsuccessfully.

"What are you talking about?"

The train car pulled into the station as they sparred. The doors opened and stayed that way for several seconds as passengers hurried on and off. At the last second, she wrenched her elbow from Charles' strong grasp and jumped inside the people mover before the doors closed. Charles dropped his briefcase and tried to pry open the doors, but they had closed and he couldn't open them. As the train pulled away, he stood on the platform watching her head toward the next stop.

All this time, they had both lied to her. Jason's fake name was Froggy Watson. She was told he killed a slave, Consuela Rivera ... Connie.

Tears ran down her face as her anger grew and her fists clenched. *How dare he use me like his personal plaything.*

As she leaned against the large window grasping the handrail, the people mover whisked her along the elevated tracks toward the next station. She considered her options and decided to visit Tara for a few days. She had been asking her to visit with her and her nana since she returned from Vancouver, but Kathleen had been swept up into Jason's whirlwind life and his need to protect her.

The people mover pulled into the last station in South Miami. She got off and walked to Tara's home. She had always felt at home in the house where Tara grew up. When they were college roommates, Kathleen had visited many times. Tara's grandmother had always welcomed her with open arms. While she didn't have a lot of wealth, her grandmother had always offered her warm hospitality. She had done an admirable job raising Tara after her daughter and son-in-law died in a car accident.

She hurried down the street toward Tara's place, looking behind her to see if anyone followed. Seeing no one, she headed directly for her best friend's home and rang the door bell. When Tara's grandmother opened the door, Kathleen smiled at her and received a big hug in return. "Hello, Nana. Can I impose on you?"

"Oh my heavens, look who's here. Come in. Tara's in the living room."

While Kathleen explained to Tara and her grandmother what happened, she paced the room. Anger filled every nerve ending. She looked down at her cell phone when it rang. "Jason's calling. I don't think I'm ready for that talk yet." She continued to pace and rant about Jason being Froggy Watson and that he killed another slave he had owned more than a year ago.

"I can't believe Jason would kill someone, especially a woman," Tara said.

"I can't either," Kathleen said. "I thought I knew him."

"You *do* know him," Tara said. "Don't let this Wilson guy spook you. That's what he wants. He wants you to run scared. I've had a dose of your reality and I sympathize with your feelings. But I'm also very angry about being used and I'm going to fight to the end."

Kathleen accepted the glass of sweet tea offered by Tara's grand-mother. "Thanks, Nana." She sat down on the sofa. "Matt will catch those guys who attacked you."

"My reputation has been ruined," Tara said. "The video is for sale on the internet. I'll never have a modeling career now." Tara sniffed and looked at her lap.

"Make bad publicity into something good," Kathleen said. "Hold your head high, learn from the experience and parlay that into some-thing positive."

"Is that what you're doing?" Tara said.

"I'm trying hard to turn my life around and you can too," Kathleen said. "We can do it together." She grabbed Tara's hand and held it.

Tara smiled at her, then winced. "If you and Jason break up, we can get a place together."

Kathleen's borrowed cell phone rang. She knew who called before she looked down at the screen. Jason was the only one who called her besides her girlfriends, and he had called at least six times already.

"Are you going to answer it this time?" Tara said.

"I might be calm enough to speak to him in a civil tone." She took a deep breath and crossed one arm in front of her belly to protect herself from the virtual blow she was about to receive. "Hello," she said in a none-too-pleasant tone.

"Kathleen, what the hell—" Jason said.

"Don't you curse at me." She stood and walked away from Tara. "I'm the one who should be cussing you out."

"For what?"

"For one thing, Wilson." She put her hand on her hip. "When were you going to tell me he skipped bail?"

"When I had to." He sighed. "Who told you?"

"Wilson sent me a box of dead roses today. The card said he was here to get me!"

"What? Where are you?"

"My life is in danger and you decide to keep this to yourself?"

"You've been shaking for three months. Why would I tell you Wilson was coming?"

"I've got news for you, Mr. Smooth. I'm strong enough to handle it."

"Mr. Smooth? Where'd that come from?"

"You're unflappable. I've never seen you ruffled."

Jason sighed. "Baby, listen ..."

"And don't call me baby. I'm not a child."

"I know that." He sounded annoyed. "It's a term of endearment."

"No kidding. You can keep your terms of endearment to yourself, until you realize I deserve to be treated with some consideration." She took another breath and continued her rant. "And the second reason I'm mad at you is Connie. What was she to you and why did your mother ask if I was her replacement?"

Jason groaned and paused. "My mother told you about Connie?"

"What matters is you *didn't*. How dare you! What am I to you, an experiment?"

"Maybe, at first. I admit I wanted to help you to overcome my guilt."

"Guilt for what? Killing Consuela Rivera?"

"What? No!"

"We were told she was punished for reporting the owners."

"I didn't kill her. The traffickers killed her and mailed me her foot and hand."

She grunted from the punch in her stomach. "You're Froggy Watson." She heard nothing but silence on the other end of the phone. "Everyone knows you killed Consuela Rivera."

"That's not true. I made Connie report them to the FBI and they killed her for it. We never found her body. Carlos is Connie's son. I promised her husband I would do everything I could to keep him safe."

"I saw the death list in Vancouver and Froggy Watson was on it."

Jason sighed. "When I was a boy, I loved frogs and my mother's last name is Watson. She called me Froggy Watson and still does sometimes. That's the fake name I use to bring slaves home."

"You used me. Who do you think you are? Now I find out that Wilson's here to kill me!"

"I would have told you when it was the right time."

"Well, I don't like being dictated to. I've earned the right to make my own decisions."

"I'm trying to heal you, sweetheart."

"Keeping secrets from me is not helping me heal. You made me feel like a slave again. Here to serve. To do everyone's bidding. No say in anything!"

"I'm sorry, baby. I didn't realize you'd gotten stronger."

"Well I have." She grabbed the phone so hard her hand ached. "I am strong." She clenched her fist in the air to punctuate the point.

"I need to see you. Where are you?"

"I'm too angry to see you. Besides, two people who care about each other don't keep secrets. You're still treating me like a victim."

His strained sigh preceded silence that filled a short void. "Where are you? I'm coming to get you."

"I appreciate everything you've done for me. I know it hasn't been easy. But I'm not coming home, at least not yet. I need to face this myself ... on my own terms."

"I need to make sure you're safe."

"I need time ..." Kathleen looked around the room at Tara's grandmother, the family photos, and Tara sitting at the kitchen table as her grandmother consoled her. "I need time to think about what I want in my life."

"Okay, you know where I am."

"Yes I do. Goodnight." She hung up the phone and clutched her throat, forcing back a sob. She walked into the kitchen and sat down next to Tara, who reached over and hugged her close for several minutes as tears ran down both of their faces. They both faced challenges that have been forced upon them, but they would both overcome them.

≈

Jason's hand shook slightly as he ran it through his hair and hissed a breath of frustration through his lips. Pressing his thumb on his cell phone, he ended his call to Kathleen. He closed his eyes, clenched his jaw and rubbed his forehead. She was angry. She would eventually calm down, think about their relationship, and come home. She didn't move out completely. Her things were still here. She didn't say she would come get them. She wasn't ending their relationship. She was angry about how he treated her. He had kept a secret from her that would have set her recovery back weeks. Maybe he should have told her. He was used to making tough decisions about telling clients everything. Sometimes clients didn't need to know every little detail. But she wasn't a client. She was his lover ... his girlfriend. He had never had a girlfriend live with him before. This experience was new to him. He felt confident he could repair things with her and she would move back home.

He pressed his thumb on his cell phone and used the GPS locator to pinpoint her location. In a couple of minutes he knew she was in a neighborhood in South Miami. He looked up from the edge of the fountain where he sat to stare at the Miami River. Where did Tara and Chandra live? He could follow them home from work. No, he wasn't a stalker. But he needed to know she was safe. He'd have his private investigator follow her and protect her if need be. If anything happened to her, he would never be able to live with himself. His guilt about Connie, his housemaid, had taken a toll on him. He could not imagine the grief he would suffer if the woman he loved ...

"You look miserable," Charles said as he walked up to the fountain by the river.

"I feel miserable." Jason rubbed the back of his neck.

Charles pondered his friend's response and sat next to him on the fountain edge. "I chased her to the people mover but she jumped on the train just before the doors closed."

Jason looked down at his phone. "Thanks for calling me." He looked at Charles. "My mother called the condo and asked her if she was Connie's replacement."

Charles groaned. "Not a good thing."

"She thinks I killed Connie."

"That's crazy," Charles said.

"Plus, Wilson sent her dead flowers today. He's here in the city. He'll probably come for me too. He won't know Kathleen isn't still living here."

"You're staying at my place until this is over," Charles said. "I know you're a big strong man who can take care of himself, but setting yourself up as a decoy is nuts."

"If he comes for her, I can keep him from killing her."

"You're staying with me."

Jason looked down at the GPS tracking on his phone. "She's in South Miami."

"Tara lives down there. Want me to call her?"

Jason paused and thought about his options. He wanted Charles to call Tara but he didn't want to involve him in his personal affairs. "They both need time alone. Let them discover what they want in their lives ... two high-intensity men or a solitary life full of peace and quiet." He smiled at Charles, squinted at the reflection off the water, and flipped down his sunglasses.

Charles chuckled. "Believe it or not, a life full of peace and quiet is beginning to appeal to me."

Jason felt doubtful and gave his friend a disbelieving look.

"If we have to start our business over again," Charles said, "I was thinking of buying the club as a second income."

"That doesn't sound very peaceful to me."

"We could run it together." Charles raised one eyebrow. "Interest in BDSM has really increased lately."

Jason shook his head. "I don't think so. The club was fun when I went with you but living that lifestyle full time takes too much work. After a hard day's work, I want some down time. I don't enjoy the power exchange like you do. Making every decision for another person full time is too much. Besides, I liked sharing my home and my life with Kathleen. We did everyday things together, shared our lives, shared secrets ..." He thought about her and wondered if she would miss him as much as he already missed her.

"Sounds like you're falling in love with her," Charles said.

"I believe I have." Jason looked up at Charles to see a smile of knowing satisfaction on his face. What could he do to win her back? Buying things for her was tacky, like buying her love. He didn't want that kind of relationship. He had ones like that before and soon discovered those were shallow and meaningless. He cherished the intimate bonding time he spent with Kathleen. Doing those silly Karezza routines for almost two weeks, he realized their evening intimate rituals had indeed bonded them together. She hadn't said she wanted to move out. She said she wasn't coming home, not yet anyway. He felt hopeful about that but he needed to make sure she was safe.

Jason called the private detective he used to protect the McDougals in the hospital and gave him Kathleen's location. His surveillance would start right away, which gave Jason a feeling of satisfaction and relief that someone would be watching over her while he couldn't.

"Want to take a walk?" Charles said. "I'd like your advice about how to treat a woman who's been assaulted."

"You're asking me for advice?" Jason chuckled and reached for his keys and phone. "I'm the guy whose girl just told him off." He forced a smile but didn't feel happy, instead he felt strained and agonized over her anger. Walking with Charles along the Miami Riverwalk, he gazed at cigarette boats, jet skis, and dog walkers while he related some of the things Dr. Jennifer had shared with him about psychological challenges of victims of sex crimes. "Are you interested enough in Tara to survive the challenge? Because a challenge it is."

"I've watched you do it and you've made it look easy," Charles said. "I'm sure it's been difficult. I don't know if I have the patience you do. Besides, Tara and I are just having fun together. We're not in a serious relationship."

"Tara might think differently now. She might not want anything to do with being dominated in bed and tied up."

Charles crossed his arms in a defensive mode. "Mutual consent between two adults is completely different than being assaulted against your will for profit."

"That's true. But the fact remains that she was violated and may not be able to deal with it right away. She's going to need more romancing now."

"There's only one way to find out." Charles nodded and smiled.

While Jason walked back to the condo with Charles, he thought about what Kathleen had said and realized he never really asked her out on a date. He never took her dancing, to see a movie, or other things that might be considered a date. They were thrown together in Vancouver and made the best of their situation. This brief separation might give them a chance to start over like two people who love each other and want a more permanent relationship. Hopes of mending his bond with her flooded his thoughts with endless possibilities. Eager to begin anew, his urgency to see her peaked.

Chapter 16

Kathleen looked both ways before leaving her office building. She stepped out onto the sidewalk, her head covered with a scarf and floppy hat. Tossed by the afternoon sea breeze, she clutched it and scurried toward the bus stop. Before she could reach her destination, tires squealed when a car slid to a stop next to her. The front door flew open and Wilson hopped out. Another car roared toward her, nearly hitting the first car when it screeched to a halt. A middle-aged man got out of the second car. When the stranger and Wilson both rushed toward her, she ran in the opposite direction, hearing gunshots behind her. Glancing over her shoulder, she saw the other man lying in the street.

Wilson shot him and had now raised the gun at her. "Stop right there, bitch."

She turned to face him. "You may as well shoot me too. I'm not going back to Vancouver."

"You won't die that easy. Get in the car!" His lip snarled upward when he moved the gun muzzle in that direction.

She raised her hands. "I'm not going anywhere with you." When she heard shouting, she turned her head to see a group of co-workers running toward her.

Wilson aimed his gun at them and pulled the trigger.

"No!" Kathleen screamed as one person fell to the ground. Her co-workers stopped advancing and surrounded the wounded person. "Stop shooting people because of me!"

"Get in the car," Wilson said in a sinister tone.

She got into the backseat of the car while Wilson got into the driver's seat and sped away. Tires squealed as Chandra and her co-workers watched her streak away. She should never have asked them to help her

236

hide from the slave traffickers. It put them at risk and she had no right to do that. She felt guilty and hoped the injured person wasn't killed. At least there were witnesses to Wilson taking her. They would call the authorities. Chandra would call Jason and he would tell her parents. The circus would start all over again. But this time, it would end. She would never survive slavery a second time. No matter what happened, Wilson wouldn't take her again.

Wilson drove to the Port of Miami where he stopped at the entrance gate, flashed some papers, and muttered to the guard. The arm at the gate rose and Wilson hit the gas, thrusting the car forward toward Seaside Shipping.

Kathleen wondered if Jason had found a link between his client and the traffickers. Tensing, she realized she might be about to find out what that link might be.

Wilson halted in front of the Seaside Shipping office where Jason had brought her months ago. He opened the back door and yanked her out of the car. Sticking his gun in her back, he shoved her through the office door. A young woman sitting at the front desk glanced up as she entered with Wilson close behind her. As he pushed her along, Kathleen kept walking forward.

"Can I help you?" the receptionist said and stood up. "You can't go in there."

Kathleen moved down the hall of office doors while Wilson pressed harder into her back. At the last door, he kicked it open and shoved her inside.

An older white man sat behind a desk and looked up with surprise as she stumbled into his office. He was meeting with another man who sat with his back to her. When he turned to look at her, his mouth fell open, his face turned white.

"Hello, Joe," Kathleen said when she recognized Joe Hargraves from the FBI human trafficking task force.

"What are you doing here?" Joe said.

"I should ask you the same question." She observed the computer reports tacked on the cork boards on the wall.

"I'm responsible for immigration and customs inspections at the port," Joe said.

"Then why are you meeting with the computer manager?" She cocked one eyebrow.

"Why'd you bring her here?" the man behind the desk said, looking behind her.

"What's the matter?" Wilson said. "Don't like seeing the faces of your victims?"

Kathleen stiffened at his remark. She immediately realized that Joe and the computer manager worked together on the slave trafficking scheme but had succeeded in washing their hands of any direct involvement, easing their guilt.

"I want you to tell the Chinese I've got the bitch that brought us down. She won't be any more trouble," Wilson said.

"I don't want to be involved in this," the man behind the desk said. "You're on your own. I told you that when they killed Consuela Rivera."

Kathleen inhaled and looked at Wilson in disbelief.

"I'm taking care of business," Wilson said to the man behind the desk. "You need to take care of your end."

"Get her out of here," Joe said. "You might have been followed."

"I wasn't followed," Wilson said. "You tell the Chinese to let my brother go and I'll take care of this bitch for them."

With shock on their faces, Joe and the manager stared at her, then saw the gun in Wilson's hand. "I didn't sign on for anything like this," the manager said. "Get out of my office!"

"You will do as I say!" Wilson shouted.

"Get out!" The manager stood up. "Ginger, call the police!" he shouted out the office door.

Wilson aimed his gun at the man and pulled the trigger. As the older man fell behind his desk, Wilson turned his gun toward Joe, who raised his hands in the air.

"Don't shoot," Joe said. "Tell me what you want and I'll do it."

Kathleen hated him even more than she already did. Weasel of a man. When she heard sirens, Wilson grabbed her hair and pulled her out of the office and down the hall past the receptionist, who cowered behind the water cooler. He pushed her through the front door toward the ship docked alongside the container terminal where a gantry crane loaded hundreds of boxes onboard.

Dock workers hurried around, trucks moved in and out of the facility bringing containers to be loaded. No one noticed Wilson had a gun in her back. Miami Police cars roared into the facility, lights flashing and sirens blaring, headed for the Seaside Shipping office.

When she reached the gangplank, she held her breath and ran across it. Crew members saw them embark and hurried toward them. Wilson pointed his gun at them and they stopped where they were, raising their hands. She mocked them in her mind. Raising their hands had no meaning to Wilson. He would shoot anyone just for the fun of it.

"Stop shooting people!"

He snarled at her. "Get downstairs where you belong." He shoved her toward the metal stairway leading below deck.

Stepping off the bottom of the stairs, she headed toward the large room where she had been so many times in Vancouver. The metal gangway door stood open, she stepped over the raised threshold into the dingy room full of folding tables and chairs. A far cry from the elegant room on the other ship the traffickers used for slave auctions. This room looked like a mess hall and socializing area for the crew.

Wilson shoved her into the center of the room. "Sit down while I think."

She complied with his orders for now. Time would tell when she could make her move. She had no intention of going back into slavery. He would have to kill her this time. Or she would kill him. Either way, her life was over. Taking another person's life went against her upbringing. How could she cope with the reality of killing him when the only alternative was to be killed? Neither prospect appealed to her but something had to be done and she would be the one to do it ...

At the same time, Jason stood in the salon of his sailboat wearing a camouflage wet suit, his weapons and equipment strewn on the table. He reached for his pistol and put it on his dive belt where another pistol already hung. Pulling his dive hood over his head, he reached for the underwater assault rifle, just in case frogmen surprised him underwater.

Charles stood in the galley. "You brought your Glock?"

"I'm not sure what I'll need. I can use it underwater but only for close-range self-defense. It works better above water." Jason removed the other pistol from his belt and admired it. "Now this baby ... it works underwater. A Heckler & Koch used by special ops teams."

"No kidding. How'd you get that?"

Jason smiled. "I know some very interesting people."

"I can see that. Are you sure you're not an undercover agent?"

Jason laughed. "I'm friends with some unique folks who appreciate my interest in the finer things in life."

Charles chuckled and removed a bottle of liquor from a cabinet in the galley. "Ready?"

"Ready." Jason picked up the underwater assault rifle, hanging the strap around his back allowing the rifle to rest across his chest. He followed Charles to the deck above where the lines on the sails gently knocked against the rigging.

Charles unscrewed the top on the bottle of liquor and poured it over his head. He stuck out his tongue as the alcohol ran down his blond hair, over his face, and trickled down the front of his clothes. He smiled at Jason. "Do I smell like a drunk?"

"You smell like one to me." Jason glanced over his shoulder. Growing more serious, he looked at his watch. "Matt said to meet him at the container ship in fifteen minutes. Let's move." He arranged his dive mask, flippers, and rebreathers on the seats around the deck while Charles moved behind the helm.

Charles started the engines while Jason tossed off the dock lines allowing the *Legal Ease* to move slowly away from her slip at the Miami Marina. A morning tropical breeze filled the sails. Charles steered toward the container ships docked nearby at the Port of Miami. When

240

he neared the ship a few minutes later, he shut down both engines and used the sails to maneuver toward the gargantuan vessel.

Jason put on his flippers and mask, held the rebreather in his hand and slipped underneath a loose sail curled on the deck near the edge of the boat. "Matt said the tugboats would leave us alone but you still need to be convincing." He ducked his head beneath the spare sail.

"Don't worry," Charles said. "I can play a drunk. Just make sure to slip over the side without being seen or we both might be shot."

"Sail close enough to the ship and I'll do the rest." Jason lowered the sail over his face, hiding in darkness. He held the flapping sail over his body as the boat headed toward the port. He lifted one corner and saw the dark hulk of the ship looming far above his head. He heard a horn sound and shouts from above.

A monotone announcement over a loud speaker blared toward them, skipping across the water. "Stay away from the ship."

Charles swayed and stumbled around as Jason held the sail just above the decking, allowing him to watch. "Hold on," Charles whispered.

The *Legal Ease* nudged into the side of the container ship. Jason visualized the mast knocking against the giant black hulk when it creaked. Men with strong foreign accents shouted from above. Jason couldn't tell what they were saying but by their tone, he knew they weren't happy.

"Get away from the ship!" one angry voice said.

Charles stumbled around the deck. "You're in my slip!" His slurred speech followed by a hiccup added to the effect. "Move your ship out of my way!"

"Move away from the ship or we'll shoot!" the angry male voice yelled.

Jason tensed. He didn't want any shooting.

Charles stumbled to the handrail. "You're parked in my slip. You need to move!" He hiccupped and waved his arm dismissively. "I paid a lot of money to dock here."

When Jason heard men shouting and running, he wondered if this plan was going to work. A boat engine roared closer to their sailboat. Rubber squeaked as the bumpers nudged against it.

241

"Captain," a stern male voice said on a loud speaker, "you're being boarded."

Jason couldn't move without blowing his plan. When lines dropped on the deck in front of him, a man stepped aboard their vessel

The man shouted to the crewmen above. "We'll take care of this."

After a pause the man lowered his voice. "My name's Capt. Fielding from the Port Authority. Matt asked us to intervene. We'll stay here until the operation ends."

"Good deal," Charles said. "As soon as the men on the ship stop watching us, my partner will dive overboard."

"We have a diver who can help him get on the ship. They're starting to move away, but wait a couple minutes to be sure," the man said.

Charles stumbled around some more to make a convincing case. "Get that rust bucket out of my slip!"

The man from the Port Authority pulled out his handcuffs, stepped behind Charles, and put his wrists in them without locking them. "We got him." He moved in front of Charles and pulled out some papers and a pen. "Okay, now I'm reading you your rights. You have the right to stand here and stumble around while we delay whatever is happening. Your buddy has the right to slip over the side now that the men have left the railings."

Jason heard him and slithered from under the sail and silently slipped over the side of his sailboat into the Biscayne Bay. He put the rebreather into his mouth and went underwater, heading toward the dark hulk of the ship's hull. Propelling himself lower beneath the ship, he kicked toward the dock side of the ship. No one could see his bubbles. They wouldn't know he was there. As he neared the dock, he looked down and saw white bones on the bottom of the bay. Assuming it was a manatee carcass, he swam lower until he realized they were human remains. When he saw the skeleton wearing a necklace with a large cross, he rose up and almost gulped water. *Connie Rivera.* He reached for the necklace and gently lifted it from her neck. One hand and one foot were missing from the bones. These remains were definitely hers. Slipping the necklace into his belt, he swam to the surface between the ship and the dock.

Before his head broke the surface, he looked and listened for anyone around the vessel and the dock. Seeing no movement and hearing nothing, he popped his head above water and saw large lines running from the ship to the dock, securing it. A huge gantry crane loaded containers, which took the attention of the crew away from his sailboat and Charles. He looked for a ladder where he could climb onto the deck of the ship but saw none.

Aware that a container ship only had thirteen crew members, he knew he could easily climb onboard and search for Kathleen, with the crew distracted. He didn't have to wait long. When he heard shouting and running along the deck of the ship, his chance to board the vessel unobserved had arrived. He slipped beneath the water's surface and kicked toward the back of the vessel. His heart jumped when he saw bubbles and the silhouette of a diver opposite him.

The other diver wore a police badge at his shoulder, easing his grip on his rifle's trigger. When the frogman saw him, he pointed toward a ladder at the back of the ship and raised his thumb.

Jason saw two rungs of what appeared to be a ladder, raised a thumb in response, and followed the other diver. Lifting his head out of the water, he grabbed the bottom rung to steady himself.

"I wondered what happened to you."

The Port Authority diver smiled and stepped on the ladder. "I'll go first in case there's trouble."

Jason nodded and followed as he climbed the enormous ship. When he and the other diver reached the engine room, he stepped onto the deck, glanced around, and pointed in the direction of the room where he remembered Kathleen and the other slaves had been auctioned. Wilson would probably do the same thing on this ship that he did in Vancouver. Jason removed the Glock from his belt and headed for the metal door ahead. Backing against the wall, he waited until the other diver stepped to the other side of the door. He nodded to the other man and hoped he wasn't too late to save Kathleen.

＝

243

Kathleen sat calmly in the large open room while Wilson watched out the portholes. He nervously fiddled with the pistol he carried. "What are you planning to do with me?" she asked.

"I'm going to kill you, like I should have in Vancouver. Too bad you were too smart for your own good." Wilson glanced over his shoulder at her. "This time you outsmarted yourself."

She clenched her jaw and waited for the rampage that was about to erupt. She knew him well enough to know that he carried a tremendous amount of rage inside. He would explode any minute as he paced nervously around the room.

Before that happened, a man in a wetsuit and mask kicked open the metal door, stepped into the room, and raised his gun. Popping sounds from Wilson's gun preceded the frogman falling to the floor.

Kathleen covered her mouth to stifle a scream but soon realized the diver was not Jason. This man's hair was brown and longer.

Wilson cursed, raised his gun toward the open door, and grabbed her from behind. Pointing the pistol at her temple, he cocked the hammer.

Jason stepped through the door with his pistol aimed squarely at them.

Wilson flinched. "Stop right there, Montgomery!"

"Easy Wilson. Let her go."

Wilson grabbed Kathleen's long auburn hair and pulled her head back. "Come after me and I'll shoot her."

"You okay, sweetheart?" Jason said.

"So far," she said and winced.

"Let her go and we'll go easy on you."

"Ha!" Wilson said. "You can't fight the whole Chinese mafia! Besides, I'll get out of jail just like I did this time. They own lots of people."

"You don't own McDougal," Jason said. "I bought her, she belongs to me." She glared at him before he winked at her. "Look Wilson. Stop now and help us fight these people."

"You can't fight them! They control everything!" Wilson pushed her toward the door. "If I change sides, they'll kill me and my brother."

Remembering that Wilson was trapped too, she briefly considered sympathy towards him. But no, he had killed too many people. And now he would kill her. She clenched her jaw and stepped through the raised threshold where Wilson pulled her backwards down the hallway.

"McDougal and I are taking a walk." Wilson stepped back to the metal staircase where he pulled her up the steps. Jason followed them with his pistol drawn. Wilson paused before emerging onto the main deck with her in tow.

Several vehicles with flashing lights sat in front of the shipping office. She wondered what story Joe would tell. As Wilson pulled her up another set of stairs leading to the next higher deck, she saw the Biscayne Bay far below and stiffened.

Jason followed close behind, his gun drawn, waiting for a chance to shoot.

"Stay back!" Wilson turned his gun toward Jason and pulled the trigger.

Kathleen screamed. Relief flooded her when Jason ducked behind a steel beam where the bullet ricocheted. She loved Jason. She couldn't bear to see him injured or killed because of her. It seemed this was the way her life was supposed to end. She had cheated death many times over the past year only to face it now head-on, one-on-one with Wilson. She wondered where all the crew had gone. The ship seemed like a ghost town. When she saw smoke billow into the air on the other side of the ship, she realized someone had set a fire. She heard shouting. This was Wilson's time and her time. She would not go any farther.

Wilson pushed her along until she stood at the edge of the ship where he spun her around to face him. "This is where you die." He raised the gun to her chest.

"Wait, I have a goodbye present." She reached into her pocket and removed the shiny metal PED that Nathan had given her. "It's a coin. You can see yourself in it." She flicked the red tab on the edge, flipped it to him, and stepped back to the railing at the edge of the ship. Clutching the Dutch slave bead around her neck, she saw a flash in his eyes as he caught it.

He gazed at his reflection in the mirrored surface when the PED

245

exploded. The force of the explosion pushed her backwards over the railing above Biscayne Bay where she plummeted toward the water ....

≈

"No!" Jason watched the woman he loved blown backwards, falling helplessly toward the water, stories below. He pulled on his flippers and stepped off the side of the ship near the place where she hit the water and sank. Slicing through the surface of the water like a torpedo, he slowed his descent with his arms and looked around for her. When he saw Kathleen, she looked unconscious. He kicked toward her, grabbed her by the arms and pulled her quickly to the surface. When his head broke the surface, he saw his sailboat. With one arm around Kathleen, he swam with the other toward the *Legal Ease*.

Charles tossed a flotation device tied to a line into the water. "Holy cow, man." He stretched out with a boat hook ready to pull Jason toward the boat. "Is she okay?"

Jason reached for the floating ring and put it around Kathleen. "Toss me a boogie board."

Charles disappeared below deck, then returned carrying the requested foam board, tossing it into the water.

Jason reached for it and maneuvered it beneath Kathleen to hold her up, then swam backwards toward his boat. "I need your skills with rope." He floated her alongside the ladder to the sailboat. "Push the mast over the water, throw a line over it and lower it down to me."

Charles lowered the line to the surface of the water next to Kathleen and adeptly moved down the ladder, lowering himself into the water. Taking the line hanging down from the mast arm, he wrapped it around Kathleen and the boogie board and tied it into a single knot above her. "You're stronger than I am. You hoist her."

Jason climbed the ladder, untied the rope from the handrail, and pulled until she dangled in the air, even with the decking.

Charles followed her up the ladder and yanked her over the deck while Jason lowered her down. He hastily untied the knots and freed her from the boogie board.

Turning Kathleen on her side, Jason thumped the middle of her back to remove any excess water she might have swallowed. Soon she gasped and started coughing. Her eyes flew open but she looked dazed.

Jason picked her up and laid her on a seat cushion. Kneeling at her head, he brushed her hair away from her face and caressed her forehead.

Charles grabbed her arm. "Do you know where you are, kitten?"

Her eyes focused on his face then looked at Jason, who brushed water from her cheek. "Yes." She coughed. "I'm with the two best men in the world." She covered her mouth and coughed a few more times.

Jason hugged her, caressing the back of her wet head. "Thank heaven, I thought I lost you."

Kathleen gasped for air. "Steady counselor, you won't get rid of me that easily."

He held her tight and rubbed her back. "I love you, baby."

She touched his face as he pulled back to look into her eyes. "I love you, too." Their lips met in a tender kiss.

Fearing he had almost lost her, Jason closed his eyes, held her close, and cherished these precious moments when he heard Matt's voice.

"We have an ambulance leaving, let's get Kathleen in it." Matt looked down over the edge of the ship.

She sat up on the cushion and looked up. "I'm okay."

"You need to be checked for a concussion," Jason said, kneeling at her feet.

"Please, take me home." She tenderly touched his face.

He joined her on the cushion and pulled her close, cradling her head in his large hand then looked up at Matt. "We're going home."

"Watch for headaches," Matt said. "Take her to the hospital right away."

"I will," Jason said.

Charles started the engines and turned the vessel toward the Miami Marina.

Jason squeezed Kathleen tight, tucking her head under his chin.

She looked up at him. "How'd you find me?"

"I traced your cell phone," Jason said. "It was in Wilson's car outside Seaside Shipping."

Her eyes looked sad. "Joe Hargraves was the mole."

"No kidding? Joe?" Jason looked at Charles.

Kathleen closed her eyes. "He's at the Seaside Shipping office with the computer manager. He admitted the whole thing."

Jason tensed. "Toss me my phone." He extended his hand toward Charles, who tossed it to him, and called Matt to make sure he arrested Joe Hargraves.

Matt answered and confirmed they found Joe with the dead body of the computer manager. "He was so afraid of being killed by the Chinese mafia, he admitted everything."

Jason disconnected the call and looked at Kathleen. "They got him." He glanced at Charles, who clenched his jaw. "I could never figure out why Joe was so hostile toward me."

"He must have been afraid you'd figure out what was going on," Charles said. "What about the computer manager? Did he admit his role?"

"He didn't make it," Jason said.

"Wilson shot him for not calling the Chinese and telling them to release his brother," Kathleen said. "Apparently the Chinese got him out of jail to kill me and threatened to kill his brother if he didn't."

"What a mixed up mess." Jason closed his eyes and stroked her back.

Charles winked and smirked. "I'm telling you, a life of peace and quiet is starting to look awfully good."

Jason laughed, pulled Kathleen closer and held her until they arrived at the marina a few minutes later. "How do you feel? Do you have a headache?"

She shook her head. "I'm fine. I just want to go home."

After securing the boat, Jason walked with his arm around Kathleen to the end of the dock through the gate, when Matt pulled into the parking lot. "Not more bad news."

"I can't take anymore," Charles said.

Matt strolled toward them. "Thanks for your help, both of you."

He shook their hands. "Between your distracting the crew and Carlos bringing his buddies to make a ruckus, the ship's crew was preoccupied enough to arrest all of them plus the folks at the shipping office on suspicion of slave trafficking. We'll question all of them until we get some answers." He turned to Kathleen. "I'd like you to answer some questions when you're feeling better."

"I'd be glad to," she said. "What's going to happen to Joe Hargraves?"

"He'll be thoroughly investigated and charged," Matt said. "He told me he needed the money to pay his wife's medical bills."

"She had cancer, right?" Charles said. Matt nodded.

"That's sad," Kathleen said.

"Sure is." Jason put his arm around her and held her close. Then he remembered and removed Connie's necklace from his dive belt. "Afraid it's my turn to give the bad news. I found Connie's remains under the ship near the dock. Here's the necklace Charles and I bought her for Christmas." He put the necklace into Matt's outstretched palm. "One hand and one foot were missing, so it's definitely her."

"I'm sorry," Matt said. "Our dive team will bring up her remains so Carlos can give her a proper burial."

"We'll pay for that," Charles said. "It's the least we owe her."

"And Carlos," Jason said.

Kathleen had her head down, peering at the dock. Jason tugged her to his side. "Connie was our house maid." When she looked at him, her green eyes reflected sadness. "Charles and I paid her to clean up after our Christmas party. When the traffickers found out she kept the money, they beat her pretty badly. The next time we saw her, she had black and blue marks all over her body. When she admitted she was a slave, I forced her to report the traffickers to the FBI. She disappeared right after that, until one day I received her hand and foot in the mail."

Kathleen closed her eyes at the painful vision and remembered what the computer manager had said. "The Chinese mafia killed her."

"How do you know?" Jason said.

"The computer manager said that to Wilson." She gave him a sympathetic look.

249

"That reminds me," Matt said. "Wilson won't be bothering you again. When the PED exploded, he fell backwards and hit his head on a steel beam. I'm not sure which killed him but the end is the same."

Jason felt relieved at their new-found freedom and knew Kathleen did too when she sighed and relaxed against him. "Your parents will be glad to hear that."

"Maybe they can move back home," she said, smiling up at him.

"What about the shipping company?" Charles said. "Is there any evidence that more folks knew what was going on?"

"None so far," Matt said. "The dock workers in Venezuela will shed some light on that. Unless we uncover something, it's between you and them whether you continue your business relationship."

Charles seemed torn about the possibility. Jason put his hand on his best friend's shoulder. "We'll schedule a meeting this week. Let's get this resolved."

Charles clenched his jaw and nodded. "That would be best."

Jason tugged Kathleen to his side and walked toward his truck. "Would you like to go out for dinner tonight?"

Her green eyes danced when she squeezed his side. "I'd like to stay home."

That made him very happy. Now, they could start their relationship over. Tonight there wasn't going to be any Karezza ... tonight there would be thrusting ...

≈

Kathleen rubbed her long auburn hair with a bath towel, drying it as best she could before dressing in her tights, a tunic top with a wide belt around her slender waist and slipping her feet into high-heeled shoes. She put on some light make-up and blow dried her hair, fluffing it in the full-length mirror before heading out of her bedroom into Jason's condo. She had moaned when the hot shower caressed her tired, aching back muscles. Not sure if it was the fall or the positions she had been in with Wilson, she felt relieved to be free of his evil ways.

When she found Jason sitting outside on the balcony gazing over the Miami River, she tiptoed behind him, bent over and kissed his cheek.

"Hey!" Jason turned, grabbed her and pulled her across his lap, laughing all the while.

She shrieked playfully and laughed as they wrestled together on the lounge chair.

"It's great to see you laughing," he said.

Kathleen smiled and laid her head on his chest, kicking her feet in the air. "I feel so happy and free. This is the best day since Vancouver." She looked into his dark blue eyes. "Since the day I met you."

Jason grinned and leaned down to kiss her, endlessly and passionately. His breathing increased as she relaxed across his lap, tasting his lips and enjoying the heat and the love she felt. "You talked to your parents?"

"Yes, it took some time to explain everything that happened, but they're thrilled not to feel threatened anymore." She kissed him with an eagerness she hadn't felt before. She had almost lost him, not to mention her own life.

Jason caressed her nipple through her tunic until it stiffened. He unfastened her belt, lifted her top, and reached up to hold her bare breast in his palm. He squeezed and fondled it until it grew in size.

Her breathing increased as they kissed and played with each other. So happy to be alive and free, Kathleen couldn't keep herself in check. When she felt his penis stiffen beneath her butt, she wiggled seductively on his lap, teasing him until he groaned.

"You're killing me baby." He kissed and nibbled her neck.

"Please make love to me," she whispered in his ear and bit his earlobe.

He lifted her off his lap and carried her into the bedroom they had shared together. Gently laying her on the bed, he leaned over her and kissed her, rubbing her body until she squirmed. He lifted her tunic over her head and tossed it on the floor, smiling at her before sucking a hard nipple into his hot, wet mouth. Pulling down her tights and tossing them and her shoes on the floor, he pulled her naked body against him and savored every inch of her.

Her breathing increased as he caressed her body. Wetness and heat engulfed her swollen folds, throbbing at the thought of him entering her. No Karezza tonight. She wanted him inside her, thrusting against her, agonizing with each heated thrust, panting, she clutched the back of his neck and held him against her mouth while he gently thrust into her, firm yet gentle.

Her nipples hardened, her breasts swelled in anticipation of his wet, passionate kisses. She could smell her arousal, heady, musky, needy, wanting him. She pulled him on top of her and reached around his back, opened her legs and raised them in the air, encouraging him to pound into her wet, swollen folds.

He took her welcoming posture and pounded into her, repeatedly, effortlessly, until she felt an increasing spiral of pleasure, the tension, the heat, the throbbing, the wanting. Her eyes opened wide as she felt an enormous orgasm raging inside her. Surrendering to her man, she conquered her fears. She screamed in ecstasy for several minutes as Jason pumped into her, holding back until she finished. Her toes curled at the intensity of her climax.

He continued to pump into her, slowly, calmly building his release until finally he ejaculated inside her as she squeezed him internally with tender muscles that milked him of every drop of fluid until he relaxed on top of her, exhausted.

They rolled over onto their sides still intact and held each other until they drifted off into a gentle snooze, holding and caressing each other.

"I want to talk to you about changing your name," Jason whispered.

She thought this was an odd time to discuss that. Finally, she had experienced an orgasm. The first one in more than a year, and he wanted to talk about security. With disbelief, she gazed at him as he lifted his head to look into her eyes.

His eyes turned dark. "How does Kathleen Montgomery sound?"

Her heart skipped a beat. Had she heard correctly? When his warm smile touched her, she realized she had. "Are you propositioning me, counselor?"

"If we're going to live together, we need to talk about making it legal."

She grinned and hugged him. "That would make my mother happy."

His warm sincere look seared her skin. "I want to make *you* happy."

"You have. I'm very happy." She kissed him, tasting his lips until he stiffened inside her. They replayed another love scene before night turned into morning. She had conquered her fears and he conquered her heart.

Chapter 17

The next morning Kathleen was awakened from a contented sleep by the ring of Jason's cell phone. He groaned and removed his arm from around her waist.

She glanced at the clock ... 6 a.m. *Good heavens, who would call this early on a weekend?*

He answered the call and listened to the caller for several minutes. "I'll be there." He placed his phone on the nightstand and gave her a sympathetic look. "There's one more thing I need to do before this is over."

"What's that?" She stifled a yawn with her hand.

"I need to save Connie's husband from the fields. Today is the first day in more than a year, it might be possible."

"Interesting ... arresting Joe Hargraves changed the game in our favor."

"Apparently he was involved in several trafficking schemes."

Feeling exhilarated, she threw off the covers and jumped out of bed. "Let's go." Grabbing her tights and tunic, she dressed, brushed her teeth, and picked up her little purse. When she came into the bedroom, she repulsed at Jason's clothes.

He had thrown on a pair of baggy shorts, a Hawaiian shirt, and a pair of brown leather sandals over white socks.

She grimaced at his appearance. "You're not going dressed like that."

"I'm playing a tourist. I need to look like one for this charade."

She looked down at her clothes. "Should I change?"

"You're fine. You're not getting out of the car." He grabbed his phone, car keys, hand gun, fake identification, and hurried toward the front door. "I'll fill you in on the way."

254

She felt excited for Carlos and for Jason. To free Carlos' father from slavery would be a great achievement for Jason. That would go a long way toward helping him deal with the guilt he felt about Connie's death. After getting into his convertible, they rode south toward the Keys, through the city and suburbs until the scenery changed to miles of agricultural fields that stretched to the horizon. "How will we know which field he's in?"

"Matt said he's in the field after the next mile marker. That should be around the next bend." As he drove past the mile marker, a big black truck with dark windows sat on the shoulder of the road. Jason honked twice as he passed. "Don't look around but that was Matt in the black truck." Kathleen gasped and looked surprised. He slowed down and checked the rear-view mirror. "I'm going to stop and let some air out of our tire. When we get to the field, you stay in the car in case something goes wrong. If it does, you take the car and leave."

"I'm not leaving you!" She felt aghast at his suggestion.

"Save yourself, baby."

"I don't want to live without you."

He gave her a loving smile. "If I weren't driving …"

"You can kiss me later." Her smile reflected the adoration she had for him.

Jason pulled over to the side of the road behind some mangrove trees. He leaned over, kissed her, and got out of the car. At the rear tire on the driver's side, he knelt down.

She heard air whistling as the car tilted in that direction.

He got back in the driver's seat, lowered the convertible top, and slowly drove forward around the mangrove trees. As they moved into a clearing, fields of tomato plants stretched to the horizon. Workers bent over plants, picking the fruit and loading them in wooden baskets.

Her body wobbled as the car limped along the roadway.

While Jason steered down the shoulder, cars whizzed past on their way to the Keys.

Kathleen shielded her eyes from the bright sunshine. "Do you see him?"

"Not yet." He peered out the windshield scanning the backs of the pickers. "It's hard to tell which one he is. I'm going to stop and get out so he can see me."

"Be careful, honey." She grabbed his forearm and leaned toward him.

He kissed her and gave her a reassuring smile. "I will." He left the car and stood at the side of the road glaring at the flat tire. "Holy cow, honey! Look at this." He ran his hand through his hair. "We got ourselves a flat tire out here in the middle of nowhere!" He walked around the car looking at all the tires. "What do we do now?" He threw his hands in the air and let them drop loudly against his ugly shorts.

She stifled a chuckle, covered her smile with her hand and turned her head away from the workers. When she composed herself and glanced back through her lowered window, she saw several farmhands looking at Jason while they picked tomatoes.

Jason walked around to the other side of the car and stared at the flat tire as if it would change itself. He put his hands on his hips and waited for what seemed an agonizing amount of time.

One of the men in the field looked around at the guards, who laughed at Jason's charade. The worker said something Spanish. The guards nodded and one tossed his head toward the car. Standing upright, the slender worker moved toward the car, stepping over several rows of plants. When he climbed the incline at the edge of the roadway, the man looked at her then at Jason. She saw a resemblance in his face to Carlos.

"Jason, is that you?" The man spoke softly, moving toward the back of the car.

Jason looked at the ground. "Buenos dias, Hernando." He put his hands on his hips and shook his head as he looked at the flat tire keeping his voice low. "Today is the day, mi amigo." He pointed at the tire. "Look at this tire! I think I have a spare. I've never used the thing! Do you know how to change a flat?" He opened the trunk, removed the spare, a tire iron, and a can of fix-a-flat spray. He leaned the tire against the bumper to block the guards' view. "Kneel like you're fixing the tire."

When Hernando knelt down, Jason opened the car door, started the car and raised the convertible top. After the top was locked in place, he went back to the bumper and knelt down next to Hernando and blew up the tire. "Get in the back seat and lie down."

Hernando crawled inside and lay on the floor behind the front seats. When the tire was full, Jason threw down the can, hopped into the car, and sped off, leaving the spare tire bouncing behind him. "Sweetheart, this is Connie's husband, Hernando."

She looked behind her. "Hello, Hernando. I'm Kathleen."

"Buenos dias, senorita." Hernando smiled with relief.

Jason sped around the next curve, reached into the center console, and took out a large knife. He passed it back between the two front seats to Hernando. "Cut off your ankle monitor. Push it under the seat."

Kathleen watched him cut through the thick plastic band around his ankle. "Carlos will be very happy to see you."

"He's what I live for." Hernando shoved the ankle bracelet under Jason's seat and handed her the knife.

When she reached for the knife, she glanced out the back window and gasped. "There's a big truck coming fast behind us."

"I see it." Jason pressed harder on the gas pedal. "Hold on. I'm going to run this red light." She inhaled sharply and held her breath. No one came in either direction so she released her breath and looked behind them. "He didn't stop either."

"Get my gun. Be ready to use it."

Her eyes widened when she opened the glove compartment and removed the pistol. The kick on this gun would knock her into the next county, but she would use it if she had to. She removed it from the holster and held it in her lap.

She looked behind them as the truck gained on them. Her heart beat faster. "Want me to shoot the radiator?"

"Not yet." Jason steered wildly around motorists who dawdled while looking at the scenery. "I'll try to lose him first. If that doesn't work, we'll put a hole in his gas tank." He sped down the road, followed by the truck, which was not as fast as his sports car. As the truck chased them, Jason looked in the rear-view mirror. "Hold on." He slammed his foot on the brake, causing the truck to speed past them. He reached for the gun in Kathleen's lap, accelerated toward the truck, and pumped several bullets into its gas tank. Streams of gasoline spewed from the holes. He swerved to avoid the fuel on the roadway and flew past the truck as it pulled to the side of the road.

She turned around to watch. "Two men jumped out of the truck."

"Good. Matt and his team are right behind them." Jason slowed to a less heart-pounding rate of speed and soon turned into a marina where he drove to the edge of the water at a boat ramp and stopped. "Get out, both of you."

She grabbed her little purse and his Glock and hopped out of the car while he opened the driver's door to let Hernando out. While she and Hernando stood safely away from the car, Jason stuck the knife point into the floor mat and jammed the handle against the gas pedal, causing the engine to roar. She covered her mouth in shock as he shifted from park into drive and the car lurched forward, splashing into the water. The open windows helped the car fill with water. It seemed odd the lights remained on.

Jason stepped quickly to Kathleen and grabbed her hand. "Hurry, more folks might be right behind us." He rushed up the boat ramp onto the dock and ran down to the end. Holding her hand, she ran alongside him while Hernando followed.

When she saw Charles and Tara waiting for them in a speed boat at the end of the dock, she gasped with fear and happiness. Jason let go of her hand, jumped into the speed boat, and turned toward her. "Come on, baby." He held out his arms while she held her breath and leapt onto the boat. He grabbed her and held her close to his chest.

Hernando jumped onto the boat behind her and quickly lay down on the deck. "Buenos dias, Senor Charles."

"Welcome aboard." Charles pressed forward on the throttle and zoomed away from the dock, flying across the surface of the water. "Where should we go, Key West?" He looked at Jason and winked.

"We have to get Hernando and Carlos to the safe house," Jason said. "As appealing as going to Key West would be ..." He looked down at her and hugged her to his side.

258

She smiled up at him. "They're going to my safe house?"

"Your family doesn't need it anymore. Matt's folks are helping them move back home today."

She felt shocked and surprised. "You and Matt are two sneaky guys." She smiled and held him with greater appreciation when he tossed his head back and laughed.

Tara came to her side and reached for her. "I'm so happy to see you. Charles told me everything that happened. Chandra was scared to death when that man took you."

"I should have called you both but it took a long time to explain everything to my parents and Sam, then I was dying for a shower …"

"We tried to call you," Tara said, "but couldn't get you."

"Sorry, my cell phone is still at the Port. I'll have to call her. I didn't get time last night." She smirked at Jason. "Where'd you get this hot boat?" She glanced at Charles, who sat behind the wheel with Tara by his side.

"We rented it from the marina. I've been thinking about getting one of these babies to race on weekends in the P1 Superstock hydroplane boat races."

Her mouth fell open in amazement at these two men who never seemed to stop, then she suddenly remembered the sports car. "Oh my goodness, your car." She turned around to see the headlights still shining underwater.

"I always liked that car." Jason watched the submerged vehicle as its lights flickered.

"Our insurance company won't be happy," Charles said. "Can we start that boring life full of peace and quiet now?"

Jason considered Hernando. "We're done saving people for now."

Charles pushed the throttle forward causing the boat to hydroplane across the top of the water, headed for the Miami Marina.

Kathleen grabbed onto the side rail as a plume of water rose behind the boat like a tail feather. He must have been cruising over a hundred miles per hour.

As they fled the traffickers who forced needy folks into agricultural jobs and never let them leave, she wondered what would happen if Americans knew how much of their food was produced using slave labor. Would things ever change?

~

Weeks later, Kathleen held Jason's hand as the elevator whisked them skyward to the fiftieth floor. Her stomach jumped as the lift came to a sudden stop at the top of the building. When the doors opened, she marveled at the magnificent views of the Miami River, Biscayne Bay, Port of Miami, and in the distance, condos along South Beach on the Atlantic Ocean.

Jason walked with her toward the tables and chairs scattered throughout the room. "You did a great job decorating." He admired the balloons and streamers she put up.

"Happy birthday, honey." She smiled and kissed him when he leaned down to her. Savoring the heat and gentleness of his caress, she touched his bulging bicep and squeezed it, sending a chill down her spine. As they stood in the middle of the room, she gazed at the scenery which encapsulated her life. She had always lived in Miami and came to realize how much she loved her hometown.

When the elevator bell rang, lots of folks who rode up together stepped out onto the shiny marble floor. Kathleen's parents arrived with Charles, Tara, Sam, and Chandra. As they made their way from the lobby into the middle of Club 50, she and Jason greeted them with smiles, warm hugs, and friendly handshakes.

"What a great idea for a birthday party," Harry said. "Where's the bar?"

"This way ..." Charles took him aside.

"I know you said no gifts," Brenda said to Jason, "but we had to get you a card."

"Thank you, ma'am. You're very kind." He smiled while he opened the card and read the amusing sentiment. Laughing, he pecked Kathleen's mother on the cheek, which seemed to surprise her.

A jazz combo began to play soft music in the background while the guests arrived. Even though it was his birthday, Jason acted as host to his own party. Kathleen didn't ask him but she figured he was paying for the party himself. While he laughed and visited with everyone, she enjoyed watching him relax with his friends and co-workers. Their relationship had been a whirlwind affair. Not the typical dating ritual like most couples experienced, but she wouldn't trade any of it --well, maybe the Wilson part.

"A penny for your thoughts," Tara said.

"Sorry." She shook her head. "I was just thinking how lucky I am to have him." She wistfully looked at Jason while he laughed with his diving friends who had just arrived.

When Matt stepped off the elevator with Todd and some of the men from the FBI dive team who recently returned from Vancouver and Venezuela, she held her breath. She tensed when they moved toward Jason to shake his hand.

Jason led them toward the bar and got everyone drinks before they started to circulate with the other guests.

She glanced from Matt and the dive team back to Tara. "I hope he doesn't bring any bad news this time. We need a break."

"Matt is a nice man," Tara said. "He was very good to me."

"Oh, I like Matt a lot. He just has a habit of bringing bad news."

"I wonder what he found out about Charles' father," Tara said. "When they exhumed his body, Charles was upset that his dad's honor was being questioned."

"Charles is an honorable man. I would hate to see his father's reputation ruined." *For more reasons than one,* she thought. *What would Jason do?* "How are you and Charles doing?"

"He's been very sweet," Tara said. "He's backed off the bondage. We're just friends, for now."

"He's a good man." She glanced to where Charles stood talking to Jason, impressed by the depth of his character.

Chandra joined them while Sam continued to speak with Jason and Charles. "This is so cool. We should do this every year."

261

"Definitely." Kathleen grabbed a shrimp from a passing tray.

While servers walked through the party passing around hot and cold hors d'oeuvres, the guests shared stories about Jason and laughed. She felt eager to join Jason but wanted to spend some time with her friends before dedicating the evening to him. "How is the man who was shot by Wilson?"

"He's doing okay," Chandra said. "He'll be on crutches for awhile."

"I'll have to send him flowers and a card," Kathleen said. "I can't believe Wilson shot someone without reason, but I shouldn't be surprised."

"It's over now." Chandra clutched her hand. "No more running and hiding from paparazzi either. They've moved on to other prey."

"After Matt held that press conference in Washington, D.C., things have almost returned to normal, whatever that is." Kathleen glanced over at Jason and wanted to join him. "Let's go see what's happening." She walked toward him, followed by her friends.

Moments later, Hernando, Carlos, and his friends stepped off the elevator and headed toward Jason and Matt. Silence fell over the room. Once they were greeted as welcomed guests, the party chatter returned to a low din.

Kathleen nudged next to Jason and received a warm smile from him. He put his arm around her shoulders and tugged her against his side. Content to be held by the man she loved, she felt happy and cherished while listening to his conversation.

"Listen, Sam," Jason said. "My foundation is getting bigger by the month. I need to refocus on my day job while still rescuing slaves. What would you say to a paid internship to help me manage the foundation?"

Sam seemed shocked, then glanced at Kathleen's broad smile. "Sure. I'd be happy to help you."

"Great." Jason shook his hand. "Stop by my office when you have time and we'll talk about it. You'll probably have lots of questions."

Sam glanced at Chandra, who stood nearby talking to another guest and contemplated something. He then looked back at Jason with a quizzical look. "You seem to be giving everyone else gifts on your birthday."

Jason looked at her, smiled, and kissed her forehead. "Oh, I have my eye on a special gift."

When a twinkle flashed in his dark blue eyes, Kathleen smiled and wondered what he was talking about. Maybe he planned to take her somewhere. Maybe they'd go back to the Keys for a get-away. She almost asked him why he was smiling like a child with an ice cream cone when her parents joined them. She swallowed her question and rubbed her Dutch slave bead necklace.

"You saved our daughter again," Harry said, shaking Jason's hand.

"She saved herself." Jason gave her a smile of admiration. "She's a strong lady." He tugged her closer.

Kathleen smiled and squeezed his waist. Jason finally thought of her as a survivor, not a victim. His eyes twinkled at her as she almost kissed him but waited.

"I know we didn't get off to a good start," Brenda said to Jason. "I'd like to start over." She extended her hand in a friendly gesture.

"Forget it, ma'am. You've suffered what no one else could ever imagine. Let's move forward." He took her hand and pecked her on the cheek.

Brenda looked surprised and flashed an awkward smile at Kathleen. Jason's face looked sincere and she felt very proud of him. Rubbing his back with loving appreciation, she flashed him a warm smile.

"How are you settling in back home?" Jason asked Brenda.

"We're very happy and glad to be home." She looked at her husband, who smiled broadly.

"There's nothing like sleeping in your own bed," Harry said.

When Matt and Charles joined their conversation, Kathleen tensed. That was a gut reaction she learned over the past several months whenever Matt came around.

"I've been talking to Charles about his father and the shipping company," Matt said. "I thought you might want to know what we discovered."

"Do I want to hear this on my birthday?" Jason only half joked.

"It's good news, buddy." Charles glanced at Matt. "Go ahead, tell him."

"We interrogated the ship's crew and all company employees. From our investigation, the slave trafficking scheme between the computer manager and Joe Hargraves didn't involve anyone else at the shipping company. They paid off workers on one ship to hold the auctions. Some dock workers in Maracaibo were paid well to put captives in the container. And Joe made sure the Customs inspections never took place."

"You're right, that is good news." Jason patted Charles on the shoulder. "What about your father?"

"The autopsy found heart failure, which runs in our family," Charles said. "There's no way to determine whether he was killed or died naturally."

"Your dad was a good man," Jason said. "He did the honorable thing by reporting what he discovered. He might have died because of his beliefs. We'll never know. But there's one thing for sure, you can be proud of him." Charles nodded, relief evident on his face.

"Sorry to hear about your car," Matt said.

"Afraid my fake IDs went down with it," Jason said. "If the traffickers trace Hernando's ankle bracelet, they'll get my IDs and hopefully assume I died in the crash." He hugged Kathleen to his side. "We've seen the end of Froggy Watson."

"We'll need to come up with a new name," Matt said. "You still want to do this, right?"

Jason looked down at Kathleen with a quizzical look. "Do I?" She waited for him to answer his own question, but he never did. When the jazz ensemble took a break, Jason removed his arm from around her shoulders, picked up a nearby spoon, and clanged it on the side of his wine glass. When the party guests stopped talking and watched him, he scanned their faces. "I know I said no gifts, but there's one gift I really must have." He turned to look at Kathleen.

Her heart skipped a beat when he handed his wine glass to Charles and turned to stand in front of her. He took her right hand and bent down on one knee in front of her. "Kathleen McDougal, I love you. Will you marry me?"

She covered her mouth, which had fallen open in shock. Goosebumps ran down her back. A sob threatened to erupt. "Yes."

Reaching into his pocket, he removed a folded cloth, opened it and removed a ring.

Tears of happiness streaked her cheeks when he took her left hand and put his ring on her finger. She wiped the tears away trying to see it but only saw a big sparkle. "It's beautiful."

When Jason stood up, he pulled her to his chest and held her. The silent room of party guests erupted in applause and whoops while she held his back.

Smiling into his face, Kathleen's auburn hair fell down her back. "I love you, honey."

"I love you, sweetheart." He kissed her passionately while his birthday guests cheered.

Consumed by his kisses, held tightly in his arms, her head swirled ... dizzy with happiness. She had conquered her fears and he had won her heart, surrounded by the love of her family and friends, old and new. His broad smile filled her green eyes with his deepening love and her heart with hopes for a long blissful life together.

Epilogue

Six months later, Kathleen and Jason sat side-by-side in a hotel suite in California. She sat back on the sofa and smiled. "That's my story," she said to the two men sitting across from her. She couldn't believe she had just pitched her story to two of her favorite movie people, Tim Hanx and Stephen Spellbound.

The two men looked at each other and nodded. "We've got to tell this story."

"I agree," Stephen said. "When is your book coming out?"

"In a month or two, it's being designed."

"We'd like to buy the movie rights," Stephen said.

"Awesome," she said, smiling broadly. "When you make the offer in writing, I want all the proceeds to go to my fiancé's foundation, Impact Ten." She reached over and squeezed Jason's leg.

"You don't want to be rich?" Tim Hanx smiled and winked.

"I have everything I need." She gazed at Jason's adoring face.

Tim shook his head. "Okay, if that's what you want."

Kathleen, Jason, Tim and Stephen stood to shake hands. "Congratulations," Stephen said to Jason. "You've got quite a woman."

"Yes I do," Jason said, smiling at her.

Tim shook her hand. "Good luck with your campaign on behalf of trafficking victims."

"We're starting a Survivor's Network," she said. "We'll have safe houses all over the country offering counseling, medical needs, job training, even language translation. We're hoping the money earned from the book and the movie will help accomplish our dreams." She smiled at Jason, whose eyes twinkled.

"We'll do whatever publicity we need to make sure the movie's a success. Have any acting experience?" Tim said.

"No way, Scarlett Jorgenson would be a better choice." Kathleen laughed. "I'm still working on my self-esteem. This is the first dress I've worn in more than two years." She spun around and turned so they could see the laser treatments had lightened the scars on her legs. I haven't decided about the slave tattoo." She pulled up her sleeve to show them her number. "It's kind of a badge of honor for survivors."

"Keep it," Stephen said. "Display it proudly." He kissed her on the cheek. "We'll be in touch."

"Have a happy life you two," Tim said, also pecking Kathleen on the cheek. "You've earned it."

Tim and Stephen left them alone in the hotel suite, a silent void left them glowing from their encounter with Hollywood royalty. Kathleen leaned into Jason who wrapped his arms around her. She returned to her place of comfort.

"Happy, baby?" He held her against his chest.

"Very."

Jason devoured her lips, kissing her passionately until she felt his erection poke against her belly. Pulling away from her lips, his dark irises reflected his passion. "Want to try out the bed?" His eyes twinkled when he grinned.

She nodded. "Can we stay a couple more days?" She had warmed to the idea of sharing some time together for sightseeing and loving.

He picked her up behind her knees and carried her to the bedroom, kicking open the door. "I'm looking forward to many years of passionate love making with you,"

She squealed when he tossed her on the bed and lay down on top of her. "Can I have some thrusting, counselor?"

"Yes, ma'am." He lowered himself onto her yielding body.

She reveled in the feeling of his weight on her. Wrapping her legs around his back, she pulled him against her and swooned to the beat of her rapid heart, eagerly anticipating another climax and many more to come.

The End

267

Acknowledgements

A special thank you to my family and friends who continue to support and encourage me throughout this exciting journey.

Many thanks to my cover illustrator, Paul Summerfield, who captured the essence of my characters and created an excellent rendering for the cover. Your outstanding work reflects the heart of my story.

Many thanks to my editor and designer, Michelle Lovi of Odyssey Books, who improved my writing and helped my story come to life. Your excellent work resulted in a more professional book.

About the Author

For more than a decade, Joy Ann Coll has been writing romance novels. She graduated from the University of Delaware and went on to pursue a successful twenty-five year career at DuPont. After leaving the corporate world, she moved to coastal Florida and began working on her writing career by taking part in conventions and contests held by Romance Writers of America. Her debut novel, *A King's Ransom*, was published in July 2012. Joy lives in Vero Beach, Florida, with Bernard, her husband of twenty-three years.

Author website: http://sites.google.com/site/romancebyjoy
Facebook: www.facebook.com/authorjoyanncoll
Twitter: Twitter.com@joyanncoll
Email: romancebyjoy@aol.com

www.ingramcontent.com/pod-product-compliance
Lightning Source LLC
Chambersburg PA
CBHW021954170626
46808CB00001B/145